Broken Silence

LIZ MISTRY

ONE PLACE. MANY STORIES

HQ
An imprint of HarperCollins*Publishers* Ltd
1 London Bridge Street
London SE1 9GF

1
First published in Great Britain by
HQ, an imprint of HarperCollins*Publishers* Ltd 2020

ISBN: 9780008358372

MIX
Paper from
responsible sources
FSC
www.fsc.org
FSC™ C007454

This book is produced from independently certified FSC™ paper
to ensure responsible forest management.

For more information visit: www.harpercollins.co.uk/green

Printed and bound in Great Britain by
CPI Group (UK) Ltd, Croydon, CR0 4YY

To Baroness Lola Young and Kevin Hyland for opening my eyes to Modern-Day Slavery . . . but mostly for all those victims of this appalling abuse of human rights.

'Once you know, you can't claim ignorance'
Baroness Lola Young

Prologue

A sharp rat-a-tat-tat somewhere near his head shattered his reassurance. Someone was out there banging on the side of the bin. Stefan held his breath and his body stiffened. Maybe it was one of the workers out for a smoke. He strained his ears. He couldn't hear anything else – no dogs, no voices. Maybe whoever it was had gone.

Then it came – a coarse singsong whisper penetrating the plastic bin – taunting and at the same time chilling him. 'Come out, come out, wherever you are.'

This was followed by ferocious yelping and Stefan knew the game was up. The lid was thrown back and a bright torch shone into the inside. In a last-ditch attempt, Stefan remained still and silent, but it was no good. Whoever shone the torch followed that by pushing a long prod through the layers of cardboard. When it connected with his body, Stefan braced himself not to react, then the electric current from the Taser had him yelping in pain as his entire body shook for a moment and then became numb. Seconds later, two of Bullet's henchmen dragged him from the bin and flung him in a heap on the wet ground. The dogs, salivating

1

and over-excited, pranced and jumped close to him, taking the odd nipping bite before they were yanked back by their owners.

'Oh dear. This makes me very sad, you know. It also makes my boss very sad.' Bullet tilted his head to one side and laughed. 'Actually, it doesn't make him sad so much as angry.'

He waved his phone in the air. 'He told me to hit you where it hurts and boy, am I going to enjoy doing that.'

SUNDAY 15TH MARCH 2020

Chapter 1

DS Felicity Springer couldn't wait to get home. She'd thrown her stuff into her case, and walked, red-faced, past her colleagues who lingered in the hallway making plans to extend the weekend. She exited the hotel on her walk of shame. It didn't matter that no one was paying the slightest bit of attention to her – she had a vague recollection of what had happened, and she felt dirty. Why had this happened? She had Stevie after all – how could she have allowed herself to get so drunk . . . so out of control?

Straightening her spine, she dragged her trolley case over to her car, blinked back her tears – she didn't do tears – shoved her luggage in the boot of her Kia Sportage and got in, just as it began to snow. Hidden from view, she rested her head on the steering wheel, wishing she could clear her brain; that the pounding at her temple would go. She wasn't even sure she should be driving. Maybe she was still over the limit but there was no way she could remain for the rest of the conference.

She'd had an awful time anyway, feeling totally out of her depth at the multi-agency 'Making Bradford Safe' conference. It had been billed as a way of working together to get the drugs, the weapons and the gangs off the streets. The first step in flushing out any of those businesses who were employing trafficked immigrants. It smacked of lip service to Springer, because she knew fine and well there wasn't enough in the coffers to finance their grandiose ideas. Still, it was worth it to get different agencies together . . . share ideas, break down barriers. On a personal level though, Springer was pissed off. Nobody, not even the bosses from her own agency, had given her contributions credence. It was all crap, crap and more damn crap. Perhaps that's why she went off the rails, but that was just making excuses and no excuse could ever be good enough for what she had done. As she'd walked through the hallway, she had felt like she had the word SLUT tattooed across her forehead and she reckoned that by the time she walked through the front door to Stevie, SLUT would have morphed into CHEATER.

Her head pounded – *just how much did I have to drink?* Last night was a blur. She'd had wine with her evening meal, but she thought she'd only had a glass. Afterwards she'd forced herself to go to the disco and she vaguely remembered dancing – *really?* Felicity rarely danced. *How much did I really drink?* Surely not enough to account for that one very big mistake. The sort of mistake she was going to feel guilty about for a long time to come. She had someone at home who cared for her. So, why had she risked that for a sleazy fumble with a lecherous loser? He was always a bit of a dick, so she couldn't quite make sense of how the hell she had ended up in bed beside him. She remembered vaguely chatting to him, and she'd ended up in his room . . . in his bed, so . . .

Thing was, she wasn't a hundred per cent sure *what* had gone on. She barely remembered the post-conference party. It was all a blur of blaring music, flashing lights, gyrating bodies and loud laughter. Snapshots of it came back to her; laughter, drinking, chanting, 'down it, down it, down it', but none of it was in sequence. As for after the party . . . in the hotel room . . . well, that wasn't clear either. She laughed humourlessly. So much for the session on monitoring binge-drinking in the Bradford district!

Her phone rang, and looking at the screen, she groaned. Feeling like a bitch, she let it go to voicemail. She couldn't face speaking to Stevie. How was she supposed to act like everything was okay when she'd betrayed the person she loved?

A wave of nausea overtook her. She took slow, deep breaths to control it, then rummaged in the glove compartment for a bottle of water. After only a few sips, her stomach heaved, and she barely got the car door open before vomiting, the warmth of her puke melting the already layered snow. Aware of a speckle of sweat across her upper lip, Felicity took another glug of water, gargled and spat it out before grabbing a tissue and wiping her mouth. *Shit, I feel rough.*

All fingers and thumbs, she leaned back against the headrest, snuggled deeper into her winter coat, soothed by its softness and, eyes closed, played the voicemail. 'Hi, you. Hungover, are we? Never mind, I've got lunch on the go. Let me know when you'll be home and I'll have hot chocolate and a hot bath ready for you. Might join you in the bath if you're lucky. Love you.'

Dropping the phone into her lap, Felicity looked out the window, only vaguely aware of other cars leaving the hotel car park, and tried to think back to that morning. She'd awakened, disorientated and naked in his bed. A trail of clothes round the room, his leering face beside her, the strange taste in her mouth, the throb down below . . . all of it told the story, yet . . . even now, she couldn't remember a sodding thing about it and she'd been too embarrassed to ask, too ashamed to admit she'd been so pissed she couldn't remember and too humiliated by his leering grin and the casual smack on the ass as she crawled out of the bed. This was the perfect clichéd situation . . . *Important male figurehead beds needy underling. Needy underling regrets it and we all know who's the butt of all the jokes!*

She didn't know how long she had sat there, but the snow changed from relentless splatters to thicker, heavier flakes obliterating her windscreen and casting a deathly tomb-like glow inside her car. She shuddered, realizing how cold she'd got and gave herself a shake. *Come on Fliss, you've got to put this behind you and get yourself home.*

Hands trembling, she tried to insert her key in the ignition, dropped it and flinched as a sharp pain went through her body when she bent over to scrabble for it on the floor. Eventually, she grabbed it and, managing to start up the engine, she set the wipers in motion, appalled to see just how heavy the snow was. Peering through the heavy flakes, she saw that the roofs of the few remaining cars were layered with a couple of inches of snow and the treads of the last cars to leave were being rapidly covered by the blizzard. *Shit! Shit! Shit!* Last thing she needed was to drive home in these conditions with a pounding hangover. The thought of waiting for a taxi and then having to return the next day to retrieve her car was too much for her. Resigned, she engaged the clutch, eased the vehicle from the parking space and headed for home.

Despite her aching head, Felicity found the heavy silence of her own disordered thoughts too disturbing, so she switched on the radio. But it was some cheesy love song by a boyband she had no desire to listen to. She turned it off. She'd rather deal with her own thoughts than this crap. Hands trembling, she wondered if she should be driving, especially as the wet snow was getting heavier and her wipers were going nineteen to the dozen.

Swinging off the roundabout, instead of taking the Bradford dual carriageway exit, she opted for the back road . . . less traffic, less likely to get stopped. And boy, did *she* want to avoid getting pulled over. Thoughts of yet another reason not to drag herself to work the next day made her slow right down and lean forward to peer out the window. Overcast clouds made everything grey and she flipped her lights on and continued at her sedate pace until a transit truck overtook her sending up a backwash of mucky slush over her windscreen, momentarily obscuring her vision. *Ass!*

But within seconds her annoyance turned to relief as she realized that having a bigger vehicle in front of her ploughing through the slush that was gathering on the road, was a godsend. She could follow the van's tracks and it gave her something to focus on. Increasing her speed a little, she glided along just behind the van.

Wipers on full blast, she peered through the grey until something caught her eye. *What the hell is that?* The van's light had popped out and now something was dangling from the hole. Wishing the wipers would speed up, Felicity, headache momentarily forgotten, leaned forward and pressed a little harder on the accelerator.

A hand? Bloody snow. Could it really be a hand? How the hell could a hand be waving it her from the space where the light now dangled?

Then there it was – not just a hand but an entire arm . . . protruding from the rear light casing, the light dangling on a wire. What the hell was going on? It was like something from a cheesy American car chase movie, or a serial killer movie. Was someone captive in that van or was it some sort of practical joke?

Uncertain what to do, Felicity increased her speed till she was closer to the van in front, mulling through her options as she drove. It couldn't be a joke. Course not. Why would someone stage a prank like that when the only car around was hers? So, if it wasn't a joke, then it must be someone's desperate cry for help. A last resort to attract attention. Whoever the hand belonged to wasn't doing this for fun, they were desperate.

For the first time, Felicity regretted her decision to take the back roads and follow the van. If whoever was driving it was keeping someone inside against their will, then they must be dangerous. She glanced in her rear-view mirror, praying for the telltale signs of car lights behind her – there were none and she realized that, as she'd driven, the road was getting narrower. Normally she was reasonably familiar with this area, but the darkness and her preoccupied state made her unsure where exactly she was on her route. Then it struck her. Stevie had installed the What3words geocoding app on both their phones telling her it might come in handy someday. Of course, Felicity had scoffed. She had a satnav, who needed a stupid app? Now she was glad of it. She hadn't put on her satnav and it would take too long to bring it up. She quickly pressed the app and got the three words she needed.

Grabbing her phone from her lap, she dialled 999 and switched to speakerphone.

'What's your emergency?'

'Police. Don't have time for all the crap. Find my location using these words Buttercup, Red, Triangle. There's something weird going on in the vehicle in front of me. I suspect an abduction.'

'Could I take your name . . .?'

But the van had sped up and was turning off. Felicity threw her phone on the passenger seat and raised her voice so the despatcher could still hear her. 'I'm following it. A white van. Don't know what the road's called but get someone here ASAP. I'll keep my phone open. I'm a police officer. Get someone here pronto.'

Letting herself lag a little behind the vehicle, whilst still keeping it in her sights, Felicity followed. The hand was still waving about from the rear light. Then it disappeared. A moment later it was back, throwing stuff out the opening, waving. Frantic. The van sped up, and Felicity suspected the driver was aware of what their captive was doing and that they were being followed.

Nausea filled Felicity's throat, but she swallowed it back. The road was now a track . . . a bumpy track and it wasn't helping the sickly feeling. The snow was getting ever heavier, big flakes masking her vision, and Felicity was scared she was going to skid. Who knew if that stupid app worked or if anyone would be able to triangulate her phone data to secure her whereabouts from here? Maybe this had been a bad decision. Pulling herself forward, she peered through the windscreen and, as a darting shadow dived in front of her, she slammed her foot on the brakes. Her phone skittered across the seat and into the footwell as the car careered to the right. The shadow – what looked like a baby deer – disappeared into the foliage to the left. Felicity, heart hammering, wrenched the steering wheel and eased her foot off the brake. With the car in front gaining distance, her car slowly righted itself. She raised her voice, hoping her phone was still connected and would still pick up her voice. 'We're on a side road now. Terrain crap, road bumpy. Visibility is poor and the reg number is obscured. The vehicle is speeding up.'

She'd no idea if the responder on the other end of the phone could still hear her, but she kept up her chatter. 'Just passed a farmhouse . . . Appletree Farm . . . series of wind turbines in a field to the right of it.'

The tinny voice from the phone told her the despatcher was speaking and she swallowed, blinking away the tears that sprung to her eyes when she realized that she wasn't completely alone. Even though the phone was on loudspeaker, the despatcher's words were distant. The van she was following was about fifty feet ahead of her. She took her eye off it for a second . . . and reached down, her fingers scrabbling across the carpeted floor. She glanced up, righted the wheel, eased off the accelerator and stretched a little deeper. If she could just find the damn phone, she'd be sure the phone operative could hear her.

Crash!

The judder and bang as she rear-ended the van, propelled her forward and, just as quickly, back when the airbag deployed.

Pinned back against her seat by the weight of the airbag, vision obscured, she blinked. What the hell? She began to push the airbag down, ignoring her breathlessness, just wanting to get out of the vehicle but before she had the chance to move, the door was yanked open and a figure in a balaclava thrust a gun into her car. Felicity looked up at the man, her eyes wide in terror. 'Please . . . don't . . .'

Bang!

'Hello . . . hello? Are you still there . . .?' The despatcher's voice faded.

11

Chapter 2

Headlights pierced the early morning dark, as the van pulled up outside Bradford Halal Chicken Factory. The men who were bundled on the floor in the back, got to their feet before the doors were yanked open and they were berated by the big hulking bloke the other men called Bullet. Their eyes adjusting to the dawn light and shivering, they stumbled out onto the frosty ground. After being locked up in the dark for the duration of the journey, it was a relief for Stefan Marcovici when the doors opened. The smell of unwashed bodies combined with their cramped positions always panicked him a bit. What if they crashed and the van exploded? What if one day their captors just parked up and didn't bother to open the doors for them?

The factory lights were on, but they were the first workers to arrive and the car park was empty bar their transport and another car that probably belonged to the night watchman. It was parked next to the huge waste containers that stood next to the roll-down warehouse doors attached to the factory. As they passed Bullet, he pushed each of them, a stupid grin on his face. They trudged on to the next man. Huddled in a huge coat, woollen beanie on his head and a fed-up weed-glazed look on his face, he handed them their lunch: a single paper-thin sandwich with a disgusting paste filling, that clagged up your mouth.

Each day, he arrived at the halal chicken factory, put on white overalls, a plastic apron, hairnet, mask, gloves and wellies and for hour after interminable hour he stood, freezing his balls off, by whatever machine they directed him to, dealing with the cold chicken corpses that moved past him on a conveyor-belt of death. All around him, the machines clanked and jolted, the men chatted and the radio played songs about love and sex, none of which held any importance for him in his current situation.

Over the months Stefan had grown immune to the putrid stench of blood clogging up his nostrils. It had become routine, just part of his day. A huge part of it. A necessary part of it. The section between getting up and going back home to bed. The bit he could measure. The squish of innards and entrails between his gloved fingers, the sound of cartilage and bone cracking beneath his cleaver and the persistent buzz of the fly catcher that hung from the ceiling above him, as he worked, were all just scene setting. Part of the cadence of his daily life.

Some of the men worked shorter shifts than he and his fellow captives – coming in later and leaving earlier. About two hours before the end of his shift, Stefan watched, heavy-hearted and envious, as they left of their own accord with a friendly wave and banter, whilst he and the other faceless people slogged in silence. Sometimes he wondered if it was just one great long nightmare. Months earlier he'd been full of hope, making plans for a future where his entire family joined him and his daughter. A new start away from the threat of the gang he'd betrayed back in Romania. When they'd taken him and Maria to a bank and helped them sign up for an account, he'd been sure everything was legitimate, all above board. Sure, he'd be able to manage his money, pay off his debt to those who'd helped him escape and build a life, but the bastards had confiscated his card and insisted he still had a huge debt to pay off.

Throwing a pile of chicken guts into the plastic waste tubs behind him and wishing it was a brick hitting Bullet's head, he went through his strategy. For days now he'd been thinking about this and now the day had come, he wanted to make sure everything went to plan. The trigger had been when he'd heard the advert on the radio. At first, he hadn't understood it. Wondered what it was about. Then, he heard it again and it began to dawn on him. The advert was about people like him and the other men. People kept against their will, unable to escape. People like his daughter being forced to do God knows what.

His captors had told them that nobody cared about the likes of them, but that wasn't true. The police were advertising it on the radio. They were asking people to contact them. They would help. So, Stefan memorized the number. All he had to do was tell someone what was happening. At first, he'd thought he'd tell one of the other men – the ones who were free to come and go, but he decided against that. They must know what was going on. They just turned a blind eye. Probably glad it wasn't them. So that wouldn't work. The more time that passed, the weaker he got, the more poorly some of the other men became, and this fuelled his determination to escape. To escape and to find Maria.

Finally, he realized the easiest way to break free was from the factory. They weren't watched all the time here. Bullet and his thugs came and went, but there were times during the day when the only supervisors were the factory ones and they didn't seem quite as threatening. He'd observed the direction the other men's cars took when they left the car park and reckoned he'd reach civilization at some point if he just got out, turned left and kept on running.

Stefan waited, nervous and scared. This could all go badly wrong, but it might be his only chance. Eventually he sloped off to the loading area by way of the toilets. Creeping slowly forward, he craned his head to either side. He could see two of the big truck drivers off to one side, smoking and chatting. If he sidled out and used their truck for cover, he could get outside. Quick as a flash, he nipped back into the toilets, stripped off the white protective covering that would draw attention on the street, shoved it onto a bin and retraced his steps to the loading bay. The men were still laughing and smoking – looking at something on their phones. Heart pounding, he took a deep breath and darted over to the truck before edging forward. He listened, but all he could hear was the regular sounds of the factory machines and the occasional shout from the men. Taking his chance, he darted to the side, using the factory wall as cover and sidled over to the bushes that lined the edge of the car park. Crouching behind them, he made his way to the main road and then took to his heels running as fast as he could along a pavement lined with car parks assigned to other huge factory buildings. He was in an industrial estate. He accelerated, the cold air catching in his chest, but adrenaline made him fly. He followed the road round and saw a main street. There was a bus stop a few yards ahead and he wished he'd had the foresight to steal some money. He kept moving past it. The scent of freedom beckoning, making him smile.

Chapter 3

DS Nikita Parekh, shoulders hunched against the driving sleet, bounced on the balls of her feet as she waited in the no man's land between the outer and inner cordons of the crime scene. Concentrating, she watched the CSIs processed the scene. The weather made it imperative that they work with speed and so they'd quickly banished any unnecessary personnel from the inner cordon and this included Nikki and her team. Not used to standing about, Nikki, Tyvek suit over her leather jacket, crime scene bootees over her boots, was doing her best to absorb what she could see of the crime scene.

The CSIs had already set up spotlights, but under orders from Gracie Fells, the head CSI, in order to make sure the heat they generated didn't compromise the crime scene, the lights had been placed at the very edge of the cordon. This lack of direct light made picking up on the details a little more difficult for Nikki. The CSIs – amorphous gender-neutral figures in their white bulky suits – held torches as they worked. The car, a red Kia Sportage, was slewed halfway across the narrow road, its front end squashed, the driver's door hanging open to reveal the empty seat. *Not so classy now.* Blood had turned the slush a rusty colour and as she watched, the CSIs were frantically trying to gather evidence as they took photos and scooped up spattered matter.

Other figures focused on the tracks that were beyond the Kia. The vehicle the car had crashed into was absent, and harvesting track marks and footprints was a race against the elements. Nikki itched to get in there and make her own analysis, talk to the CSIs, get a real feel for the scene. Already the memory of the resigned but annoyed atmosphere that had descended on her family, when she'd grabbed her jacket and headed for the door, was fading – almost, but not quite. It was a year since her daughter had been abducted and she and her partner Marcus had nearly lost their lives; still, every time she was called away from a family gathering, the memory of that horrific time was triggered for all of them. *But this is my job!* Her justification didn't always sit too well with her family, but they had to be aware that she'd been trying her best. Charlie knew first-hand how important her job was . . . didn't she? Trying really hard to be more present in their lives, more giving of her time . . . that, she decided, just had to make up for her dashing off halfway through the Sunday dinner that Marcus had so painstakingly cooked. But as the guilt soaked in, she realized that was just part and parcel of having to balance two sets of responsibilities.

Resolutely, she pulled her thoughts away from the kids' disappointed and slightly worried faces and back to the scene before her. The presence of blood with the absence of a body combined with the car owner's frantic call to emergency services was chilling. What the hell had she seen? A hand through the back light of the vehicle in front? One that she was unable to give a registration number for. One that she had only described as a white van. Nikki hoped the CSIs could work their magic on the rapidly melting slush . . . CCTV was non-existent in these back roads and besides, they meandered for miles, criss-crossing other roads and back roads. Who knew when the reported van would hit mainstream roads again, if ever? There were so many snickets, hidden roads and premises around this area, the van could be holed up in any number of locations waiting for them to divert their searches elsewhere. Their only other option would be a police appeal for a white vehicle, but with the lack of a better description, they'd be inundated with a raft of pointless sightings. What made it worse was that Nikki was acquainted with the woman who'd made the phone call . . . It had become personal for West Yorkshire police and, whether she could stand the woman herself didn't matter, she was one of theirs and that counted for something. Cupping her cold fingers round her mouth, Nikki blew into them, trying to ease the numbness in her joints and simultaneously stamped from foot to foot. Springer had made her life hell for a while the previous year, but that didn't stop Nikki feeling sorry for her now. Springer had clearly been taken by whoever was in the van she'd been pursuing and who knew what state she'd be in. Nikki wasn't used to standing idle at a crime scene and her patience was wearing thin. The sooner they got a look at the scene the sooner they could crack on with finding Springer.

The weight of a hefty elbow nudging her as she watched, had Nikki spinning round, arms already up to shove back when she realized it was her DC, Sajid Malik. 'For goodness' sake, Saj. What the hell are you playing at?'

Beyond him, in the lane, Nikki could see he'd parked up his Jag, but had had the good sense to turn it round so it was facing back the way they'd come. The crime scene had prevented through traffic in order to preserve any evidence left by the departing van and as more and more officers came to the scene, the chances of Nikki being able to spin her old Zafira round was getting slimmer. Sajid carried a Tyvek suit, which he was shaking out, ready to put on. He grinned at her and Nikki's scowl deepened. Of course, he'd had the sense to wear a winter coat and . . . was that a bloody polo neck? A shiver ran through her. She almost wished she could rip the damn jumper off him and put it on. As the thought crossed her mind, her fingers lifted to the rough scar on her neck and she shuddered. The last thing she would do was wear a polo. Too damn suffocating; a scarf, even loosely draped was bad enough but the very idea of her neck being enclosed was claustrophobic. Her own Tyvek suit offered little warmth in addition to her leather jacket and she had the distinct feeling of dampness in her socks – had her DMs finally given up the ghost and developed a hole in the sole? Just what she needed right now when the leak in her car still wasn't sorted. 'Wish they'd hurry up. I need to get in there.'

Ignoring her tetchy tone, Sajid pulled his suit up over his jeans, tucked his – probably cashmere – coat in and inserted his arms in the sleeve. 'Heard it's Springer.'

Nikki nodded. 'Yep. The call came in from Springer. Seems like she was on her way back from that Community Liaison Conference in Wakefield and took a detour to avoid traffic . . .'

Sajid moved closer to the demarcation tape, eyes scanning the scene. 'That blood by the driver's door's a bit ominous.'

'You don't say.' Nikki's tone was snippy. Saj was only articulating what she'd been thinking, but it irked her. She was cold, pissed off and eager to get on. 'Blood, yes, but the fact that she's been removed from the scene might be a good thing. The fact they've taken her might mean she's still alive.' Well, that's what Nikki hoped anyway.

'What do you make of her saying she saw a hand and then an arm sticking out from the taillight?'

'Don't know . . . but the fact that she's been lifted makes that seem even more ominous.' Wrapping her arms round her upper body, Nikki focused her gaze on the scene, ignoring the glance Saj sent in her direction. There was no love lost between her and The Spaniel, but that wouldn't stop her doing her best to find her.

A commotion near the outer cordon had both her and Saj spinning round.

Voice low, Saj exhaled. 'Shit, it must be bad if Archie's here.'

Nikki moved forward to meet her boss. DCI Archie Hegley was a large man, with a brusque Scottish tone and right now, his bulbous face was bright red and his breath came in quick pants sending off little puffs of vapour as he thudded over. 'Parekh, this is a bloody mind fuck. Right got ma proverbials in a lather, this has. Now, I ken you dinnae get on with Springer, but you need to put that behind you. We've got to find her . . . find out what the hell is going on.'

Oh yeah . . . I'm just supposed to forget that she accused me of killing my husband, as if all she did was swipe a sweet from me. She snorted but on seeing Archie's glare, tried to turn it into a cough. 'Yes, sir. Course, sir'.

She lowered her head. She'd heard the tape of Springer's call to the emergency switchboard and although she disliked the woman, she could clearly hear her puzzlement at what she was seeing. Nikki gave her bonus points for following the vehicle. It's exactly what she would have done herself, yet she would have put money on it that Springer would have pulled into the side of the road and waited for back-up. Maybe the woman wasn't quite as much of an arse as Nikki thought she was.

Archie was speaking again, his voice loud, harsh against the mumbles of the CSIs working the screen, causing them to look over. 'Get to get to the bottom of this, Parekh. Right! They not done yet?' He glowered over the inner cordon tape and Nikki thought for a moment that he was going to burst through the tape. Instead, he took a step back and exhaled. His entire body seemed to deflate like a burst balloon. He raked his fingers through his hair and cleared his throat. 'Did something awful tae her at the weekend at the conference.'

Nikki and Sajid exchanged glances and waited. What the hell could he have done that was so bad? Archie Hegley was a straight shooter, but he was fair. Not often he was nasty for the sake of being nasty. Nikki nudged Saj and nodded towards their boss. Saj was better at dealing with the emotions side of stuff. With an exaggerated, but silent sigh, Saj shook his head and stepped forward. 'Weren't you leading one of the sessions, sir?'

'Yep, that I was, Malik . . . that I was.' He glanced up, his eyes lasering Sajid. Nikki shuffled her feet in the snow, feeling more dampness soak into her socks.

'I was a bastard to that woman. Told her she needed tae show a bit of guts.' His gaze moved from Sajid to Nikki. 'Told her she needed tae be a bit mair like you.'

Ah! Nikki got it. Archie was wondering if Springer had only followed the van because of his harsh words . . . inside Nikki wondered if he was right. Had his casting her up to Springer been what had sent her off acting unpredictably? Voice calm, she looked at Archie. 'Well, we'll just have to find Springer then, won't we?'

'Felicity . . . that's her name. Felicity!'

Felicity? She hadn't known that. She'd never really thought of her as having a first name. Of course, she knew she must have, everyone did, but Nikki just hadn't given it any thought and if she had, she'd have thought it might be something tough like Hilda or Eva – as in Braun or maybe like the big boss, who was cold to the point of iceberg.

She held her boss's stare until they were interrupted by a yell from Fells. 'Right, you lot. We've done all we can for now. Get your freezing arses over here and we'll walk you through what we've got. Stick to the treads though.'

Yanking her gaze away from Archie's, Nikki smiled a tight smile and squeezed his arm once. 'Get back to Trafalgar House and get things sorted at that end, boss. Saj and I have this.'

'Yeah, I've ordered the police helicopter out. It'll be up soon and maybe they'll find something.' Pausing, he bit his lip. 'Soon as yer done here, Parekh, I want you wi' me when I speak tae her family.'

Family? The Spaniel? Really? Nikki bit her lip as shame washed over her. The woman had been abducted, was clearly injured, possibly dead and she was behaving like a witch. 'Better if Saj goes with you, Archie. He's more . . . you know . . . touchy-feely than me.'

She ignored her partner's mumbled, 'That wouldn't be hard.'
'Not that I couldn't do it, you know, but . . .'

Archie cut her off. 'I asked *you*, damn it, Parekh. For once in your bloody life just do as yer told, will you?' and not waiting for her response he stormed off, coat wafting behind him in the slight breeze that had started.

When Saj snorted, Nikki rammed her elbow into his side. 'Shut up . . . just shut up.'

She watched Archie trundle back to his vehicle, before ducking under the tape with Saj to approach Gracie Fells, who was standing beside Springer's car. As soon as Nikki crouched to peer inside the vehicle, she could smell the lingering cordite in the air and her eyes were drawn to the driver's seat. She flicked a glance at the CSI. 'Gunshot?'

The CSI nodded. 'Yes, difficult to estimate where she was hit because of the impact, but if she was sitting upright in the seat, chances are, it went straight through her chest or possibly her shoulder.'

Neither option was ideal, but if it had hit her shoulder, she might still be alive. The question was, how long would her abductors want to keep an injured woman alive? And if they dumped her in this weather, even if she was alive, the chances of her staying that way for long, were next to zero. 'What did you find inside the car?'

'Her phone was in the footwell of the passenger seat.'

That tallied with Nikki's estimation of the recorded phone call. Springer seemed to somehow have lost her phone although thankfully it was on speakerphone so, although faint, they managed to pick up what she was saying.

'Her bag's in there too. Doesn't look like it's been rifled. A whole load of used tissues – more like she'd been crying than that she had a cold. We'll find out when we get them back to the lab . . . not that her crying will necessarily have anything to do with what happened to her.' The CSI moved back and pointed to the bloody slush. 'She was dragged out of the vehicle. Blood trace on the car and onto the road. Difficult, because of the snow, to gauge exactly how much blood loss. Looks like they moved her to a larger vehicle – some sort of transit van, I reckon, judging by the car tracks. We'll narrow that down when we get the casts back to the lab. But, if she saw a hand waving through the back lights, I'd reckon it was probably one of those ones you can borrow from any company, like Enterprise or the like. Those have an enclosed back and the doors open at the rear.'

'That's not going to make it any easier. We'll have to check out van rental companies in the district as well as owners. Sooner you can get the make and model narrowed down the better.'

Ignoring Gracie's annoyed tut, Nikki studied the rest of the scene as the CSI continued. 'You can see blood drops and smears as her feet are pulled through the slush, then it looks like she was put into the back of the van. The vehicle skidded as it set off making these tread marks too blurry to cast effectively, however, one of my team got some better prints twenty yards down there.'

Nikki's phone buzzed. She took it out and saw it was a text from Archie. Opening it she frowned. *What the hell?* Saj, who'd completed a circuit around the Kia, re-joined her. 'You okay, Nik? Bad news?'

Nikki flicked her phone shut and smiled. 'No, nothing like that. Just Marcus griping because I missed Sunday dinner,' she lied.

Seeing that Saj looked sceptical, Nikki turned and perused the rest of the scene. She'd deal with Archie's weird text later. Trying to replay what had happened, she cast her mind back to the recorded conversation she'd listened to numerous times on the drive to the scene. Seemed like Springer had a near-miss seconds before the final crash. The recording had clearly picked up the impact of the two vehicles. Now, seeing the scrunched-up front end of Springer's car, it was clear that Springer had rammed the vehicle in front. Had she done it to try to stop them? If so, that was madness. On the other hand, had she been trying to retrieve her phone and not noticed that the van had stopped? Or there was another option that seemed more likely, for it was what Nikki would have done if she'd been the van driver. She'd have slowed imperceptibly, waited till Springer's car was close and then slammed on her brakes, so the smaller vehicle would hit the larger one, engaging the airbags and disorientating the driver. Stupid woman hadn't thought about how conspicuous she would be on these roads on a night like this. What the hell had possessed her to go rogue? Archie's words rang in Nikki's ears . . . was she to blame? Had Archie's taunt about her needing to be more like Nikki, been what sent her into danger? Fuck! Springer was ill-prepared for any sort of fresh case. She dealt with cold cases . . . victims long dead . . . a desk jockey, who didn't see a lot of active duty. *Idiot! She should have waited for the damn back-up.* Someone had been in the back of that vehicle . . . Springer had seen a hand and then an arm protruding from the taillight – someone trying to attract attention . . . someone who wanted to escape.

If she'd been driving a van with a prisoner of some description in the back and someone on her tail, she'd have waited till they were in an isolated space and done exactly what they did. Brake hard, hope for an impact, but not been totally reliant on that alone – quick out of the van, run to the car before the driver had the chance to get orientated, yank it open. That was it – maybe . . . 'Fingerprints on the handle?'

The CSI winked. 'Doing my job for me now, are you?'

'Take it that's a no?'

'Gloves probably, only picked up smudged prints.'

Nikki let out a half-laugh. 'Ha! Well, worth a try.'

Sajid followed the tracks a little down the road and stood talking to one of the CSIs.

Nikki turned to Gracie and, voice low, said, 'You manage to get blood samples?'

'Yeah, course we did.'

Glancing down to make sure Saj was still out of earshot, Nikki continued. 'Orders from above, get it tested for these.' She turned her phone so Gracie could see Archie's text. 'Keep it on the QT, eh? Results for my eyes only, okay?'

Gracie glanced at Saj who was striding back, blowing on his hands as he surveyed the area around the crash, and nodded. 'Very mysterious, but you got it. Your eyes only . . . very 007.' And she began humming the theme tune.

Nikki scowled; now she'd be humming the damn tune too for the rest of the day, no doubt.

Saj glanced at the CSI's departing back with a quizzical expression. 'Something you're not telling me, Nik?'

'Loads . . . but I didn't think you'd be interested in my sex life.'

Saj snorted, and catching her eye, waited before speaking. 'Really? You're going with that?'

With a shrug, Nikki grinned. 'Can't share everything with you, now can I?'

'Yeah, but if it's to do with the investigation then you should, yeah?'

Nikki mentally cursed Archie. Why the hell the secrecy? She wasn't used to not sharing things with Saj. He was her partner and she trusted him, but Archie was her boss and she trusted him too. Feeling like a shit, she shrugged. 'Don't know what you mean. You know what I know.'

'Okay. If that's how you're playing it. Nothing else for us to do here and it's bloody freezing. Let's head back . . . see if we've been lucky. Maybe someone else saw something odd. Maybe a van with a dented rear end has been spotted on one of the feeder roads.'

Sighing, Nikki nodded and did a slow circle of the scene. How the hell would Springer survive this? They just had to hope she'd been alive when they took her, but who knew what condition she would be in now. 'Yep, right, let's go.'

As they walked together to their vehicles the faint sounds of a helicopter approaching got louder and both Nikki and Sajid placed their hands on their foreheads and followed its progress.

'Hope they have some luck.' Her tone betrayed her lack of conviction and once she'd shrugged out of her overalls and got into the car, Nikki waved bye to Sajid, who was already driving down the snowy lane. She flicked her key in the ignition, only to hear a grating sound. Great! Damn battery was dead. She slammed the heel of her hands on the steering wheel and screeched. If there was one thing Nikki hated, it was to ask for help with her car. Stepping back out onto the wet road, she glared at the young PC who approached carrying a set of jump leads and a huge smile. She glowered at him. 'Just get it started and if this gets round Trafalgar House, I'll know whose guts to add to my garters, right?'

Chapter 4

Running along parallel to the industrial estate, the only sounds Stefan could hear were the wind, the sound of his own breathing and the occasional swoosh of cars as they passed him, their beams lighting up the path in front of him. After the third car passed him, stirring up a flurry of slush and drenched his thin trackie bottoms in the process, Stefan realized he was too visible on the main road. He should have stuck to the periphery of the estate where shadows and bushes offered some cover from any would-be pursuers. He'd just changed direction to head back into the estate via a gap in some bushes when he heard the sound of a larger vehicle approaching. The hairs on the back of his neck sprung up and he dived flat onto his belly. He had no idea if they were after him or not yet, but he couldn't help feeling on edge. From his prone position on the grass he eyed the van as it neared. It was a white transit and it was driving more slowly than the weather conditions necessitated. Stefan held his breath, praying they wouldn't see him and, when they continued past the spot where he lay, he exhaled slowly. He was sure it was Bullet and he was equally sure he was looking for him, so it was just as well he'd decided to head back into the estate. How the hell had they been alerted to his absence so quickly? Then he puzzled it out. One of the men he worked beside, slept beside, was a snitch.

He'd just decided that he could risk moving when he heard the sound of a vehicle revving up and sure enough the white transit was revving backwards. In a panic, Stefan crawled over to the gap in the bushes and slid through. He'd just re-entered the estate when he heard the van doors open, followed by frenetic barking and Bullet's guttural tone breaking through the night.

'Go get him, boys.'

Shit, they'd brought the bloody dogs. Legs pounding, Stefan tore between buildings looking for some way to escape, the barks and growls growing nearer as he ran. Finally, he saw a huge industrial bin and, wondering if he was sealing his fate, but having no other choice, he pulled himself up, slid the rolling lid back and dropped in on top of a pile of cardboard boxes. After closing the lid, he burrowed to the bottom of the bin, covering himself with layers of cardboard and once more prayed the dogs would lose his scent.

Sounds from outside were muffled and it was difficult to decide if his pursuers were coming any closer or not. He could hear barking and yelling, but it was distorted. The heat generated by the cardboard warmed Stefan up slowly and he began to think that his safest bet was to remain here till the dead of night and then make another bid for freedom. He could catch some sleep and he'd be dry and warm. He smiled. The mere thought of not having to move for a few hours, not having to listen to other peoples' bodily functions, not having to smell the great unwashed, was like a gift to him. He sighed, reassured by the silence that had descended outside.

A sharp rat-a-tat-tat somewhere near his head shattered his reassurance. Someone was out there banging on the side of the bin. Stefan held his breath and his body stiffened. Maybe it was one of the workers out for a smoke. He strained his ears. He couldn't hear anything else – no dogs, no voices. Maybe whoever it was had gone.

Then it came – a coarse singsong whisper penetrating the plastic bin – taunting and at the same time chilling him. 'Come out, come out, wherever you are.'

This was followed by ferocious yelping and Stefan knew the game was up. The lid was thrown back and a bright torch shone into the inside. In a last-ditch attempt, Stefan remained still and silent, but it was no good. Whoever shone the torch followed that by pushing a long prod through the layers of cardboard. When it connected with his body, Stefan braced himself not to react, then the electric current from the Taser had him yelping in pain as his entire body shook for a moment and then became numb. Seconds later, two of Bullet's henchmen dragged him from the bin and flung him in a heap on the wet ground. The dogs salivating and over-excited pranced and jumped close to him, taking the odd nipping bite before they were yanked back by their owners.

'Oh dear. This makes me very sad, you know. It also makes my boss very sad.' Bullet tilted his head to one side and laughed. 'Actually, it doesn't make him sad so much as angry.'

He waved his phone in the air. 'He told me to hit you where it hurts and boy, am I going to enjoy doing that.' He gestured to his thugs who dragged Stefan, feet trailing through the deserted industrial estate to where the transit van waited. As they flung him in and slammed the door shut, Stefan was glad that he was the only one to be punished. He couldn't bear it if Maria had to suffer any more at the hands of these brutes.

Chapter 5

It had taken Xavier over an hour to drive to the old farmhouse in the middle of the moors and it was only courtesy of his police scanner that he'd been able to avoid the patrol cars and the crime scene itself. He took a moment to get in character. His code name, Xavier, made him feel quite sophisticated. Xavier in the X-Men was a visionary . . . an intellectual . . . a leader – all the qualities he himself rated highly. He allowed himself a grin as he acknowledged that his aims were more in line with Magneto's than Xavier's. It amused him to subvert the idea of a superhero; after all, heroes were all in the eyes of their beholders, weren't they?

Looking through the windscreen at the snow-covered yard, Xavier's good humour dissipated a little. The weekend had started off fine . . . in fact, until this morning, it had been great. The Community Liaison Conference had been amusing. He'd been asked to speak at the session on modern-day slavery and that had given him a buzz. All those people from social services, policing, education, local government, politicians and the like hanging onto his every word. Then there was his down time . . . that had been satisfying, or rather *she'd* been satisfying.

When the phone call came, his rage had clouded his mind for a moment. *Bloody Stefan Marcovici!* Xavier made a point of not knowing their names – too bloody many of them to remember anyway – but Stefan Marcovici had become a risk to the entire operation and so Xavier had to sanction drastic action. That in itself didn't bother him. No, what bothered him was that he'd not been there to witness it, but Cyclops, his right-hand man was right. Bullet and his cronies could deal with it. In fact, they'd enjoy it. Besides which, he needed to distance himself from this and just as well, because now he had these two fools and their mess to deal with and that was on top of the existing problem of Adam Glass's betrayal. Seemed like trouble did come in threes, but by the end of the night his minions would have cleaned it all up and it would be back to business as usual.

The one sensible thing the idiots had managed since picking up the bint who was following them, was to get as far away from the scene as possible and head for safe house number two. Why they'd shot her, he didn't know, and why they'd decided it was best to throw her in the back of the van and cart her here was beyond him. *That's what comes when you have to rely on lowlifes.* He inhaled deeply and took a moment, releasing his breath slowly.

Now that he'd switched off his headlights, the only light source was the moon and the few stars visible between the snow-heavy clouds. It was like some dystopian wilderness and that was just what he wanted; silence with no nosey parkers around to meddle.

No sign of the van, so they must have hidden it in one of the outbuildings. Smart move. Not that there were many passers-by, but best to be safe. They'd done well, he supposed, to black-out the windows. No light escaped from the sides and the gas heaters they'd transported up weeks ago negated the need for an open fire and the subsequent telltale smoke. To the casual eye, the building and outbuildings looked deserted, just as they should. He'd chosen this old house because of its location. Far enough from the touristy moorland walks, yet not so far that he couldn't have the goods transported to anywhere in the district in record time. His men had been trained to be on the lookout for over-curious nosey parkers and as per his instructions, none of his deserted properties were used to store his assets for more than a few weeks at a time.

He employed a random rotation model that had served him well: neither his rivals nor the authorities had shown any interest in his doings so far. He smiled. Even if they had, he was so far removed from the dirty end of things that nothing could be traced back to him. Even the goons inside were unaware of his true identity and that was the way he intended to keep it. What was it they called it? Plausible deniability?

Before exiting his 'borrowed' vehicle, he got his game face on. Well, actually it was a balaclava, but it served the same purpose. He wasn't exactly pissed off by what had happened today. Other than a minor inconvenience for himself and the waste of a Sunday afternoon that could have been better spent screwing his mistress, it was mere irritation, but combined with the other stuff, it niggled. Not because he personally felt under threat – he was secure in the knowledge that nothing could end up at his doorstep – but because he hated incompetence, hated needless complications. In his experience, complications left to their own devices could unravel and that's why he'd elected to come here himself. If he couldn't deal with Marcovici, he could deal with this cock-up . . . make sure it was tied up with no loose threads.

However, he had a role to play and play it he must. The fact that he enjoyed taking on a bullying persona was just an added bonus. He stepped out of the vehicle into a couple of inches of snow, glad that he'd changed his clothes before heading off here. Even without the snow, none of his premises were what you'd call muck-free and as he found himself up to his ankles in mucky slush, he grimaced before heading to the door and rapping three times.

The door opened a crack to reveal a wide-eyed Danny Boy. Immediately the door opened all the way to allow him access. 'Hi, boss.'

The lad's tone was high pitched and the way his pistol shook, despite being pointed at the ground, betrayed his nervousness. The X-Man smiled. It was always good to keep them on edge. No point in letting them get complacent. They needed to know exactly who was boss. He grunted and brushed past the lad making his way into the dimly lit living room where Danny Boy's brother, Jason was huddled on a rickety wooden chair in front of the heater. Jason jumped to his feet as soon as the door opened, casting a nervous glance at his brother.

The two of them were fairly new recruits and this was their first solo job. The fact that it had gone so awry was clearly making them antsy and Xavier intended to capitalize on that. 'Tell me!'

As Xavier grabbed the chair, whipped it round and straddled it backwards, Danny shuffled over next to his brother. 'We picked up the package like we were supposed to and were heading to the safe house to await further instructions. Then Jase noticed we were being followed, like. She kept coming up close and then lagging behind and then right up close again. She were on her phone and . . .'

'You panicked?'

Relief flooded Jason's face as he nodded.

Keeping his tone conversational, Xavier inclined his head slightly to one side. 'And do I pay you to panic?'

Again, the boys exchanged worried glances and Xavier had to swallow a chuckle. This was such fun. He hardened his tone. 'Then what happened?'

Words splurged out of Jason's mouth like diarrhoea in a shithouse. 'We braked really hard and she rammed into the back of us and Danny got out of the van and shot her. But she wun't dead and then we saw that the package had punched out the back light.' He gulped in a breath before continuing. 'And so we shoved her in the back with him and kicked him a few times till he conked out. Then we came here instead of the first safe house.'

'Why did you do that?' Xavier jumped to his feet, his body full

33

of bristling anger as he paced the room, nervous energy zapping off him like thunderbolts as he moved. The two idiots in front of him had no idea what to tell him . . . no idea at all. That's what happened when you relied on inexperienced yokels. They made mistakes and then had no idea how to rectify them, so instead they compounded them.

'What possessed you to bring her with you?'

Danny Boy bit his lip, like a 2-year-old. 'Thought she might talk otherwise? Thought it best to keep her close, like.'

Give me strength. 'And who is she?'

This time the colour drained from Danny's face and Xavier thought he was going to be sick, so he looked at Jason. 'Well?'

Jason blinked. 'Dunno.'

Lowering his voice till it was barely a whisper, Xavier, punctuated each word with a pause. 'You . . . don't . . . know?'

Both men shook their heads and Xavier jumped to his feet, sending the chair toppling across the floor and began pacing. They'd had one simple transportation job to do. Not rocket science, not complex, not requiring more than a half-functioning brain and yet *still* they'd messed up. Messed up big time. Okay, so it wasn't disastrous, but *they* didn't know that. They had to be taught a lesson. Mistakes could be fatal and they needed to learn not to make any more. He stopped pacing and spun round to glare at them. The younger one backed up a step, glancing at his brother, looking for guidance.

'It's stupidity that gets us into this sort of mess. Things have been under the wire and I'd intended to keep it that way until we had full control. Now you imbeciles have scuppered that. Now we have to react and if there's one thing I hate doing it's reacting. Reacting implies a lack of control. Reacting adds variables over which we have no control.'

He glared at the vacant looks on the boys' faces. Before this day was over, they would no longer be reacting, they would have learned their lesson . . . the hard way.

Xavier kicked the toppled chair and it crashed against the wall, making the brothers jump. 'Take me to them.'

It was almost comical the way they scampered to the door, in their willingness to please. 'They're in the van in the barn.'

Xavier smiled. He'd already decided that they needed to dispose of Glass, after all it was his stupidity in trying to escape that had landed them here in the first place. Now that they'd got the bank account codes off him there was no need to keep him alive. How he'd had the gall to syphon money from his deals, Xavier couldn't understand. The idiot would pay dearly for trying to cheat him, but perhaps nature would have done its job and the cheat may have frozen to death. That still left the problem of the woman . . . but hell . . . they'd just have to dump the bodies separately.

Using torches, the three men made their way through a fine drizzle of rain to the ramshackle old barn. Xavier was pleased to see that despite the isolated location, they'd still padlocked the doors shut. Maybe they weren't quite as useless as he'd first thought. Perhaps he'd give them the benefit of the doubt this time. After all, he, Xavier, was nothing if not merciful and help was hard to come by these days.

Danny Boy opened the back door and Xavier jumped up. His torch danced over the male body sprawled near to the door.

'What you waiting for? Get the fuck up here. Find out if he's still with us. Then get the body disposed of. Get a move on.'

Jason jumped up. 'Yes, boss.'

'He dead?' Xavier's tone was hopeful.

Jason went over and held two fingers on the man's neck, before looking up at his boss, shaking his head. 'Nope, still alive.'

Ah well, that wouldn't last. Xavier turned to the other figure, his torch dancing over her face taking in her blood-soaked coat and blouse, the paleness of her face. *Shit! It's her! Would you fucking believe it?* 'She's a pig, you idiots.'

Jason placed his fingers on her neck, then looked up, all colour wiped from his face. 'Aw crap, boss. She's a dead pig.'

Dumping the body of a lowlife was one thing but killing a police officer and then disposing of her was another. Xavier didn't feel quite as generous towards his two goons, now that he saw the extent of the mess they'd created. But he had more to worry about . . . much more. He couldn't be sure that there was no forensic link back to him. The last thing he needed was to be drawn into the investigation of a murdered police officer and held up to any sort of public scrutiny. Not when he had a family and a legitimate job as well as his other sidelines to consider. 'You got a spot in mind?'

'Leave that to me and Jase. We've got the dump spot all sorted, like. We won't let you down. Not again.'

'They both need to be disposed of. But separately. She needs to be dumped where she won't be found for months – the middle of the moors or somewhere. And him . . .' Xavier kicked the prone man. 'Finish him. And make sure you use the usual forensic measures – yeah?'

'Eh?' Jason looked puzzled, but his brother nudged him and said, 'Bleach, ya tosser. Bleach.'

'Okay, I'm counting on you. Get on with it.'

Chapter 6

By the time Nikki, with the help of the young police officer, had coaxed her Vauxhall Zafira back to life at the crime scene and managed to set off back to Trafalgar House, it was getting dark and although the snow had stopped, the clouds still looked heavy with the promise of more to come. In truth, whilst the young lad had got out the jump leads Nikki always kept in her boot for such emergencies, and managed to manoeuvre a patrol car into position that allowed the leads to reach both vehicles, Nikki was on the phone barking instructions to the officer Archie had commandeered to oversee things till Nikki and Sajid got back. She was more than capable of jump-starting her car. She'd had to do it on numerous occasions recently and was now seriously considering bumping the purchase of a new car battery higher up her priority shopping list than new DMs for herself. *Damn car!* Her hands were freezing, her toes were numb, and she was better employed sitting in her marginally warmer car organizing things than fannying about in the slush getting colder. Besides, as her car engine sputtered to life, the officer, unlike herself, was dressed for the weather. She gave him a thumbs-up as she backed down the narrow lane, and stopping when she drew level with him, she wound down her window. 'Remember, no telling DC Malik about this, okay?'

As the grinning officer shook his head, Nikki frowned. 'In fact, no telling anybody, yeah?'

'Lips are sealed, Detective, lips are sealed.'

Satisfied, Nikki nodded put her window back up and, wishing that her vehicle would choose today to spontaneously burst heat from its contrary fan, set off.

By the time she reached the station, the promised snow had started again and Nikki was glad she'd missed driving in it. Entering the Trafalgar House car park, she was pleased to note the absence of the media. Last thing they needed was this leaking before they had a chance to speak to Springer's next of kin. She ran up the steps to the officers' entrance at the back of the station and jogged up to the incident room, bursting through the door, causing it to bang against the wall and rebound back almost hitting her in the face. Dodging it, she moved into the room and cast her eyes round. Apart from Sajid, a couple of uniformed officers momentarily looked up from their computers at her entrance. Otherwise the room was deserted. Everybody else was either at home or out following up the limited leads they had on Springer.

'Ah, you're back.' Sajid, alerted by her dramatic entrance, turned around from the crime board he was creating. At the top he'd scrawled, 'DS Felicity Springer' and underneath 'Abducted/ Missing?' 'Was beginning to wonder if that chunk of metal you call a car had finally given up on you.'

Hoping that the officer who'd helped her would keep his side of the bargain, Nikki tutted. 'Oh, ye of little faith. Course it didn't let me down. Pure gold, that car.'

Ignoring Sajid's disbelieving snort, she bent down, undid her DMs and peeled off her sodden socks before swiping a discarded newspaper from one of the cluttered desks. Scrunching it up, she stuffed pages of it into her boots and then placed them and her socks onto the heater.

'Fire risk.'

Nikki raised her middle finger at her colleague and glanced round. 'Archie?'

Sajid tilted his head towards Archie's office. 'In there.'

Nikki began to march towards it, but Sajid's next words stopped her in her tracks. 'Wouldn't go in. He's not alone and he's not a happy bunny.'

'Oh? Who's he with?'

'The big boss.' He lowered his voice. 'Something's going on, Nik and whatever it is, it's serious. You should've seen Archie. I thought he was going to explode.'

Nikki looked at the blinds that now obscured whatever was going on inside the room. That was strange in itself. Archie rarely lowered the blinds, preferring an open-door policy, or, as Nikki suspected, he really liked to keep an eye on what was going on in the office. Archie had been acting strangely all day. Agitated and off-kilter. Then, of course, there was that really strange and secretive request he'd made. Now he was ensconced in his office with the big boss, blinds closed. Detective Chief Superintendent Eva Clark was pretty much a hands-off boss. If she wanted to see Archie, she'd normally request his presence upstairs in her office, so what had prompted her to come down here? *What the hell's going on?* 'How long they been in there?'

'She arrived just as I got back.'

Nikki exhaled and then walked over to stand beside Saj. 'Okay, let's deal with the Archie situation later. We need to focus on Springer. Did we get some officers sent over to interview the hotel staff? We can't rule out that it may have been a planned and targeted attack.'

'Yep, I asked them to grab any CCTV footage they could, just to be sure. Everything from Friday afternoon through to ten o'clock this morning, when the conference officially ended.' Sajid frowned.

Nikki knew her partner well enough to sense his discomfort. 'Spit it out then.'

'It's just, apparently someone else already requested copies of the hotel's CCTV of the conference.' He paused. 'All of it.'

Nikki shrugged. 'No big deal. As long as we've got it, that's fine. Maybe Archie was on the ball and requested it.'

Saj nodded. 'Yeah. It was Archie who requested it.'

Nikki nudged his arm. 'There then. No big mystery.'

'Well, that's just it, Nik. Archie made the request at 10.47 a.m.'

As his words sunk in, Nikki exhaled. She pulled out a chair and sank into it. 'You sure?'

'Yep. I even phoned the hotel myself to double check.'

'Shit! What's going on?'

'No idea, but it's damn weird that Archie put in that request almost an *hour* before we got the call from Springer.'

Nikki agreed. This was strange and if she and Saj were to be able to do their job, Archie needed to start sharing with them. There was something off about all of this and Nikki needed to get to the bottom of it. She cast another impatient glance at Archie's office and for a second considered barging in then and there and demanding to be told exactly what was going on. Fortunately, good sense prevailed and instead she focused on the task in hand. She'd deal with Archie later. 'Have we got a copy?'

When Saj nodded she said, 'Well, let's at least have a look at Springer leaving the hotel. We can start following her journey from the hotel to when she disappeared.'

They huddled over the computer with the largest screen and Saj fiddled to get the recording to the right spot. 'She signed out at 9.57 a.m., so here's the footage of the front entrance and hotel car park from eight-thirty.'

They fast-forwarded the recording, keeping an eye out for any transit vans or anything else that stood out. At one minute to ten, Felicity Springer exited the hotel, pulling a trolley case behind her.

'Pause it and zoom in.' Nikki rarely looked at Springer, prefer-ring to pretend the other woman didn't exist. Now, it felt a little strange observing her without her knowledge. She frowned. Did Springer look upset? Hard to tell really with the fuzziness of the CCTV, but her body language seemed off. Her head was down, her shoulders, hunched. 'Try to get a shot of her face, Saj.'

Saj fiddled a bit, fast-forwarding, and finally managed to get a shot of Springer's face. 'She looks upset.'

Nikki shrugged. 'Maybe. Or perhaps she's just hungover. Difficult to tell. Let's play on. What I want to know is where she went after this. No way did it take nearly an hour and a half to get to where we found her car.'

They watched as Springer approached her Kia and after slinging her trolley into the boot, got into the driver's seat. Nikki tried to swallow the pang of envy when she mentally compared the glossy sleek bodywork to her dented wreck. Then she remembered the state of it as she'd seen it earlier with its front end all bashed in, a bullet hole in the driver's seat and blood on the upholstery. Maybe her own Zafira was preferable after all.

'Smooth ride.'

Nikki grunted and ignored Sajid's comment. 'What the hell's she doing? Why's she not moving?'

Sajid fast-forwarded, minute after minute scrolled past on the screen yet the car remained, engine on but unmoving. Then the door opened.

Nikki pointed to the screen. 'Quick, she's getting out.'

Saj rewound a little and replayed it on normal speed. The door swung open and then Springer's head appeared as she vomited onto the concrete. 'Ah, hungover it is, then.'

'Looks like it,' said Nikki. 'Perhaps that's why she chose to take the back roads despite the snow. Maybe she wanted to avoid getting stopped if she thought she was still over the limit.' She looked at Saj and saw her own disbelief mirrored on his face. 'Doesn't seem like The Spaniel though, does it?'

'Nah, she doesn't strike me as a get-pissed-at-a-conference sort of woman.'

'Right. Anybody managed to get in touch with her sidekick? Bashir, is it?'

Saj shook his head. 'Extended annual leave. Gone to Pakistan. Grandad's poorly apparently.'

At that point, Nikki's phone rang. She looked at it and groaned. 'It's my mum.'

'Well, you gotta answer it, Nik. See what she's been up to.'

Nikki's mum had gone to India with her elder sister, supposedly to shop for Nikki's cousin, Monika's wedding. But they'd been gone over a month already. In that time, they'd celebrated Holi with relatives in Gujarat, visited the Taj Mahal in Agra, the Red Fort in Jaipur and Gandhi's ashram in Ahmedebad and now had returned to Gujarat to shop. Nikki missed her mum and would be glad when she returned to Bradford, but right now she didn't want to have the conversation she suspected her mum wanted to have. 'She's going to Navsari tomorrow.'

'And?'

The phone continued to ring. 'Bloody sari shopping.' Nikki frowned and answered it, resigned to the conversation about colours and textures and designs that she would have to have. 'Hi Mum, you okay?'

Sajid yelled, 'Hi Lalita. Don't worry, I'm keeping Nikki under control whilst you're away.'

Her mother sent her love back to Sajid, and then Nikki, with a half-smile on her face, listened to her mum describe the meal she'd had the previous night and a proposed trip to a hill station for the following week, before the conversation turned to clothes. 'You need to give me some idea of colours, Nikita. Anika, Charlie and Ruby have all given me detailed lists. Even Sunni and Marcus have chosen a few suit designs.'

Nikki grimaced and stuck out her tongue at Sajid who was grinning at her, seemingly enjoying her discomfort. It was okay for the others, Anika and the girls. They liked flouncing around in saris and Indian suits. Nikki hated it. It wasn't her style. She always felt uncomfortable. Hoping to reach a compromise, she put a smile into her voice and said, 'You know what I'd really like to wear for the wedding?'

Her mother snorted and Nikki thought she heard her say 'jeans' but she ignored that and said. 'A suit. A nice simple shalwar kameez. That's what I'd like to wear.'

With a raised eyebrow, Sajid mouthed, 'Really?' at her.

Nikki turned her back on him. Of course, she didn't want to wear a suit either, but it would be more manageable than a sari.

'Nikki, it's a wedding. We need to sparkle. Tell you what. I'll get you and Anika similar saris. Five or six each should do.'

Nikki's voice rose. 'Five or six?' Shit, no. She had three perfectly good ones at home, why wouldn't those do? But her mum was already blowing kisses down the phone and giving instructions to pass her love onto the rest of the family before hanging up.

'You look like you've been nuked.'

Nikki tightened her ponytail, grazed her fingers over the scar on her neck and exhaled. 'Bloody feel like it too. Let's get back to Springer.'

They spent the next twenty minutes going through the ANPR footage. They caught sight of the van Springer had described but as she'd said, its registration plates both front and back were obscured.

'It doesn't look like it targeted her. It was in front of her most of the way from the Wakefield roundabout onwards. Do you think she saw something peculiar before she phoned it in and that's why she followed it?'

Nikki shook her head. 'That doesn't tie in with her call. It seems to have been completely arbitrary. Which means we've got to look for a needle in a haystack. Bet there's thousands of unmarked plain-white transit vans in the district.'

Saj nodded, looking as fed up as she felt. 'I'll action it and get a couple of uniforms trawling through it. Any word from the helicopter search yet?'

'Nah, probably too soon.'

'Okay, we need to interview everyone at the conference too. Not that I think her disappearance is owt to do with that conference but still, better to cover all our bases.'

Sajid was already scrolling down a list of delegates and conference attendees. 'This lot are a right motley bunch. We've got your Anika's boyfriend, the ever so moral – and married, I hasten to add – Yousaf Mirza. Also, that homophobic friend of yours from vice, DI Joe Drummond. Archie's on the list as is his mate DCI Eddie Capaldi and a whole load more dignitaries.'

His voice trailed off as Archie's office door slammed open and DCS Clark stormed past them with barely a nod of acknowledgement as she left. Archie, red-faced, with his hair spiked on top of his head like two devil horns on either side of his bald patch followed her into the room, staring after his boss with a frown that was enough to have Nikki hesitate before approaching him.

He seemed to realize that Sajid and Nikki were staring at him and growled out a 'Well?'

Nikki told him what they had, including the fact that someone had already requested the CCTV footage from the conference hotel. If she'd been expecting Archie to slam the heel of his hand against his brow and say 'Och aye. That was me Parekh, slipped my mind,' she'd have been mistaken. His expression didn't change, not even when she wondered aloud about the fact the footage had been secured before any crime had been reported. This was so unlike Archie and it chilled her. Even Sajid looked flustered and he only knew half the story.

'Need a word with you, Parekh.' Archie lumbered back into his office. As she followed him, Nikki noticed the blinds were still down and she hoped she wasn't about to be pulled any deeper into whatever was going off. If she was, she'd no intention of keeping Sajid out of the loop and if Archie requested that, then he could go and jump.

Choosing to stand, hoping it would speed things up, Nikki

waited till Archie had lowered his sizeable frame into his chair and attempted to keep her expression neutral. She realized she hadn't succeeded when Archie, studying her for a long moment finally said, 'Face like a slapped arse, Parekh. Something up?'

Nikki gestured to the door that DCS Clark had left through and raised her eyebrows. 'You tell me?'

Archie wafted his hands in front of him, his tone tired, almost defeated. 'Sit, Parekh. Yer putting my proverbials on edge standing there like a bloody high court judge. No, scrap that. Yer mair like the damn executioner and after the morning I've had I can dae withoot it.'

Giving in, Nikki sank into a chair and waited. However, when Archie began to speak, it wasn't what she'd expected to hear. She'd expected some semblance of an explanation about all the weird subterfuge, but instead . . . 'You're aware that it's unlikely DI Ferguson will return. Medically speaking, he's not fit for the job.'

Archie's piercing eyes met Nikki's and her heart fluttered. Why was there a brick in her stomach? She shook her head as if to ward off whatever words Archie was about to come out with, but to no avail. Ferguson had seriously hurt his back earlier in the year on a car chase and had been off since.

'I've spoken with the chief and, perhaps a wee bit reluctantly if I'm honest, she's agreed you can step up to acting DI for the time being.'

This was the last thing she'd been expecting and she was stunned. DI? Her? Yeah, the money would be handy, but she had to consider her family too. She already put so much into the job, this just seemed like a step too far for her. Besides, she liked working with Saj. She shook her head. 'No way, boss. No chance. You know fine and well I'd hate that. I'm an on-the-streets sort of officer. No way I want to be DI, acting or otherwise.'

Archie just nodded. 'I was afraid ye'd say that, Parekh. So, what I'm going tae do is gi' you a bit of time. Let you think aboot it.' As Nikki opened her mouth to object, he raised a finger. 'Don't say another word. We've got tae get our arse in gear and speak to Springer's next of kin before they issue a statement tae the press.'

'You mean you and Saj, yeah? You'll take Saj with you. He's good at all the touchy-feely stuff.'

'No, I mean you. I told you earlier. Stop trying tae squirm out of it. Now, hop it. I need to check her file for the address. Five minutes, okay?'

What? That was it? No mention of him ordering the recordings, no explanation of the strange request he'd made earlier and still a whole load of secrecy. This was rubbish. She glowered at Archie, making her feelings known, but he didn't even glance her way as she moved to the door. She'd just stretched out her hand to the handle when he cleared his throat. 'You ordered that other test, Parekh? The one I texted you about?'

Not bothering to turn round, she nodded. 'Course, though I'd rather have been able to tell Saj. What's the big mystery?' She hesitated, waiting for Archie to respond, but all she heard was the rustle of papers. She half-turned and looked at him. 'We pulled the CCTV footage from the hotel the conference was held at.'

After long seconds, Archie replied with a grunt. 'Good. Let me know what you find, eh?'

Heart sinking, Nikki pulled the door open and walked through, desperate to escape the suffocating secrets that hung in Archie's room. Even the stink of the big office with all its ambient variants was an improvement.

Chapter 7

Felicity's arms ached. In fact, despite the biting cold, her entire body ached. She thought she'd felt crap when she woke up, but right now, the only thing keeping her from giving up completely was Stevie. Stevie wouldn't cope without her so, there was only one option. She needed to get out of this mess.

She lay still for a few moments, thinking. She was on her side, on top of a metal surface, in the dark and the cold, with an itchy blanket half over her. So, they'd probably dumped her in the back of the van and driven her somewhere. The van was silent so unless they were being ultra-quiet in the driver's cab, she thought she might be alone. Her nostrils twitched at the oily petrol smell that wafted off the cover and she regurgitated a little bit of alcoholic vomit. If she wasn't so damn cold, she would have kicked it off already. Her arms had been pulled behind her and her wrists were bound. When she moved them, whatever was binding them became tighter, scouring her flesh and sending shooting pain up her arms and into her shoulders. *Cable ties.* What should she do? What could she do? She moved her legs and discovered that her feet were bound together and only the presence of her jeans was saving them from chafing her skin.

She wanted to close her eyes and give in to the pain, but instead, a glimmer of a thought flickered into their mind. At first, she was resistant and then as the flicker persisted, she realized she had no other option if she wanted to survive. At the conference, Archie had looked at her scathingly and told her she should be 'more like Parekh' and that might be exactly what she needed to do to stay alive. She was no Nikita Parekh, yet, much as she despised the woman . . . distrusted her even, she knew that the tenacious thought niggling inside her throbbing head might be the only thing that would get her out of this mess. *What would Nikki Parekh do?*

Against her better judgement, Felicity Springer considered her options. Parekh would probably assess her physical condition. Felicity had no real knowledge that her supposition was true. She hardly knew Parekh – not really. Any interaction was always acrimonious, yet with a conviction born of these observations and office gossip, she knew that Parekh would *not* just curl up and die. She would fight. That's what she'd done the previous year and that's what she would do in this situation. Parekh was nothing if not fearless and determined. Keeping that thought in mind, Felicity hardened her resolve and began to assess her own physical condition.

Her shoulder ached like a bastard, and she suspected the bullet had gone straight through it. The smell of fresh blood made her feel a little nauseous, yet the fact that she was conscious and relatively clear-headed told her someone had staunched the bleeding. Her right arm felt useless by her side. Every movement was like a million pinpricks concentrated on her wound and she wanted to scream. *Bet bloody Parekh would just suck it up and be on her feet already.* Still feeling groggy, both by her hangover from the previous night and by the waves of nausea that rolled over her every few seconds, she tried to complete her injury inventory. On a scale from one to ten, her shoulder was a definite eight – no way would she consider it a ten; she had to think like Parekh, had to keep some reserves in play, so she couldn't allow her bullet wound to be a ten. Using her newly devised criteria, she decided that her entire body, arms, shoulders, legs, crotch . . . all of that was a six.

The sound of her own breathing roared in her head, disorientating her. She needed to channel Nikki, so she slowed her breathing right down, long slow breaths and gradually she was able to focus on listening. She held her breath and strained her ears to see if she could hear the faint breathing of anyone else beside her. Nothing. There'd definitely been someone in distress in the transit van she'd followed. Had they been injured in the impact? Was she lying next to a dead person? The thought freaked her out and she began to drag in big breaths that increased her pain tenfold. *Get a grip, Fliss. Get a bloody grip. You deal with cold cases, skeletonized corpses and bodies every day. Get a damn grip.* The only difference was, she was in control then. Now she was at the mercy of some unknown assailant, in the middle of God knows where, channelling her inner bloody Parekh. If nothing else told her how bad the situation was, that one thing did.

'Hello?' Even to her own ears her voice sounded tremulous. She tried again a little louder, but not too loud in case someone *was* in the front cab of the van, 'Hello? Is anyone there?' Still nothing, so either she was alone or the person whose arm she'd seen through the taillight was unconscious. With determination she pushed away the addendum . . . 'Or dead.' She was *not* going to think that way. She was alive, she was able to move a little, she was alone. All of the above were things she could use to her advantage.

She rocked a little on her side – tentative and controlled. A groan escaped her lips as she fell back into her original position. *Body, six and a half more like – not a seven though.* No, she couldn't allow the rest of her body to be a seven. It had to be well below the most painful injury on the pain scale. This was going to be hard. She took a deep breath and tried to roll onto her back, so she could see better. It wasn't quite absolute darkness. There were shadows and shapes looming around her, some larger than others and some smaller. All she had to do was focus and she might find something to help her escape from her current predicament. All she had to do was overcome her pain and move round the vehicle, surely there would be something in here to help her.

Using her bound feet for leverage, Felicity began to push herself backwards to where she thought the front of the van was. Maybe she'd find a tool, something to cut her ties, something she could use as a weapon. Her head banged gently against a solid surface and she tilted her head, trying to work out what it was, but the light was too dim. Using her feet to propel her round so her hands could feel the surface, she ignored the warm blood that trickled from her shoulder and ended up pooling at her wrists. She got herself in position and strained her shoulder upwards, so her hands could touch the surface, and almost cried when she realized that instead of heading to the front of the vehicle, she'd slithered herself to the back instead.

She was at the door, but there was no way she could either stand up or reach the handle to open it, which, knowing her luck would be locked anyway. Her shoulders slumped, and the sensation of sticky blood on her bare hands and wrists was gross. She hated dirt, hated gore, hated anything like that. Stevie often teased her about nappies and baby sick. Not her fault if she had an aversion to all that crap. The glimmer of Nikki Parekh was in danger of fading; pain was hitting a nine. *Can't let it hit ten. If it gets to ten, I might as well give up.*

She moved her wrists, tried to wipe some of the blood off onto her sleeve. It strained her shoulders, but she was prepared to bottle the pain if she could just get rid of that horrid stickiness. At the back of her mind she was aware that she was becoming a little hysterical . . . a little panicked, still she kept flexing and unflexing her wrists, desperate to get rid of the cloying gunge. It was invading her nostrils with its coppery abattoir smell. Tears streamed down her cheeks as she kept frantically moving. It wasn't a sudden awareness that the cable ties were shifting with her movements, more of a gradual dawning. Her moving hands slowed as she savoured the fact that the ties moved up and down her wrists without causing quite so much pain – a four now instead of a six. She tried twisting them to the right and then to the left – definitely slacker. The blood from her shoulder was lubricating the cable ties making it easier for her to move them. If she could only persevere a bit more – channel a bit more Parekh – then maybe she could get out of them. Separating her wrists as wide as she could, she began moving again – this time more frantic. It was sore – course it was – a seven, maybe nearly an eight, the cable ties were digging into her wrists, despite the lubrication, but the gap between her wrists was getting wider. Finally, breathless, sore and tired, Felicity reckoned she had created enough slack.

First, she tried to yank both hands out together, but all she succeeded in doing was hurting her wrists even more. It was then she had the idea of manoeuvring one bloody hand out at a time. Keeping her fingers as close together as she could, and tucking her thumb in, she pulled her right hand up whilst sliding her left down trying to maximize the space between them. It took a few attempts and when she finally succeeded, her right arm jerked, causing a sharp dagger to shoot through her shoulder. Dizzy and gasping in pain, her breath rasping in her throat, she couldn't quite believe she'd managed to get out of the cable ties. Her fingers were numb as the blood flooded them – ten fat sausages on the end of her hands. *A definite eight. Not a nine though, definitely not a nine. Take that Parekh. Just take that!*

Now what? Freer now, Felicity rolled onto her back and brought her hands round to rest on her stomach. Forcing herself to block out the pain, she wiggled her digits, willing her circulation to do its job, willing the numbness to go so she could use them. After what seemed like ages, she rested her elbows on either side of her body, and minimizing the pressure on her still recovering hands, she got herself into a sitting position, leaning against the door. Her feet didn't have the same numbness she had experienced in her hands and it took her a moment to realize that the ties weren't as tight around her feet. If she pulled the material from her jeans up that would loosen them even more and if she removed her ankle boots, she'd be able to get them off completely. She'd be untethered.

The thought spurred her into action and she forced her clumsy fingers to first pull her jeans out from under the ties and then she was able to pull the ties further up her leg as she unzipped her boots. She took frequent breaks to rest her shoulder which, though she was loathe to admit it, was now hitting nine, possibly even nine and a half. She needed to get out of there. Needed to get out of this damn metal coffin. Needed to get back to Stevie. She'd never admit to anyone that she'd channelled Nikki Parekh of all people to help her. No, that would be her secret – one she'd take with her to the grave. Unable to bend down one more time, Felicity jiggled one foot at a time until her boots were nearly off and then, with a final effort, managed to flip them off completely, before manoeuvring one foot, then the other from the cables.

The relief was like a tsunami knocking her backwards against the metal panels. But it was short-lived. She gasped as she realized time might not be on her side. Felicity shuffled over to her boots, rammed them on and clambered to her feet, her hands outstretched and feeling for the handles that would guarantee her release.

Her hand latched onto the mechanism at the same time as a grinding sound reached her. Someone was coming in. Someone was nearby. Fear flooded her body as she wondered whether they would check on her, and if they would look to make sure that she was still secured. Falling to her knees, Felicity grabbed the cables and put one foot in, lay on her left side facing the door with her hands clasped behind her and shrugged the smelly fabric half over her body, praying that they would assume that if her position was changed it was done en route to wherever they were. She closed her eyes. Better if they thought she was still unconscious.

The door opened, and torch light bounced around the van. Focusing on keeping her breathing steady and not flinching, Felicity waited. A slight dip of the vehicle told her someone had entered, and seconds later she smelled the faint but familiar tang of a citrusy aftershave that made her stomach lurch. *Please don't notice the cables, please don't notice the cables. What is he doing?*

'What you waiting for? Get the fuck up here. Find out if he's still with us. Then get the body disposed of. Get a move on.'

Felicity froze. That voice . . . did she recognize it? Was it someone she knew or was she just imagining it?

'Yes boss.' The second voice was raspy, like he'd smoked too many full tars over his lifetime and then the van dropped again as a second man entered. 'Nope, still alive.'

The words chilled Felicity; they were going kill her. Kill her and dump her. The vehicle dipped once more, and shoes scraped against metal. A third person. So at least three in total. The familiar citrusy scent was replaced by sweat and stale smoke. Felicity tried to think. What the hell would Parekh do? Should she try to make it to the door? She was weak and stiff. She could barely stand upright without effort, there was no way she could use the element of surprise – not in her condition. The only option she had was to play dead. Maybe if they thought she was dead, or even just unconscious, they'd just dump her and not bother killing her. Maybe then she'd have a chance.

Cold fingers touched her neck and Felicity forced herself not to flinch as she held her breath and Felicity closed her mind. If she shut everything off, maybe she'd survive.

Tar man replied, 'Leave that to me and Jase. We've got the dump spot all sorted, like. We won't let you down. Not again.'

'They both need to be disposed of. But separately. She needs to be dumped where she won't be found for months – the middle of the moors or somewhere. And him . . .' Xavier kicked the prone man. 'Finish him. And make sure you use the usual forensic measures – yeah?'

Felicity recognized the voice itself but couldn't place it. Without a face to go with it, she just couldn't remember. She couldn't risk looking, had to play unconscious. Keep her eyes closed and focus on keeping still. Not that it would do her any good, not with a bullet through her brain. So much for channelling Nikki fucking Parekh!

Citrusy man snorted and then the van lifted again. 'Okay, I'm counting on you. Get on with it.'

The click of a semi-automatic pistol being cocked echoed in Felicity's ears. Her breath caught in her throat and it was all she could do not to scream out loud. She sent up a final prayer that Stevie would be all right. She needed to believe that Stevie would be all right . . . especially now. She hadn't quite finished her frantic prayers when the shot fired out, extra loud in the van . . . followed by silence.

Chapter 8

Felicity Springer lived in Eccleshill, just behind The Oddfellows Arms on Harrogate Road. As Nikki turned onto Springer's street, the sight of the pub made Nikki realize that she and Sajid still hadn't found a new pub to make their local. Although The Mannville Arms was supposedly opening again under new management, Nikki doubted that she'd ever be able to set foot in it again. Not after everything that had happened. A year on and still the very thought of the place made her shudder. Dreams of rats chasing her through the underground tunnels soon morphed into a human assailant and even now, Nikki often woke up drenched in sweat, her breath ragged, her heart thudding. Marcus, half asleep, would stretch out an arm and pull her to his chest, holding her tight till she felt safe enough to drift off to sleep again.

Now wasn't the time to think about that though. She'd something far worse on her mind and the very thought of it chilled her to the marrow. Her mum had confided in her once that her biggest fear was the thought of two police officers landing on her doorstep to deliver just the sort of news Nikki was going to deliver now. The chances were extremely slim, she told her mother, yet history told her that you could never be too sure of that.

Her clapped-out old Zafira felt overcrowded with Archie

rammed into the passenger seat beside her as she pulled up onto the kerb a few feet from number thirty-six. The car's erratic heating system had dried their snow-covered outer garments, leaving a damp smell lingering in the air. The fact that Archie kept fidgeting and practising his words under his breath was distracting and Nikki wished the whole thing was over. There were, after all, only so many ways you could tell a relative that their loved one had been abducted and was injured, possibly dead. Apart from that, Nikki was still angry with Archie, but she had to get over that before they approached the house.

'What do we know about The Spaniel, Archie? She married or what?' Although Nikki and Springer had worked in the same building for years, Nikki knew nothing about the other woman's home life. Truth was, Nikki avoided Springer as much as possible and she suspected Springer did the same. They were more enemies than friends and that niggled at Nikki. It was difficult enough to be present when a relative was notified of something like this, but having to offer insincere platitudes about how popular Springer was and what a good officer she was went against the grain. She'd do it though. It was part of the job. She was just relieved that Archie was the one doing the talking. All she'd need to do was to nod in the right place and look suitably solemn.

'Don't know much.' Archie's voice was gruff. 'Records say she's married, but nobody, not even DC Bashir kens anything about her. Next of kin is down as her spouse Stevie Blake. Shit, Nikki. How am I going tae dae this? What if I get ma proverbials in a knot? It's ages since I've delivered a . . .'

He hesitated, and Nikki knew he had been about to say death notice. She turned off the engine, leaned across and squeezed his arm. 'We've no evidence to say she's dead yet. You know that. We need to keep it upbeat. Get the lay of the land. She might have kids, for all we know.' Although the very thought of Springer deigning to go through childbirth seemed very unlikely to Nikki. 'Tell you what, Archie. I'll do it.'

Archie's lips twitched as he extricated himself from his seat belt, opened the door and stepped onto the road. 'Since when have you been Ms Sensitive, Nikita Parekh?' he said over the top of the car when Nikki had emerged from the other side. 'Nae chance, hen. I'll dae it myself.'

Nikki opened her mouth to argue and then sighed. Archie was right, she was definitely not Ms Sensitive. But she could make the tea. 'Okay, you win.' Then, grumbling as she joined him on the pavement, added, 'That's why I said Sajid would have been a better choice.'

Together they opened the gate and walked up to the door. Springer's house was a modern-built semi with a drive with enough room for two cars. It was occupied by a sporty-looking vehicle that Nikki assumed would be well above Springer's pay grade, and she wondered what exactly Springer's partner did for a living. Parallel to the drive was a paved area with a few plant pots and some covered garden furniture. It was strange to think of the missing woman as a person and not just a colleague she didn't get on with. No matter what her personal feelings for Springer were, she felt sorry for the poor sod – her husband – whose life they were about to disrupt. The lights were on, but the curtains were only half shut and before Archie and Nikki reached the front door it was wrenched open by a striking woman. With a mane of red hair cascading over her shoulders, she was at least a foot taller than Nikki. And she was pregnant.

Archie, eyes automatically drawn to the woman's belly, coughed. 'I'm DCI Archie Hegley and this is DS Parekh. We work with DS Springer, can we come in?'

The woman looked from Archie to Nikki and then back again, before her hand flew up to her mouth. Without uttering a word, she stepped back from the door and ushered them inside. Exchanging a quick glance with Archie, Nikki stepped through the door, taking care to wipe her feet on the mat before she followed the woman along the cream-coloured carpet and into a living room that smelled of roses and something spicy. Clearly this woman was at home here.

Once inside, the woman gestured to the sofa and Nikki sat, only to almost be catapulted back off when Archie's weight descended on the other side. The woman stood before a flickering wood burning stove, and Nikki's glance was drawn to a framed photograph on the wall above the fireplace.

Wringing her hands, the woman finally spoke. 'Has something happened to her?'

Archie cleared his throat and began to speak. 'I need to speak to Felicity's, I mean DS Springer's hu—'

Realizing the mistake her boss was about to make, Nikki jumped to her feet, and putting her arm round the other woman's shoulder, guided her to a chair. 'You must be Felicity's wife . . . Stevie, is it? We need to talk to you.'

Nikki glanced pointedly from Archie to the photograph of Felicity Springer and her wife in matching wedding dresses, arms round each other, love shining from their eyes, hoping he'd get the hint. Nikki had never seen The Spaniel look so human. Discarding that thought, she focused on the woman before her but before she had a chance to speak the woman said, 'I know something's happened. Fliss should've been home ages ago.'

Fliss? For a moment Nikki was confused then she caught herself. *First Felicity, now Fliss? Really?* Today was throwing up all sorts of surprises about DS Springer.

'I left her a voicemail earlier, but haven't heard back from her. Even accounting for the weather, she should've been home ages ago and she's not answering her phone. It's so not like her.' She gripped Nikki's hands in both of hers. 'Please tell me she's all right.'

Nikki swallowed, glanced at Archie and cursed inwardly, wishing she'd paid more attention to his practice attempts in the car. Archie nodded at her giving her permission to break the news. Nikki broke out in a sweat. Trying for her most sensitive tone, she removed her hands from the other woman's and crouched beside her. 'It seems that on the way home from the conference in Wakefield, DS . . .' She cleared her throat. 'I mean Felicity . . . Fliss saw something untoward in the van in front and followed it. She alerted the police by phoning 999 and we were able to ascertain her location using the What3words app.' Nikki swallowed, wishing the other woman would stop staring at her like her life depended on her. 'By the time we reached her, there had been a car crash and DS, I mean Felicity, was absent from the scene, as was the vehicle she was pursuing.'

Stevie held Nikki's gaze for what felt like hours before responding. 'But she gave you the reg number, didn't she? You've traced the reg number and you'll soon find the vehicle. They've not hurt her . . . tell me they've not hurt her.'

Archie moved behind them and Nikki prayed he would answer, but he remained silent. *Up to me then, is it?* 'The thing is, Stevie. DS Sp . . . Felicity couldn't give us the vehicle registration. She told the emergency services operator that it was covered in some way and unfortunately when we got to her car, there was evidence that Spri . . . I mean, Felicity was hurt.'

Tears began to roll down Stevie's cheeks and with a sigh, Nikki stood up and relocated herself to the chair arm, putting her arms around the now crying woman. 'We're doing all we can to find her and the initial analysis indicates that the blood loss is non-fatal.'

'Blood loss? Was she hurt in the crash?'

'No . . . not in the crash.' Nikki wished she didn't have to say the words, but there was no other way. She had to be honest. Stevie had to be prepared. 'We think she may have been shot.'

As Stevie collapsed in her arms, Nikki held her, looking over the other woman's head to Archie, who sat motionless on the couch, hands trapped between his knees, an expression Nikki had never seen before on his face.

What the hell wasn't Archie telling her?

Chapter 9

The atmosphere in the incident room after Nikki and Archie had left to speak to Springer's partner was calm, but still a heaviness lingered, as if warning Sajid that things were going to get worse – much worse. The other two officers who'd been working on their computers had disappeared. Whether they'd signed out or just gone for a break, Sajid wasn't sure, but the quiet was a welcome change from the tension radiating from both his partner and his boss.

Flinging his pen across the table, Sajid stretched his arms up, trying, and failing, to release the knot at the bottom of his spine and ease the taut sensation in his shoulders. He was fed up with Nikki. It had been obvious that she was keeping something from him earlier at the crime scene and equally obvious that she and Archie had disagreed over something before they left, yet she just shook her head at him when he asked. With her lips tightly pinched, she put her socks and boots back on before heading out of the room with a curt. 'Tell him I'll wait for him at my car.'

Now, looking at the crime board, he was aware that he was prevaricating. It was time to go home. There was nothing else they could do now and anything that came in later would be caught by the night shift. Home meant Langley and he wasn't entirely sure he was ready to face him just yet. He sighed before logging off his computer and tidying up his desk. It was okay for Langley. He'd been brought up in a very different family to Sajid's. Langley's family couldn't care less about his sexuality. They supported it even and that made him comfortable in his own skin. Saj was only too aware that he lived a sort of double life. One where he was always slightly conscious of where he was, whose company he was in and who knew about his private life. He was only truly relaxed when at home with Langley, at Nikki's or on the job.

However, Langley was getting pissed off – no, that was too strong a word. Langley didn't do pissed off, no, it was more exasperation, with being, in his words, 'the hidden partner'. Saj couldn't blame him really. If Langley were with someone other than him, he could be as 'out' as he wanted. The mere thought of Langley being with someone else made Sajid shudder. He couldn't bear it if his boyfriend got so fed up with him that he dumped him. But what was the alternative? Come out to his parents and family? Yeah, he knew exactly how that would go down – lead balloons would be an understatement. The entire family would be horrified, the extended family and the community would be consulted and Saj would be evicted from the family . . . if not worse. It was the worse he was worried about. Although *his* parents were mild-mannered, there were members of his family from Birmingham who'd been part of the demonstrations against the No Outsiders education programme, outside the primary schools in their area. Mouthing off, using the Qur'an to justify their bigotry towards gay rights without even fully understanding what the school curriculum is about. He doubted they'd be receptive to his sexuality and the worst thing was, some of them were already angry that he'd become a copper. This would be the last straw.

Although, he was concerned about his own welfare, that wasn't his priority. Saj was more than able to look after himself, but Langley was a different matter. Langley was a bloody doctor for

God's sake, not a fighter. Hell, Langley was so oblivious to his surroundings, unless of course it was the damn mortuary, that he wouldn't even see them coming. Did Saj really want to expose the man he loved to that? The only options available to him were to either break up with Langley or confide all of his fears and convince his boyfriend to keep their relationship on the low down. After all, there wasn't a huge distance between Bradford and Dewsbury. All he needed was some uncle or auntie spotting him with Langley and putting two and two together. He supposed they could move, but that was like giving in, giving up.

The message he needed to get over to Langley was that he wasn't ashamed of their relationship or his own sexuality. That was the fear he saw lurking in Langley's eyes all the time; that he was ashamed of *them*.

Grabbing his coat from the hook by the door, he left the office. If he was being one hundred per cent honest with himself, he'd admit that a lifetime of anti-gay rhetoric did cloud his happiness. If his parents could be as accepting as Langley's were, things would be better. They'd like Langley. He was sure of that. What wasn't to like – other than the fact that he wasn't female, that is?

Deciding that he couldn't put things off any longer, that he had to make some sort of attempt to talk to Langley, try to make him understand, he swung by the One Stop in Heaton and grabbed a bottle of wine. Langley had cooked, but not knowing when Saj would return home, he'd texted to let him know he'd eaten and that his food could be reheated when he got home. The thought of Langley's Yorkshire puds and roast beef would normally have Saj salivating, but tonight his stomach felt fragile. What was wrong with him? Too much time spent with Nikki, that's what it was. He'd absorbed her inability to confide, her inability to articulate her feelings to those she loved. He was normally the one who was more in touch with his feelings. It was what he was good at – talking to witnesses, making them feel at ease – so why the hell was this so difficult?

By the time he arrived in the underground car park and got out of his Jag his nerves were fried. So much depended on this and the last thing he wanted was to mess it up. All too soon, the lift whooshed him up to his floor and then he was at the front door of their flat. As he pushed the door open, the sound of some documentary or other drifted through from the front room. Taking his time, he hung his coat on the coat stand and walked through to the living room where Langley lay sprawled on the couch, so engrossed in his programme that he didn't hear Saj enter.

Saj looked at him for a moment. He was wearing the jumper Saj had given him for his birthday and he'd clearly just had a shower as his hair was still damp and flopping over his forehead. *What a geek!* Despite his anxiety, a smile tugged Saj's lips and the knowledge that he'd do anything to protect this man barrelled into him like a rhino on speed.

He walked over, placed his hands round Langley's shoulders and plonked the red wine in his lap, savouring the way Langley's eyes crinkled when they saw him. The big discussion could wait for now.

Chapter 10

Nikki needed to unwind after the emotionally charged business of telling the heavily pregnant Stevie Blake what had happened to her wife. She forced her shoulders to relax as she drove round the Listerhills Estate streets. This was something she often did before heading home for the evening. Keeping an eye on her patch as she drove had two benefits. One, she kept her finger on the pulse and two, she didn't take as much of her work home with her as usual.

Fliss! For God's sake, Fliss? Who'd have thought jagged, cold Springer would be called Fliss? She frowned. Who'd have thought jagged, cold Springer would have a pregnant wife? Shit, Nikki had suspected she ate children for breakfast but that whole scenario was turned on its head. Now that she'd met Springer's pregnant partner and liked her, it was even more imperative to get Springer home. She was invested in this now.

Her headlights picked up figures scurrying into the darkness of the ginnels. That was something else to worry about. Franco and Deano, the dealers she'd got rid of last year, may be gone, but there was always another rat ready to pop up from the sewers . . . no wonder she hated the vermin so much. Deliberately, she turned off the side street and into the cobbled back alley that separated two lines of terraces, and trawled down it in second gear. It was three streets over from her own home yet this was always one she kept an eye on. It backed onto one edge of the Rec and was prime land for drug deals, besides, there had been a worrying increase in machete attacks nearby in the last two weeks. Where there were machete attacks, Nikki's experience told her there were also Class As, other weapons and gullible kids to get caught up in the bravado and cheap sell of a Lamborghini, a snazzy wristwatch and posh mobile. She'd spoken to the drug squad before and although they were keeping an eye open and supposedly receiving intel about the new kingpin, nothing seemed to be confirmed. Well, nothing her contact, Joe Drummond, was willing to share. In the meantime, there was an air of expectancy, like a toxic cloud hovering over her estate and Nikki wasn't going to stand for that. She reached the bottom of the ginnel, hoping her exhaust wouldn't fall off – she'd no spare cash to replace that, not if she was going to replace the battery – and waited, looking to her right and left.

A figure dodged out from a back yard further down, didn't even look in Nikki's direction and loped off down the ginnel, dodging the puddles, shoulders hunched and hood up. As he dipped under one of the few still-working streetlamps she cursed. 'Fuck's sake Haqib. Do you never learn?' and she was out of her car, leaving the engine running and her door open as she darted after him. 'Haqib?'

He hesitated, seemed to consider whether to speed up or turn and face the music. Thankfully, for him, the latter instinct won.

'Whassup, Aunt Nikki?' He splayed his hands in front of him, sulky mouth drooping, attitude in the way he hunched his shoulders.

'What you doing out at this time? It's after ten and *you*, I believe, are still grounded after Fingergate.' She was well aware that she was being harsh. The lad's finger had been amputated and reattached nearly a year ago. Sometimes though, it paid to remind him of what his last brush with drugs had resulted in.

Haqib winced and flexed his little finger. 'That's a bit tight, innit? That were last year. I've not been grounded for months now.'

Hands on hips, Nikki inhaled slowly. 'I'll tell you what's tight, Haqib Parekh. Skipping out of the house behind your mum's back – that's what's tight. Breaking your word – that's tight too, hanging out here—'

'Yeah, yeah, I get it. That's tight too.' Haqib mimicked his auntie's tone.

Nikki reached over and gently cuffed the back of his head, 'No, that's not bloody tight . . . that's stupid. S.T.U.P.I.D. Stupid – got it?'

'I ain't doing drugs, you know. I'm not that mental.'

Nikki raised an eyebrow, not caring how harsh she was being. Haqib worried her. A young Asian lad trying to be cocky, trying to be a big man, was a worry for her. Her sister Anika, Haqib's mum, seemed content to leave it up to Nikki to sort her son out. Not that she had a reliable good male role model to offer Haqib. But that was another story. She studied the bloom of red that spread across his cheeks. That was guilt all right, but not the sort of blasé, fast-talking guilt she was used to from her nephew. 'So, spill!'

A voice from behind her had Nikki spinning on her heel.

'It's me he came to see, Mrs Parekh.'

The girl was tall – taller than Haqib, skinnier than was healthy, blonde with blue eyes and a dimple in the middle of her chin. At present her eyes looked worried as she darted glances towards Haqib and each hand worried at the sleeve of her jacket. The girl looked familiar, but it took a minute for Nikki to place her and when she did, she groaned inwardly. *Fuck's sake Haqib, if it's not drugs, it's inappropriate relationships.* 'You're Glass's sister, aren't you?'

The girl nodded. 'Michelle – Chelle-to-my-mates.'

The words ran together and for a second Parekh thought she was telling her she had a different surname to her brother. Chelle-to-her-mates indeed. Who did she think she was – bloody royalty?

'Haq isn't doing drugs. He knows it's for idiots, don't you, Haq?'

66

Haqib, mouth hanging open, looking exactly like an idiot himself at that precise moment, nodded. *Lovestruck, that's what he is.* But did he *have* to be lovestruck over Adam Glass's sister? Of all the girls on the estate, her nuisance of a nephew had to go for the one most likely to have him losing another digit – if not something worse.

'So . . .' Nikki chewed her lip, trying to come up with something auntie-ish to say, but could only manage, 'You're both bloody stupid. Do you really think your white-supremacist brother, office holder in Albion First, Yorkshire's answer to the EDL, is going to sit back and let you date an Asian boy . . . a Muslim boy?'

Michelle's eyes darted to the ground and then almost immediately straight back up again. She met Nikki's gaze. 'We love each other, me and Haq. We're like Romeo and Juliet, aren't we, Haq?' Her face flushed, her lips turned up, her eyes full of love as she looked at her boyfriend.

Looking a little embarrassed, Haqib managed a mumbled, 'It's not like I'm proper Muslim anyway, is it? Dun't go to mosque or owt.'

Nikki somehow managed to swallow her snort of laughter, but one look at Haqib's hurt expression told her that her face had given her away. The lad was right, he wasn't Muslim, apart from when Anika decided to try to impress her married lover and Haqib's dad. 'Look, I'm sorry. Really, I am. I can remember being your age and thinking I was in—'

'Told you she wouldn't understand and if *she* dun't understand, Chelle, then my mum won't stand for it either. We're doomed.' Haqib looked ferocious, his eyes flashing, and Nikki sighed. There was no need for her to be such an arse. No need at all. Especially when she should be pleased that Haqib wasn't involved with the druggies. Still, going out with Adam Glass's sister wasn't a whole lot safer for him. Glass was an upstart thug . . . but he was an upstart thug with friends – organized friends!

Aw, for goodness' sake. Nikki was beginning to wish she'd gone straight home and not done her usual trawl of the area. She hated this sort of crap. Marcus, on the other hand, was good at this. Maybe she could get him to have a word with Listerhills' answer to *Titanic*. She scowled, wishing she'd opted for a simile that didn't involve the male lead losing his life. Mind you, Michelle's analogy to Romeo and Juliet was no more promising.

Using every reserve of patience she had, and channelling a little of her memory of the feelings she'd once had for her deceased husband, Nikki smiled. When the girl took a step closer to Haqib and grabbed his arm, angling herself slightly behind him, Nikki realized her 'smile' was less reassuring than she'd hoped. 'Look. I can't be all warm and fuzzy about this. Your brother is a racist scumbag.' *Oops, should've toned that down a little.* But when Nikki looked at Michelle, the girl was nodding, a slight smile on her face.

'He is, Adam's a racist. He's a thug. But . . . I'm not. I don't mind Pakis. Anyway, Haqib's not pure Paki. He's a half-caste.' The girl's smile widened as if she was expecting a pat on the back for her enlightened views.

Flinching at the 'P' word that had so glibly dropped from Chelle's mouth, followed as quickly by the equally offensive 'half-caste', Nikki was amazed that her nephew didn't even seem to register it. 'Eh. I think you mean Pakistani, not Paki and we don't use half-caste either. It's a racist term. Mixed race or dual heritage are better.'

Chelle wafted her hand in a 'whatever' gesture and continued. 'Anyway, what I'm saying is, my brother in't here any more, so Haqib and I can be together properly.'

Haqib blushed again and Nikki decided not to wonder what 'properly' entailed for the two kids but she made a mental note to ask Marcus to get in a supply of condoms and do the 'dad' chat with Haqib. She was more concerned with wondering where Adam Glass was going and for how long. She liked to keep an eye on idiots like Glass and it was always useful to know where they were. As for the racist crap – she'd have a word with Haqib later about appropriate use of language and not falling into the 'you're not like the others' trap that white racists often used to justify their own prejudice. 'Heading off somewhere, is he? Your brother?'

Haqib stepped forward, fingers linked through his girlfriend's, tone eager. 'He's been demoted like. No longer head honcho of Albion First.'

Eyes narrowed, Nikki studied Haqib. Why wasn't this common knowledge? Why hadn't her snitches told her this? This was big, with widespread implications for Bradford and beyond. 'You sure?'

It was Michelle who answered. 'They came for him in the middle of the night two nights ago, dragged him from his bed. Me and my mum were bricking it, but they just told us to keep schtum. She won't say it, but Mum's as glad as I am to see the back of him. Couldn't stand the idiots he brought round to the house. Hated them.'

'Who came for him?'

'Albion First. They all had masks on, but who else could it be? They said summat about laundry and that if he didn't spill the codes, he'd be a goner.'

Laundry . . . Could that be laundering? Was Glass laundering money? She hadn't had him down for that and Joe Drummond, her eyes and ears in vice, hadn't alerted her to that either. Maybe he was doing it for someone further up the chain? Albion First had little cells all over the region and they were being funded somehow. Perhaps Glass was doing more than just being a henchman. Possibly he was involved in ensuring their economic viability. If she was heading up an extreme right-wing party, she'd use someone like him as her patsy. 'And you've not seen him since then?'

'Nope, but he texted. Said he had to leave the country.'

'Why would his own thugs come and take him away? That doesn't make sense.' Nikki was talking more to herself than the two kids, but Haqib answered like he thought she was losing it.

'Duh, because he was double dealing, *everyone* knew that. On the one hand he's heading up that Albion First shit and on the other he's cutting deals with that new guy from Wakefield that's taken over from Franco. Word is he's into some bad stuff, but nobody knows his name.'

This was all news to Nikki and she didn't like it. She always kept her finger on the pulse of Bradford and on her estate in particular. The fact that this had escaped her notice vexed her. Had Drummond kept her out of the loop? Surely not. They'd done favours for each other for years now and he'd always kept her informed. Well, she'd soon find out. She turned to love's young dreamers, trying to ignore the fact that they had their tongues down each other's throats and coughed loudly. When she had their attention, she tried out a friendly grin. 'You two need to skip off home, right now. Listerhills isn't safe till we suss out what's going on.' Nikki took out her mobile and as the kids sidled away in opposite directions, she phoned Joe.

The phone rang for ages, before it was answered by an annoyed voice, 'Yeah, Parekh. Bad timing, as per usual.'

Nikki could hear the sounds of a disgruntled female voice complaining in the background and choosing to ignore Joe's words, jumped straight in. 'Did you know about this mysterious guy from Wakefield?'

The silence on the end of the phone told her all she needed to know. 'You bastard. You knew there was someone new on my streets and you didn't tell me?'

The unmistakable sounds of someone getting out of bed reached Nikki's ears. 'Look love, all we know is this boss is well under the radar. Seems like the fucker wears a damn invisibility cloak. We've no idea if he's from Wakefield. None of our snitches are spilling, we've got reports of human-trafficking, rumours of huge weapons stashes, lorry loads of heroin dispersing throughout the district.

'What about Glass – where does he fit in?'

'Glass?' Joe sounded surprised, so Nikki continued.

'Word is he was picked up from his house and has gone AWOL.'

'Shit! Glass has been picked up from his house? Things are unstable in Bradford . . . really unstable and we can't seem to get a handle on it. Thanks for passing on your intel. It's useful, but you need to focus on that Springer case, yeah?'

Nikki frowned. What wasn't Joe sharing? 'You will keep—'

But he'd hung up and Nikki wanted to throw her phone at the wall. Who the hell was Joe Drummond to hang up on her! Okay, so what if it was a Sunday evening and he was with his latest girlfriend? He owed her. Stamping her feet, causing slush to drench her jeans, before spinning on her heel, she trudged back to her vehicle, got in and resumed her nightly rounds. Something was off in this area and, even if it killed her, she'd find out what it was. An invisible kingpin was worrisome. She much preferred the ones that she could see. The ones that were in the open. It was the insidious ones that caused more damage.

A half-hour later, shoulders aching with being hunched over her steering wheel, Nikki turned into her own street and parked up in the only space she could find which was just outside her mother's house. Her sister's and Nikki's homes were half a dozen doors further down on the opposite side of the road. Since everything that had happened before, Nikki had got into the habit of sitting in her car for a few minutes to clear some of her work from her mind before entering the house. That way she was able to be present in Marcus's company. He appreciated it and it was working for them now they'd moved in together.

The kids too were happier. So what if on occasion she resented not having her own space, resented not being able to lie on her bed and work through things in peace. Overall, things were better . . . and Marcus was alive. A movement out of the corner of her eye made her glance up. A man in a parka with the hood up was sidling down the street. When he stopped at Anika's gate and cast a glance at Nikki's house, Nikki cursed. *Bloody Anika is seeing Yousaf again. Will my sister ever learn that Haqib's dad is bad for her?*

She inhaled through her nose and exhaled through her mouth, using the technique shown her by the psychiatrist she had to see in order to be cleared for work. Despite her initial misgivings the therapy had proved beneficial. Hands resting at ten and two o'clock on the steering wheel, eyes closed, Nikki repeated the action, consciously releasing the tension from her shoulders and across her back. When the passenger door opened and someone slid into the seat, she continued breathing, but this time with a slight smile on her lips. 'Caught me again, Marcus.'

'Couldn't stand to be away from you a moment longer.' Marcus's tone was light and teasing. 'You eaten?'

Nikki thought about that, then opened her eyes. 'Not since I had to miss half of that stupendous Sunday dinner you cooked.'

'Just as well I saved you a plate then, isn't it?'

He settled in and the two of them savoured the companionable silence. She was so lucky. So damn lucky to have him. She reached over and squeezed his arm. They weren't like normal couples, not like Saj and Langley for example who kept no secrets from each other. She and Marcus had more than a normal quota of secrets and an unspoken agreement that it wasn't necessary to talk about them. She frowned. Well that was what she thought. They'd never actually *talked* about it. She'd just assumed Marcus got it. As she looked through the windscreen, it began to niggle her that perhaps he did want to share. Marcus was completely different from her – more gregarious, much more open. Maybe he didn't confide in her because she closed it down.

Nikki, focusing on the empty street ahead, said, 'You know I don't talk much. You know, dwell on stuff and do all the, well . . . the baring my soul and all that.'

Nikki swallowed hard as Marcus turned to face her. Thank God for the shadows. Last thing she needed was to get this off her chest with him looking at her.

Marcus prompted her. 'And?'

'Well, like. I just want you to know that you *can*. If you want, that is. You can tell me anything. I'll listen.'

Amusement running through his voice, Nikki could imagine Marcus's smile, as he replied. 'This about last year, Nik? Cause if it is, we're all good. You know that.' And he threaded his fingers through hers.

It wasn't just about last year though; it was about everything. Her childhood, his childhood. Her dad, his parents. She bit her lip, realizing she knew nothing about Marcus's folks. She cleared her throat. 'Erm, you know . . .' She hesitated, unused to this sort of conversation, but determined to spit her recent thoughts out. 'We don't talk about other stuff either.' She waved her hand in the air as if that explained the sort of stuff she was referring to.

'Eh?' In the light cast by the streetlights, Marcus's frown was visible. 'What *other* stuff?'

Moving her body till she was leaning against the door, so she could see him better, Nikki tried again. 'Like stuff we've done . . . you know before. Like the boxes I keep in the bedroom about my dad.' She risked a glance at him and tried to keep all inflection from her tone as she added, 'Or your family.'

Marcus's pursed his lips and Nikki not sure what that implied wafted her hand in the air. 'Well, I just want you to know, we can talk about it. If you like, that is . . . just saying we can . . . you know . . . share stuff if you like.'

The frown cleared off Marcus's brow and a small smile played across his lips. The sort that told Nikki he was still amused by her attempts to delve deep into her inner psyche and she had an urge to prod his arm. It had taken her a lot to work up to this and here he was amused at her, but before she had the chance he spoke.

'I know enough about your dad, Nik. I get why you keep an eye on where he is at all times. That's how you make sure you're protecting your family. Me? I'm a foster kid. No desire to rehash all of that.' He smiled. 'You know, Nik, sharing stuff from the past may well be overrated don't you think? If it feels right, we can talk about it, but it doesn't need to be like some therapy session. Let's just be us. We're good being us.'

Nikki could have kissed him. Why had it taken her so long to realize that Marcus got her . . . warts and all.

'Come on. It's freezing here. Let's get you fed and watered.'

Nikki got out of the car, yawned, and after glancing towards her sister's house, looked across the car roof at Marcus. 'You noticed him too? Yousaf?'

Marcus's shrugged his lips tight. 'He'd have been less noticeable if he'd driven a quad bike down the street. Tosser, what did he look like in that bloody parka?'

Nikki grinned. Sometimes it was good to be part of a team. 'You thought I'd storm over there and cause a scene?'

'Well, I thought the temptation to tie his balls round his neck and strangle him might prove too much for you to resist, that's all.' Marcus walked round the car and slipped his arm through hers. 'We could still do it if you like? How would the lying piece of shit explain that to his wife?'

Nikki laughed, the sound feeling good as it left her chest. Today had been crap, but here she was able to laugh and that was good. She was getting there. 'Haqib's dating Glass's sister.'

Marcus stopped and turned to look at her. 'So that's where the little shit's been sneaking off to these past few nights. He's going to end up mince, Nik.'

It felt good to share so she filled him in on what had happened. She hadn't quite sorted out her feelings about the Felicity, Fliss, Springer abduction, so she glossed over that with a 'Can you believe that woman's called Fliss? Fliss? I'm not lying, you know?'

Marcus threw his head back and laughed, the sound warm and rich, and Nikki's heart thrummed.

Not sure what had made her broach the subject, Nikki squeezed his hand. Maybe it was Springer's abduction, maybe it was Haqib's love life, maybe it was the unknown threat that hovered over

Bradford's streets or maybe it was seeing that her sister was still in a relationship with an idiot who didn't deserve her. Whatever it was, she just needed to let Marcus know that she was there for him. That although she only gave him snippets of her past, he could tell her anything. They'd been together off and on for twelve years now, but over the past year their relationship had settled into something permanent. Nikki wasn't good at permanent, but she didn't want to fuck this up. She didn't want to lose Marcus, because she couldn't share . . . she needed him to know she was there for him. That she was all in.

'Nah, not just about that. Just stuff. I . . . you know . . . like . . . I care about you.'

Marcus. Leaned over and kissed her cold cheek. 'I love you too, Nikki Parekh.'

How lucky was she to have a man who understood her so completely? She turned until their lips met and kissed him back. Funny she no longer felt hungry. 'I'll trade your Sunday roast for breakfast in bed tomorrow if we can go straight upstairs now.'

Marcus didn't need asking twice.

MONDAY 16TH MARCH 2020

Chapter 11

'Aw no!' Nikki flung the pillow over her head to drown out the sound of her phone ringing. 'No, no, no, no, no.' It was the middle of the night. It was too cold and she was too damn sleepy to answer now.

It stopped ringing and she breathed a sigh of relief only for it to start up again almost immediately. Marcus nudged her with his elbow, his voice sleepy. 'You gonna get that, Nik? Must be urgent. Maybe they've found Springer.'

Nikki sat up, threw her pillow at the wall. Shit, she'd forgotten about Springer, so relaxed was she after making love with Marcus. With bad grace she answered the phone. 'This better be good!'

Saj's voice, tinged with amusement, drifted through the phone. 'Spoil your beauty sleep, did I?'

Nikki was already half out of bed, shivering in the early morning chill as she groped around in the semi dark for her jeans and jumper. A quick glance at the clock told her it was only two o'clock. No wonder she was tired. 'What have we got, Saj?'

'Woman's body reported dumped naked in a street in Denholme.'

Nikki's heartrate accelerated as she one-handedly pulled her jeans over her legs. A quick glance at Marcus told her he'd rolled over and covered his head with his own pillow. She bent down, grabbed the rest of her clothes and made her way as quietly as she could into the hallway. 'Springer?'

'No ID yet, but what're the chances?'

Exactly, what were the chances? It wasn't every day they had a murdered body dumped on the street and it was far too coincidental not to be Springer. Nikki's heart contracted momentarily in sympathy with Springer's wife and then she shrugged her emotion aside. It wouldn't do anyone any good if she let emotions taint her investigation. 'Archie know yet?'

'Yep, he's on his way. Says he'll meet us there. I've just pulled up outside yours. You nearly ready?'

'One minute.'

Nikki ran into the bathroom, slurped a mouthful of Listerine straight from the bottle, sat down and peed whilst she sloshed the mouthwash around her mouth. Jumping up, she it spat into the sink, washed her hands, splashed her face and bounded down the stairs. In the hall she shrugged on her jacket, grabbed her house keys and without doing up the laces, rammed her feet into her DMs and was out of the house, slamming the door behind her. True to his word, engine purring gently, Sajid's Jaguar waited double parked by her front door. Raising a hand in greeting, she ran round to the passenger seat and jumped in.

As Sajid drove off, she allowed herself a moment to absorb the delicious warmth that seeped through her shivering body from the heated car seats and ignored her partner's grin as a satisfied groan left her lips.

'Almost better than sex, eh?'

Eyes still closed, Nikki grinned. 'Almost . . . but don't tell Marcus, eh?'

Warm and more awake now, Nikki slid the seat back to give her more space, bent over and sorted out her laces. She wanted to be ready to get out as soon as they arrived at the scene. 'Who found her?'

'An old bloke out walking his dog, apparently.'

'At this time of night?'

Saj shrugged. 'That's all I know. We'll find out more when we get there. But we're keeping the CSIs busy, aren't we?'

Nikki looked out at the snow that had melted into a mucky slush and with the plummeting night-time temperatures begun to re-freeze. 'Well, at least it's not snowing any more and hopefully the rain'll hold off till we get the crime scene secured.'

Ten minutes later, Sajid drove along Denholme Main Street and following the satnav took a right into a street before turning left into another smaller street called Hill Top Lane and pulled up behind police cars and a CSI van. The street had been marked off by a fluttering string of crime scene tape, beyond which streetlights illuminated the ghostly figures of the crime scene investigators already at work. They'd already erected a tent around the body and Nikki could see that the uniforms had managed to contain the rubberneckers in their own gardens. Some had taken to the upstairs windows where their tired faces peered down from the darkness like vultures on the scene below. Nikki could never understand this morbid curiosity. Was it relief that they weren't part of the drama or a sneaky wish to insert themselves into it? Only a few of the spectators would push themselves forward when the journalists crawled out from under their stones, giving their own, sometimes skewed, take on things. The rest would satisfy themselves with snatched moments of glory in the workplace over the coming weeks as they described their tenuous link to something exciting.

Caught in the quandary of hoping it wasn't Springer in the tent and realizing that by wishing that, she was, in effect, consigning another woman to death, another family to the sharp pain of grief, Nikki tried and failed to dispel the images of Springer's pregnant wife, her stricken expression, her tears. It was always worse when you'd met the missing person's family, sat in their homes, seen the photos on their walls, made a connection. It was easier to wish, however fleetingly, for it not to be them. That perhaps, by some miracle, the person they were about to view didn't match those smiling framed images. It was worse because Nikki was conflicted. On the one hand, despite the current situation, she was unable to shake off her resentment that Springer had made her life hell for a few weeks the previous year and on the other, she *knew* the woman, had met her wife, worked in the same station as her – hell, she was one of them.

Nikki and Sajid moved over to the uniformed officer who was monitoring the cordon and signed themselves in. They each put on an overall from a box full of them, covered their shoes and ducked under the tape. A yell from behind made her turn and when Nikki saw their boss waddling towards them, she waited for him to suit up too.

Approaching the crime scene tent, she spotted another officer who was clearly in charge and made a beeline for her. Nikki flashed her badge and said, 'What can you tell us, Officer? Do we have any ID on the dead woman?'

'Sergeant Anwar,' said the officer. She took a few moments to collect her thoughts before continuing. 'The woman was naked and so far we've not been able to ID her. A Mr Malcolm Nichols found the body. He's an old man, well into his eighties. He's an insomniac so he sometimes takes his dog out for a walk at night-time. Thing is, he didn't contact us direct. When he saw what was happening, he pressed his panic button.'

Nikki was puzzled. 'Panic button?'

Anwar rolled her eyes and screwed up her face, half in admiration, half in disbelief. 'Well, he's quite infirm, is Mr Nichols. He's not really supposed to leave the house because he uses a Zimmer frame and he's not very stable walking. Social services gave him an emergency panic button that he wears round his neck in case he falls over . . .'

Nikki nodded and a smile tugged at her lips. She got it. She'd come across hordes of folk just like him over the years. The old man was a stubborn old bugger who had sneaked out despite his infirmity. Thanks to him snatching a night-time walk, they'd got to the crime scene earlier than they otherwise would have, which meant hopefully forensics would pick something useful up. Although she was keen to get to the body, she knew that until the

CSIs had processed it, they wouldn't get near, so she wanted to find out as much as she could about the people who'd dumped her. 'Seems like our Mr Nichols is a bit of a character, Sergeant. Go on.'

'Well, they arrived within about half an hour, during which time, Mr Nichols had taken off his jacket and covered the body.' Anwar nodded, 'Yeah, I know not ideal, but the old bloke thought she might still be alive, so he did what he could.'

'You can't blame him for that,' said Saj. 'It's human instinct to try to help.'

'Well' said Anwar, 'that's all fine and well, but because he'd given his coat, he ended up getting chilled to the bone and we've had to have him taken to Bradford Royal. We got a bit of a statement from him before he left and I've sent an officer with him and his daughter, who arrived just in time to go with him in the ambulance. Basically, he says he was just heading back to his house with Loopy.'

'Loopy?' The word shot out of Archie's mouth like a bullet and Anwar flinched, before Archie shook his head, 'Sorry, sorry. I take it Loopy's the dog?'

Nikki and Sajid exchanged glances. Archie didn't usually come to crime scenes and now here he was making the on-duty officers feel awkward. They all wanted to confirm the ID of the victim, but these things couldn't be rushed. Archie knew that.

Anwar nodded. 'Yes. He'd gone three houses along and was on his way back when he heard a car speed up and skid into the street. This street is a through way. You can enter it from either end. Don't worry, I've cordoned off the other end too.' She pointed behind her and Nikki nodded.

'You've done a grand job. What else did he see?'

'Well, he says the car slowed down just beyond his house and he saw something being shoved from the back seat. He's a bit short-sighted so he thought it was rubbish and he was annoyed by that. Got a bit of a bee in his bonnet about fly tipping has Mr Nichols. He said the car zoomed straight off, leaving the bundle in the middle of the road. It was only when Mr Nichols got closer that he saw it was a woman. And the rest you know.'

'I don't suppose he saw who was in the car? Or has any ideas on the make or colour?'

Anwar shook her head. 'We asked him, but he really had no idea, poor soul. I've started officers knocking on doors to see if any home security CCTV angles onto the street at all or if anyone else saw or heard anything. So far, no luck, except for a couple of people complaining about being wakened up by the car roaring down the street. None of them admit to getting up or looking out the window.' She snorted. 'Although they're all doing a good job of managing that now, aren't they?'

Nikki had to agree; the street was awake now, and agog to find out what sort of human drama had played out in their neighbourhood.

Archie extended his hand. 'Good work. Report back to DS Parekh on this one please.' He swivelled on his heel and began marching towards the tent. Nikki and Saj fell into step behind him as he was greeted by Gracie Fells.

'Timed that nicely, DCI Hegley. We're done here and you can have a look at her in situ before we transport her.'

Archie hesitated by the entrance and then swallowed loudly. 'You go, Parekh. You go.'

Seeing her boss's anguished expression, Nikki nodded once and moved forward, sweeping the door flap aside as she stepped through. In the powerful light the woman's nakedness made her look like an alabaster statue and the cruelty of that wasn't lost on Nikki. This wasn't a work of art; it was a travesty. No woman should ever end up naked and discarded like a piece of trash on a wet street in the middle of the night. Lying on her side, with her spine curved and her legs bent as if in a foetal position, she faced away from Nikki. Bruises pixelated her body. Her hair, wet though it was, matched Nikki's recollection of Felicity Springer's.

The image of Springer's wife insistently pushed itself to the forefront of her mind as she approached, wishing she was anywhere but here. She moved round the body, her heart hammering, dreading what she was going to see, took a deep breath and immediately her nostrils were filled with the overpowering stench of bleach. Caught off balance, she swayed on her feet, momentarily transported back in time. *'I'll make her swallow it – all of it if you don't do what I tell you, bitch.'* Grounding herself, she pushed the memory from her mind and focused on the here and now . . . the woman before her . . . the victim. *This is what is important.*

She moved closer; a strand of hair had fallen over the woman's face, partly obscuring it. Nikki knelt beside her and with shaking fingers gently moved the strand away, tucking it behind the woman's ears. She stayed motionless for long seconds, aware of both Archie and Sajid waiting by the entrance watching her. Tears sprung to her eyes, but she blinked them away, bowing her head till she was sure her composure had returned. Then, she stood up, met her colleagues' questioning looks and shook her head once before striding from the tent, brushing Archie and Sajid aside. Not wanting to see the relief on their faces, hating herself for the relief she felt when she saw the woman wasn't Felicity Springer.

That woman was someone's daughter, sister, mother, friend and Nikki had no right to feel relief because she wasn't someone known to her. What sort of person did that make her if she was relieved that the victim was a stranger? *I'll find who did this, I promise you, I'll find whoever did this to you and I will make them pay.*

Clearing her mind of everything, Nikki sought out Sergeant Anwar, but before she had the chance to speak, the other woman shrugged. 'Not your officer then?'

'Nope.'

'Didn't think so. Seemed too young to be DS Springer. Also, some of her bruises are quite old. I presumed that Springer, being in the police and all, wouldn't stand for domestic violence, not that that's a given, unfortunately.'

Nikki agreed. Domestic abuse could happen in any relationship and being a copper didn't give you a free pass if your partner was that way inclined.

Nikki turned as Gracie Fells joined them, stripping away her mask as she walked. 'You seen enough, Parekh? They want to move the girl.'

Truth was Nikki had seen more than enough, but there was no point in sharing that. Fells, by the look on her face, had also seen more than enough for one night. 'What can you tell me about her?'

'You know all of this is off the record, don't you? You'll have to wait till Campbell's done the PM, but here's my unofficial take on things. She's been beaten, violated and dumped. Something's been inserted into her mouth . . . If you want my honest opinion, this is a warning . . . a warning to others not to do whatever this poor woman did. In terms of anything else at the scene – nothing. No tyre tracks, nothing. We'll have to hope someone calls in with some evidence or that the fuckers haven't been quite as savvy as they thought with the forensic measures. Maybe we'll get something from the body . . . you know, Locard and all that.'

Nikki was indeed familiar with Locard's principle of forensic transference and although, given the overpowering stench of bleach, it seemed unlikely in this instance that they'd retrieve anything useful, she could still hope. She raised a hand in farewell, nodded for Sajid to follow her back to the car and left the scene.

Once huddled into her jacket, shivering as she waited for some warmth to circulate in the Jag and appreciating the soothing heat from the seat that was beginning to seep into her frozen body, forcing her back muscles to relax despite themselves, Nikki exhaled a long breath. 'What the fuck is happening in our city, Saj?'

They sat, Nikki's words hanging unanswered between them for a few moments, before Sajid clipped his belt in place and started to drive. 'I'll drop you at home. We both need to grab a few hours' kip, because I have a feeling that things aren't going to get any better tomorrow and there's nothing more we can do right now.'

Chapter 12

By the time Felicity Springer came round again and realized that the bullet hadn't been for her, the petrol fumes had been replaced by the coppery stink of blood, tinged by the smell of her own urine. The vehicle was moving. She kept her eyes closed for a moment, assessing her pain levels. Her shoulder was edging up to a nine and a half, but the cold had numbed the rest of her body to a five, maybe a five and a half – not ideal, but manageable . . . just.

Darkness pressed against her, weighing her down as she waited, listening for long minutes to be sure that nobody else was in the back of the van with her. When she was as certain as she could be that she and the dead body were alone, she suppressed a shudder and began to slowly, making as little noise as possible, shuffle in one direction. When the thick gloop of blood soaked into her trousers, she knew she was close. Stretching out a shaking hand she tentatively felt for the body. When her fingers touched fabric, her hand jerked back and vomit rose in her throat. She swallowed it down and took a deep breath, which was a mistake as the smell of blood and the increasing odour of excrement hit her full in the face. This time she couldn't contain the flow of bile that splattered onto the metal floor. Groaning, she shut her eyes and counted to ten, breathing slowly through her mouth. When she'd done, she opened her eyes and, mouth set in a determined line, spoke under her breath. 'Come on Fliss. Come on. You can do this. For Stevie. For the baby. You can do this.'

Once more she reached out and touched something soft. Whether it was a trouser leg or the arm of a jacket she couldn't tell. Her fingers traced along the fabric until she came to a shoulder. Suppressing her shudder, she reached up to where she thought his neck might be and tried to find a pulse. Nothing! Moving her fingers upward, she touched a stubbly chin – *so, a man then.* What had this poor soul done to deserve this?

Exhaling, she considered what that might mean. They must be taking them both to be dumped but where, she had no idea. Would they try to dispose of the bodies for good? The best way to get rid of forensic evidence on a corpse was to burn it. *Oh God, please not that, please don't burn me alive.* Her mind flicked back to her most recent cold case. The corpses discovered underneath the Odeon car park had been buried. Her breathing accelerated. *Oh no, not that either. It would've been better if they'd shot me through the heart.*

The van lurched to the right sending Felicity rolling. She landed on her right arm, a jolt of pain spiralling from her injured shoulder through the rest of her. A yelp escaped her lips, followed by a groan as her pain level reverberated around the ten. *Shit, please don't let them have heard me.* The van slowed down, engine still thrumming as it rolled to a stop. Felicity cursed herself again. Up till now they'd thought she was dead, and now she'd given herself away. But the van began to gain speed again and sagging with relief, Felicity pinched her leg with her good hand.

'Focus, Fliss. Focus. What would Parekh do?'

She'd stay alive, that's what she'd do. She'd never wish she was dead. She'd fight to stay alive, fight for her family and that's what I'm going to do.

'I'm coming home, Stevie. I'm coming home.'

That decided, Felicity edged her way back to where she'd originally lain. She was going to play dead and when she saw a chance she was going to escape. It wasn't much of a plan, but it was the only one she had, and she needed to make it work.

Making sure her feet looked like they were still tied together and the cables round her wrists, she waited, forcing herself to remember happy times with Stevie: their first scan, the first time baby had kicked, the trips to buy pushchairs and Babygro's, rather than the overwhelming stench of death.

The texture of the road surface changed, and Felicity realized they were on a windier road, with more potholes. Her heart began to hammer against her chest. She was sure they were getting close to whatever dump spot they had in mind. Firmly putting aside her earlier thoughts of burials and death by fire, she focused on flexing and unflexing her leg and arm muscles. She needed to be ready. She would only get one shot at this and she needed to take her chance when it arose. She exhaled and began her mantra: *Channel Parekh, channel Parekh.*

The van came to a stop and Felicity was sure her heart was going to explode in her chest when she heard the slam of two car doors telling her there were indeed two captors to deal with. She heard the guttural sounds of males talking, a sharp laugh and then they were at the back door. Felicity, eyes shut, held her breath, willing herself to stay perfectly still. When the doors finally swung open the men were preceded by the smell of cigarette smoke. For some reason the fact that they'd stopped for a smoke before disposing of the bodies incensed Felicity. How bloody dare they treat human life in so cavalier a fashion. It was like they were dropping some recycling off at the bottle bank, not dumping a once living, breathing person.

Their weight as they entered the van made it dip and as they passed Felicity to reach the dead man a waft of sweat reached her nose. She held her breath, straining her ears to work out what they were doing. Muffled curses followed by, 'I'll drag him, you grab his legs when we get to the door,' told her their intentions.

Please don't come back for me, please give me a chance to escape.

They jumped down from the vehicle and took the corpse with them and Felicity waited. What were they doing? From outside came the sound of liquid sloshing . . . shit they were going to torch him. Next, they'd be back for her. Then the smell hit her . . . not petrol – thank God! – just bleach, plain old bleach. A nervous laugh hitched in her throat as relief flooded her. Straining her ears, she heard them moving outside the truck, their breathing heavy as they lifted the body. When the sounds faded to nothing, Felicity knew it was time for action.

She opened her eyes. It was still dark, but they'd left the back doors open, and moonlight flooded in. She struggled to her feet, supporting her injured arm with the other and stumbled towards the doors. Peering out, Felicity saw the two figures moving slowly away from her in the distance, down a narrow path. Taking her chance, she sat down and gently lowered herself to the ground. Her legs wobbled and dizziness told her that she'd lost a lot of blood. Ignoring the pain, she slipped off her coat and pressed it against her shoulder which was oozing blood again. Last thing she wanted was to leave a trail of blood.

Realizing that her best bet was to move out of sight of the men when they returned from their macabre task, Felicity edged her way round to the front of the van, using it as cover and took a few seconds to take in her surroundings. To her right was a canal. In the distance the moonlight shone on stationary barges. Having no idea how long she'd been unconscious, Felicity had no way of knowing which canal she was near, but that wasn't her immediate concern. She needed to hide and quickly, before her captors returned and, more importantly, before the adrenaline that had given her the energy to act thus far, ran out. To her left was shrubbery and as far as she could see, it spread quite a distance and merged into a copse of trees. If she could just get off the track and hide herself in the shrubbery, maybe, just maybe, she'd make it.

In the night air, the sound of the men's voices told her they were returning, and as quickly as she could, Felicity edged her way into the shrubbery, and began crawling awkwardly. She'd barely gone a few yards when once more the smell of cigarette smoke wafted in the night's breeze. Her stomach clenched. *The bastards were having another smoke! They'd dumped a body and now they were rewarding themselves with another smoke. Had they no conscience?*

Feeling vulnerably visible, Felicity pressed herself into the dank earth. Her vision was cloudy and she wanted nothing more than to just curl up and sleep. The sound of the van doors slamming shut roused her. Disorientated, she considered for a moment whether she had passed out, then panic filled her body. *Had they noticed her missing?* The engine started up and the van reversed its way along the path passing the spot where Felicity lay.

'Told you I'd be okay, Stevie,' she said just before darkness engulfed her once more.

Chapter 13

Xavier rolled over in bed, and glancing at the woman snoring peacefully beside him, he threw the duvet off. He grabbed the pile of clothes he'd left neatly folded at the bottom of the bed where he left them every time and, padding softly across the floor, he exited the room. The woman wouldn't be surprised to find him gone when she woke the next morning. It was only on very rare occasions that he spent the full night there and tonight wasn't one of them. She'd served the purpose of exercising some pent-up energy, but now he had work to do.

Making as little noise as possible he got dressed, then, by the light sweeping in from the streetlights through the window at the end of the hallway, he made his way downstairs and out through the front door. He was as familiar with this house as he was with his own so, even in the semi-dark, it was easy. On the doorstep, he flicked up his hood, scrunched his shoulders and cast a glance up and down the street to check for any observers lurking in the shadows before heading off in the direction of his vehicle. Except for a slight movement at the far end of the street followed by the flash of a mobile phone being activated, he saw nothing. Last thing he needed was for anyone to be logging his nocturnal comings and goings, but that was what he paid his flunky for. The phone had been a sign to let him know he was unobserved and could move onto to his next destination without fear of being watched.

He smiled and took off at a slow jog, hoping to offset the bite of the frosty morning air. After the minor upset earlier, things were back on track and beginning to run again like a well-oiled, if very illegal, machine. He'd waited a long time for this. Set all his ducks in the proverbial row, kept a watching brief as his competition was eliminated one by one and all the time he was networking; making contacts both here and abroad, spreading out feelers, whilst always maintaining the anonymity that would save him in the unlikely event his little ventures would go tits up. Only one person knew Xavier's real identity, and that was Cyclops. And even he was unaware of just how far his business ventures extended. Besides which, his power over the man who protected him was absolute . . . that was the very first thing he'd made sure of. He'd even on occasion supplied Cyclops with the women to torture for his sordid recordings. It had been the only way to safeguard himself and, well . . . needs must, eh?

A couple of streets away, he cast another quick glance around him before pulling on a pair of gloves, opening the car door and getting in. It wasn't his own car. No, this was one of several which his contacts had procured, in order for him to keep his movements under the radar. As always, he took further necessary precautions. Not wishing to attract any attention to himself, he didn't turn the key in the ignition. This wouldn't take long and he could withstand the cold for a few minutes. He pulled two pre-paid, untraceable phones from his jacket pocket, and using his teeth, pulled his glove off before activating the first of the two. A text message. Good. He brought it up:

Message delivered, loud and clear. Goods disposed of. No witnesses!

He typed a cursory reply:

Good. You know what to do now.

Then slipping his glove back on, he opened a tub of antibacterial wipes that sat ready on the passenger seat and wiped the phone down. He'd dispose of it later, but he'd trained himself to always cover his bases as soon as he could. Tossing the clean phone on the seat beside the wipes, he lifted the second one from his lap, repeated the manoeuvre with his glove and activated the phone. Almost immediately, a frown spread across his face. Shit! What was it with some people? You give them a second chance and they still fuck up. He slammed his palm on the steering wheel and tried to get control of the anger that had surged into his chest. The confined space of the car made him yearn to fling open the door, jump out and run back to his mistress's house. But that wasn't really an option. He knew better than to risk bruising her. Best to take his anger out anonymously, on someone who wouldn't come to the attention of the authorities, someone too scared to report a bit of rough. Thornton Road might feature in his plans later, if he had the time . . . that or one of his warehouses.

The thought of how he could dissipate his anger later, calmed him somewhat and he looked once more at the text.

Urgent! Bint's gone missing. What shall we do?

Sighing, willing himself to hold it together until he'd dealt with these idiots, he dialled. It barely rang once before it was answered with a breathless. 'Yes?'

Wishing to prolong the agony of the idiot on the other end of the phone, Xavier waited, allowing only the sound of his steady breathing to drift across the line.

'Boss?' The tone had progressed from breathless to terrorized, strangulated even.

Xavier silenced the tut that was on his lips and instead opted for minimalist interaction as he shot a single word into the air. 'Explain.'

'We . . . well . . . we did what you said, like. You know, got rid of . . . you know disposed of . . . Well, disposed of him, like.' A rasping wheeze punctuated the man's stammering.

Time for another bullet. 'And?'

'Well, we got back to the farmhouse, like, and we were going to clean up, like. You know hose out the back o' the van, like, and that's when we noticed.'

Xavier closed his eyes and imagined himself punching the two brothers into oblivion, their blood spattering out with each punch. The image was so vivid he could almost smell it and he felt himself go hard and lowered his hand to readjust his burgeoning crotch. Yes, a trip to Thornton Road was becoming more of a probability than a possibility. Still, *he* wouldn't be the one to administer the punishment. No, that would be tasked to someone else on the food chain, Xavier would have to find his release elsewhere.

'So, she's gone?'

'Do you think someone took her?'

Xavier rolled his eyes. 'Who the hell would be there in the middle of the night to steal a dead body from the back of a van?' His eyes narrowed. 'You checked. You said she was dead.'

'Yeah, like. Well, dunno. Must've made a mistake. She must've got out when we dumped the . . . you know . . . at the canal, like.'

'You didn't think to double check before leaving her unattended?'

'Eh?'

Xavier rolled his eyes – seemingly the concept of double checking was anathema to the two men. 'You didn't make sure she was dead?'

Truth was, he knew this was partly his fault. *He* should have checked himself at the farmhouse, but he'd been rattled when he saw her. Anyway, why take the blame yourself when you pay idiots for just such a purpose?

'Well, like she looked it. Covered in blood and all . . . *and* I checked her pulse, didn't I?'

He stopped for a moment. Hadn't there been cable ties round her wrists and ankles? 'Thought you'd tied her up?'

The rasping wheeze grew heavier and Xavier imagined Danny glancing at his younger brother for help – to provide a plausible excuse. *Good luck with that, Danny Boy.*

Finally. 'They were still in the van . . . she must've managed to get them off.'

And there we have it! The extent of their incompetence. Even when they had a captive secured and confined in a metal coffin, these two idiots couldn't even bother to double check, make sure she was dead.

'Enough!' Xavier wasn't going to waste time on these jokers. 'Someone will be in touch. Sit tight.'

Yes, someone would be in touch all right and if these two fools were stupid enough to hang around to find out who, they'd be in for a painful, if somewhat short night. And if they ran . . . well, the pain would still be there, but the duration would be extended, exponentially. Tonight was shaping up to be eventful for many people. All good and necessary disciplinary precautions, but boy was the body count increasing. He grinned. Just as well he was untouchable.

Xavier shut the phone, cleaned it and tossed it beside the other one, before retrieving a third mobile from his jacket pocket and texting.

Extermination required; Dumb and Dumber. ASAP

Chapter 14

A hand descended on Stefan's shoulder and flinching, he jerked away. Shards of pain seared through him as his body tensed. He waited for the punch or the kick to his stomach that was sure to follow. But instead, words in Romanian, his mother tongue, were uttered quietly, for his ears alone. 'It's me, Stefan. It's Rogin. You're safe. It's the middle of the night and you're back in the barn with the rest of us.'

Rogin? Thank God! The red-haired Romanian was his friend. He'd thought he might never see him again. Eyes still closed, Stefan focused on the familiar orchestra of snores that punctuated the cold air, the smell of twenty-some unwashed bodies combined with human waste and mould was quietened by the stench coming from Stefan himself. Nearby, the sound of someone pissing in one of the buckets that had been left out for that purpose reassured him that there was no immediate danger. His tension dissipated, making each tortured muscle protest as it drained from his limbs. If they'd brought him back to the barn it seemed his punishment was over for now.

Then the memory of what he'd witnessed over the long hours hit him and a low groan left his lips. *Maria!* Why had he thought for even one moment that he could escape? That he could rescue Maria and get away from here. A single tear dropped onto his bloody hand. There was nothing left to live for now . . . nothing. This barn and the halal chicken factory were his life from now on.

With difficulty he lifted his arm and rested his hand on Rogin's. He tried to speak, but his throat was too dry, the taste of blood sour in his mouth, the sickening stench of his own urine and excrement shaming him. Dizzy now, Stefan was aware of Rogin moving beside him on his own single tattered mattress, whispering to someone. Then, gentle hands removed his soiled trousers, cleaning him up with freezing cold water, moving him a little, hushing his protests with quite reassuring words.

Rogin swore repeatedly as he worked. 'Câcat! They have worked you over big time, my friend.'

Finally, dressed in dry trousers, Stefan groaned as Rogin put a sturdy arm round his shoulders and hefted him to a half-sitting position. Rogin's helper pushed a bottle of water to his lips and in accented English said. 'Drink.'

It was the young boy, Denis, that he'd taken under his wing. He was barely thirteen and Stefan had watched helplessly as over the weeks the light in the lad's eyes had faded. He didn't go to the chicken factory with the older men. No, he and the other young boys with equally dead eyes were taken elsewhere. He heard them crying in the early hours of the morning when they returned and he knew exactly what was done to those boys. The same things the monsters did to his Maria

Stefan sipped the water until the bottle was removed from his mouth and Denis shoved two pills between his lips before the bottle was replaced. 'Take! Pain!'

He gipped as he swallowed them and was relieved when Rogin and Denis lowered him back onto his thin mattress on the ground and covered him with a foul-smelling blanket. 'Thanks.'

Rogin shrugged as Stefan peered at him through his swollen eyes. 'They caught you.'

It wasn't a question, but Stefan nodded.

'And Maria?'

Stefan, breathing in shallow half gulps of air through his mouth, looked away. 'They killed her, Rogin. *That* was my punishment. They killed my daughter.' And at once he was back there, being hauled out of the bin before being transported to the warehouse where Maria was waiting. His poor Maria was out of her head on whatever cocktail of shit they'd given her. But that wasn't the worst of it. He shook his head, but he couldn't dislodge his daughter's screams as they tortured her, her eyes becoming more and more dull with each new horror they inflicted.

Rogin was talking, tucking the blanket round him. 'Sleep now. You need to rest.'

Stefan closed his eyes against the half-light, resigned to being alone with his pain, resigned to storing it like toxic waste seeping out killing him slowly. Eventually he slept.

The sound of the barn doors being flung open, followed by the sound of something being banged against the metal door frame, woke Stefan instantly. The glare of the harsh light, like scorching pinpricks driving straight through his retinas into his skull, sent electric shocks down to his toes as he peered at the three men who stood, outlined against the glare behind them. The guns they held in their hands cold and threatening in the early morning sun. They stepped forward, their faces screwed up in protest at the stench that greeted them. Three Rottweilers snarled at their heels, looking ready to attack at a moment's notice.

'Fuck's sake, what sort of animal are you? Cowering in your own shit. GET UP! Work to be done.'

It was the one called Bullet, presumably partly because his oversized head was shaped like a bullet on his disproportionately small neck and mostly because he had a light in his eye that warned them that he was the one most likely to pull the trigger on them. The other two were minions. One was Asian and the other Polish. Both big fuckers . . . but the silent implacable type. They didn't move unless Bullet told them to, but at least they didn't seem to derive quite the enjoyment from their job that Bullet did. As the other men scrambled to their feet, shivering in the cold morning air, their skinny frames hunched, their eyes cast downwards, Stefan felt two sets of arms under his armpits and he was hefted to his feet and supported by Rogin and Denis. Unable to contain the growl of pain that left his lips, followed by the choking coughs as he tried to catch his breath, Stefan found himself on the receiving end of Bullet's gaze.

Holding his rifle in front of him. Bullet stepped forward and prodded Stefan hard in the ribs, eliciting another yelp. Stefan's body folded over, hacking coughs bringing tears to his eyes as he tried to draw in some breath. The two men holding him upright railed against his weight and Bullet laughed. 'Let him go!' His tone brooked no argument and as Rogin and his mate released him, Stefan folded onto the cement ground, his entire body shivering as he continued to suck small gulps of air into his throbbing chest.

Bullet strolled over to the centre of the barn and nodded at the two other men flanking him. 'Drag him here so everyone can see . . . so everyone can learn.'

The other two men grabbed his arms nearly yanking them from his sockets as they dragged him across the floor, adding bruises to his already enormous collection of purple, green and yellow patches. They dumped him in a heap before Bullet, who took the opportunity to kick him in the stomach. The release of air emptied Stefan's lungs and had him wheezing on the ground, with Bullet's foot resting on his aching hips. If he was just a bit stronger, he would have grabbed Bullet's leg and yanked it hard. Bullet would respond with violence and, never had 'death by Bullet' seemed more appealing.

Stefan's eyes flicked over the gathered men. Each one a prisoner, each one in this sorry state because they'd made a mistake. He could see sympathy in some of their eyes, those who hadn't been here as long, but others were dead behind the eyes and they were the ones that wouldn't last much longer. It was because he'd seen the hope fade in other men that Stefan had tried to escape. He wondered how long it would be before his face reflected that dull emptiness.

Bullet removed his foot from Stefan and began pacing back and forth behind him, addressing his audience like a politician on an election trail. The only difference was most politicians didn't carry a rifle or prod their audience with it.

'See this idiot here?' He used the rifle to make sure they knew he referred to Stefan. 'He is not an example you want to follow. He is a traitor . . . I said a TRAITOR . . . What is he?'

Stefan, dizzy and feeling as if he was floating above the proceedings, wanted to laugh. The idiot was talking to the men, yet only a few of them had any idea what he was going on about. Most of them spoke only basic English and relied on the others to translate for them, but Bullet was prone to these grandiose demonstrations of his oratory skills. The men were unsure what he wanted from them when he raised his hands, rifle in one and the other palm upwards.

A weak chorus of 'Traitor' trickled from the few who'd kept up with his rant.

Bullet shook his head and spat on Stefan. 'I said WHAT IS HE . . .?'

Catching on now, the reply came back louder. 'Traitor!'

'Again. WHAT IS HE?'

This time, the roar of twenty men sycophantically appeasing him seemed to satisfy him for Bullet nodded, a smile exposing his rotten teeth as he raised his hand for silence. The chant of 'TRAITOR' was swiftly subdued and Bullet continued '*He* has escaped prison in Romania by coming to the UK. *We* helped him with his transport, *we* fed him, found him work and what do you think *he's* done . . .?'

A gurgle of hysteria caught in Stefan's throat, making him cough so much he spewed up a trickle of bile.

Bullet kicked him and continued his rant. '*He* has been ungrateful, trying to escape and so *he* has been punished . . .'

There was a bit of a pause in Bullet's ranting and then screams rent the air – shrill and spine-tingling. *Maria!* Stefan lifted his head an inch from the floor and looked up. All three of his tormentors were standing in front of their captives, their phones held high in the air and the screams and pleas and barbaric sounds from the previous night reverberating through the barn. The men looked on, their gazes drawn to the phones, horror and disgust in all but the deadest of eyes.

With no strength left, Stefan's head fell back to the floor. With his breathing shallow and laboured, he fainted.

Chapter 15

'Gonna sign this, mum?' Sunni held out a paper form, folded so that only the line requiring Nikki's signature was visible. His face was slightly flushed and he wouldn't quite meet his mother's eyes. Had he been naughty in school? Maybe this was for a detention. But that was so unlike Sunni. Yes, he was boisterous on occasion, but he was also very amenable – like his dad. Marcus was placid and even-tempered too. Nikki'd only made it back a couple of hours ago. Time enough to grab an hour's sleep and a quick shower before having breakfast with the kids before school. As a result, her brain hadn't quite kicked into gear yet. She cast a quick look at Marcus who smiled at her from behind his coffee mug, telling her nothing. Why did she have the feeling that the two of them were in this together?

She held out her hand for the form, catching the sideways glance Sunni aimed at his dad. What were they up to? 'What's it about, Sunni? You know I won't sign my life away without knowing why.'

Sunni shrugged, his lips turning downwards, his face sullen as he shuffled from foot to foot.

'Told you, Sunni. Told you, she'd never just sign it without at least reading it, and when she's read it, she'll say N.O. – NO!'

Ruby, chin raised challengingly, stared at Nikki as if daring her to contradict her. 'It's because she's a big fat scaredy cat, that's what it is. She tells *us* to face our fears, but when it comes to her, well it's a different story.'

Frowning, Nikki looked round the breakfast table. How the hell had something that started as a pleasant family breakfast to start the week disintegrated into a sullen Sunni and a carnaptious Ruby? Her gaze rested on Charlie, waiting for her to insert her tuppence worth.

'Yep, you're right, Rubes. She can dole out the advice, but, the sad fact is, she can't take it herself. Not even for Sunni. Look how upset he is. Poor kid. Aw, never mind Sunni. She can't help it if she's too scared to do this *one* teeny little thing for you.'

Nikki's gaze swung round and rested on Sunni, whose bottom lip now trembled alarmingly, his huge brown eyes awash with unshed tears. What the hell were they talking about? She stood up, rounded the table and put her arms round her youngest child. 'What is it, *beta*? You can tell me.'

Snuffling now, Sunni's words came out in a snotty indecipherable mess. '. . . hamster . . . Easter holidays.'

Nikki looked to Marcus for help, but he was gathering up the breakfast things and, she thought, deliberately ignoring her. He'd pay for that later. 'Look Sunni, I can't hear what you're saying. Stop crying and just spit it out. I'm sure I can sort out whatever it is that's upsetting you so much.'

'Brilliant!' Charlie clapped her hands together. 'You heard that Sunni. You can stop crying now. She's said she'll sign your permission letter. I'll help you carry the hamster home when school breaks up.' And she turned and shared a high five with her sister.

Hamster? What bloody hamster? Nikki barely managed to suppress a shudder. Surely she hadn't just agreed to allow Sunni to have the hamster he'd always wanted. There was no way she could live in a house with a rodent. No way at all. Could she convince him to opt for a budgie instead? Budgies were nice.

Maybe she could convince him that it would be fun to teach it rude words. Yes, that was a viable argument . . . a budgie that he could teach to swear! Okay, that wasn't perhaps the route most responsible parents would take, but she *had* been pushed into a corner. She opened her mouth to begin her budgie argument but stopped. Three sets of hopeful brown eyes were trained on her and her heart sank. They were right. She often told them that facing their fears diminished their hold on them, so how could she not face her own fears for the sake of her kids . . . for Sunni. She reached out and ruffled his hair and attempting to keep the terror from her voice, she said, 'Okay, give me the damn form.'

Marcus came over and put his arm around her. 'We know it's hard for you, but it is only for a week. Only for the Easter break. Sunni knows he can't have a hamster forever, but we thought bringing home Jemima for half-term was a good compromise.'

Jemima? Jemima? Who in hell would name a rodent Jemima? Jemima was a nice name. A friendly, loveable, cuddly sort of name . . . The animal she was just about to sign into her home for a week should have been named . . . Demon from the Sewer or . . . a Rotten Rodent. Nikki's stomach contracted, the hairs on her arms rising at the mere thought of it. Thank God, it was only a week. She could manage a week . . . just. She scribbled her name on the form, before she reconsidered, wishing the tingle up her spine didn't unsettle her quite so much as it made her think of claws creeping along her back. 'Jemima stays in your room the whole time, Sunni. I don't want to see it at all, okay?'

'Yippee.'

Charlie and Ruby grabbed Sunni and danced round the kitchen with him. 'Told you it would work,' Charlie said, winking at Marcus.

Nikki glared at him, well aware that she looked petulant, but reckoning she had every right to be. 'You too, huh? Played by my entire family. How is that fair?'

Laughing, Marcus kissed her cheek, 'Aw but look at their faces. You can't grudge them this.'

Sunni, Charlie and Ruby immediately put their heads together and plastered angelic smiles on their faces.

'You're not getting round me that easily.'

'Aw mum, you'll love Jemima when you get to know her.'

'Jemima is the last animal I will be getting to know. I've told you. She stays in your room.' She shuddered and tried to think of something other than scratchy feet and swishing tails . . . Okay, maybe hamsters didn't have tails, but they were still rodents and they still had twitchy noses and whiskers. The thought of having one in her home, even for a short time, was horrid. She glared at the kids and Marcus, grabbed her jacket from the back of her chair and as she headed out the door said, 'I mean it. I don't want to see that animal at all, got it? You all owe *me*, you know? Big time. Cups of coffee on demand, hoovering, dusting, evening meals . . .'

With their, 'We do all of that anyway, Mum' drifting after her, she grinned. She was happy and safe. Her family was happy and safe . . . life was good. Then she remembered Springer. Life wasn't good for her, or her wife, Stevie. She doubted there had been any updates, or Archie would have been in touch. The officers from the night shift were still chasing down leads, checking the limited CCTV footage and scouring the roads around the vicinity of the car wreck. They had little to go on and looking for Springer with no conclusive plan, seemed like a thankless task. Still, maybe the police helicopter had come up with something. With that in mind, she sprinted to her car through the slight drizzle that was turning the morning's snow flurry to slush and once inside, headed to Bradford Royal Infirmary, where she was to meet Sajid later.

Chapter 16

Felicity's eyelids fluttered against the sunlight. She groaned and stretched her arm out, reaching for Stevie. A poker of pain surged up her arm and into her shoulder and at once she was transported back to reality. A sob caught in her throat as she opened her swollen eyes fully, fighting against the dizziness that threatened to spin her into unconsciousness again. She was lying, shivering in the middle of lank, sodden shrubbery, in pain and alone with no energy to move or call for help. Her clothes were soaked, her head throbbed and the silence around her was eerie. What if the men had come back and were looking for her? What if nobody ever found her? Favouring her right arm, she rolled onto her back, her entire body throbbing and gave herself up to the heaving weeping that wracked her frame.

Finally, spent, she tried to settle her breathing. She needed to do what she'd done earlier, for Stevie's sake, for her unborn baby's sake. If she was going to get herself out of this mess, she needed to channel Parekh again. That decided, she cast her mind back to the previous night. When the gun had gone off, she'd been sure she was dead, but instead she'd heard a thud as the bullet entered, followed by a shallow whoof, as if air had escaped a balloon and, at exactly the same time, she'd fainted.

The rest of the events of the previous night played out like a cartoon animation in fast forward. Who was that woman? She looked like Felicity, but she must have been someone else. Felicity giggled hysterically then began to cough, her dry hacking sending electric currents of pain through every nerve ending. Her head pounded and her parched throat ached. Parekh – what was she supposed to do with Parekh? Again, the giggle. Punch her lights out, that's what she wanted to do to Parekh. Something niggled in her head. That wasn't what she was supposed to be doing though. Why was she thinking about Parekh? She hated Parekh with her bouncy ponytail and scruffy DMs and her sarcastic mouth. Stevie. She'd think about Stevie instead. Stevie was kind and beautiful and loved her . . . She smiled. 'Love you Stevie.' And then she drifted into unconsciousness again.

Despite shivering, Felicity was hot. Beads of sweat dappled her brow and she had the vague idea that she should do something, but for the life of her, she couldn't remember what. Blinking against the light, her brow furrowed as she tried to concentrate. She should be in bed, yet she had the growing suspicion that she was outside . . . in a field? A forest? The air smelled damp, like it did after a rainfall and, as a slight breeze ruffled the shrubbery that cocooned her, she remembered – the community liaison conference, the weird looks, Stevie's text, the drive home, the arm waving from the rear light, the crash, the shot and another shot.

She tried to sit up but couldn't move. It was like she was paralysed, and a wave of panic skittered like cockroaches from her stomach to her chest. She turned her head sideways and saw that she was lying in a furrow of sorry-looking wet weeds.

Starting with her toes, she attempted to move her body . . . nothing. She tried again and as her toes flexed, she almost cried at the pain the movement sent up her leg. If she didn't manage to drag herself from this concealed position, she might never be found till spring and then she'd be a dead body, scavenged by foxes and other wildlife and Bashir would have to investigate what had happened to her. Sobs hitched in her throat and she tried again to move her toes and her fingers. Not quite as painful this time, but she really needed to keep going . . . it was so hard. She shut her eyes . . . just for a few minutes . . .

Chapter 17

Despite feeling unrested, tense and slightly delayed by her family's antics, Nikki was determined to get a head start on the day. So, by eight-thirty, still feeling rough from lack of sleep, Nikki headed for BRI. With no word on Springer, she was filled with a nervous energy that meant she couldn't sit still, so she'd already contacted Sajid's partner, Langley, who was also one of Bradford District's pathologists, to see if he would be doing the post-mortem on the dead woman. When he said he was, she arranged to meet him there and delayed meeting Sajid till a little later.

Nikki wasn't sure whether they would be kept on the investigation into the dead girl's death or whether it would be given to another team in light of their ongoing investigation into Springer's abduction. However, the unidentified woman, so vulnerable and alone, had got to Nikki. Her injuries and that smell of bleach had transported Nikki back to a time in her life she could never forget – a lifestyle that a child had no business being part of and one her mother's ultimate strength had eventually got them out of.

That woman might not have an ID yet, but she wasn't alone. Nikki was determined to make sure that whichever monsters were responsible for this woman's death were brought to justice. After all, twenty-five years ago that woman could have been Nikki's own mother. The very thought brought a rawness to Nikki's throat. If she believed in God, she'd probably use the phrase 'there but for the grace of God', but she couldn't reconcile a God who would allow this to happen with being full of grace.

It angered Nikki that the unidentified woman had been discarded like trash, and, even if the case was allotted to another team, she would keep a close eye on it. Ultimately, that's what had prompted her to attend the post-mortem. Afterwards, she and Sajid were going to head up to see Mr Nichols who had been kept in BRI overnight for observation. She justified her decision by telling herself she was heading to BRI anyway. Two birds, one stone and all of that.

As she drove to the hospital, Nikki flicked the radio on, hoping for some boppy music to lighten her spirits. *Even Justin Bieber would do!* Thinking of Justin Bieber made her think of the scene at breakfast with the kids. *Bloody hamster – glorified domestic rats, that's all they are.* She grimaced, nothing she could do about it now anyway. She'd signed the damn form.

'The missing police officer, feared abducted and injured has not yet been found. West Yorkshire police are . . .'

Nikki tapped her steering wheel, wondering when the hell Springer was going to turn up and more to the point, what condition she would be in. Flashing back to Springer's wife's blotchy tear-stained face from the previous night, Nikki hoped that Stevie wasn't listening to the news. Stevie had rejected the presence of a Family Liaison Officer, preferring her own company, something Nikki could empathize with. The very thought of even a highly trained individual, but a stranger nonetheless hovering about was the worst thing imaginable. However, a uniformed officer would have visited Stevie to reassure her that the woman found overnight wasn't her wife.

'. . . early hours of this morning in a quiet residential street in Denholme, the naked body of a woman . . .'

Vultures! Already on the case. Like it being a residential street makes it worse.

'. . . neighbours are horrified that their secluded neighbour-hood could be used so . . .'

What about the victim? Doesn't she get a look in? Where's the concern for her, eh?

'. . . police say the victim has not yet been identified . . .'

Scowling, Nikki turned it off. The way the two women had been portrayed in the news report was telling. One was a responsible member of society whom we should get behind. The other was a blight on a residential neighbourhood – a bit of unwelcome fly-tipping on an otherwise unblemished landscape. Feeling the injustice of it all, Nikki vowed to make sure both women were respected. As she swung into the front entrance of the hospital car park, her spirits only marginally lifted when she got a parking spot with little trouble.

The BRI mortuary and post-mortem suite had been given a much-needed makeover and this was the first time Nikki had been in this part of the building since it had been opened with much falderal by the Mayor of Bradford, the previous month. Now, all startling white, with clinical pastel blues and greens that matched the scrubs worn by the various pathologists and techni-cians that worked in the department, it was blindingly new and convincingly high tech.

Entering the viewing room which enabled observers to view proceedings without having to get too up close and personal, Nikki stood by the partition. Langley was just about to start with the Y-incision on the unidentified woman and had picked up a scalpel. Nikki shuddered. The scalpel would be followed by the saw and she hated the sound of that. She didn't usually mind the rest of the PM, but the sound effects she could do without.

Laid out on the trolley, under the harsh hospital lights, the dead woman looked smaller than she had the previous evening. Nikki's fingers played back and forth across her scarred neck as her eyes traced the damage inflicted on the other woman's body. The unidentified woman's long hair was dry now and had been combed through, to find any trace evidence it might hold. It had a shiny, reddish hue to it. Her eyes were swollen and even from this distance, their glassy stare seemed to penetrate Nikki's soul. Bruises stood out dark and violent against the translucence of her skin . . . on her face, her chest, her legs. Some bruises were the size and shape of a booted foot, others more punch-sized. The fingers on her right arm had been broken and now jutted out at odd angles. The girl must have been in horrible pain. And judging by the number of bruises, her beating had lasted quite some time.

Trying to drown out the sound of Langley operating the saw, Nikki focused on the bloody stumps that were all that was left of the fingers on the body's left hand. This was more than just a beating. This was torture and whoever had done it, had clearly enjoyed their work.

Langley glanced up. His eyes, while smiling above his mask, weren't quite as sparkly as usual. Who could blame him when he was faced with such a needless act of violence? He paused with the saw in his gloved hand. 'Hi, DS Parekh. Nice to have you here. I'll give you a quick rundown on my findings so far.'

His voice coming through the speakers into the viewing room was strangely disembodied and, unsure whether he could hear her reply or not, Nikki nodded.

'I'd put her at roughly between 16 and 21 years old. Significantly underweight for her height. Her body had been doused in bleach, presumably as a forensic measure, which although crude, is extremely effective in terms of DNA. However, fragments of metallic slivers obtained from her hair may be useful in determining the type of building where she was tortured and will hopefully add to the weight of evidence when you find the crime scene. Those have been sent off for analysis.

'One good thing is that, although forensically savvy to a degree, our killer or killers neglected to consider her fingernails . . . well, the ones on the fingers they didn't hack off. I've taken scrapings of skin cells from under them and those too are awaiting analysis. Of course, as you can see—' Langley moved round the table and lifted one of her arms '—she has scratch marks down both arms. It may turn out that the skin cells from her nails belong to our victim herself. Who knows though, we may be lucky? I counted nine, what I believe to be, dog bites. I will take casts of those, which, should you find the animal, will corroborate that.'

Placing her hand back down on the trolley with a gentleness that made Nikki want to hug him, he looked up again and sighed. 'I sometimes wonder if there's no end to the inhumanity of some people, you know.' He gestured to a series of labelled plastic bags on top of the cupboards at the side. 'I extracted samples from her feet. Squished between her toes to be specific. It's faecal matter . . . canine, I believe, and presumably from the same animals who bit her. Find the animals and we can match DNA'

Nikki closed her eyes. Pressure surged through her, right from the soles of her feet and up into her chest. It had nowhere to go and it was building and building, suffocating her, making her dizzy. She wanted to scream and thrash her fisted hands against the Perspex separating her from the post-mortem suite. As Langley continued the PM, Nikki, trying to control her shaking, thrust each hand inside the sleeve of the opposite jacket arm. Her fingers slid up beneath her jumper, finding the warm soft skin beneath and when she thought the pressure could get no stronger, she plunged her nails into her bare flesh as hard and as deep as she could. Digging them in, she savoured the pain, and pushed harder, breathing into it enjoying the image in her mind's eye of her skin splitting open beneath her nails, the stickiness of her blood as it oozed up around her fingertips. The compression eased, her chest became less constricted, and a trickle of energy faded down past her stomach, through her pelvis, into her legs and eventually dissipated through her toes. Marginally calmer now, she released the pressure on her arms, let her fingers relax, her nails disengage from her skin and as her heart rate slowed, she pulled her hands out. Holding them by her sides, she clenched her fists to hide the telltale traces of blood on her fingers. 'Send me your report when you're done please, Langley.' She was amazed that her voice sounded so normal when seconds before she'd thought she was going to lose it.

Langley glanced up and nodded. *So, it is a two-way microphone.* 'Will do.'

Fists still clenched, Nikki left the room, and headed for the nearest bathroom. Once inside, she ascertained she was alone before disappearing into a cubicle with a damp paper towel to examine the damage to her arms.

Sitting on the loo lid, she rolled up her sleeves. Her jumper had already begun to stick to the blood and she gently peeled it off, before mopping the blood away. It wasn't as bad as it could have been. Yes, there would be bruises and yes, she'd broken the skin, but the scratches weren't very deep and they were only on one place on each arm and they'd stopped bleeding. She hadn't inflicted the marks in multiple places. She'd have to tell Marcus. He'd be disappointed, of course he would, but more than that he'd be worried. She hadn't self-harmed for months and now she'd started again. Okay it wasn't a blade this time, but this wasn't any better. She knew what her trigger was. It was that woman, girl really. The way she'd been treated like she didn't matter, like she was worthless . . . and the bleach, both here and at the crime scene hadn't helped either. Her chest tightened and she closed her eyes and began a slow count, just like her therapist had taught her, synchronizing her breathing with each number. She could control this. She'd done it before, and she could do it again. As soon as she got home that evening, Nikki would cut her nails and keep them really short just in case the urge to do this again was too strong.

Her phone buzzed.

Sajid: *At the main entrance. Where are you?*

Nikki stood up slowly, making sure her sleeves were pulled down and stepped out of the cubicle. Washing her hands, making sure there were no traces of blood under her fingernails, she looked at her reflection. *Come on, Nikki Parekh. You can do this. Time to kick some ass.*

Marching to the front entrance, Nikki kept an eye open for her partner. It was early, still before nine and well before visiting time, but she hoped she'd be able to convince the hospital staff to let them in to see their witness for a short time. Along the corridor, near the front entrance, Saj leaned against a wall, phone to his ear. She raised her arm and waved. 'Sajid!'

Glancing up as she approached, he held one finger up to warn her to wait till he'd finished his call. Nikki leaned against the wall beside him and waited. When he hung up, he was frowning, his lips in a tight line. 'Bad news, Nik. Mr Nichols passed away overnight. We've lost our witness . . .' He exhaled and Nikki sympathized with his anger.

'. . . and gained another victim,' said Nikki, finishing off his sentence. 'Poor old soul was trying to do the right thing and look what happened to him. What was it?'

'Heart failure. They didn't say it, but it was no doubt exacerbated by last night's events.'

Spent by the adrenaline slump after her anger in the morgue, her knees weak, Nikki closed her eyes, stretched her head back and hit it gently on the wall behind her. 'He put his jacket over her, Saj. That old man put his jacket over a stranger in need and died for his trouble. It's just not fucking fair.'

'I'll tell you something else that's not fair.'

Something in his tone alerted Nikki and she jerked her head forward, eyes following the direction of his gaze and groaned. *As if this morning couldn't get any worse.* Pushing herself away from the wall and heading towards the main entrance, Nikki hissed from the corner of her mouth, 'Quick, Saj. She's not seen us yet.'

However, just as they reached the doors, two elderly men came through and stopped abruptly, blocking the exit as they debated whether they'd locked the car, got the right entrance, or knew which ward their friend was on. Nikki went to dodge past them, but every time she tried to go around them on one side, the men changed their position . . . until finally, damn them, they decided to walk in front of her over to the main desk. Behind her, the pitter-patter of high heels on the linoleum floor told her she was imminently in danger of being spotted. Nikki edged her way to the side and, hoping that the old men would obscure her, she attempted to make her small frame even smaller. Like a hunched-over gargoyle, she cowered by the wall with Sajid beside her, eyes wide and with stupid grins on their faces. What the hell was it about Lisa Kane that had this damn effect on her? A mere glimpse of the woman knocked her off balance and had her behaving like a primary school kid and what was worse, she now had Sajid behaving like a moron too.

Holding her breath, it was no surprise when she heard the, 'Well, Nikita Parekh, if I didn't know differently, I'd think you were trying to avoid me . . .'

Trying to release the air that was now desperate to escape her lungs from between her gurning lips without producing an inelegant whoof, Nikki straightened up, thrust her hands into her pockets, lifted her chin in the air and ignored Sajid's 'I knew she'd spot us' snort. Lisa Kane was with her sidekick, cameraman Max Ashton. The pair were practically inseparable although he rarely said much, preferring to be silent with an inscrutable expression and let Lisa mouth off. Kane had been in Nikki's registration group at high school. A tall slender girl with long blonde hair, loads of friends, loads of money for the latest clothes and the confidence to strut around the school like she owned it. Lisa had been the direct opposite of Nikki and had taken delight in drawing attention to Nikki's small stature and her hand-me-down, secondhand clothes. Nikki had learned to ignore her and leaving Lisa Kane behind when she left high school was one of the things she rejoiced in most of all. Little had she known at the time that their lives would interlink only a few short years later when Nikki joined the police and Lisa worked her way up to be the main crime reporter for the *Yorkshire Enquirer*.

'Didn't notice you there Lisa, but we're in a rush, you know. Catch up later.'

But the journalist wasn't to be deterred and Nikki swallowed her annoyance as the woman fell into step beside her with long strides, forcing Nikki to speed up. Turning to Saj, Nikki glared, but with a cheerful wave of his hand, he stepped back and fell into step behind them, leaving Nikki to face her foe alone.

'Shame about your colleague DS Springer. Any word on her yet?'

Keeping her tone level, Nikki shook her head. 'Aw, Lisa, you know I can't say anything. There'll be a press conference later.'

'Well, what about the "naked girl"? You on that investigation, Nik?'

Something about her tone when she said 'naked girl' irked Nikki. The slight inflection on the word 'naked' was like a label of guilt, like the girl had been to blame for what happened to her, like she'd somehow inappropriately, crudely even, in an affront to civilization, displayed herself in a residential area. Not ten minutes earlier, Nikki had seen with her own eyes what had been done to that young girl and residual anger from that experience still lingered. She came to an abrupt standstill, and Lisa had taken three more steps, still chuntering on about 'residential area and family streets and the shock of such an awful happening in such a secluded neighbourhood, before she realized Nikki was no longer beside her. She turned, pulled her coat tightly round her and folded her arms over her pert breasts.

Almost a foot shorter than her, Nikki held her quizzical gaze, until Lisa frowned. 'Is something wrong, Nikita?'

Exhaling, Nikki shook her head and walked past Kane, deliberately bumping into her arm as she did so. 'You know the score, Lisa. It's an active investigation so, no comment.'

Saj caught up with Nikki and fell into step beside her as Kane called after them, 'Have you got an ID yet? Was she a prostitute?'

Nikki stopped and mumbled under her breath, 'Don't react, Nik, don't react.'

Saj, equally quietly, said, 'Yeah, don't react Nik. The woman's toxic, but don't fall for her crap.'

His strangled, 'Awww no,' when Nikki spun round and glared at the smirking reporter was resigned.

Nikki took a step forward, her cheeks warm, despite the cool spring air. Hot blood surged through her veins, fuelling her fury. 'I'll tell you what she was.'

Despite the quietness of her tone, Nikki's anger resonated with each word. 'She was a victim. Someone's daughter . . . maybe a sister or a girlfriend or a friend and now she's dead.' She lifted her hand and prodded Lisa Kane on the arm. 'Instead of focusing on how her death has horrified a privileged area or sensationalizing it for a few extra clicks on your website, perhaps you should focus on what her death says about the monsters who did this. About the people who live on the fringes with no protection, who become click bait fodder for unscrupulous journalists like you, out only to grab a headline, not to try to help find a solution to the problem . . .' Nikki was in full flow now, and nothing could stop her. 'But instead to incite indignation and criticism and . . .' Nikki had moved even closer, her hand still raised, finger pointed as if about to prod Kane again. Then she stopped and allowed her hands to fall to her sides. 'You know what? It's just not worth it. People like you don't get it. You make me sick, the way you devour misery and wrap it up like a present to sell your trashy rags . . .' Nikki's voice rang out across the car park, the reporter's patronizing lipsticked smile compounding Nikki's ire.

With a, 'Sod off Lisa' she gestured to Saj and the pair of them marched towards Nikki's car. Fed up with herself for succumbing to Kane's provocation, Nikki kicked her car tyre a few times and then spun round to Saj. 'You could've bloody stopped me, Saj. What sort of partner are you?'

'Eh, the sort who wants to remain attached to his balls.' He flung his head back, showing off his perfect teeth and laughed 'You were magnificent Parekh . . . truly magnificent.'

Nikki nudged him none too gently and then started to laugh too. It had done her good to offload and Lisa Kane had had it coming for a long time . . . 'Not too much then? I didn't go overboard?'

Saj snorted. 'Oh yeah . . . you went overboard. It was brill; "devour misery and wrap it up like a present". It was pure Parekh pulling no punches.' Still laughing, he walked off shouting over his shoulder, 'I'll meet you in Trafalgar House in a bit, yeah?'

Nikki waved and, once in her car, she took a few minutes to think about everything that had happened in the space of the last twenty-four hours. When she got to the station, she wouldn't have a moment to herself. Springer's abduction followed by the dead woman being dumped, Joe Drummond's sketchy behaviour on the phone, Haqib's girlfriend's revelation that her brother, a known racist and suspected illicit dealer of drugs and weapons, had gone underground . . . all of it made her uneasy – really uneasy. Was the dead girl the person whose hand Springer had reported seeing waving for help from the back of the missing transit van? Or, was that a different victim? If Springer was still alive, which Nikki thought unlikely, the chances of her remaining so for much longer were slim . . . very slim. Something had to be done. She needed information and if Joe Drummond wasn't prepared to come up with the goods any more, then Nikki knew someone who might . . .

Chapter 18

Sajid had worked with Nikki for long enough to gauge her moods accurately. Yes, they'd laughed at the interlude with the reporter, but he'd seen the tension lines around her mouth and the pulse thrumming in her neck. It didn't take an expert to realize that Springer's abduction followed so closely by the horrific torture and murder of the young girl had affected her. Springer's abduction was the first major case they'd had since Nikki had nearly died at the hand of a serial killer the previous year. That, combined with the shared animosity between Springer and Nikki and then topped off by the young girl being dumped the previous night, was enough to send anyone into a spin, never mind someone with the baggage Nikki carried.

Sajid had seen her face when the bleach smell had hit her at the crime scene. She'd frozen, her jaw slack, her eyes bruised, terrorized – just for a moment and nobody else would have noticed it, but he did. Langley had told him she'd asked to attend the post-mortem although she didn't have to. But that was pure Nikki. It didn't surprise him one bit that she'd feel obligated to follow things through with the dead girl. It had affected her though. When she'd strode along the corridor to meet him, she'd been flushed, tugging at the sleeves of her leather jacket and some instinct made Sajid remember when he'd caught her self-harming the previous year. Had she started that up again? Of course, there was no way he could ask her. Nikki didn't do tea and sympathy or sharing her emotions . . . she was more of a bottle-it-up and wait till it all bursts out in a toxic spew kind of girl and of course that's what had happened with Kane. If she hadn't managed to control herself, who knows what else Nik would have said?

Why did they have to run into bloody Lisa Kane, of all people? Like that wasn't the last person Nikki needed to have up in her face right now. The woman was unpleasant and seemed to enjoy goading Nikki. Normally Nikki was able to ignore it, waiting till later to vent her anger, but today she'd been caught off guard and had allowed the journalist to get under her skin. Saj was glad Kane's puppy-dog photographer hadn't managed to snap off a photo. That was a headline photo he didn't want to see anytime soon.

Sitting in his car, he observed Nikki from his parking space in Bradford Royal Infirmary car park, wishing for once that he'd driven a pool car rather than his flashy, extremely obvious Jag. Call it gut instinct or a sixth sense, but he was sure Nikki was about to do something off the radar and, although she kept him out of the loop to preserve his plausible deniability, he wasn't about to let her cut him out completely. Therefore, if he was going to follow her, he'd just have to be even more canny about it than usual.

She appeared to be thinking . . . weighing things up. Knowing Nikki, she was plotting and planning but if she thought he'd let her blindly go off on her own, then she had another think coming. As she pulled from the car space and followed the one-way system that lead down to Duckworth Lane, Sajid allowed another car to go in front before slipping his own car out and following her. She hadn't even glanced towards him, so he was counting on the fact that she wouldn't consider that she might be followed to keep his surveillance covert.

At the first traffic light, she indicated left to go up Little Lane and Sajid smiled. If his guess was right, he knew exactly where Nikki was going. *Not as smart as you think Parekh, eh?* But he gave her top marks. If she wanted to find out what was going down on the streets of Bradford, who better to put on the case than her friendly neighbourhood taxi owner mate, Ali Khan?

He followed, not bothering to keep too close. His suspicions were confirmed when she turned right at Toller Lane junction. She was definitely heading to Khan's Taxis. Turning off into the street before the taxi rank, Saj did a U-turn and parked up at the top of the row of terraced houses, where, providing she headed straight back to Trafalgar House after meeting with Ali, he'd be able to see her car pass.

Ali wasn't a criminal, but that didn't mean that he and his drivers didn't hear things on the streets. Nikki had told Saj about Adam Glass going underground and how Joe had clammed up on her and now this woman's body had been found. Hopefully Ali would be able to do a bit of digging for her. The only thing was, if Nikki chose to be closed-mouthed about it, Saj didn't know how he'd manage to prise the information from her. He bit his lip and thought about it. Nikki was an obstinate cow when she wanted to be. Then a thought came to him. He took out his phone and dialled a number. If she wouldn't share with him, then he'd just have to enlist the cavalry and bypass her.

Chapter 19

The usual floral scent greeted her as Nikki entered the concrete single-storey building that housed Ali Khan's taxi rank. Jenny, his personal assistant – who knew if they were any closer than that since Ali's wife had passed a few years ago? – glanced up in response to the tinkling bell that that announced a visitor. Seeing it was Nikki, her face broke into a wide smile and she nodded at the man sitting beside her to take over as she stood up. Walking round the front of the counter, she hugged Nikki. 'It's been far too long, Nik. Ali was just saying the other day that he'd not seen you for ages.'

She always seemed to visit Ali when she needed a favour and he deserved better than that from her. He never let her down and he always helped her out without question. She should be a better friend to him. 'Sorry, I've been busy.'

Jenny wafted her excuses away with a grin and a shake of her head. 'Of course you are. You've got those gorgeous kids to look after and you work full-time. And . . . well . . . you've had a lot to deal with, haven't you?'

Not wanting to dwell on the things she'd had to deal with, Nikki just nodded. 'Ali around then, is he?'

'For you? Always, me dear.' She turned to the bloke on the desk. 'Give Ali a buzz, will you, Imran. Tell him Nikki's here.'

In under a minute the door to the back offices opened and Ali was there, large and reassuring with a grin that made Nikki feel better than she had all morning. 'Come through, come through, Nikki. Jenny, bring some tea or coffee for us!' He quirked an eyebrow at Nikki and Nikki said, 'Coffee would be good, thanks Jenny.'

Ali's office was as untidy and homely as she remembered it. Jenny kept the outer offices spick and span, but her influence clearly didn't extend to Ali's workspace. He moved piles of paperwork from a comfy chair opposite his desk and gestured for Nikki to sit down. Once she was engulfed by the huge soft cushions, Ali nodded, seemingly satisfied that she was comfortable and retreated behind his old wooden desk. For a moment he studied Nikki and, used to this rite of passage, Nikki allowed him to. He steepled his fingers under his chin. 'You look pale and you've got skinny.'

Nikki laughed. Ali was always to the point and that was one of the reasons she loved him. 'And you've got plump and tanned. Heard you went to Pakistan for a holiday.'

Ali grinned. 'Yes, I did. I left Haris in charge – well, when I say Haris, I mean Jenny. It was hot and nice to meet family, but . . .' He shrugged. 'Bradford's my home. I got homesick after the first month and came home early.'

Jenny knocked on the door and entered carrying a tray. She put Nikki's coffee next to her on a small wobbly coffee table and placed Ali's drink on the desk before leaving with a 'Eat the biscuits, Nikki, or Ali will eat them and he really shouldn't, you know.'

Ali's guffaw made Jenny smile as she left the room. 'So, what can I do for you, Nik? Is it something to do with that poor woman they found last night in Denholme? Or that officer that's gone missing? It's all going to shit in Bradford at the moment, in't it?'

Not surprised that Ali had already heard about the body in Denholme, Nikki nodded. 'Both actually and also something else. I heard from Adam Glass's sister that he's gone underground, been ousted from Albion First for some sort of laundering or something. You know anything about that?'

Ali shook his head. 'Glass, I feel, is the least of your worries. He's not a kingpin, but rather a small cog in a very large and, from what I'm hearing, complicated wheel.'

So, Ali had been aware of something going on. 'Go on.'

'I thought your colleague in vice . . . what's his name, Joe or something. I thought he would have been able to tell you more than the odd bits of gossip my drivers pick up for me.'

From his tone of voice, it was clear that Ali was fishing for confirmation of some kind and Nikki thought she knew what it was. 'Joe's shutting me out, Ali. Clamming up on me. I know there's a lot going on in Bradford. It's like a tinderbox just ready to explode. Women abducted, murdered. Talk of gangsters from outside the region stepping in, uncertainty, fear on the streets. It's all positively combustible and I can't get a handle on it.'

'I have the same feeling. It's like things are being tightened and tightened. Less inconsequential low-level crime filtering through. It's as if the boss, whoever that is and wherever he's from, is putting a stranglehold on Bradford. People are scared. They're not talking. The new people on the streets are careful to keep themselves hidden and it seems that whoever is the puppet master is always one step ahead. Even Haris has been unable to get a proper take on what's going on.' Ali bit his lip. 'But, drink your coffee. I will get my most trusted drivers to dig a little deeper . . . but you understand, Nikki, I can't have my men risking themselves. They have families, you know?'

Nikki nodded. 'I wouldn't want them to, Ali. Just do what they can as long as they keep themselves safe.'

He rummaged in a drawer and took out a phone. 'Take this. I'll be in touch, if I find owt.'

Nikki slipped the phone in her jacket pocket, hugged Ali and left, wondering if Saj was still waiting for her or if he'd got fed up and driven back to the station. Outside there was no sign of his Jag. *So, chances are he got fed up. Idiot, did he really think I wouldn't spot his bloody Jag trailing me?* Her thoughts went to

Springer again. The more time that passed without her being found, the less likely they were to find her alive. It was after ten, now. Soon she'd have been missing for a full twenty-four hours. Sliding into the car seat, Nikki thought for a moment, then took out her phone and dialled.

'No more fobbing me off, Joe. You need to start sharing. We got a police officer missing and then another girl turns up beaten and tortured.'

'Aw, for God's sake Parekh. You're like a dog with a bone and I've got nowt for you.'

'Yes, you do. The dead girl lying in the morgue tells me you do. That girl was tortured. She was dumped as a message. Are you really telling me that your department is so far away from the pulse that they assume crime's dead? This must all tie in with Springer's disappearance . . . unless you know something I don't?'

Sounds of movement over the line told her Joe was on the move. 'Gimme a second . . .'

Tapping her fingers on the steering wheel, Nikki waited, watching a fat black and white cat dissect whatever remains it had found in a discarded polystyrene chip packet.

'Look, I can't talk now. Meet me in the Lidl car park tennish tonight, okay?'

Nikki snorted. 'As long as it's not boy racer night there tonight.'

The Lidl car park on Ingleby Road had got a bit of a reputation for hosting Pakistani lads who showed off their souped-up vehicles, revving their engines and generally strutting their peacock feathers.

'The only boy racer likely to be there tonight will be your shirt-lifter mate with his gay as fuck Jag.'

'Tolerant as ever, Joe, I see. Just keep your nasty homophobic shit to yourself, eh? Wouldn't want to have to lie for Saj, when he beats you to a pulp. See you at ten.'

She pocketed her phone, took a moment to silently curse Joe and then headed back to the station, pleased that she'd managed to snark a face to face with the man. It was always easier to exert pressure in person. Mind you, it might be that Joe thought *she* had things to share with him . . . well, who knows? By tonight she might have a whole load of tradeable info at her disposal. *A girl has to live in hope, doesn't she?*

Chapter 20

When the phone vibrated in his pocket, Xavier knew it was a call he needed to take in private. Today he was in a number of meetings and he'd already fielded a series of awkward calls today. It was going to be one of those days when the two conflicting sides of his life collided and the last thing he wanted was his colleagues getting suspicious, but some situations just had to be dealt with. So, he smiled and chatted and edged his way to the exit, before dodging out and heading to the men's toilets two floors up.

As expected, the lemony-scented loos were empty because half the staff were downstairs at the meetings he should have been in. He spun the lock on the outer door and settled himself in a cubicle, ignoring his distaste at being forced to conduct business in a toilet. Mind you, it could be worse. It could be the public ones at Bradford Interchange or the ones in City Park – who knew what degenerates frequented those public conveniences?

Taking out the burner phone he looked at the text he'd received. *Call me. Urgent!*

He pressed call and waited. Thank God for burners, last thing he wanted was anything traced back to him. It was answered almost immediately.

'Hey boss. Dumb and Dumber have been taken care of.

You want us to spread the word like we did this morning with that bitch?'

Xavier thought for a moment and then he grinned. 'Not just yet. Let's apply a bit of pressure, eh? Have them chasing their tails . . . their little curly piggy tails.'

A low laugh rumbled over the line and Xavier's grin widened. He just loved Cyclops. There was a man who shared his vision, his sense of humour. Not that he'd give him too much rope . . . just enough to keep him in line and on side, not enough to give him real power.

'What you got in mind, boss?'

'Let's spread them thinly . . . force the police to pressure point . . . see if the bastards explode. Then, when they're on their knees we'll show them who's boss.'

Again, Cyclops's laugh rumbled in his ear.

'They're already stretched, looking for that woman pig and following up on the dead bitch. My sources say they haven't a damn clue what's going on. We'll wait till tonight and then you'll dump the boys – in two of the most remote areas that are still in Bradford district – then you phone them both in anonymously within half an hour of each other. Let's keep piling on the pressure . . . make them work. The busier they are with form filling and procedure, the more they'll miss what's going on right under their noses. Besides, by my calculation they're behind still. Let's keep them running.'

The handle on the outer door rattled, and a muffled 'For fuck's sake, why do they keep locking the toilets, do they think we're gonna swipe the loo roll?' drifted through the door.

Xavier lowered his voice. 'I'm counting on you. Get it done.'

Now he'd have to hang out in here for half an hour till the coast was clear. No point in making anyone suspicious. He took out another unused burner phone and, using a password he'd stolen from one of his colleagues, signed onto the Wi-Fi. Settling back, leaning against the cistern, he scrolled through some porn sites, till he found one he liked the look of. *Just the way to pass twenty minutes or so.*

Chapter 21

Weak rays of sunshine broke through the gaps in the barn walls catching the dust motes that hung in the stagnant air. Stefan's eyes flickered; straining to stay conscious. Even this dim light made his head ache and as for the rest of him – well, even the slightest movement was agony. After a while he realized he was alone in the barn. The others, he presumed, had been transported to the chicken factory. The silence was interrupted only by the rain on the corrugated roof and the persistent drip from the gaping rusty holes that years of intemperate weather had eroded. It was soothing. It took him back to when he was a child and his mum had given him and his sister some lentils to play with in his sister's toy pots and pans.

He and Ana had been in a corner of the flag-stoned kitchen, sitting on the rug his mum had put out for them whilst she baked *alivenci*. Stefan could almost smell the vanilla, taste the plump raisins that his sister picked out, but he devoured. It was a special treat for them and on that occasion, it had been his father's birthday. But his parents were now long gone. Still, the memory persisted. Whilst his sister had created an imaginary dinner for her dolls, Stefan had enjoyed the sounds the lentils made when he poured them into the different containers from

131

different heights and in different quantities. He could create anything from a thunderstorm to a gentle drizzle with those lentils and in his mind, he became the weatherman. The person who could control the rain with just his small hands. His sister had scoffed at him as she rattled her spoon around the pot telling him she was cooking *balmos*, a buttery cheesy delight he would do almost anything for right now. Their mother had told Ana to leave him alone. That he was having fun. And he was!

What am I doing thinking of things long past? Stefan needed to focus, but every time he tried to move, tried to form a constructive thought, his mind drifted back to Maria and what they'd done to her. It was easier instead to think of the past. To before he'd got married, had kids. That way, for a little while at least, he could block out what his stupidity had done to his daughter. But he didn't have that luxury. The men would be back sometime after dark and, of course, Bullet and his thugs and those vicious dogs would be with them. Which made him wonder what was in store for him. He was no good to them in his current state. There was no way he could work and that meant he couldn't pay off his debts. Would they write off the debt and just dispose of him? There was no way they would risk getting him any sort of treatment.

Beside him on his thin mattress was a bashed bottle of water and a packet of pills. *Rogin!* The thought that he had at least one friend couldn't replace the hollow where his heart had been, but it gave him a little hope. But, what about Denis and the other kids? Maria may be gone, but he couldn't just forget about the young boy. He wished he could do something, for, from what he overheard in the warehouse, Denis and the other boys were going to face something far worse than they'd already endured.

In his weakened state it took him ages to unscrew the bottle cap and when he finally managed to drink some of the icy cold liquid, it seared his throat as he swallowed. For a moment he contemplated taking all the pills that Rogin had left. He'd no idea what they were, but he reckoned that they might be enough to finish him off. Maybe that would be the best solution. Why should he let Bullet have his fun? But a memory stirred. He was back at home, his hands cupped round his wife's cheeks as he kissed her lips. 'You look after yourself, Daria. We will be in touch as soon as possible.'

Stefan hugged her close. '*Te iubesc atat de mult.*'

She sniffed and pulled away from him, her eyes as blue as their daughters' and as full of love as any man could wish for. '*Si eu te iubesc.*'

With one last tight hug, Stefan moved on to his son, Luca who was waiting by his mother's side, his lips trembling, his eyes covered by his riotous dark curls. Where his daughters took after his wife, Luca was indubitably his son, dark-skinned, dark-eyed and dark-haired – *a mini me.* Even at 10 years old, Luca was trying to be strong for his mother and sister. Stefan ruffled the boy's hair and then grabbed him into a tight hug. 'You be a good boy for your mum. Do everything she asks . . . look after them for me.'

Luca was only a little younger than Denis. His son nodded, keeping his head down, but Stefan caught the splash of the boy's tear as it landed on his hand and wondered, not for the first time if they were making the right decision. Frowning, he glanced at Daria, but although her hands were clasped so tightly her fingers had gone white, she smiled and nodded. 'This is our only chance, Stefan. We have no other option.'

'Come on Dad, we'll miss the bus and then we'll be late for the flight.' Stefan's eldest daughter Maria was eager to start their adventure and Stefan wondered when he'd begun to be so cautious. Maria had completed her farewells in a matter of minutes and although she'd miss her family, she was eager to get started on their journey. *Ever the adventurer, my Maria!*

As the memory faded, Stefan wiped the tears from his eyes. Maria was gone and that hurt. But he still had a family out there. A family who would be worried about them. Daria deserved to know what had happened to Maria, the children should know their sister had died and it was his responsibility to tell them. With difficulty he popped two pills from their foil wrap and after a few efforts he managed to swallow them. A paroxysm of coughing wracked Stefan's frame. When he took his hand away from his mouth there were speckles of blood all over it. He wiped it on his trousers. He had little time left, but he would do his best.

Chapter 22

In the mood for company as she drove to Trafalgar House, Nikki turned on Capital Radio, hoping that a dose of light-hearted banter might boost her mood. She was disappointed when the final strains of Ed Sheeran's latest, segued into one of the depressing public awareness ads about being vigilant against modern-day slavery followed by the local news.

'A police spokesperson has stated that the dead woman tossed from a car in the rural village of Denholme, just outside Bradford city was not, as was originally assumed, that of missing police officer Detective Sergeant Felicity Springer. Needless to say, Bradford's police are under pressure to identify the victim and to locate the whereabouts of one of their own officers . . .'

Nikki prodded her finger at the radio controls, relieved when the news reporter's superior tones were abruptly replaced by BBC Radio Leeds' interview with a local graffiti artist, who was set to be the new Banksy, but without the anonymity. *Wonder how that'll work for you?* Nikki prodded the controls again and silence pervaded the car. She presumed Sajid would have made it back to the station by now, as she hadn't spotted him as she retraced her route along Toller Lane. She wasn't annoyed that he'd followed her. On the contrary, she was rather impressed.

He'd clearly picked up on her intention to go under the wire for information and he'd had her back in the same way she would have, had the circumstances been reversed. The thing was, should she give him the satisfaction of coming clean and admitting she'd cut him out of her plans, or put up with his petulant comments and pretend she had no idea why he was being a dick?

She grinned. She was in the wrong, no two ways about it; she should have kept Saj in the loop. Should have told him about that weird text Archie had sent yesterday. Still, she couldn't pass up on the opportunity to yank his chain for a short time – just till the end of the day, when she'd come clean and make nice with her partner. That'd teach him to follow her. Satisfied that she'd made a decision, Nikki turned into the station car park, past a group of journalists who crowded her vehicle as she waited for her ID to activate the electronic gates. Lisa Kane was among them and Nikki took great delight in glaring at the woman. *Hope she bloody freezes out here or, better still, that the heavens open and drench the lot of them.* As the gates opened, she edged forward, regretting her nasty thoughts. Until The Spaniel was found, she should be hoping for a heatwave not adverse weather. Who the hell knew what conditions the other woman was being kept in, if she was still alive that is?

Parking up in the empty spot next to Sajid's Jag, she got out and, bracing herself for the busy day ahead, made her way into the station. If anything important had been discovered overnight, either Saj or Archie would have contacted her, so she wasn't holding out much hope of any major breakthroughs on either case.

After the nippy coolness of the car park, Trafalgar House felt overly heated, claustrophobic even, as Nikki strode through the corridors to the incident room. Her leather jacket, which had seemed inadequate for the outdoor temperatures, now was too heavy and as she swung into the room, she shrugged it off, ready to toss it on a desk only to be met by Archie's brusque tone. 'So, Parekh. What have you got?'

Barely through the doorway, jacket still hanging from one arm, Nikki took a moment to observe the scene before her. Uniformed officers were stationed at desks around the edge of the room engaged in various admin type activities, the crime scene boards had been started for both Springer and their new unidentified victim. So, the investigation into the unidentified woman's death hadn't been taken from them yet. That news satisfied Nikki. She wasn't ready to give up on her – not yet. Mind you, depending on what happened with Springer, the unidentified woman could still end up being given to another team. As she was still a few minutes early for briefing, Nikki took exception to Archie's snarky tone. After all, it wasn't like she'd just rolled out of bed was it? She'd been out of her house at the crack of dawn attending PMs and trying to take witness statements.

Biting her lip so as not to make one of her usual smart-ass comments, she logged into her tablet to see if any reports had come in since she'd last checked, as Archie paced the room, hands on hips, a tortured expression on his face. He'd clearly not been home since the previous day. A faint tang of sour sweat hung in the air and the stains visible on his shirt when he raised his arm to rake his fingers through his hair confirmed he was responsible for it. His desk was littered with used mugs and empty crisp packets. Like yesterday, his colour was high, his eyes bloodshot and a pulse throbbed at his temple.

Nikki was used to Archie being larger than life . . . being loud and bossy . . . being full of short sharp orders. She wasn't used to this. She wasn't used to him being less than his upbeat self, less controlled, less together. She cast a glance at Sajid who lounged in a chair by Archie's desk, one leg slung over his knee, elbow resting on it and his hand cupping his chin. He raised his eyebrows but made no attempt to respond, his gaze clearly saying 'over to you Parekh.' But Archie was still ranting.

'Bloody press vultures hovering outside, desperate tae hear that we've got her body.' Pausing, he glared round the room as if it was the fault of the officers working at their stations. 'They're not after a fairy tale ending, the bastards. Oh no, that won't sell their papers will it? Right this minute they're planning their damn soundbites, ready tae persecute Springer and us for that matter. I'd hang the lot o' them by their proverbials given my way. And their irresponsible reporting of the death o' the poor lassie from last night . . . have they nae scruples?'

Stepping further into the room, Nikki allowed the door to swing shut behind her and narrowed her eyes at Sajid before moving closer to Archie. Close up, he looked even worse. His shirt was loosened at the neck, his tie flung on top of his jacket over the back of his chair and a sheen of perspiration coated his forehead. Deliberately keeping her voice low so the other officers wouldn't hear she said 'You need to go home, Archie. You need to rest. You're no good to anybody like this.'

Nikki had aimed for concerned yet calm, but judging by Archie's glare, she'd missed the mark. He snorted, his belly wobbling as he lurched forward and leaned his fisted hands on his desk. 'Don't you . . .' He stopped and swallowed, colour draining from his face as he held her gaze.

His chest heaved and for a second Nikki wondered if he was about to have a panic attack . . . or worse. She glared again at Saj and was relieved to see that he too was standing now and was studying Archie, his face a mask of concern.

Archie heaved a rasping gasp before finishing his sentence. '. . . tell me what to do, Parekh.' He sank to his chair and waved a hand in the air. 'What have you got?'

Nikki hesitated. He looked ghastly and she wanted to do something to make him listen but he looked implacable. *Fuck, Archie, don't you bloody have a heart attack on me!* She glanced at her tablet and flicked the screen. 'Definitely Springer's blood in the car and outside . . . no other blood trace found. No fingerprints other than Springer's either.' She risked a glance at Archie before continuing. 'They've managed to match the tyre tracks to a specific size. The bad news is that there are at least ten transit makes that use that specific tyre and each has at least three if not more models.'

'I need something, Parekh . . .'

God's sake, what the hell's got into you? 'They've analysed the paint flakes that were transferred to Springer's car on impact. That excludes a few makes, but it's still over twenty possible models, Archie.'

Archie lumbered to his feet, his chest still heaving. 'She's still missing . . . we've still not found her. Where the hell is she? She's one of ours.'

Nikki wracked her brains for something else they could be doing and came up blank. They'd put out a BOLO, they'd made a media appeal both for sightings of a white van with a dented rear end and for anyone who may have spotted anything odd on the route Springer had taken from Wakefield and so far, they'd come up with zilch. The police helicopter also hadn't come up with anything and the weather had made the chances of anyone spotting something untoward less likely. Apart from everything else, she couldn't work out exactly why Archie was so affected by this. That he'd been a bit sharp with Springer at the training session didn't account for this extreme reaction. Keeping her voice level, she spoke again, wondering if she'd survive this meeting with her head still attached to her shoulders. 'Look, Archie, we're doing all we can . . . what more can we do? You *know* how it is with these things. Something will break, it's bound to. In the meantime, we keep positive, yeah?'

Sajid moved forward. 'Yeah, sir, Nikki's right. We need to keep positive, something will break . . .'

Gee thanks Saj . . . about time too. Nikki would have tutted but now wasn't the time. She'd have words with Saj later for leaving her to smooth things over.

Archie swung his chair so he could look at the board with Springer's photo on it. Her mouth was pressed into a humourless smile that didn't reach her eyes and it was a look she'd regularly thrown at Nikki. It was the complete antithesis to the loved-up gaze she'd shared with her wife in their wedding photo. Seemed like Springer was deeper than Nikki realized. Pointing to one of the uniformed officers – a tall, skinny lad with a smattering of acne across his forehead, who Nikki vaguely recognized from around the station – Archie barked out instructions. 'Get that board up tae date, laddie.' Before swinging his chair to look at the picture of the previous evening's victim.

'What's the update on our unidentified woman, Parekh?'

Nikki swallowed. Whilst Springer's photo had been bereft of emotion, it had still held some animation – the coldness in her eyes spoke to her prickly personality, her slightly raised chin challenged you to disrespect her at your own peril. This unidentified woman with her death picture being the only one available was empty and pitiful. Her life snuffed out with no evidence that she'd ever been alive. Nikki swallowed hard, composing herself as the image of her on Langley's table, bared to the world and violated, once more flashed into her mind. 'I've got an initial report from Dr Campbell's post-mortem this morning. The full one will arrive by this afternoon, he assures me.'

With another wave of the finger, this time to one of the nervous-looking PCs standing at the edge of the room, Archie indicated he wanted her to fill in the noticeably empty board as Nikki spoke.

'First of all, it is with sadness that I report that Mr Nichols, the elderly gentleman who reported finding her body and who used his own coat to cover her, died in BRI this morning just before DC Malik and I arrived to take his statement.'

A murmur of regret went round the room and Archie grabbed a tissue from his littered desk and blew his nose before nodding at Nikki to continue. Although they hadn't expected much elucidation from the old man, his statement would have tied up a loose end.

'I attended the post-mortem this morning. I'll go through

the salient points here and make sure the full report is available in the case files. Our unidentified victim is between the age of 16 and 21, cause of death is strangulation after serious torture over a prolonged period of time. Langley noted all the injuries caused immediately peri-mortem and also documented a further list of injuries accrued over a period of months prior to this final beating. Again, I'll append the list to the file as it's extensive. The main and notable injuries were beatings with a blunt object, which caused numerous breakages, cigarette burns and other violations.' Reading the list made Nikki's mouth dry. She grabbed the bottle of water Sajid handed her and took a drink before continuing. A respectful silence filled the room, with all the officers' eyes either drawn to the photo of the dead girl or respectfully lowered to the floor.

'Langley found evidence of long-time sexual abuse, again that will be documented in the file. As we know the perpetrators took forensic measures by dousing her in bleach, but Langley took some scrapings from under her fingernails, which we hope will show bring results. There was little other forensic evidence although.' Forcing herself to remain expressionless, Nikki 'Langley found traces of canine excrement between her toes.' She glanced up. 'That's dog poo.'

A collective shudder went round the room as Nikki continued. 'Campbell is sending it off for testing. He says we might get lucky. If the perps own the dog, and we find them with the canine, it could link them – circumstantial, I know, but we take what we can at this stage.'

'Any word on an ID?' The spotty officer's question was tentative and biting down her instinct to snap 'let me finish' at the lad, Nikki gave him a slight nod instead. The lad was keen and there was no need to take her own mood out on him. 'Her fingerprints have been run through the system, but with no hits, so far. Her photo has been distributed to Missing Persons and we've got a police artist to sketch a more animated version to distribute through media channels throughout the day. However, Campbell, judging by the quality of dental work, suggested she might be from Eastern Europe and so I have been in touch with Interpol and her photo is now being matched against missing person reports throughout Europe. I am hopeful that one of those avenues will bear fruit.'

Nikki hoped that her expression didn't betray the lie in her final statement. She had a strong conviction that this girl, so disrespected in death, had been just as disrespected in life and wasn't holding on to any hopes of reuniting her body with a loving family, although if that were to be the case, Nikki would be pleased to have returned their daughter to them. Lack of closure tore families apart and Nikki knew first-hand the agony of not knowing.

Archie's phone rang, and Nikki released a long slow breath, stretching her neck to loosen the tension that had gathered there. The air of expectancy in the room as she delivered her report, had left her knackered and it was still early. The truth was, they didn't have much to go in either investigation.

'Yes?' Archie's tone was still sharp as he barked into his phone and Nikki again wondered just what was making him so antsy. Seconds later that thought was driven from her mind as her boss lurched to his feet, his face even paler than before. 'They've found a body. Saltaire Canal. Get cracking.'

Nikki's first thought was, *I hope to hell Stevie's not got the news on.* Those vultures would be on it in no time. She turned to the spotty officer. 'Get a FLO to Stevie's house pronto. I don't care if she objects, I want someone with her. Make sure she keeps off the news.'

She glanced at the huge clock on the wall; eleven-fifteen. Barely a day since Springer had gone. She shook off the wave of exhaustion that flooded her. Despite the odds, she still held out some hope that they would find Springer, as well as the perpetrators who had taken her. As Archie grabbed his jacket and headed for the door, Nikki grabbed his arm. He tugged it away impatiently, but she whispered, 'Wait.' He glared at her and then stopped, his breathing heavy, he allowed the room to clear and hissed, 'What? You got something?'

Nikki nodded. 'As you requested, I got an analysis on Springer's blood. The stats came back. Low alcohol – just a trace, enough to show she'd had a drink the previous night, but nowhere near enough to charge her with if she'd been breathalysed.' She hesitated, shuffling her feet, unsure how to handle the next bit. 'But there *were* traces of Rohypnol in her blood.'

Archie exhaled and then rubbed his fingers across his forehead. 'Shit.'

'What's going on Archie? You can't keep us out of the loop like this. We need to know everything if we're going to find her. How the hell did Roofies get in her bloodstream and, more to the point, how did you know to look?'

She held his gaze, using her willpower to try to force him to confide in her. Archie had been at the same training event as Springer. He'd spoken with her *and* he'd been worried enough or suspicious enough to suspect she had been drugged. Nikki knew Rohypnol only remained in the bloodstream for around twelve hours after ingestion, so they'd been lucky to catch it . . . which made Nikki's question even more imperative.

Archie's face crumpled into an angry mask. 'You accusing me Parekh? I'll have your proverbials if you are.'

Nikki snorted. 'Don't be stupid, boss. You could have left her blood untested for date rape drugs, but you didn't – that alone lets you off the hook. Now you need to tell me what's going on.'

Sajid's face appeared in the doorway. 'Come on, you two. We need to get moving.'

Archie waved Sajid away and in a low voice said, 'Later, Parekh. Later. Let's see if we've found her first. By the way, you thought about the DI job?'

Nikki stormed past him without a word. Bloody DI job. Where the hell had that stupid idea come from? She was so *not* DI material and she wouldn't be forced into it. She hated dealing with people, hated doing the paperwork and hated having to toe the line. Archie bloody well knew that too.

Chapter 23

The only things that made this crime scene a little more bearable than the previous two was the absence of snow, the fact it was daylight and there was a slightly warmer temperature in the air. Otherwise it was dire. The drive over to Saltaire had been punctuated by Archie's heaving breaths and mumbled curses. Nikki had encouraged Saj to drive and had opted for the back seat. She was worried. Worried about the investigation. Worried that they were going to find Springer's body. Worried about their stretched resources and most of all she was worried about Archie.

There was something going on with him and whatever it was seemed to be affecting his health. He'd been useless last night when they'd told Springer's wife what had happened, had clearly had a sleepless night and, this morning, both she and Saj had thought he was going to keel over. Despite her lack of affection for Springer, she feared that the body in the canal would be hers and she didn't think she could break that news to Springer's wife. Judging by Archie's laboured breathing, he wouldn't be able to deliver the bad news either and as Stevie hadn't even met Sajid, it seemed the task would definitely fall to her. She was also irked by Archie's offer of the DI position. She thought he knew her. Knew that she wouldn't want to be tied to a desk. Knew that she wasn't a pen pusher and yet he'd sprung that on her. 'What the hell is going on?' seemed to be her constant lament at the moment and she hated it.

Work was usually uncomplicated for her. Just nab the bad guys, but all this other stuff was an unnecessary complication. By the end of the day, whether she had managed to squeeze every last bit of information from Archie or not, she was going to come clean to Sajid. Maybe he'd be able to help her get more of a handle on what was going on.

Driving down Victoria Road, through the centre of the village named after the famous philanthropist Sir Titus Salt, Nikki, despite her subdued mood, smiled. This was one of the delights of Bradford – a lazy village with its own busy street festival and the renowned Hockney art gallery housed in the refurbished Salts Mill. She loved that it was a short drive or bus ride from the city centre. Sajid managed to snag a parking spot just outside Don't Tell Titus, a pub whose tongue-in-cheek name was a nod to the teetotal rules employed by Sir Titus for his workforce.

Further down the road a line of police cars and CSI vans already lined the streets and a crowd had gathered around the bridge at this side of the canal. Nikki jumped out, itching to get moving, but waited for Archie to get out too. His pallor worried her, yet his expression was so forbidding she dared not broach the subject with him.

'He's not well.' Sajid's voice was barely a whisper. 'He shouldn't even be here, Nik. What are we gonna do?'

You don't say, Saj! Watching Archie lean heavily on the car door to steady himself before slamming it shut, she ducked a nod of acknowledgement in Saj's direction. The tension lines around the boss's lips showed how much effort the simple movement had taken him and neither she nor Saj were fooled by his attempt at casualness. A pang of guilt hit Nikki in the solar plexus. The team was short-staffed. Their DI, John Rankin was off on long term ill health with little likelihood of returning to the job. Archie had asked her to step up as acting DI, but she'd refused, the thought of being stuck in the office, being a desk jockey wasn't for her. Archie, rather than enlist a new acting DI from another team, had taken on the extra workload himself, saying he was waiting for Nikki to cave into his little nudges and guilt trips. Was it the extra work that was finally taking its toll on the man? *Bloody Archie!*

Saj stepped closer and offered his arm, but the boss waved him away. 'You two go on ahead. I'll catch you up when I've caught mah breath.'

Nikki hesitated for a moment, torn between getting to the scene by the canal to see the body in situ before the CSIs with the help of the police divers moved it onto dry land and making sure Archie was all right. 'You stay with him, Saj. I'll go on ahead and phone up if there's anything happening.'

Tightening her ponytail, she set off at a jog down the street to the bridge that led to the canal. As she reached the bottom of Main Street, where an outer cordon had been created, preventing the few journalists who'd already got wind of police activity by the canal and the general public from wandering too close, she nodded to the two officers who were controlling the area. She had just signed herself in when the police divers' van pulled up and triple parked as near to the cordon as possible. Thank God, she was in time to see the body before they moved it. Speeding up, the wind whipping her ponytail, Nikki waved to the divers as they exited their vehicle and ducked under the tape. First impressions of a crime scene were essential and Nikki wanted to absorb as much as she could from the fact this body had been dumped in the canal, before it was moved to the mortuary.

At the bottom of the incline more crime scene tape cordoned off the bridge leading to the skateboard park and the Shipley Glen tramway. From here, the tape extended round to block access to and from The Boat Inn pub, a family pub that nestled on the banks of the River Aire which ran parallel to the Leeds/Liverpool Canal where the body had been discovered. She assumed that a team of officers had been sent to tape off the canal walkway further away from the site to contain the crime scene. Nikki paused by the tape and looked around. The concrete walkway beside the canal tailed off into a muddy dirt path a little further along. Three barges lined the waterway and one of them had smoke drifting from a small metal chimney, so at least one of them was inhabited. The first of the three was the Ice Cream Boat that she'd bought ice cream from for the kids on many occasions. The boat was shut for now, but would probably open for business for half-term, next week.

In the summer, this area was heaving with walkers and families. At this time of year not so much. According to the officer who'd called it in, it wasn't a dog walker who'd discovered the body, it was one of the barge owners. Nikki spotted some police activity near the pub. No doubt that's where their witness was, hopefully getting warmed up and calmed down. The area had a dark sinister feel to it and Nikki couldn't help shuddering. Maybe it was the skeletal leafless trees or the brooding clouds that seemed to hang threateningly low in the sky. Nikki had only ever visited this area when it was filled with laughter and family activity. The knowledge that a body had been dumped so unceremoniously tainted it somehow.

The duty crime scene manager was Gracie Fells again, so after shrugging into her suit, Nikki headed past the Ice Cream Boat towards the other two barges. 'Where is it, then?'

Gracie nodded to a gap between the two other barges. 'Face down in there. The old bloke who noticed it said this barge—' she pointed to the newer of the two, painted a shiny royal blue and going by the name of *The Prince's Son* '—came in and berthed up early this morning. They woke him up with all the racket they made. He got the impression they were inexperienced boatmen on a bit of a break. Reckons the barge is a hired one. When he and his partner got up, the other barge was in darkness and he got the feeling the family had left.'

Nikki nodded to the second barge with *The Sailor's Wife*

scrawled in swirly yellow writing on top of the pillar-box red paintwork. It had tarpaulins secured over the bow and its jaunty floral curtains were tied back showing a tidy interior. 'That the witness's barge then?'

'Yep, two of your lot have taken the two elderly gentlemen down to the pub and got them drinks.'

A gangly officer wandered over. 'We're trying to contact the rental company to get details of the family who rented it, ma'am. See if they spotted anything untoward.'

'You spoke to the witness yet?'

The officer blushed and seemed to straighten his spine. 'Yes ma'am, I took a preliminary statement, but told him and his . . . er . . . gentleman friend . . .'

'Partner.' Gracie rolled her eyes. 'It's his partner not his friend, although I suppose he could be both friend and partner.'

Nikki shook her head slightly at Gracie, who responded by raising one arm like a trunk in front of her face and edged away, speaking in a Dalek voice. 'Backing off . . . backing off . . . backing off.'

Nikki laughed. 'Ignore her, Constable . . .?'

'Williams, ma'am!'

'Drop the ma'am and we're fine. She's been working too many hours over the past few days and has lost the few marbles she had to begin with. Continue.'

Williams swallowed; his flush had now blossomed over his entire face and down to his neck. He'd have to toughen up, if he was going to succeed on the job. He glanced at the CSI, who had now turned and was speaking with one of her colleagues. 'Nah, she's right ma'am. The old bloke said it was his partner and I should've gone with that. Anyway, I told him someone senior to me would be down to take another statement later. But this is what he told me . . .'

He cleared his throat and took a moment before continuing. 'Mr O'Donnell heard a ruckus at around four or half fourish.

He heard nothing else overnight.' His lips twitched. 'Except his partner snoring that is. They had a cuppa and a bacon sandwich around eight. And around nineish, they decided to wander up to Saltaire Village, buy some milk and suchlike. When they got back, Mr O'Donnell remembered the racket the previous night and decided to check to make sure they hadn't scratched his barge and that's when he found the body.' He turned and pointed between the two barges. 'Down there.'

Nikki edged closer and peered over the edge. She could just see the back of a head with longish hair of indeterminate colour wearing some sort of winter jacket. She leaned further over, trying to see if it could possibly be Springer. Still unable to see clearly, she knelt down and stretched closer.

'Want me to hold your legs?' Gracie's voice was full of amusement, but at least she'd lost the Dalek tone.

Nikki grunted, 'Aw piss off, I'm not going to fall in.' She peered down past the wooden curve of the prow into the dark glimmer of the canal. Something moved to the right of her and her head jerked towards it at exactly the same time as she heard a scrabbling sound. Panic sent her heartrate speeding. *For fuck's sake! No! Just No!* Her hands gripped the edge of the bank for a second, then she released them placing her palms on the concrete slab and jerked her upper body backwards. The back of Nikki's head cracked against something solid. *Shit!'*

'Ouch, watch what you're doing, Parekh!'

Nikki, terror still gripping her at the thought of creepy crawly talons and a swishing tail, kept pushing back sending the two of them tumbling to the ground, just as a massive rat jumped onto the sidewalk, skittered over Nikki's hand and disappeared under the bridge. Her heart thundered as she stared, open-mouthed, at where the rat had run over her. She stretched back shuddering, wishing she could disassociate her hand from the rest of her body, wishing that she'd put her gloves on, wishing that she'd stayed with Archie and sent Sajid in her place. She'd just about gained control of herself and was on the point of moving, when, clearly disturbed by the unusual human activity near the wall, three more rats, bigger, with twitchier noses and scratchier claws jumped up, ran over her hand again and followed their leader. Nikki yelped and jumped to her feet, shaking her hand as if she could loosen it from her arm, and hopped about. 'Rats, rats, damn rats and more damn rats!'

It took her a few seconds to realize that the three divers in wet suits were now lined up just in front of her not even bothering to hide their grins, whilst two CSIs were openly chortling at her. Gracie glared at her over her mask, her gloved fingers palpating her nose. 'If you've broken my nose Parekh, you can do your own bloody lab work. Now, out of the way. The diving team has a job to do and thank God *they're* not scared of a few damn rodents.'

Nikki closed her eyes and swallowed. What the hell had just happened? It would take no more than half an hour for her panicked encounter with her rat-enemy to be exaggerated and circulated round Trafalgar House. Stepping away to allow the divers space to work, she glanced round and saw Saj grinning at her from the bridge whilst Archie seemed to be focusing more on his breathing than her stupid antics. As she cast her eyes round the accumulated group, a couple of the officers beyond the cordon slipped their phones back into their pockets. She raised her voice. 'Don't even bloody well think about circulating that . . . I see you. I've got your names. I'll make your lives hell if that hits the internet.'

Turning her back to the crowd, Nikki edged further away from the canal bank and tried to put the memory of the rats touching her from her mind. *Pull yourself together Nikki. You're working. They're only little – can't hurt you.* But even as she thought the words, she shuddered again and couldn't help her eyes darting around the shrubbery and down the tow path. She half expected to see an army of the damn things descending on her, elongated claws out, like rodent Edward Scissorhands, wild grins on their twitching whiskered faces and tails long enough to strangle her should they desire. Then another thought struck her. Would they have made themselves acquainted with the body by the canal? *Yeuch, gross!*

A splash signalled the entry of one of the divers into the canal and Nikki, hands thrust behind her back, watched as another black suited body slithered over the edge too. The third diver remained on the side and shouted instructions to the other two in the water.

'Bet it's freezing in there, Nik.'

She glanced at Saj, who'd now joined her on the canal bank, her frown deepening when she saw his grin. No way would he let her forget this . . . no damn way. 'Archie okay?'

Saj's grin slipped from his lips. 'I think he needs checking out. He's clearly struggling. Keeps rubbing his chest . . .'

'Tell me about it. You heard anything on the grapevine? Why's he so aerated about Springer? There's never been any love lost between those two, yet he's acting like he cares about her personally.' If anyone knew any inside info it would be Sajid. He always had his ear to the ground and because, unlike Nikki, he was so sociable, he was often privy to gossip that passed her by.

He shook his head. 'Not a damn clue. Gunveet was on duty yesterday and said there was a bit of toing and froing with Archie and the big boss after some phone call or other . . . but that was before this all kicked off.'

Apparently speaking to her again, Gracie approached. She'd been hovering near the divers keeping an eye on proceedings, ready to process any evidence handed over by the divers as they worked to untangle the body. 'Divers reckon the body got tangled up somehow on some rope and may have been dragged along the canal a fair bit. The canal boat owners might never even have noticed it in the dark.'

Nikki nodded towards the divers. 'Is it . . .?'

Gracie shook her head. 'Nah. It's not your woman. It's a bloke, apparently. We'll know more when we get him out of there. But they identified a gunshot wound to the chest, probably close-range. Scorch marks on his T-shirt. They reckon it'll be another half-hour or so.'

Shit, not Springer. Nikki didn't know whether to be relieved or not, for this dead male body put the body count at two, *plus* a missing police officer. How long would they be able to maintain all three of these investigations at the same time? Sure as fate, the bloody news vultures would be quick to question whether the Springer investigation was garnering more hours than the other two. If they were lucky, maybe they'd see a clear link between this body and the woman from yesterday.

'Saj, get on the phone to Stevie. Let her know that the body doesn't belong to Springer. The press will soon have this all over the media and I don't want her worrying any more than she already is. Tell her I'll drop by later.'

Whilst Saj made the call, Nikki observed the divers and the CSIs working together like they did this sort of stuff every day. Gracie took photos at various angles every time the divers moved the body, ever the consummate professionals.

'Well, done that. She's upset, but relieved.' Saj shuffled his feet to keep them warm, 'The good thing is, the canal's fairly straight-forward. If we find where this barge was docked overnight, we'll be able to work our way back from there, checking out any likely dump sites. The body must have got tangled between their last barge spot and their current one.'

Nikki turned to PC Williams. 'Chase up the family who rented this barge. I need to know ASAP where they were last berthed. Can I count on you?'

The lad nodded, already pulling his phone out. Nikki handed him her card. 'ASAP, yeah?'

But he was already speaking to someone and responded with a smile and a thumbs-up.

Nikki glanced back up at the bridge, where Archie was peering over, his gaze intent on the divers in the water below and shook her head. His face visibly relaxed as he took her meaning, but his body was still hunched over the wall by the bridge as if he'd fall down otherwise. Turning abruptly, she dipped under the crime scene tape and jogged up to Archie with Sajid following. Up close, Archie looked even worse than he had earlier. Despite the cold, a sheen of sweat covered his forehead and his breathing was laboured.

'Right.' Nikki, hands on hips, glared up at her boss. 'Enough is enough. I don't know what you're playing at.' As Archie opened his mouth to reply, Nikki extended her hand palm towards her boss. 'No, I'm not listening to you. *You* need to get checked out. I've not got time for this, Archie. I've got to focus on co-ordinating the investigation into Springer's abduction and, now I've also got two dead bodies on my hands. *You* need to go and get checked out. You're a hindrance . . . you hear me? A hindrance. And I'm not having it.'

Archie blinked, and rubbed his chest. 'It's complicated Nikki . . . I . . .'

But Nikki wasn't listening. She turned to one of the PCs who were guarding the outer cordon. 'DCI Hegley needs to be taken to Bradford Royal Infirmary. He'll argue and he'll moan but that's where you are going to take him, okay?'

The PC cast an uncertain glance to Archie, then seemingly realizing how poorly their mutual boss was, gave a quick nod. 'I'll get the car.'

Glad that she hadn't had to exert too much pressure on the young officer, Nikki started to walk back in the direction of Sajid's car when Archie's voice, stronger than it had been moments earlier, stopped her. 'I need to talk to you Parekh. This thing could blow up in all our faces . . . we need to talk.'

Nikki exhaled, nodded once and kept walking. 'Yep. When you've been checked out, but for now, Saj and I are off to look for possible dump sites.'

Chapter 24

Maybe this is what it feels like to be dead. All floaty and like you're not in your own body. Felicity giggles. It is a little bit like some of the scenes she'd seen on the telly. The corpse is lying on a stretcher or a hospital bed or something and the person's floating somewhere near the ceiling, looking down on their own body. All around, the nurses and doctors are talking in muted voices, inserting tubes, injecting stuff and then there's the ECG. The body spasms on the trolley, as they all look at the machines . . . no heartbeat. DEAD!

Felicity's eyes flutter and her fingers try to grip the edge of the hospital bed, expecting soft sheets. *That's not right.* She forces her eyes open and realizes that she's outside, lying on wet grass. Where's the hospital? Then she gets it. She's dreaming. That's all, it is a dream. Some horrid dream where she's hurt and alone.

She should get some sleep. Stevie would tell her to rest, so would the doctors. But it's so hot. Why's it so hot? Couldn't they open some windows? Let in some fresh air?

She looks up to see if she can see her other self floating above her, but all she can see are grey clouds flitting across the sky in the slight breeze. It's then she becomes aware of the grass moving . . . like whispers in the dark, soft and comforting, 'go to sleep, go to sleep' and she drifts off into unconsciousness.

Chapter 25

As they walked up Saltaire Main Street from the canal, the young officer charged with escorting Archie to hospital drove past, tooting as he went. Saj and Nikki shared a grin, albeit a worried one, at the sight of Archie, huddled in the front seat, hand extended and middle finger raised at them.

Sajid pointed his key fob at his car and unlocked it. 'Looks like he's not lost any of his usual charm, eh?'

Nikki snorted. 'Charm. That's what you call it?'

Sajid swung into the driver's seat and when Nikki was settled beside him, the antibacterial wipes he kept for emergencies in her hands, he turned to her. 'Gonna tell me what's going on with him? It's not like anybody's doing a great job of pretending they don't have secrets.'

He was right, of course. All the clandestine meetings, the surreptitious whispering and stuff was stupid. Saj was no fool and she hated that perhaps *he* thought that she considered him one. 'I have absolutely no idea what the hell is going on with Archie and the big boss, but you're right something is going on and I'm determined to get to the bottom of it.' She hesitated, unsure how much she was at liberty to share. *Sod it!* Saj was her partner, he deserved better. 'I don't know how and I'm not even sure about this, but I'm beginning to think that it's got something to do with Springer's disappearance.'

Saj flicked the wipers on and looked through the windscreen

at the light drizzle outside, his fingers tapping the steering wheel. 'What makes you think that?' He turned and met her eyes.

Nikki flushed and bit her lip, hoping she didn't look as guilty as she felt. 'Just . . . stuff.'

'Stuff? Gimme a break, Nik. What bloody stuff?'

'Just . . . stuff. Like the way he was when we went to Springer's house. Like the CCTV footage . . . that sort of stuff.'

Nikki was pleased to see that Saj looked less probing.

'You ask him about that? The CCTV?'

'Not directly. I told him we'd accessed it and . . .' She glowered out the front window making the woman with a pushchair who was trying to cross the road in front of their parked vehicle glare back at her. Waving her hand at the woman's back, she shook her head. 'What the hell was all that about?'

'I suspect she thought that demonic glare of yours was directed at her.'

'Shouldn't be so damn paranoid then, should she?'

'CCTV?'

Damn! She'd half hoped that the byplay had distracted him. She opened the tub of wipes and began wiping her hands. 'Well, he just didn't say anything. No mention of already accessing it . . . nothing.'

'And you didn't ask.'

'For goodness' sake, Saj. I was still reeling from him offering me an acting DI job instead of Ferguson.'

'Wait a minute. Archie offered you acting DI last night and you're only just getting round to telling me?'

'Not like I'm taking it, is it? Next, he'll be wanting me to take my inspector exams and all that shit. No, I'm fine where I am.' She leaned over and prodded his arm. 'With you!'

Saj flicked the radio on and a few seconds later said, 'Yeah well, you could show me a bit more appreciation sometimes, you know? Instead of just hassling me all the time . . . and using up all my wet wipes. Hope PC Williams hurries up with an overnight location for that damn barge soon.'

Nikki agreed. They needed to be doing stuff, not sitting waiting for intel. She'd barely completed a deep clean on her rat-infested hands using most of Sajid's antibacterial hand wipes, having threatened him with any amount of disastrous consequences should he be the instigator of any rodent jokes at Trafalgar House, when the text came in. She glanced at her phone and smiled. 'The gangly blushing guy came up trumps.'

Sajid quirked an eyebrow. 'You mean PC Williams?'

Nikki frowned. 'Yeah, yeah that's what it says here anyway.' She knew fine and well Sajid was pointing out her lack of social skills and gently criticizing the fact that she rarely remembered the names of the uniformed officers they met at crime scenes. He had a point and she was working on it . . . but no need to tell him that in the past two days there were two uniformed officers names she'd remembered, one being PC Williams, and the other being Sergeant Anwar from the previous night's crime scene.

She always remembered the ones that impressed her, just didn't see the need to store up a whole load of names that she'd probably never see again and who she would never trust to be part of her investigation. She didn't know how the hell Saj managed to keep all those names in his head, but he did. Shit, sometimes she ran through each of her own kid's names before hitting on the right one. Down to business now, Nikki thrust the used wipes in a plastic bag and belted up. 'We need to head to Five Rise Locks. The family parked their boat up a few hundred metres this side of it. Your PC Watson's already told Fells and she's sending a team out as we speak.'

'Berthed, barge and Williams.'

'Whatever.' Nikki grinned. It was so easy to take the piss out of Saj. 'Let's get moving. According to DC Wilson, Gracie's sent a team to meet us there and the Saltaire team are going to start work from this end. Hopefully, before too long, we'll have established exactly where the body was tipped into the water.'

'Williams.' said Sajid, his tone long suffering.

Chapter 26

The longer Stefan stayed in the barn, the less chance he would have of escaping. Not that he was convinced that he could break out anyway. He was so weak. He suspected he had internal bleeding. Had one of his broken ribs punctured something inside? Or had one of Bullet's well-aimed kicks ruptured one of his organs? Whatever, if he remained here like this, he would either just get weaker and weaker and die a victim, or worse still, Bullet might enjoy a long slow torture before killing him and then it would all have been in vain. He and Maria would have died for no reason and his family back home would be forever tormented wondering where they were, perhaps thinking they'd forgotten them. However, if he at least tried to get out, he might just do some good. Perhaps he'd be able to save Denis and the other boys. Maybe for once luck would be on his side. But he'd have to move fast.

Stefan had never been alone in the barn before. It was disconcerting not to have the constant shuffle of his fellow captives moving on their makeshift beds, their low mumbling conversations in a variety of languages, the hacking coughs and groans. It made every movement Stefan made seem extra loud. He had no idea if anyone remained in the unfurnished farmhouse when they were transported to the factory, so he'd have to be aware of that if he made it outside.

He was fairly sure that Bullet's dogs weren't around at the minute because he could hear no barking and those dogs yelped at the slightest opportunity and that was another reason to act quickly. He wouldn't stand a chance if those monsters returned. He wracked his brains trying to recall what he could of the journey to the factory. They were locked in the back of the van in the dark, but he had a vague idea that the bumpy track from the yard didn't last long and was then followed by a smoother road. From his recollection they rarely stopped until they got closer to the factory. Did that information help him? He wasn't sure, but he hoped it meant that a bigger road, hopefully with some traffic wasn't far away.

The first thing he had to do was find out if he could actually escape the barn. With agonizing slowness, he managed to roll himself onto his hands and knees. Peering round the gloomy interior, an expanse of soiled bedding and dotted tin buckets were the only furnishing. Studying the structure, Stefan saw light spilling in at intervals as his eyes moved round the walls. Breathing heavily, he kept his eye on the biggest chunk of light and began to crawl towards it. Within seconds, searing pain made him fall forward. Taking only shallow breaths, he lay still until it dissipated, wondering how the hell he was going to get out if he couldn't even move.

At last, he was able to manoeuvre himself bit by bit into a sitting position. The only thing he could think of doing was to bind his torso tightly in the hope that would minimize the agony. Taking a sheet, he wrapped it round his chest twice then, taking a deep breath, he yanked the ends as tightly as he could and tied the sheet in place. By the time he'd done it, sweat dotted his brow and a pool of foamy bile pooled on the ground. Conscious of the time passing, he again rolled into a crawling position and took a tentative shuffle towards the hole in the wall. It was sore, but not quite as bad as before. Moving as quickly as he could, he approached the crevice, praying under his breath that the wood around it would be rotten and he'd be able to pull it away and escape that way.

After what seemed like a very long time, he reached the wall and took a few moments to catch his breath and retighten the sheet round his body. Finally, hands shaking, he stretched out to touch the wood. The hole itself was too small for him to squeeze through, but hopefully years of neglect had rotted the planks. Jagged splinters pierced the skin of his fingers as he wiggled the timber, willing it to fall apart in his hands, but it refused to give.

Stefan began to crawl to the next largest hole and repeated the process. Tugging at the shards of wood, ignoring the blood dripping from his hands and the pain that wracked his body with every move, he persevered, tears streaming down his face. Still no joy.

'*Fute!*' He rolled onto his bottom and leaned against the wall. He had little strength left. How could he go on? He closed his eyes, imagining the life ebbing from his battered body and he ached to just give in to it. To end this suffering. Nothing was more appealing than the thought of easing himself to the ground, resting his head on the hard ground and just drifting away . . . to peace.

He didn't know how long he had sat there. It could have been hours, but the light still spilling through the gaps reassured him. His body was shaking as he tried to summon up the strength to continue, when an image of his wife flashed into his mind. She was laughing, her head thrown back. She was taunting him to finish painting the ceiling in their unborn Maria's bedroom.

'You'll regret it if you give up, Steffy. Give in to your vertigo and it has won. Come on darling, make this little one proud.' And she'd patted her burgeoning abdomen.

He'd cursed, loud and long, annoyed that she was right. Daria was always right. She'd waited patiently till he got to his feet and when he picked up the roller and climbed the ladder, she said, 'I'm proud of you, darling.' And all at once, his dizziness seemed unimportant.

A sad smile pulled at his lips. He'd give anything to see Daria again. To beg her forgiveness for not taking care of their daughter. Sighing, he got to his knees and pushing through the pain, crawled to the third biggest cavity. Maybe this one would be the one.

Chapter 27

Nikki had used the drive from Saltaire to the Five Rise Locks to direct a detective to interview the family who'd hired the barge. They lived in Wakefield, so one of the Kirklees coppers had said he'd drop over and take their statement. She'd spoken to one of the police divers who, after teasing her about head-butting Gracie, had intimated that the inexperienced bargers had left a looped rope trailing behind them and that their dead body had lodged there by pure fluke. This had been the family's first foray into canal boating and they'd had little idea of the complexities of the barging life . . . *and why would they want to?* Nikki thought. Especially so early in Spring. It was freezing out and despite the cosy looking smoke drifting from some of the other canal barges, Nikki wasn't convinced.

CSI Gracie, her usual professional self, had worked out the best strategy to scour any vehicular accessible routes to the canal from Five Rise Locks back to Saltaire in order to ascertain exactly where the body had entered the water. Accordingly, she'd dispatched teams of CSIs to start cordoning off areas of interest along the canal. She'd also told Nikki that the dead man had been taken to the morgue and that Dr Campbell had promised to do the post-mortem later in the day.

Just up from Five Rise Locks stood the The Bargers' Butty Café, which Gracie had identified as the first possible point of vehicular access. Situated within eighty metres of the canal, the car park was close enough to the basin to allow the body to be carried down and dropped into the water.

After Sajid parked behind a CSI van in the road just outside the cordoned-off car park, they got out, Nikki shivering in the breeze. She pointed at the solitary vehicle in the car park. 'Wonder if that belongs to the café owners? Poor sods won't be able to move it till we clear the area and they're not going to get any customers till after that either.'

'Oh, I suspect they'll get their fair share of custom from the uniforms and the CSIs once they've processed a walkway to the café.'

Realizing that she was hungry, Nikki's stomach rumbled on cue. 'Okay, you've convinced me. We can have a coffee after we've spoken to the CSIs.'

When Sajid's face lit up it reminded her of Sunni's delighted look that morning when she'd signed the hamster consent form and she all but rolled her eyes. 'Come on. Stop looking like Oliver bloody Twist.'

The CSI in charge of this area was a tall slender Welsh man called Blake. He was an organized man of few words and most of them were pessimistic.

'We're starting here and ascertaining if this could be where the body was transported from. I've got two investigators trawling the area down there to see if they can see an entry spot, but as I say, I think we're pissing in the wind, here. It's unlikely we'll be able to discover whether the body was in a vehicle here, but we're looking for blood and suchlike. Slow process, mind, but that can't be helped.'

He turned away and began to shout instructions to one of the other suited-up figures before turning back.

'Not much you can do here really unless we find the area. But if you follow Fletch here, he's about to put out treads so we can access the café, you know for toilets and suchlike. I'll give you a shout if we find anything.'

Shit! Another body and still it was as if her hands were tied. She'd set everything in motion that she could, but the hanging around endlessly was getting to her. Nikki huddled into her jacket. 'Looks like it's the café for us then.' And the two of them followed Fletch as he created a path to the café that would not disrupt any potential forensic evidence.

Warmth and the delicate aroma of homemade baking hit them when they opened the door of The Barger's Butty. Nikki's tummy rumbled again, and she thrust a twenty-pound note at Saj. 'You get them. I want a cappuccino and some carrot cake.'

'Always the gopher,' moaned Saj, but he obediently went up and made their order whilst Nikki chose a table near the window.

Pulling out her phone, she dialled the admin staff on their team at Trafalgar House to see if the house-to-house enquires near the crash site had thrown up anything useful. She was concerned at the lack of progress on finding Springer. If she was dead, she'd have expected her body to have been dumped and if she was still with her abductors, Nikki dreaded to think what was happening to her. And now they had two actual murders to investigate as well and no Archie to co-ordinate. It wouldn't be long she reckoned till the big boss dragged in another team for one or other of the cases and Nikki suspected Archie would want them to retain Springer's case. Which was another conundrum she'd mull over as she indulged in her cappuccino and carrot cake.

Saj deposited a tray on the table and shuffled into the seat opposite her. 'You checked in with the boss yet, Nik?'

Stuffing a chunk of cake into her mouth, Nikki closed her eyes. It was heavenly, and she realized, it was also the first thing she'd eaten today, having discarded her toast during the hamster fiasco that morning. 'I told that officer to give me a bell when he knows something. I'll ring later. You know what A&E is like.' She laughed. 'Don't envy the poor sod. Bet he's on the receiving end of Archie's tongue. D'you think they'll award medals for putting up with Archie's shit?'

Saj snorted. 'Archie will have run him ragged before the end of the day.' They sat in silence for a bit, eating cake and drinking. 'He'll be okay won't he, Nikki?'

Nikki had been pondering that herself. Archie had looked deathly, but now at least he was in the safest place. If he had heart trouble, he'd get the help he needed there. Still, that was another worry. Two dead bodies, an abducted colleague and a hospitalized boss . . . everything was far from hunky-dory. What worried her was that, with the development with Archie's health, she may be manoeuvred into taking the interim DI position. 'Yeah, sure. He'll be fine.'

'You think he'll be staying in?'

Nikki shrugged. 'Don't know, but he sure as hell looked crap, didn't he? Besides if they keep him in, he'll be out of our hair.' She just wished that she meant that last part. Archie was a great sounding block and a brilliant boss. If he wasn't back soon, she didn't know how well she'd cope.

Interrupting her gloomy thoughts, the door burst open and a young CSI, mask pulled down, excitement all over her face, approached. 'They think they've found where they parked up to dump the body. It's only about fifteen minutes' walk away along the canal path. The boss told me to tell you.'

Stuffing the last remaining chunk of cake into her mouth, Nikki jumped to her feet and followed Saj out. At last something was going their way.

Chapter 28

Why was Parekh's face zooming in and out all googly-eyed and intimidating? Getting in Felicity's space, making her feel nauseous. What was she *doing* here anyway?

Felicity tried to move, thought then stopped. Everything was fuzzy and it was sooo damn hot. 'If you've got to be here, Parekh, why don't you help me take my coat off?'

Had she said the words out loud? She wasn't sure, but Parekh was drifting away. Felicity giggled. She could see right through her and there was nothing inside. She'd no heart and that was oh so funny. Parekh had no heart.

Something was niggling in her mind. Something to do with Parekh? Was she supposed to be doing something with Archie Hegley's favourite? No. Surely not.

It was all so cloudy – no wait a minute, those were clouds. Felicity smiled. That one looks like a castle. A princess castle . . . 'Look Stevie, a castle.'

She moved her head. Where was Stevie?

Too hot . . .

'Waken up Fliss. You've got to waken up. Do the Parekh thing.'

Ah, there she was. Stevie. Everything would be okay now. No need to worry about Parekh any more . . . she'd gone.

Chapter 29

Despite the chill in the air, it was pleasant walking along the canal towpath from Five Rise Locks towards Saltaire. Accompanied by the occasional insistent duck quack and the sound of the breeze whispering through the overhanging trees, Nikki and Saj strode along in silence. Looking upwards – was that cloud in the shape of a Disney castle – Nikki saw a large bird swoop and soar, wings spread, proud and elegant against the light grey sky. Who'd have thought silence could be so noisy?

With only a few barges, which appeared to be closed up, on their left and a steep grassy embankment to the right, adjoining an expanse of fields stretching out for miles, Nikki could see why this stretch of the waterway was inaccessible for their killers. However, further along, the embankment flattened out and the never-ending fields were replaced by small rows of terraced houses, separated by grass verges and high fences. Again, not the ideal access point for body dumping.

'How much longer?' Although they'd only been walking for about ten minutes, Nikki was beginning to wish they'd driven. All this was taking up too much time and that was one commodity that was in short supply. They'd have the same distance to walk back to retrieve their vehicle and who knew where they might have to go from the site.

'Chillax, Nik. We're nearly there.'

Nikki let his teasing 'chillax' go and kept plodding on. He knew she hated the phrase, because she distinctly remembered ranting at him about Charlie and Ruby's use of it. Of course, that was precisely why he'd chosen it. Up ahead, two CSIs were working near the water's edge. Nikki sped up, leaving Sajid to trail behind. Thank God, they'd arrived!

Stopping outside the new cordon set up by the CSIs, Nikki noticed that this stretch of the canal was easily accessible via a much trampled and thankfully muddy shortcut down to the canal about fifty metres ahead. Hopefully, their killers would have left nice clear prints for them. Another fifty metres or so beyond the track was another cordon. The CSIs were giving themselves plenty of area to cover. Dotted around the area from the bottom of the track towards the edge of the canal, were various numbered yellow markers. Nikki crossed her fingers. With any luck, that meant forensic evidence.

The incline appeared reasonably shallow from where Nikki stood, making it easy to transport a body. Hell, perhaps they'd even rolled him down the hill, like she and Anika had done as kids in Lister Park. The two images sat uneasily side by side in Nikki's mind for a moment and then she thrust the childhood memory aside and peered up the track. The top of the incline tapered away and Nikki, although able to hear voices drifting down in the breeze, was unable to see beyond it.

She alerted the CSIs with a loud 'Hallooo!'

The CSIs looked up from their work and one of them raised a hand and sauntered over. 'We've no suits down here, so unless you've brought your own, you'll have to scramble up the hill at your side and circle round to the topmost cordon.'

Shit! In her haste to get to the crime scene, Nikki hadn't even thought to pick up the damn suits that Saj had in the back of his car. *Idiot!* Eyeing up the overgrown sodden foliage that spread up the hill, she swore under her breath and took a step towards it. It was thigh high and by the time she'd scrambled to the top, her socks would be soaked again and as for her jeans? There was nothing worse than damp jeans. Sajid nudged her and handed her a Tyvek suit from the man bag he always carried. 'Hobbit size as per usual for you.'

Ignoring his smug impression but thankful at least one of them had thought ahead, she got into her suit, with considerably less elegance than he did. Then guided by the CSI, who'd watched their interplay, amusement sparking in her eyes, Nik and Saj ducked under the tape and listened as she talked them through what they'd found so far.

She gestured to the track where another CSI was kneeling halfway up, taking photos. 'We got some shoe prints from the muddy path. Two sets. Doesn't mean they belong to your killers, but the chances are, they do. We'll take casts. Halfway down, there's a flattened mark, as if something was laid down in the mud for a short while. We're thinking maybe they stopped for a rest. There were a few forensic bits, hair and fibre fragments. That's getting tested too.'

Nikki peered up the track. She'd been right, it wasn't a steep incline, perfectly manageable for two people to carry a corpse down. Once the CSIs had completed their work, she'd have a proper look herself. She turned to the markers. 'What did you find there?'

'Ah, well that's a bonus. Despite the drizzle we found blood drops, there and there.' She pointed with her gloved hand to a marker near the bottom of the trail and another closer to the canal. 'But the real find was here.' And skirting round the markers she stopped on the narrow verge next to the waterway. 'We found two cigarette butts, which of course we've bagged and tagged. We're hoping they belong to the guys who dumped the body.'

How cold is that? They must have dumped the body and then stopped for a fag afterwards. Did they laugh and joke about what they'd just done? All in a day's work for these two. Nikki came across badness often in her line of work, but some things stuck in her throat and this was one of them. Perhaps it was just that she'd seen enough careless undignified death in the last twenty-four hours. Enough evidence that to some, human life was disposable without a backward glance; like fly-tipping on a more grotesque and devastating scale.

Her limbs became heavy as fatigue trickled through her body. Her fingers flicked up to her scar, running along its rough ridges. *Get a grip Nikki! Get a grip!* Lack of sleep combined with the pressure of Springer's continued absence and worry over Archie's illness, weighed her down. Pushing her shoulders back, she closed her eyes, inhaled a long deep breath through her nose and as she exhaled, pushed Sajid and the CSI's bemused glances out of her mind. This was no time to lose it and again she was grateful to the technique her counsellor had helped her practise to ground her.

Opening her eyes again, she scowled at Sajid. The trick had worked. Okay, the headache that lurked at the side of her head hadn't disappeared completely, but that brooding tiredness was allayed a little. 'No need to look so damn worried. I'm not losing it. Just recharging my batteries a bit. You could do with doing it too. You look like crap.'

Sajid rolled his eyes and made a bad attempt at looking offended. 'Crap is *not* in my wardrobe, I'm afraid, but all I was going to say is that you'd think these two tossers would have just lobbed their butts into the canal, wouldn't you?'

'Hmm. So, not forensically aware . . . or just plain dumb?'

'Either works for me,' said Saj.

'Except . . .' The CSI rolled the word out. 'That doesn't add up with the bleach in the car park.'

Sajid and Nikki exchanged glances. More bleach! 'Right, well, we best head up there now. Thanks for your time.'

'Yeah, best head out of the cordoned area to make your way up. We haven't processed the area around the track yet.'

Walking to the area that Nikki had already attempted to climb, Sajid spoke. 'Bleach followed by discarded fag butts? Doesn't make sense.'

'Unless the butts belong to someone else.'

'Yeah, but unlikely don't you think?'

Nikki shrugged. 'Forensics will tell. What I'm more interested in is the use of bleach. Could the two bodies be linked? Do you think it's the same suspects?' She hesitated. 'And where the hell is Springer?'

'Don't know about Springer, we're doing all we can. As for the other – yeah it is a bit coincidental, I'll grant you. Not often we have two murders and a missing police officer all in the space of two days.'

Ducking back under the tape, Nikki pondered her partner's words. Could two . . . or even three of their current investigations be connected? It seemed unlikely, but then Bradford was in the midst of a major criminal reshuffle from which Joe Drummond, her source in vice, had kept her out of the loop. Coincidental? Well, she'd find out later on when she met up with him. She was determined not to leave that meeting without a proper handle on what was going down on her streets. 'Right, let's get up this damn hill.'

She'd almost reached the brow when a yelp from behind her made her pause and look round. Sajid, who'd been at her heels the entire way up, urging her to go faster and taunting her for all but crawling up, was now six feet behind her and flat on his face.

'Bloody grass, damn rain, stupid . . .'

Not bothering to hide her amused grin, Nikki adopted a mock concerned tone. 'Oh, dear, Saj. Are you okay? Did you slip? Aw, what a shame.'

'Piss off, Parekh.'

As Sajid struggled to his feet, Nikki laughed out loud. The entire front of his white Tyvek suit was wet and muddy, with grass stains. On anyone else this wouldn't have been half as amusing, but Sajid never, ever, unlike Nikki, got his overalls dirty. Even in the muddiest environments, like the pig farm last year, Saj somehow managed to keep his suit pristine. She whipped out her phone and took a few surreptitious snaps. Always good to have some bargaining chips up her sleeve.

Leaving him to moan his way up the hill, Nikki approached the group of officers and CSIs who had congregated in the car park. Actually, car park wasn't the right word for the potholed area with space for only half a dozen vehicles at a push. Still, it seemed well-used, if the condition of the road was anything to go by. It was tucked off a single-track road, that appeared to exist only to allow access to a farm about a mile and a half further along. The road from this point on veered away from the canal into farmland.

A single vehicle, a Mazda, was parked at the topmost corner. A woman sat in the driving seat and a dog with lolling tongue and oversized ears, nose poking out the open window was watching the scene, punctuating his excitement with friendly barks.

Gracie detached herself from the group as Nikki raised her hand in acknowledgement to PC Williams. That lad was on the ball. 'You got here quick, Gracie.'

'Yeah, we'd just finished up in Saltaire when we got the call. Want me to talk you thr—' She stopped mid-sentence and mopped her brow in an exaggerated motion. 'Bloody hell, you been traipsing through the Amazon or summat, Saj?'

Nikki, enjoying Saj's embarrassment, allowed herself the slightest of giggles. His face was contorted into a frown and close up, he looked even muckier and sweatier than he had from a distance.

'Shut up, Fells.'

With a wink in Nikki's direction, Gracie continued where she'd left off. 'Come on, I'll show you what we found.'

'Hold up a minute, DS Parekh.'

Nikki turned towards Williams who was approaching at a half jog. 'Just wanted to let you know, the woman in the car over there walked her dog over the fields this morning. She usually walks along the canal, but fancied a change today. I took her statement. She didn't see any other vehicles, didn't walk near this end of the car park and CSIs have taken prints of her shoes and all that they want. She's clear to go, if you agree.'

Nikki glanced over at the woman, who was huddled in the driver's seat on her phone. 'Yeah, that's fine. Let her go, but write up her statement for the files. Good job, Williams.'

Her face turned into a scowl and Williams' smile faded from his lips. 'Bloody press!'

Williams turned and together they watched as Lisa Kane pulled up across the cordon and exited her shiny red car, her photographer, Max Ashton, following. He was a huge man, who always seemed about to burst out of his tight-fitting clothes. *Bulked out with steroids, trying to impress Kane, no doubt.* That's when the idea struck her. 'This road a dead end, Williams?'

Grin returning, Williams nodded. 'Ends at the farm, I believe.'

Nikki's scowl vanished in an instant. 'Get her to move that vehicle of hers. Tell her she needs to move forward to let us have access to the car park and she needs to move . . . oh, I don't know, two hundred metres . . .?' She quirked an eyebrow at the PC.

Getting her drift, he nodded. 'I think two hundred metres will be ample.'

'Yes, just out of harm's way. Two hundred metres it is. Tell her it's so necessary vehicles can park up and once she's parked up again, place the outer cordon, just this side of her car.'

Sajid, all signs of his earlier bad mood gone, laughed out loud. 'You are evil, Nikita Parekh . . . pure evil. But I like your style.'

'Yeah well. I aim to please. Now, Gracie, talk me through this scene.'

Gracie escorted them towards the start of the track. 'We reckon they parked up here, parallel to the trail. Either they already knew this area or someone had told them where the best entry spot was. No CCTV for miles. Quiet spot, no houses, pubs or anything except the farm and that's quite a distance away.'

As they neared, the smell of bleach, not as pungent as it had been at the Denholme scene, but still strong, drifted towards them. Expecting it, Nikki schooled her mind to zone it out and began taking short breaths through her mouth.

'They were very liberal with it. It's sloshed all over this area. However, apart from the bleach we also found a few drops of blood here, by the side of the vehicle.'

'This wasn't the kill site.' Nikki was certain of that. No amount of bleach would eradicate that amount of blood. 'He was killed elsewhere, which means we have yet another crime scene out there somewhere and the bastards have, more than likely, obliterated any forensic evidence leading to it.'

Gracie walked them over to where some markers were dotted. 'We've got more blood drops here and here, which is strange. They wouldn't have carried him down the side and then round the front of the vehicle unless they were stupid. Much quicker to take him straight from the back and over to the track.'

Nikki flashed back to the cigarette butts. Were they stupid? Perhaps they were following orders which was why they used the bleach, but messed up with the cigarette ends because nobody had told them otherwise. Another thing to consider. 'What else?'

Gracie was beaming now. 'Tyre tracks. Faint, but just enough to get a make and model. I'll get back to you on that, but, don't hold me to this and don't let it influence you unduly.' She waited until Nikki and Saj nodded. 'I'm leaning towards the vehicle being the same make as the van at Springer's crime scene.'

Wow! All of Nikki's earlier conjectures seemed less unreasonable now. If Fells was right, more and more things seemed to be linking up the three investigations. But what was worse was the persistent image of a stopwatch relentlessly spinning onwards. Nikki wished she could stop it. It was twenty-four hours since Springer had disappeared and that was the crucial time span for solving missing persons. What made it more ominous was that they'd had no ransom demand, so it was looking more unlikely that they'd find Springer alive. Nikki's bones ached, her mind was fuzzy and there was so much to process. So much had happened in such a short space of time and what she needed now was some downtime to absorb the implications of everything they'd discovered about the two bodies and Springer's abduction. She couldn't allow her vision to be clouded, no matter how tired she was. *Keep an open mind Nik. Focus. Mind over matter!* She gave herself a mental shake, stretched her limbs and did her breathing trick.

Chapter 30

It wasn't too cold to be sitting in City Park. Xavier could have chosen to go to the Wetherspoons or the Cake'Ole café for his late lunch, but he wanted to make a couple of phone calls and wasn't overly keen on being overheard, so instead he got a takeaway latte from Starbucks and plonked himself on a bench. They'd offered him one of their fancy flavours, but he'd just laughed and winked at the waitress. 'Too much for me, don't want to lose my figure now do I?'

She'd laughed. 'You look trim enough to me.'

Too right he did. All the weights and shit he did. Three times a week at the gym. That was him. Leaning back, he sipped the hot drink and watched the two lads huddled behind the newspaper kiosk doing a deal and thinking they were so subtle. Idiots. They'd soon learn that huddling in corners and surreptitious glances got you noticed. By acting confident you could get away with a whole load of stuff in plain sight. That's what he did anyway and so far, it had worked.

He looked to his left. There was that hot totty from accounts in City Hall clip-clopping through the park, skirt nearly up to her arse. He knew where she was heading. Thought she was so discreet, but he'd seen her before. That was one of the many things he was good at – noticing things. You never knew when a piece of intel would prove useful. And there he was – Mr Unhappily-Married, also from accounts and, surprise, surprise, they were heading in the same direction. To the taxi rank, from where they'd head, separately of course, straight to the rent-by-the-hour hovel on Canal Road. They liked to indulge in a little bit of rough of a lunchtime. In an hour's time they'd saunter back all flushed and a little dishevelled, thinking nobody was aware of what was going on. In reality though, they were the talk of the entire building.

Coffee almost finished, Xavier pulled out a phone and dialled.

'Yes?' Cyclops's tone was abrupt and Xavier could hear some background noise . . . music . . . a woman's voice? 'Give me a minute.'

He heard the sound of a car door opening and then slamming, putting an end to the background noise. 'Okay.'

'They found him yet?'

The deep laugh that rumbled through the phone told Xavier they had. Good, that would keep them busy and by tomorrow morning Parekh and the rest of them would be reeling, not sure which way to turn. His idea of muddying the waters was inspired, truly inspired. 'What about the women? Any word on them?'

'Not yet, but I'm keeping my ears open. They're working two scenes along the canal. Maybe the second one's hers. Nobody can get close enough and nobody's spilling.'

'Okay, keep me updated. All set for tonight?'

Again, the rumbling laugh. Xavier smiled. Talking to Cyclops always raised his spirits. 'You'll make sure it's covered? Got to have media coverage for maximum impact.'

'I'm on it, don't you worry.'

Xavier heard another voice, then Cyclops was back on the line. 'Gotta go.'

'Let me know when it's all done. I want to watch the chaos descend.'

'Sure thing.'

Putting his phone away, Xavier noticed a rumpus kicking off opposite him. He grinned. The two lads from earlier were being escorted towards the police car parked outside the In Plaice fish and chip shop.

Ah, the folly of youth!

Chapter 31

Still reeling from everything Gracie had shared with them, Nikki considered her next move. It was getting on for two o'clock and there was nothing much for her and Sajid to do here now. All she could action was routine procedures, like checking CCTV on the surrounding streets, talking to the farmer and putting out a media call for witnesses, all of which was uniform officers' and the media department's work. She pulled down the zip of her overall and fished her phone out from her bra where she'd put it earlier. It was easier to access that way. 'We should get back to the station, but I really want to check on Archie first.'

His phone rang three times before Archie answered. Muffled curses, some indefinable shuffley sounds, and more or less subdued oaths came down the line. For a moment Nikki thought he'd managed to convince the officer to leave him at the crime scene. But then he was there. 'That you, Parekh? Waste o' damn time me being here and the buggers say they're keeping me in.'

Nikki rolled her eyes. *What a baby.* 'I'm sure they wouldn't be keeping you in if they didn't think it was necessary.'

'Aye right. Bastards just want tae check mah proverbials int going tae pack in. Idiots. I'm fine.'

There were more noises as Archie presumably repositioned

himself on his bed followed by his querulous '. . . and a cup of decent bloody tea too, laddie.'

Nikki smiled. That poor PC would be glad when he could leave Archie and get back to more rewarding policing. Thing was, Archie's wife had died and his daughter was in Australia so he was on his own and she couldn't trust him to stay put. Looked like the young officer was going to have a long day. 'Archie? Archie?'

'Aye, I'm here Parekh. Just making sure that young idiot gets me a decent cup of tea. Nurses say I'm not tae have one but I'm parched. They can't have me dying of thirst.'

'They're probably waiting till your test results come back Archie. Do as you're told, yeah?'

'Whatever. Now, what have you got?'

'We're at Five Rise Locks which is where the family started their journey. And it looks like we've found the dump site. The CSIs are processing it as we speak. I've drafted all available officers in to establish a cordon all along the canal and to prevent it being breached until the CSIs clear the scene. Thing is, there's similarities in the tread marks between the van that we think abducted Springer and the ones they've found at this site. Also, they've used bleach.'

'Like we found on the wee lassie last night?'

'Exactly.'

'Any ID on her or the dead guy?'

The lack of ID was pissing Nikki off. When they had that, they could move the investigation forward. Question their friends and relatives, track their movements prior to their deaths. But, so far, it was like trying to peer through the darkest of shadows. 'No ID for either so far. I'll chase up Interpol when I get back to the station and I've already got uniforms checking missing persons. The divers thought it looked like a gunshot wound to the heart. We'll know more later. Langley's going to do the PM later on.'

'And Springer?' His voice had lowered to a whisper and Nikki had to strain to hear him.

What's all that about? She sighed. *Bloody secrets!* 'No, nowt on Springer, boss. Things aren't looking good. We're at over twenty-four hours missing and not a bloody thing.'

Archie's rasping breath floated down the line and Nikki imagined him, florid-faced, mouth screwed up in concentration. He sounded rough and Nikki was pleased she'd insisted he go to BRI. At last he spoke. 'Right, Parekh. It seems like you've got everything in hand.' Then, he lowered his voice again. 'I need you to come here, on your own soon as you can. No Sajid, no anybody else. I need to speak to *you*.'

Shit, Saj's gossip about secrecy and her own observations at Trafalgar House solidified in her mind. Something was off and whatever it was, it had got the normally unflappable Archie Hegley in a lather. But how the hell did all of this figure into everything? More to the point, how was she supposed to escape to Bradford Royal without Saj?

At that minute, Saj sauntered over and pointed to something behind Nikki. She held up a hand, signalling she needed a moment to finish off her conversation with Archie. Thinking on her feet, Nikki hoped Archie would understand that Saj was nearby and not question her in his ultra-loud voice. 'So, you want Saj at the post-mortem? Yeah, that's fine. While he's at the PM, I'll pop up to see you. Cheers, boss. See you later.'

Saj scowled at her. 'Why the hell do I have to do the PM? Surely they'll take this body off us as we've already got one and a missing person to boot.'

Nikki knew that Saj hated working with his partner, Langley. He was a bit paranoid about being the topic of gossip and being a gay British Muslim wasn't something he wanted broadcast. This was a constant source of friction between Saj and Langley who was out and proud. Nikki sympathized with her partner. She knew, coming from an Indian family herself, that things could be difficult. 'Don't be such a baby, Saj. Someone has to, and it can't always be me.'

179

Lips drooping in sulkiness, Saj looked like Sunni had this morning when he thought he couldn't have the hamster for a visit. If he hadn't been a grown man, she'd have stifled a laugh and teased it out of him. Instead, she whacked him on the arm. 'Man up, Saj. Life's full of disappointment!'

Rubbing his arm, he glared at her. 'There's something going on with the boss and Springer! You know what it is? I know you. No way would you send me on my own to the PM if he hadn't told you to. So, if we're partners you better just spill.'

Grateful that she didn't have to lie, Nikki looked straight at him. 'I'm as in the dark as you are, but it's beginning to irritate the hell out of me too. Soon as I know anything, I'll let you know, okay?'

With a reluctant nod, Saj agreed, then his face broke into a smile as he looked over her shoulder. Nikki frowned. What was her partner up to?

'You might want to deal with that.' And he pointed behind her again.

Nikki spun round and groaned. Bloody Lisa Kane and her sidekick Max Ashton with his damn camera. They'd clearly walked over the fields to get here after being trapped on the other side of the cordon.

'DS Parekh!' Lisa's voice was loud and caused the CSIs to halt their work and glance her way.

Before Nikki had a chance to respond, PC Williams had taken off at a trot, crime scene tape fluttering in his hand as he pushed them back and erected another cordon, just before them, effectively keeping them at a distance from the scene being processed. *God, that boy was good!* Nikki grinned and pointedly turned her back on the woman just as a shriek from the opposite direction splintered the air.

Saj and Nikki wheeled round as a sobbing woman, in a bobble hat and wellies, ran from the overgrown grassland that led to a copse of trees on the other side of the lay-by, a small yappy black and white dog yelping at her heels. The two CSIs, who were just heading over to process that area, ran towards her with Nikki and Saj close behind.

Gasping for breath, the woman bent over resting her hands on her knees for a moment, before raising her arm and pointing behind her. 'Back there. A woman . . . think she's dead.'

With no regard for preserving the crime scene, Nikki ran past the dog lady, through the long tangled grass and clumps of weeds and soaking wet vegetation, with Saj following. Over her shoulder, she yelled. 'Ambulance. Now!'

Who the hell was this? Springer? Somebody else? Nikki pushed herself to run faster, following the trail the woman's progress had left through the wilderness, her eyes flitting from side to side, desperate not to miss anything. Twenty-four hours, twenty-four hours, tattooed in her brain as she ran. Please let it be Springer . . . but not if she's dead.

'Over there. To your left.' Saj overtook her running at a slight angle and Nikki could see a shape nestled in the foliage.

Torn between wanting to find out who it was and dreading it, Nikki took a deep breath and approached. Saj was on his knees. He'd yanked off his nitrile glove and tossed it aside as his fingers touched the woman's neck feeling for a pulse. Holding her breath, Nikki moved closer. The woman looked so like the young girl who already lay on a mortuary slab and Nikki hoped that they weren't about to send another one to the same destination.

'Got a pulse.' Sajid's voice was filled with relief.

Nikki turned and yelled back to the CSIs 'We need blankets or something to warm her up.' Then, she joined Saj at the other side of the woman and studied her. Peeling her sodden hair away from her face, Nikki saw it was Felicity Springer. The bullet hole in the woman's shoulder and her blood-soaked clothes suggested it, but it had to be confirmed.

Her heart contracted. Springer's complexion had a blue tinge and Nikki suspected it might be touch and go for her. Nikki peeled her overall down to her waist and slipped her jacket off and lay it over the unconscious woman, leaving her shoulder uncovered.

'She's been tied up. Hands and feet. Cable ties, I suspect.' Saj spoke in snappy sentences, which barely concealed his anger. Wordlessly, Nikki handed over her phone and he began snapping photos of Springer's wounds and the surrounding area.

When Gracie appeared with a couple of blankets, Nikki took them and laid them down gently. 'Scissors?'

Gracie handed over a pair of scissors and a couple of evidence bags. Nikki began to cut away at the clothes around the bullet hole, popping each piece of fabric into the bags. When the wound was exposed, Nikki groaned. It had been unattended for hours and was inflamed and angry-looking. Gracie handed her some bandages, which Nikki placed over the wound, hoping she wasn't doing any more harm to it. There was nothing else they could do until the ambulance arrived. 'Get dog lady's statement please and her details.' Then, as an afterthought added, 'And keep those vultures away from here. Don't give them a sodding morsel of information. Suppose it's too much to expect that she didn't hear what the witness said.'

Williams' grimace told her all she needed to know. Bloody insensitive bastards.

The next ten minutes were the longest Nikki could ever remember. Springer's eyes fluttered open a couple of times, but her pulse was weak and Nikki thought they'd lose her before the ambulance arrived. When it did, the paramedics were all efficient speed, nudging Nikki out of the way and slipping an oxygen mask over Springer's mouth and firing questions at Nikki and Saj.

'What's her name?'

'Springer, Felicity Springer. She's a police officer.'

'Any idea how long she's been exposed like this? Allergies, conditions we need to know about?'

Trying to focus, Nikki shook her head. She knew next to nothing about the other woman. Barely anything at all and certainly nothing that would help the paramedics. 'She could have been dumped in the early hours of yesterday morning. That's all we know. No idea about allergies or conditions.'

One of them slipped an intravenous tube, into Springer's arm, whilst the other checked her over, presumably for breaks and other injuries.

'She'd been shot.' The words were out of Nikki's mouth before she could stop them. Saj nudged her and rolled his eyes.

One of the paramedics nodded. 'Yeah, we got that. We'll deal with that at the hospital. Priority is stabilizing her enough to get her there and gunshot isn't bleeding.'

Covered with a huge silver blanket, Springer looked as if she was already dead and Nikki found herself taking back every bad thought she'd had about the woman. Then, she exhaled. Now that they'd found her, Nikki needed to focus on finding out who shot her and how she ended up dumped in the middle of an overgrown grass verge.

After what seemed like ages, but was probably only a matter of minutes, they'd secured Springer to the stretcher and were carrying her to the ambulance that waited in the lay-by.

The CSIs stood in a line, faces sombre as DS Felicity Springer was secured inside.

'You coming?' One of the paramedics looked at Nikki.

For a moment, a wave of dizziness threatened her, then she pushed it aside. This wasn't back then. It wasn't her friend Margo . . . This was Springer and she shouldn't be alone. Nikki stepped forward and scrambled into the ambulance. Strapping herself in, she caught Saj's eye. 'Tell a uniform to get Stevie to BRI pronto. I'll see you there after the PM and after I've settled Stevie and seen Archie.'

As the ambulance doors closed on her, the last thing she saw was Max Ashton snapping away and Lisa Kane glowering at her, eyes narrowed.

Chapter 32

As the light began to darken and shadows stretched across the floor, Stefan Marcovici, exhausted by his failure, had collapsed by the side of the barn wall. His bones grated against one another as if they were trying to break through that last gap. Shivering wracked his skinny frame and his vision was distorted. He'd take the pills – all of them. That was the only option left. He rolled onto his side and lay for a moment, as the daylight receded, wondering how long he had left. If he took them now, the pills would take effect before the others got back. That was the best he could hope for – a doped-up end to his life. At least it would be more peaceful and less painful than the last six months had been.

Ready to move towards his mattress where the pills lay beside a water bottle, Stefan opened his eyes. There was a hint of grey light seeping around the door. The more he looked at it, the more Stefan wondered if perhaps he should give it one more shot . . . for Denis's sake. Maybe he could prise wood from the door. Maybe he could escape. Dragging himself across the barn floor, Stefan prayed that Bullet wouldn't return just yet. This was his last opportunity – his very final chance. He owed it to Daria to at least try. She deserved to know what had happened to her husband and daughter. He would try once more. For her. Straining for sounds of the van returning, Stefan edged closer to the door. It looked solid, yet there was a gap round the outside. He reached over and pushed his fingers between the frame and the door, yanking as hard as he could. His upper body protested, and blood seeped from his already wounded hands. Then, just like that a chunk of rotten wood broke off making him fall backwards. He threw it to the side and scrabbled forward, uncaring of the pain in his hands now as he pulled more and more chunks from the door until there was a big enough gap for him to squeeze through.

A slight breeze cooled his face as he lay, catching his breath, bracing himself for the next leg of his escape. Using the door for support, he crawled his way up into a hunched but standing position. Peering out into the overgrown farmyard, he tried to work out a strategy. He couldn't walk without support and he wasn't sure when Bullet would return with the men, so the best plan was to skirt around the barn, away from the road, using the walls to keep him upright.

Dragging the door closed behind him, with his back against the wall, he inched sideways, small steps at a time. When he reached the corner, relief spurred him on. He'd soon be out of sight from the farmyard. Peering through the gloom, he spotted a quad bike standing under a lean-to. Often, overnight, he and the other men had heard the sounds of Bullet and co screeching about on some sort of vehicle. The noise deafening against the usual deep silence.

His spirits lifted. Would they have left the key in the bike? They were stupid enough to underestimate him when they left the barn door unlocked, would they also be stupid enough to think no one could access their toy. Stefan forced himself forward. When he got to the bike and saw the key in the ignition, his eyes filled up. Gripping the handle bars, he dragged himself up and onto the seat and took a moment to familiarize himself with the controls. He'd never driven one before, but he was sure if he could get it started he could manage. All he needed was to get far enough away from here and to reach some sort of civilization where he could report his plight.

His hand shook as he tried to turn the key. It felt so stiff and his fingers were numb, but he persevered. The first time he turned the key it made a loud revving noise and then stalled. Shit! Was anyone in the farmhouse to hear him? Concentrating, he tried again and the engine flipped into life. Thanking God that all the controls were hand-operated, he released the brake causing the quad bike to jolt forward. His numb fingers found it hard to control the acceleration and gear shifts, but he was moving, holding onto the handle bar for dear life. He steered the quad bike out of the lean-to and headed for the fields at the back of the farmhouse, hoping to put space between him and his captors.

Chapter 33

Sajid was still fed up with Nikki. She'd gone with Springer in the ambulance and once she'd settled her with Stevie and found out her prognosis, she was going to visit Archie. Alone. He'd circled round the hospital car park for ages trying to find a space and that annoyed him even more. Not that it was Nikki's fault that parking was so crap at BRI, but still it felt good to blame her.

It irked about Archie. So what if Archie wanted to talk to her in private? He, Sajid, was her partner. The one who bailed her out, had her back. They should both be there. It was as if the boss didn't trust him. Even when Nikki had promised to keep him in the loop, it unsettled him. What if she didn't keep him updated? What if – typical Nikki – she went off on her own and left him looking stupid because he didn't know what was going on with an investigation he was supposed to be part of? Didn't she think she owed him something? After all, it was Langley and him that held her together last year. Oh, it was okay then for him to bend the rules and work with her to clear her name, but still she wouldn't stand up to Archie when it mattered.

Ignoring the niggling little thought that perhaps Nikki was just treading lightly round Archie because she was worried about him, he sneaked into a car space and looked through his windscreen at the back end of Bradford Royal Infirmary. Beautifully done up, the back of the building had a bustling welcoming clinical feel, whilst the front had kept many of its original features. One of the busiest hospitals in the region, BRI was always in perpetual motion. He got out and jogged down, happily absorbing the warmth that hit him as the doors swished open to a cast of characters all living their own experiences of BRI, like ants on a treadmill, just going about their business.

Saj sometimes liked to step off the treadmill and just absorb his surroundings. It grounded him, cemented his connection with humanity and here in BRI were the most diverse range of people and experiences you could get. The elderly Muslim man, quietly sitting on his own on an incongruously bright red plastic bench, his shoulders hunched, head bowed, weeping silently as all around people bustled past. He reminded Saj of his own dad and his heart twanged. Right now, he couldn't afford the time to worry about his dad or the pressure Langley was exerting on him to tell his parents the truth.

Easy for Langley to say. He didn't come from a Muslim background. He hadn't been brought up with the same expectations as Sajid had. He wasn't being fair to Langley. He knew that. Langley wasn't insensitive, course he wasn't. He *was* aware of the conflict that raged inside Saj. The battle between letting his family choose whether thirty years of being a good son, being a good Muslim, working hard, making them proud, counted for more than him being gay. The thing was, he suspected none of them would understand. His dad would be angry, his mum shocked, his sisters and brothers ashamed and even if a glimmer of love made them want to keep a door open for him and perhaps his partner, they would all be forced to turn their backs by the extended family. It was too big a step to take. How could Langley ask him to risk losing his family? He looked away from the old man, feeling like he shared his grief, even though he didn't know the reason. Instead, as he strode along the corridors, he tried to see only the bouncing 'It's a Girl' balloons and luxurious bunches of flowers. It didn't have to be all doom and gloom . . . not even on his way to a PM.

In the bowels of the hospital it was cooler and the disinfectant smell was stronger and mingled with other chemicals. Saj didn't mind post-mortems, although, unlike Langley, he didn't enjoy them either. He rapped on Langley's office door, and breezed through, pleased to see that the other police officer, a young lad called Grey, was already waiting. Langley looked up and smiled, his entire face lighting up. Saj wished his own smile could be more natural, but it was stiff and stern. Langley had to put up with a lot.

'Hey, DC Malik. You all set for the PM?'

Saj's smile loosened a bit. This was Langley's way of telling him he wouldn't be too familiar with him in front of the younger officer. 'Ready as I'll ever be.'

'Great, let's get to it.' Langley led them out of his office and into the scrub room. Saj was familiar with Langley's process of suiting up before a PM and guided the young officer through the side door that led to the observation suite. A custom-made room with seats and a window where observers could watch the post-mortem without having to get too up close and personal. For Saj the addition of this room was a blessing. No need to endure the smells that accompanied Langley's work, although the sounds still filtered through the speakers, keeping them in touch with the nitty gritty. 'This your first PM?'

The lad grinned. 'Yep, but I had a Saturday job at a butcher's so I'm not too squeamish.' His grin faded. 'Well, I don't think I am.'

'You'll be fine.' Langley's strangely tinny tone was kind as he winked up at them from the PM suite. 'Take one of these metal bowls – just in case. I don't want puke all over my pristine floor. Not like DC Malik did when it was his first PM.'

Sajid had told Langley this nugget of information in a moment of weakness and now heartily regretted it, for it was raised at every possible opportunity. Still, he took it in good spirit, merely raising an eyebrow and shaking his head as Langley walked over to the body from the canal which was laid out on a trolley and gently removed the covering sheet.

Flipping through a chart, Langley began. 'Ah, they found ID in his wallet in his jeans. Our cadaver is . . .'

'Adam Glass.' finished Sajid. It had taken him only a moment to recognize the man. Being submerged in the icy canal had blanched the colour from his face and, although not the worst floater Sajid had ever seen, his skinny body was beginning to bloat and his extremities were beginning to wrinkle. It was as much the tattoos all over his arms and torso, as his face that Sajid recognized. The conversation he'd had earlier with Nikki about Glass going AWOL and Haqib dating his sister seemed more than coincidental. Seemed like Glass had got up somebody's nose big time. Hadn't Nikki mentioned something about codes? The little tosser had probably been skimming money from someone he shouldn't have been meddling with.

'A friend of yours?'

Saj snorted. 'With those tatts? Nah, don't think either one of us would be his cup of tea.'

The tattoos in question were swastikas, English Lions and Union Jacks. Every time Saj saw the combination of these emblems his blood boiled. Everything they stood for was oppressive and dark, just like their owner. He wouldn't be missed by many. Certainly not by Bradford police. Adam Glass was a thug his mother could barely love. With studied nonchalance he kept his voice bland. 'How original. This artwork puts Banksy to shame.'

'It's funny,' said the younger officer. 'You'd think the first thing I'd notice would be the gaping hole in his chest, but in actual fact my eyes were drawn to the crap on his arms. Wonder if he'd envisaged that the ones observing his dissection would be Muslim and gay.'

Sajid froze for a moment. Shit. How did Grey know he was

gay? Had Langley said something? Eyes wide, he flicked a glance at his partner whose slight shake of the head confirmed that he hadn't said anything. But Grey, looking at Saj, continued. 'Oh, didn't you know I'm gay? Shock you, did I?'

Saj shook his head. 'Doesn't matter to me either way, but it does make me feel better that his hate is somehow being subverted.'

'Subverted?'

Langley laughed and began to circle the trolley, as his aide, Jess, came in with a camera and switched the recording equipment on. 'What DC Malik means is that, despite him being a racist thug in life, we'll still all of us work to find out who did this. He'd be turning over in his grave, if he was already buried, to have gays and Muslims as his avenging angels.'

Saj snorted. 'Very fanciful, I'm sure. I don't really see myself as an angel, avenging or otherwise.'

'I know it's difficult for you to see the detail, so I'll get Jess here to enlarge the photos she takes on the big screen.'

Jess moved in and began taking close-ups of the areas Langley pointed at and almost immediately they appeared on a screen positioned at an angle on the observation room wall. Langley began examining Glass's torso. 'It's clear from the condition of the body that he's not been submerged for very long. Hours maybe. Which, of course, ties in with the timings of the barge being moved. I'll know more when I open him up.'

Langley lifted one of Glass's hands and turned it palm upwards with a nod. Ducking down to have a better look, he grinned. 'Well, well, well. You may be in luck, Detective Malik. There's debris under his nails, which may give us some results. Thought you said they used bleach?'

'They did. The CSIs found evidence of him being doused with bleach in the lay-by. Despite these forensic measures, we also found fag ends near the spot they threw him in. Presuming they belong to our boys, they don't seem fully au fait with all things forensic.'

'Well, let's hope their idiocy reaps rewards for you.'

Langley replaced the hand on the table after directing his assistant to bag the nail clippings and moved to look at Glass's feet. 'Minimal wrinkling of the palms and soles corroborates the timings and from the look of that bullet wound, I'd almost certainly rule out death by drowning. This guy was more than likely dead before he hit the water.'

He moved up the body and began pointing to various marks on the torso. 'Beneath the tattoos and the beginnings of bloating from being submerged, you can see evidence of extensive bruising.'

The photos flipped in turn to the different areas Langley pointed at. 'By the colouration, I'd say he'd endured sustained beatings over the course of a few days, but what intrigues me more is this.'

He gestured to Jess, who obligingly zoomed in. 'These cuts look remarkably like bite marks.'

A fleeting image of Nikki diving backwards, a look of sheer horror on her face, made Saj smile. 'Rats?'

'Hmm. Yes, rats have certainly had their go at him, no doubt about that. But some of these are bigger . . . I'd say dogs.'

'Like the Jane Doe from yesterday?' Saj's interest was piqued. This was too much of a coincidence. How often did they find corpses with dog bites, never mind two in the space of twenty-four hours?

Langley took a moment to study various areas on Glass's arms and legs. 'Some of these are just bite marks, so who knows, we may be lucky enough to get enough detail to compare. Do you have reason to believe the two are linked?'

'Early days, but we can't rule anything out. As you say, there was evidence of the body being doused in bleach before being dumped in the canal and we know for certain that the Jane Doe was also covered in bleach cause we could smell it on her when she was found. Thought for a minute Nik was going to lose it. You know how she is with bleach.'

Grey, listening in with interest, pursed his lips. 'Is it that DS Parekh bint you're talking about? Heard she's a real ball breaker. Can't believe she'd bowl out over a bit of bleach at a crime scene.'

Despite his annoyance with Nikki, it irked Saj when people bad-mouthed his boss. Nikki was misunderstood and he wasn't about to let this little upstart get away with anything. 'DS Parekh is no "bint". And if you want to discover her ball breaking skills, just repeat that sort of sexist crap around her – you'll soon be singing an octave higher.'

He glared at the younger officer, satisfied when he lowered his gaze and shuffled on his feet. Nikki clearly wasn't the only ball breaker in the team. 'Also, for your information, DS Parekh is one of the best officers Bradford police have and I for one find it a privilege to work with her. Got it?'

Grey gave an abrupt nod and moved closer to the screen as Langley, head to one side said, 'So, can I continue now?'

Sajid noticed the sparkle in the pathologist's eyes and subdued a snort. Langley had enjoyed watching the little scat. With a surreptitious wink, Saj nodded. 'Yeah, good to go on, Dr Campbell.'

'If you look where the bites are positioned, it's clear that Glass used his arms to protect his face from the dog . . . or dogs. The padding from his clothes mean that some of the bites haven't broken the skin, so the rats have concentrated on the open bites instead. Lucky for us, the dogs have left bruises and teeth marks on the skin.'

At last! Saj had been beginning to wonder if they'd get any sort of break in the case and now it looked like they might have. 'What about the gunshot?'

Langley moved up and studied the entry wound. 'Small calibre gun. Close range. There's a bit of scorching to the wound and when I looked at his clothes earlier, you could see it more clearly on his jacket. Help me roll him, Jess.'

As the pair rolled him onto his side, Langley continued.

'Through and through wound. Probably nicked various arteries, but I can confirm that in a bit. He'd have bled out quickly.' Damn! They could do with some bullets for comparison purposes. The CSIs, when they took Springer's car apart in the workshop had finally found the bullet that shot her embedded in the depths of the driver's seat. Perhaps they'd be able to compare entry and exit wounds. He shot off a quick text to Nikki telling her to be sure to get official photographic evidence of Springer's wounds. Not that she'd reply – Too damn busy sharing secrets with Archie whilst he did the real work.

The rest of the PM went by in a blur of weighing, sawing and measuring, with Grey marvelling at every aspect of it, whilst Saj tried his best to look unconcerned. Why did the lad have to be so overly enthusiastic? This wasn't a pleasant part of the job, after all, and Saj just wanted it over with. He kept glancing at his phone to see if Nikki had contacted him and with no updates from her, he became more frustrated with each passing minute. *She'd better not be off doing something else on her own.*

Springer had looked in a bad way and he'd have appreciated being told how she was doing. Maybe if she wasn't as ill as she'd looked they'd be able to interview her later – find out what had happened and possibly even what the link between her, Adam Glass and the Jane Doe was.

At last the PM ordeal was over and Grey had scuttled off to share all the gory details with his mates, leaving Saj and Langley alone in Langley's office.

'So, basically what you're saying is that he died from a gunshot wound to the chest, but had been tortured prior to being shot?'

'Exactly that. His injuries indicate severe beatings over a period of days. He had a severe haematoma to the brain and I suspect that, had he not been shot, death would have followed very quickly anyway.'

'So, the poor bastard was a dead man walking.' Despite his words, Saj felt nothing but contempt for the corpse. He would work to discover who'd deprived him of his life, but he would not mourn his death.

Langley laughed. 'Not so much walking as lying unconscious. Now, how do I know you don't really mean the "poor bastard" bit?'

Saj's scowl lifted and was replaced by a grin. 'You got me. I won't lose any sleep over his death, but we'll still get to the bottom of it.' He paused, tapping his finger on his lip. 'Thought for a moment you'd outed me back there with PC Grey.'

'Surely you know I'd never do that, Saj. I would never be so crass . . . although . . .?'

Saj lifted a hand to wave goodbye. 'Yeah, I know, I know, I need to out myself to my family – but not today, eh? Got to dash, Nikki's just texted we need to go. Catch you later.'

Saved by the bell – now was not the time to discuss his 'coming out' parade. Shoving the errant thought 'when would it be a good time?' to the back of his mind, he dropped a quick kiss on Langley's frowning forehead and left.

Chapter 34

The ambulance trip to the hospital had been fraught. The paramedics had lost Springer's pulse and started CPR. When that hadn't worked, they'd used the defibrillator. Everything had played out at a hundred miles an hour, with the sirens screeching and the lights flashing, it had been a scary fifteen-minute drive, where Nikki was completely out of her element.

Now, Springer had been spirited off by doctors in blue and green scrubs, to be stabilized. One of the nurses assumed Springer was a friend of Nikki's and had escorted Nikki to a waiting room. She appeared moments later with a sugary drink and sat opposite, explaining what they were doing to save Springer's life; some sort of IV with warm fluids to deal with the hypothermia and apparently after she was stable, they'd deal with the gunshot wound which, although not the most pressing of her ailments, would need to be X-rayed to check for errant bone fragments before being stitched up, before bustling off to do her duties.

On her own for a few minutes, half-drunk cup of tea on the small table beside her, Nikki exhaled. They'd found Springer and she was alive. That was good. She only hoped they'd be able to keep her that way. Now she needed to push forward with the investigation. Find out what linked Springer, canal man and the dead girl. She lifted her phone and got through to the forensics lab. 'I need all the lab work from both yesterday's crime scene and the two today in Saltaire and by the canal, ASAP.'

'Good afternoon to you too, DS Parekh. Was that *a please* or a *thank you* I heard?'

Rolling her eyes, Nikki made her tone sugary sweet. 'Pleeeeease can you do that for me, Iftikhar Mobeen, most gracious of graciousness. Thank yooooou soooo much.'

Ifty guffawed, long and low. A deep belly laugh that tugged a smile from Nikki. 'I'm on it already, Parekh. You know I've got a soft spot for you. Don't know why, cause you're usually such a cowbag.'

Ifty was a huge, bald man over six foot seven tall which necessitated him getting his lab overalls custom-made. Still, they always seemed too short for his arms, making his body seem disproportionate. For some reason, he'd taken a liking to Nikki, and somehow he'd managed, over the years they'd known each other, to break down her defences.

'Aw come on Ifty, you don't mean it. I'm all sweetness and light, I am. Ask Saj.'

'Hmmm. I'll reserve judgement on that. But I'll get back to you when I have summat.'

Nikki, still smiling, was just about to text Sajid, when the door burst open and Stevie rushed in, coat flying open, her belly reminiscent of Archie's as it preceded her into the room. Saj would have to wait for now.

'Where is she? Where's Fliss?'

Nikki wiped the smile from her face and jumped to her feet. 'In surgery. They're working on her now. They're mostly worried about the hypothermia at the moment, Stevie. They'll deal with the bullet wound when she's stable.'

Nikki led Stevie to a seat. Stevie was panting, her breath coming in rasping gasps, which Nikki assumed was as much to do with anxiety as exertion. Bags under her eyes told their own story and the way she rubbed her back told Nikki she was suffering third trimester backache. A family liaison officer hovered behind Stevie, her expression full of a sympathetic wholesomeness that had Nikki instinctively recoiling. She hated fussy do-gooders.

The middle-aged woman, all upbeat brusqueness said, 'I can stay with her, if you want to get off. Stevie doesn't want me with her overnight, but I'll stay here with her and then make sure she gets back home later. After all –' she leaned over and patted Stevie's abdomen before continuing in a patronizing tone '– baby needs its rest.'

Yuck! Nikki glanced at Stevie's face, but saw she was too distressed to object to the FLO's inappropriate touching and stupid baby tone. *Where the hell do they get them from?* Nikki was aware she was being unreasonable and that most of the FLOs were extremely capable and a real asset to the families they served. However, this woman had rubbed her up the wrong way. She'd hated people thinking it was okay to bump pat when she was pregnant. She'd hated even more that some people, usually the older male officers, had assumed that pregnancy had robbed her of her brains. She nodded at the FLO and sat next to Stevie. 'Are you okay with that, Stevie?'

Stevie gripped Nikki's hand. 'Fliss and I will never be able to thank you enough for finding her. She'll get through this. I know she will. We've got this little one to look forward to, after all.'

Wishing she shared Stevie's certainty, Nikki smiled and patted the woman's hand, hoping her expression wasn't betraying her doubt. 'I'll let the nurses know you're here, so they can keep you updated.'

Squirming, Stevie tried to get comfortable in the plastic chair. 'You'll find who did this, won't you?'

'I'll do my best.' And the first thing she had to do was see Archie. Now that they'd found Springer, she was going to make him tell her everything that was going on.

Getting to her feet, Nikki turned to the FLO. 'See about getting her a comfier chair, please. It may be a long day.'

And she left in search of answers.

Chapter 35

Why was it that on the rare occasion he managed to return home early, his wife went off on one? She was in one of her moods and the entire house seemed to be waiting with bated breath for her to erupt. Xavier was fed up with it. He provided for the family, they had a good house, better than most of their friends and family, and still she found cause to have a go at him. She didn't complain when she was maxing out his credit card though, did she? Oh no, *then* she was happy, but he comes home early and she's got that look on her face and she wants to 'talk'. As if he didn't have enough on his plate to deal with right now. Things were at a critical level and he needed to exert his dominance. Take control once and for all and he could do without her stupid nagging. *She is turning into her mother, the old cow.*

What he really wanted to do was slap her face. He'd done that and more before, but not recently. He'd decided that was too dangerous a game to play. He was too much in the public eye to risk her looking like he'd backhanded her. So, he'd just taken his temper elsewhere, where nobody complained. The result was that she thought she could push him a bit more. Thought she had protection, and to an extent, she was right.

He'd snarled at her, told her to back off and pinched her hard on the upper arm. No reason not to give her a gentle reminder of what he was capable of, if he so chose. Then he'd gone to his office and locked the door behind him. He was seething. *Ungrateful bitch.* After everything he'd done for her.

He threw himself onto his spinning leather office chair and thought of all the ways he could punish her that wouldn't leave a mark. That helped and by the time his phone rang, he was calmer. 'What's up, Cyclops?'

'They found Springer. She looks in a bad way, but who can tell? Parekh's up at BRI with her and Springer's wife.'

'So, what you're telling me is that the bitch might survive?'

'Yep, she might.'

'And, of course, we can't get to her at the hospital.' Xavier's anger was returning. This was not good news.

'No.'

Xavier thought for a moment. 'We don't know for sure that she can't identify me from the farmhouse with those two idiots. I had my mask on, but I spoke. She knows me quite well, so if she heard me, maybe she'd recognize my voice. Idiots! I should have checked to see she was dead myself.'

Cyclops didn't respond and Xavier couldn't blame him. There was nothing to say. He'd made a mistake, but now they had to rectify it. 'Okay, we can't get to Springer, but we can get to her wife. Maybe exert a little pressure on her to make sure Springer keeps her mouth shut.'

'Can do. I can send Bullet to keep an eye out for when she leaves BRI.'

'Good man.' Xavier smiled. He trusted Cyclops to get the job done and if he thought Bullet was the man to do it, then that was fine with him. 'Everything else in place for tonight.'

'Oh yes. Tonight chaos will reign; you can be sure of that. The pigs will think their tails have been amputated and all our competitors will see just how far we're prepared to go to control the city.'

Xavier hung up, unlocked the bottom drawer of his desk and extracted a bottle of gin. Might as well start the celebrations now!

Chapter 36

Nikki pasted a smile on her face and walked along the corridor to the side room that Archie had been given. She suspected he'd been isolated because he was being such a pain in the arse. The police officer had looked visibly shaken when she passed him at the nurses' desk and relief had bloomed in his face like he'd been given a trip to Disneyland, not been relieved of his duties.

When she walked in, she knew she'd done the right thing in sending Archie to BRI. Despite his gruff voice earlier on the phone, he looked somehow diminished in his floral hospital gown, hooked up to a heart monitor and with an oxygen clip on his finger. His huge belly was covered by a pale blue cover folded over at the top with a slither of white sheet visible. He was propped up on a mountain of pillows and was prodding at his phone with a stubby finger and all the while a stream of invectives, proverbials and snippy mutters left his lips.

Nikki hesitated at the door, taking in his pallor and schooling her face to mask her concern as the heart machine beeped his vitals in red and green lines. It was all so alien, so horrible. This less than vital Archie worried her, made her realize just how much she'd come to depend on his irascible support and now look at him. Weakened, confined to bed, reliant on the skill of the medical staff and there was nothing she could do. Her fingers reached up and gently traced the rope scar that ringed her neck until, realizing what she was doing, she dragged her hand away and forced it back by her side. She was not going to get stressed by all of this. She had too damn much to do. Shaking her maudlin thoughts from her head she pasted a grin on her lips, stepped into the room and grabbed a plastic chair which she then pulled right up to the side of the bed and plonked herself in it.

Archie glanced at her, then continued prodding at his phone, no doubt texting his assistant to get updates. 'No grapes, Parekh?' He flung his phone onto the bedsheets and glared at her. 'I'm stuck in here up tae my proverbials in bloody nurses with a wittering PC at my side and you can't even be bothered tae bring grapes.'

Nikki's grin widened, became more natural. This was more like it. More like the Archie she knew and loved. 'You want me stopping off to buy grapes for you or keeping on top of the three investigations I've now got to juggle?'

'I'm getting O'Malley's team tae take over the murders. I want you focused on Springer.'

As Nikki opened her mouth to complain, he waved his hand at her. 'No! Parekh. I may be laid up in here while they monitor my proverbials, but I'm still your damn boss and I'm telling you.'

As a flush flooded his face, Nikki risked a surreptitious glance at his heart monitor and saw that his heartrate was increasing. Taking a deep breath, she held out a placating hand and kept her voice even. 'Okay, okay. You're the boss. But, just so you know, we think the three cases might be linked and now we've found Springer, we can really make progress.'

She paused, glanced at the monitor again and was relieved to see his rate had decreased again. She was reluctant to affect that adversely, but aware that if she was to push forwards, she needed to know everything Archie knew about Springer.

'How's she doing?'

Nikki shrugged. 'It's a waiting game. Hypothermia's their major concern and they're trying to bring her back from that.'

'Did you get them to do the rape kit?'

Archie had texted her whilst she was en route to the hospital insisting they get one done. After his demand to have her blood tested for Roofies, Nikki was getting increasingly concerned. What the hell was he going to tell her now? She couldn't investigate blind. So, taking a deep breath she leaned forward. 'Course I did, but now I need to know everything, boss. I need to know what you know. I need it all. I can't investigate blind, now can I?'

Archie bit his lip, his eyes narrowed and said nothing. Nikki sighed. The old goat was going to be stubborn and that really pissed her off. If he wasn't lying in a hospital bed attached to a heart monitor, she'd push and push and push. Her chest tightened as a bubble of frustration expanded Damn him. Damn him for not trusting her. Damn him for not sharing when that was something he was always onto at her about and damn him for being poorly. Her breathing grew shallow as the pressure in her chest mounted, the intake of air reduced to tiny staccato gasps like popping bubble wrap. If she didn't do something it would grip her and Archie would see how worried she was about him. She jumped to her feet, the chair scraping behind her and headed for the door, all the while trying to slow the popping bubbles down. Trying to burst them and stretch them into longer breaths.

'Sit! For God's sake sit, Parekh, before you keel over. Sit!'

Fingers gripping the door handle, Nikki stood, back straight, eyes shut, and schooled herself to breathe. Long and slow . . . long and slow . . . in and out . . . in and out. After a couple of minutes the bubbles stopped popping, her chest eased and her fingers relaxed their hold on the handle. She turned around, her movements stilted and walked stiffly back to Archie's bedside.

His eyes, piercing, yet kind, raked her face. 'I'm not dead yet, you know.'

Nikki shrugged, not quite prepared to let him off the hook

yet. Where the hell did he get off, assuming her slight blip was because of worry over his health condition? 'You're not sharing either, so you'd be as well dead for all the good you are to me if you keep secrets. You know it's an offence, don't you? Impeding an investigation.' She banged the heel of her hand against her forehead. 'What am I thinking? Of course, you do. You're the DCI after all. No *way* would you risk the favourable outcome of an investigation by keeping things from your detectives. How stupid am I?'

Her breath came in quick gasps, but this time it was anger driving her – anger and frustration. How could he be so damn stubborn? Did he think he couldn't trust her? A flicker of pain sparred at her heart with that thought, but she thrust it away to deal with later. She would not allow her personal emotions to impede her. Especially not after her near panic attack. 'We have a really ill officer upstairs, who was abducted from the scene of a car crash after she reported seeing an arm waving from the rear light of the vehicle in front of her. That's not mentioning the two corpses cooling their heels in the mortuary. If you have anything – anything at all that remotely impacts on this or eluci- dates anything, we – me and Saj – need to know.'

Archie waved her to the seat and as Nikki slipped into it, he began. 'A council worker, a Jackie Dobson, came into Trafalgar House on Sunday afternoon after the training session in Wakefield was over. She made certain allegations which . . .' He hesitated, mouth pursed in disgust before continuing. 'Which, until they can be verified, must be kept strictly confidential. It's just unfortunate that Springer had disappeared until now, as we desperately need her account in order to continue.'

Nikki frowned. 'Springer's been accused of something . . . for God's sake what the hell has she been up to now? You'd think she'd have learned her lesson after that Kowalski thing, when she nearly got sacked for defending him.' Kowalski had been Nikki's previous boss and he'd been as corrupt as they come. Whilst

Nikki had been the whistle-blower who exposed him, Springer had defended him and, as a result, some of the shit from the fan had stuck to her, hence her sideways move to the cold case unit.

Still indignant and prepared to think the worst of Springer, Nikki continued, 'Then there's the way she treated me over the Khal thing last year.' She exhaled, shaking her head. She'd taken to referring to the death of her bigamist husband as the 'Khal thing' rather than attempt to put another label on it.

'You've got the wrong end of the stick, Parekh. Springer has done nothing wrong. It's what may have been done to her that we need to ascertain.'

Nikki's eyes narrowed. They knew Springer had been shot, they suspected she'd been abducted, but how did any of this relate to this Jackie Dobson from City Hall, Roofies and rape kits? Whilst the evidence pointed to one thing and one thing only, Nikki couldn't work out where Springer's abduction and Jackie Dobson fitted into the jigsaw that was beginning to form in her mind.

A sprightly nurse, with the a name tag that read Janet Olson pinned to her uniform, opened the door with a smile on her face and proceeded to move towards Archie. 'Time to check your chart, Mr Hegley.'

'Get out!' Archie's voice shot out like a bullet and hung in the air before ricocheting round the room.

Nikki's mouth fell open. How could he be so rude? Even she had better manners and she had to concede that was saying something.

'This is confidential police business. You need tae leave, right now.'

The smile faded from the nurse's face, her head tilted to one side, she straightened her body up to its full five foot two and fastened her eyes on Archie. When she spoke, her tone was pure acid laced with sarcasm. 'Is this a police station?' Nurse Olson stared at him, waiting for an answer.

'No.'

'Is this a hospital?' Again, the gimlet stare.

Archie's tone was grudging, but less abrasive. 'Yes.'

'Are you a patient in this hospital?'

Patience, clearly on its last legs, Archie's scowl deepened, 'For goodness' sake, yes. You can see I am. That's why I'm laid in this bed, strapped to these bloody beeping machines, wearing a woman's open-arsed goonie.'

The nurse tutted. 'Are you my boss?'

Archie waved his hands in the air, shaking his head like a demented cocker spaniel, his Scottish accent more pronounced now said through gritted teeth. 'No. No. No, bloody no. You satisfied?'

'Perfectly. We're on the same page now. So, Mr Hegley, whether you choose to be rude or not, I *will* be taking your vitals right now and filling in your chart, because *my* job is to keep you alive. Your confidential police business will have to wait five minutes.'

She grabbed Archie's chart, cast a wink in Nikki's direction and ignoring Archie's sullen expression and hefty sighs, she proceeded to document his vitals, before leaving with a jaunty, 'See you in a couple of hours, Mr Hegley. Maybe your mood will have improved by then.'

Nikki burst out laughing. 'Looks like Nurse Olson takes no prisoners.'

The interlude with the nurse had given her time to readjust her thoughts. Springer hadn't done anything wrong. Nikki's surprise was quickly replaced by dread at what she was about to find out.

Archie humphed and folded his arms across his chest. 'Bloody fusspot. I'm fine and they keep coming in and interfering – interrupting me. Bloody nuisances, getting their proverbials tied in a knot if mah blood pressure's up.'

Nikki, in the interests of getting the information on Springer quickly, kept silent, allowing his moans to run to a natural halt before prompting him. 'Springer?'

Picking up his phone and twirling it between his index finger and thumb, Archie looked out the window. Finally, as if he'd come to a decision, he turned to Nikki, dropped his phone on the bed and exhaled. 'Dobson came into Trafalgar House to make a historical complaint against a notable public figure.' Tight-lipped, Archie tutted. 'The complaint was a serious one. An extremely serious one and Dobson came forward only now because she believed that Springer had been subjected to the same offence as she herself was two years ago.'

Archie's hesitancy in spitting it out was making Nikki nervous. What could be so awful that Archie would have difficulty telling her? After all, she had called out her previous boss for criminal activity. Surely, he knew she'd treat whatever complaint had been made professionally. Then she bit her lip. Shit! Had the complaint been made against Archie himself? Was that why he was having difficulty spitting it out? Is that what had brought about his heart arrhythmia? She'd always considered Archie to be as straight as a die and it would take a lot to convince her otherwise. Still her own track record in trusting men wasn't that good. But Archie? Nah, surely not. She looked at him. If he denied whatever he'd been accused of, then she'd be on his side. Definitely. No doubt about it.

'Don't worry, boss. I've got your back. Saj and I will get to the bottom of this. All you need to worry about is getting better.'

Archie looked at her as if she'd told him aliens in bikinis were running Trafalgar House. 'What are you on about? Got my back?' Then he laughed. A huge rolling guffaw that had Nikki glancing at his monitor in panic. But it beeped strong and steady. 'It's not me she'd complaining about. She came to report it tae the police.' He glanced at Nikki, his eyes sparkling, 'Had you worried though, didn't I?'

Nikki was embarrassed by her mistake. 'If you'd stop pussy-footing about and just spit it out, nobody would be making bloody mistakes. For God's sake, have they doped you up or something?'

Archie rubbed his chest, winced a little. The monitor made a couple of alarming beeps then settled down again. Serious now, he continued. 'Thing is, Dobson accused this public figure of drugging and raping her. She said she was certain he'd done it with other junior workers in the past and was nearly a hundred per cent convinced that he'd done the same to DS Springer on Saturday night. She said Springer displayed all the side effects on Sunday morning of having been roofied. Dobson saw her leaving the hotel and heading to her car in a disorientated state and vomiting next to her vehicle. She says the male in question was with Springer most of the evening and that Springer hardly drank. Seems this Dobson has been keeping an eye out. When they disappeared, Springer looked inebriated and was being helped out of the room by this man. She felt there was nothing she could do as she had no proof.'

Allowing herself time to digest his words, Nikki crossed her legs and leaned back. Dobson was accusing someone of raping her and alleging that DS Springer had been subjected to the same experience by the same man at the training event. This was bad. Really bad! She lifted her head and met Archie's eyes. 'Who? Who is she accusing?'

A pulse throbbed in Archie's cheek. 'That's just it. She won't give us a name. Says she wants to be sure Springer will prosecute before she gives up the name.'

Nikki exhaled. 'What the actual . . .?'

'I ken. It's frustrating, but that's why I wanted the Rohypnol test and the rape kit. After twenty-four hours, Roofies are undetectable in the blood.'

Nikki understood. She only wished Archie had shared it with her. She stood up and stretched her shoulders. Her disturbed sleep and busy day was catching up with her and she still had a lot to do before she could go home. She could do without a woman making rape accusations and not following through with a name.

Archie held out a slip of paper. 'Here's her details. You'll need to meet up with her tomorrow, see if you can get her tae name names, even if Springer's in no condition tae talk.'

Nikki took the paper, looked at it and then slipped it into her pocket. 'Right Archie. I'll try and pop in tomorrow, but I'll keep you updated anyway.'

'Eh, Parekh?'

Archie's fingers plucked at the bedsheet and Nikki hoped he wasn't going to ask her to help him to the loo. Last thing she needed was to be subjected to Archie's naked ass. There were some things that underlings should never witness in their bosses. She'd see if she could grab a pair of jammies from somewhere and deliver them tomorrow. 'Yeah . . .?'

'You thought any more about the DI job?'

'Aw, Archie. No. Don't try and pressure me. I'd be rubbish at it; you know I would.'

'Thing is, Nik, if you dinnae step up, they'll take these cases away from the team and pass them onto O'Malley or some other fucker.'

Nikki groaned. Archie wasn't playing fair.

'I've been on the phone with the big boss and she's agreed that, in my absence you can add two more officers tae the team and you'll have a dedicated admin tae mop up some of the paperwork. Plus, you'll get a pay rise. Go on, Parekh. Just till I'm back on my feet. I'd feel better knowing you were on the case.'

She didn't really have much choice. Saj would never forgive her if she lost their cases and she had two in mind, who'd slot in nicely. 'Right. Get back on the blower and tell her I want DC Williams and Sergeant Anwar reporting to duty first thing . . . and the best admin person you can recommend.'

She headed for the door and then turned around, 'It's only temporary, Archie. Soon as you're back you can start the interview process for a real DI. I'm not cut out for desk work.'

Chapter 37

Nikki caught up with Sajid at the Costa café at the back entrance of BRI. He was nursing a cappuccino and had an untouched blueberry muffin in front of him. His shoulders had a slump to them that Nikki had noticed more and more often recently. Something was up with Saj, but she didn't have the time to deal with it. Not right now.

She went up to the counter and ordered a drink and a flapjack for herself. If she was lucky, she'd be able to have Saj's muffin too. Didn't look like he was going to finish it. Mr Doldrums, that's what he looked like. Maybe she should just ask. No harm in asking if he was all right, was there? That's what friends did, wasn't it? As she studied him, he took a sip of his drink, grimaced and pushed it away, so Nikki ordered him a replacement. No, if he wanted to talk to her then he had a tongue in his head. Besides, Langley was better at that sort of stuff than she was – more touchy-feely. He'd be better talking to Saj than she would. *But what if Langley's the problem?* Nikki thrust the thought aside because if she gave it head room, she'd have to deal with it and she hated dealing with stuff like that. She could barely navigate her own personal life without trying to advise Saj on his.

Anyway, Langley wouldn't be the issue – no way. Nikki had

never met such a loved-up couple. Besides, she knew a sure-fire way to cheer Saj up. Balancing her flapjack in her saucer she transported the two drinks to the table. 'I've got news.'

'Oh, you want to share now, do you?'

Nikki flinched at his cutting tone. This wasn't going exactly as she'd planned.

Saj was on a roll. Breaking a piece of muffin off, he crumbled it through agitated fingers. 'All afternoon I've been waiting for an update, but, hey, everything's okay now because DS Parekh wants to share. Let's give her a prize, shall we?'

She eyed the decimated muffin hoping he wasn't going to subject another chunk to the same treatment. 'I've been busy, Saj. You know that. Lighten up, eh?'

As Saj pulled his drink towards him, Nikki grabbed the muffin and took a bite. Maybe she was going to have to man up and just ask him. 'You okay? Summat happened? Langley okay?'

Okay, it wasn't the subtle enquiry Marcus would have used, but it was the best she could do. A smile tugged at Saj's lips and she knew he was pushing whatever was bothering him aside for now.

'It's family stuff. Langley wants to meet the family.'

Nikki opened her mouth, then shut it again. That was a big deal. Saj's family didn't know about his sexuality and she suspected they wouldn't react well to him introducing his boyfriend. 'Shit!'

Saj smiled again. 'Exactly. Shit it is. But let's not talk about it now. What's your news?'

'Well, I think your news trumps mine any day of the week. You're looking at the new—'

'DI.' Saj grinned, clearly pleased to have taken the wind out from Nikki's sails. 'Knew Archie would convince you. He wraps you round his little finger, Nik.'

'We're getting two new officers. Williams and Anwar *and* admin staff so I don't balls up the paperwork and it's only till Archie's back on his feet and can interview for a responsible DI.' She blurted the words out in a rush.

211

Saj shook his head. 'You might enjoy it, Nik and not want to go back to being a DS.'

Nikki was adamant. 'No way. It's a favour and that's all. You're not getting rid of your old partner that easily, Malik. Anyway, fill me in on the PM and then I'll tell you about Archie.'

'Got an ID. You'll never guess who.'

Nikki hated it when he did this. Couldn't he just say the name? How was she supposed to guess who it was? Could be anybody. The only person she knew it definitely wasn't, was Felicity, Fliss, Springer, but that was another story. Chewing steadily, she waited till he got the message that she wasn't about to guess and ignored his eye roll as he pulled himself forward, elbows on the table, to make his big announcement.

'Adam Glass, that's who.'

'Glass? You're sure?'

Saj picked up what was left of his muffin and Nikki watched, eyes narrowed as he shoved it all in his mouth. *Greedy bastard!*

'Recognized his tatts.'

Nikki thought about that for a moment. *What the hell does that mean?* Glass was involved in some dodgy deals with some new kingpin that nobody would tell her anything about. He gets snatched from his home, supposedly contacts his mum to say he'd taken off and now he's turned up dead with a hole the size of Mick Jagger's gob in his chest.

'That's not all.' Saj grabbed her flapjack, broke it in half and paused, with it part way to his mouth.

Nikki, seeing her moment, reached over, grabbed it from his hand and shoved it in her mouth, ignoring Saj's protest.

'He'd been tortured. Systematically, according to Langley, over a period of days. His spleen was shot, his kidney's bruised, five broken ribs, teeth knocked out. Brain bleed – you name it, he had it. Langley reckons he was all but dead before they even shot him.'

Nikki didn't like the sound of that. It seemed very much like whoever was edging to take over from the last kingpin was exerting his authority on her patch and that was not good. What she couldn't understand was why she was being edged out by Joe Drummond, although she'd definitely make him tell her when they met up later on. If things hadn't been so manic at the minute, Nikki might have been persuaded to postpone her meeting with Drummond. However, if he had information pertaining to any of the cases, then she needed it ASAP. It wasn't every day she had to pull a long shift like this one, but no matter how tired she was, she had no option. People were dead, Springer was in a coma . . . and they had nothing.

'But, and this is the best part. Langley found dog bites on him and he reckons they might be able to match them to the bites on the Jane Doe. Assuming of course it was the same canine that bit both.'

That was interesting and could potentially tie up the different murders in a Houdini knot. She drained her mug and scraped her chair back. It was time for her to fill him in on what she'd learned from Archie, but not here. For this, they needed to be out of earshot of anyone. All it took was some ballsy journalist with a long-range microphone and accusations of rape against an as yet unidentified public figure and it would be all over the front page of the local rag. She stood up. 'Come on. I need to fill you in big time.'

An hour later, they were parked in the Trafalgar House car park watching the rain dapple the windscreen and the wind whipping up crisp packets and sending them flying across the ground. Whistling through a plastic bag caught in the phone cables the wind emitted an eerie whirring sound that set Nikki's teeth on edge. Sajid was deep in thought, presumably still mulling over everything Nikki had told him. Nikki was trying to work out how to handle this Jackie Dobson.

'Public figure. Rapist!' This was about the fifth time, Saj had repeated the words, shaking his head and slamming his palms on the steering wheel as he did so. As he opened his mouth, presumably to repeat them yet again, Nikki grabbed his arm. 'Ssh. If you can't say something other than that, just shut up and let me think.'

Inhaling deeply, Saj ran his fingers through his hair. 'You think this public figure had something to do with her abduction? Springer's, I mean?'

'Doubt it. When she left, according to Dobson, the public figure was still in the hotel and Springer had signed out.'

'Could've ordered it though, couldn't he?'

'Doubt it. Why would he? If he's got away with it before, then why would he? I think it is just lucky for him that Springer got abducted or we'd be trailing his arse right through every corridor in Trafalgar House right now and showing the slimy bastard, whoever the hell he is, up for what he is.'

'Don't understand why she's not giving us a name, though.'

Nikki shrugged. 'You and me both. It's downright irresponsible and, more to the point, if she suspected what was about to happen to Springer, why the hell didn't she stop it? There was a hotel full of police officers there. It's all really weird. The whole argument that she didn't actually know that a rape had occurred – not beyond a shadow of a doubt – is weak.'

Nikki could understand why it would take Dobson so long to tell anyone what had happened to her. It was an emotional process to go through and sometimes it was just too much. But not to intervene when she suspected another woman was about to be subjected to the same trauma was difficult to understand. But then again, Nikki was no therapist and the human brain worked in mysterious ways. They'd find out more tomorrow and hopefully be able to take a serial rapist off the streets before too long.

She'd just decided that it might be time to leave the warmth of Sajid's car when her phone went. 'DS Parekh.'

She listened for a moment before replying. 'That's brilliant news, thank you. Yes, send it all over to me.'

Turning to Sajid, unable to keep the smile off her lips, she punched the air. We got an ID from Interpol for the dead girl. Name's Maria Marcovici. She came to the UK around six months ago with her father to work as a nanny. Her father was going to be gardening. The rest of the family were supposed to be joining them when they settled, but other than a couple of phone calls and a postcard right at the start, the Marcovicis heard nothing more from them. That's why the wife reported them missing.'

'Wonder where the dad is?'

Nikki opened the car door and climbed out. 'Yeah, me too.'

Chapter 38

It was dark now. That sort of deep dark you only got in the countryside, the sort of dark that made the silence reverberate round you like a threat. Stefan remembered this sort of darkness from his work on the family farm. Only there, it hadn't been threatening at all. Back then, he'd been safe and cossetted by the dark. He'd been at one with it, enjoying the stars twinkling and the different phases of the moon reflecting time and seasons moving onwards. The rustles and swishes of wildlife in the shrubbery, birds and bats enjoying their night-time freedom. He'd loved sharing his enjoyment with the kids and Daria. But that had been before things went so disastrously wrong.

He had a decision to make. A crucial one and he was reluctant – or scared, did it matter which? – to do it. He'd come so far and a mistake at this point would be the end for him. He'd driven the quad bike cross-country through fields for as far as he could. The noise from the machine was amplified in the country air and he kept glancing behind him to see if he was being followed. Instead of his fear diminishing as he got further away from his captors, it increased. The closer he got to freedom, the more he sweated, the harder his heart beat.

Although he'd turned off the engine and allowed the satiny

night to camouflage him, he felt exposed. Every sound elicited images of those damn dogs jumping on him, drooling over him, their jaws snapping round his limbs. Or worse, Bullet with his crazed eyes and evil mind. He needed to find cover. He wouldn't survive outside overnight; he was barely surviving as it was.

The moon was almost full, yet a cold March wind sent clouds flitting across it, obscuring its light periodically. Peering through the trees, he debated what he should do. A few hundred yards in front of him stood a farmhouse, smaller than the one he'd left. There was a light on in the kitchen and in one of the bedrooms upstairs. On the one hand, he wanted to crawl towards it, hammer on the door and beg for protection. On the other, memories of all he'd been through in the other farmhouse made his stomach clench. What if the people in this one were just like Bullet? What if there were loads of farmhouses dotted around and all of them kept people like him locked up? He suspected he was being paranoid, yet he couldn't shift the thought.

He could climb back onto the quad bike and drive further. But his shivering body and pounding head told him that wasn't really an option. He'd been lucky to make it this far without falling off or crashing. He couldn't see straight any more. He blinked, but his vision wouldn't clear. It looked like there were two farmhouses in front of him. Pushing himself upright, he tottered forward, keeping his eye on the wavering farmhouses before him. *Come on Stefan, you've got to take a chance.*

It could have been hours or days or seconds, but Stefan reached the side of the farmhouse and edged his way to the front door. His knees were trembling, but he smiled as he reached the door. Grasping the freezing cold brass knocker, he rapped it as hard as he could on the sturdy wooden door and leaned his forehead against it – waiting.

When the door sprung open, Stefan fell forwards into the warmth and collapsed.

Chapter 39

They were hardly through the door to the incident room when Nikki got an email from Interpol with a lead on the murdered girl's father. Having ID'd her and having a possible lead on her father, they wanted to crack on. The file that had been emailed to Nikki was quite comprehensive. After a bad crop and an arctic winter, Stefan Marcovici, in desperation, had borrowed money from a dubious Romanian money lender with connections to organized crime. When he couldn't pay it back, he accrued heavy interest and of course, his debt escalated with threats ensuing. In the end he had to run drugs for them.

It was a story Nikki had heard many times before and was standard procedure for many gangs to groom people to work for them. *Poor bugger!* There he was, just trying to feed his family and keep a roof over their heads and one bad decision had sent him down a wrong path. It was this sort of thing that worried Nikki about her nephew. He was easily swayed as the events last year showed, but hopefully with his newfound love interest and the absence of her brother, he'd be able to steer clear of trouble.

With Sajid peering over her shoulder, she read on. The long and short of it was that after seeing jobs in the UK for labourers and nannies with travel expenses covered, Stefan, in desperation, had made the decision to take a chance and move to the UK with Maria, with the intention of bringing the rest of the family over at a later date. From the safety of the UK, he intended to pay off his Romanian debts.

'Shit, when he hadn't contacted her in a month, his poor wife risked exposing herself to his creditors and travelled to the city to find out what she could from the agency he'd used to arrange his trip and, surprise, surprise, what does she find?'

Saj banged his palm on the table upsetting a pot of pens and making the computer screen wobble. 'Bloody agency had conveniently shut up shop and moved on without trace.'

'I hate to say this, but could we be looking at human-trafficking here?' Nikki's voice was gruff. She'd seen enough exploitation of vulnerable people when she was a kid. She snapped at the elastic band on her wrist, trying to synchronize each snap with the start of a new breath.

Saj laid a gentle hand on her arm and she looked down at the angry red welts on her wrist. Releasing the band one more time, she savoured the sting as it hit her skin. 'Let's read on, maybe we're jumping the boat. Maybe he just wanted to escape his debts and wasn't that fussed about leaving his wife in jeopardy – some husbands can be bastards after all.'

They read in silence for a few more minutes. Daria had, after two more months with no communication from either her husband or daughter, initially reported her concerns to the local police. After checking out everything Daria had told them and being unable to make contact with the employment agency Stefan had supposedly used, they sent the file on to Interpol.

'So, the Marcovicis landed in Manchester, and their file was assigned to Manchester police, who traced Stefan to Bradford where he used his passport combined with a confirmation of employment letter from the halal chicken factory on Thornton Road to set up a bank account. Even got an address in Frizinghall for him. Worth checking if he's still there and when he last saw his daughter.'

Nikki raised an eyebrow. 'It all seems remarkably legit. Other than the fact Maria ended up dead, of course.' She pointed to a paragraph on the screen. 'It even says here that the police spoke to Stefan and that he said he was drawing a line under his past and wanted nothing more to do with his Romanian family and that as soon as they landed, Maria took off. The constable noted that Stefan seemed unconcerned about his daughter.'

'Bit of a dick then.'

'Hmm.' Nikki pushed her chair back and folded her arms across her chest. 'Seems that way. Although Daria doesn't buy it. She still insists that something isn't right. That'll be a job for Williams and Anwar when they report to the team tomorrow. At the very least we need to bring him in.'

As she spoke, the door opened and DC Williams and PC Anwar walked in together. Williams spoke first. 'Thought we'd report in for duty now, Sergeant Parekh.'

Nikki smiled. She was glad she'd chosen these two to join the team. They were enthusiastic and hard workers. 'I wasn't expecting you till tomorrow, but if you're sure, we do have a job for you.' She turned to the computer and set it to print some images of Stefan Marcovici, before scribbling on a scrap of paper which she handed to Anwar. 'We ID'd the woman found in Denholme. She's Romanian and entered the UK with her father about six months ago. Here's his last known address and place of employment. Can you go and bring him in? Don't do the death notification, I'll do that, but I'd like to speak with him sooner rather than later. We've got absolutely no record of Maria after she entered the country and that worries me. We need to hear what her father's got to say about it. Before you go, grab one of the printouts so you can ID him.'

As the two turned to leave, Nikki raised her voice. 'Keep me informed at all times, yeah?'

Williams flashed her a grin and Anwar waved before speaking in uniform, 'Yes boss.'

Nikki scowled at their retreating backs. Being called boss reminded her that she wasn't just their senior officer, she was now acting DI for the team and with Archie out of commission for now, the buck lay with her. The responsibility weighed heavy on her and she was glad that an experienced admin would be there tomorrow to relieve her of the paperwork that came along with being DI. The sooner Archie was back to get someone else doing this, the better.

With time to kill before heading off to their meeting with Joe Drummond, Nikki plonked herself down on a chair in front of the crime boards in the incident room and tried to work the knot out of her neck by bending her head this way and that, whilst rolling her shoulders backwards. Marcus would be able to work the tension out. He was so good at massages. Maybe she should have headed home for a quick massage instead of coming here.

'New dance?' Sajid plonked a coffee on the table before her. 'I'm just going to touch base with Langley. Let him know it'll probably be a lateish night.'

The room was empty now . . . and quiet for once, except for the irritating buzz of the fluorescent lighting. Nikki glanced around, making sure nobody was lurking behind a computer screen and then unlaced her boots and kicked them off. Lifting up her phone, she dialled, her lips twitching when a familiar voice answered. 'Hey Marcus. Just touching base to let you know I'll be back late tonight.'

Aware that she was repeating Sajid's words, she shook her head. Who cared if Saj's phone call to Langley had prompted Nikki to do the same? The thought was there and after all that had happened last year, she was trying really hard to be a better, less elusive figure in their lives. In the background she could hear the telly and the sound of Sunni and Ruby arguing and it made her long to be with them.

'You okay, Nikki? Saw on the news you've found Springer. Kane had a face like a slapped arse and was going on about why it had taken the investigation, led by DS Nikki Parekh, so long to find her.' He paused. 'You got Kane's back up again?'

Nikki sighed. There was no point in denying it. Marcus knew her too well so she told him what she'd done at the crime scene earlier and was rewarded by his rich baritone laugh over the line. 'You're priceless, Parekh, you know that?'

'But you love me and you wouldn't have me any other way.'

He lowered his voice. 'Course I love you. You know that.'

For a moment the familiar denial rushed to her lips and then she shook her head. She *was* worthy of love. Her fingers stroked her neck as she smiled and whispered. 'I love you too, Marcus. Now, put one of the bickering monsters on, will you?'

After five minutes of small talk with her children, Nikki's tiredness had decreased. Sunni was full of annoying facts about hamsters, Ruby insisted on singing the chorus of 'Photograph', the song she was practising for a solo in the school Easter concert and Charlie moaned on about homework and how annoying Mrs Bland was to have forced her to take off her eyeliner. The normality of it all lifted Nikki's spirits and set her up for the hours ahead.

Unaware that Sajid had returned, she began humming the chorus of Ed Sheeran's 'Photograph' and jumped when he spoke. 'You trying to tell me you want a photo of me for your desk?'

'Piss off, Saj. It's the song Ruby's singing in the school Easter concert and you and Langley are definitely coming.'

'Bloody great. As if Langley doesn't go overboard enough at Easter. He'll be all Easter Egg hunts and hot cross buns before too long.'

Distracted from her knotty aches and pains, Nikki turned again and looked at the crime boards. A photograph of Adam Glass had been added to one and Saj had filled in the relevant details from the PM. Nikki had added Maria Marcovici's details to her board and added a photo of her wearing a summer dress and laughing up at the camera. Her face plumper, her expression giving nothing away of the horror that was to end her short life. She'd been only eighteen. Next to her, Nikki pinned an image of the father, Stefan Marcovici, whom the wife had also reported missing. Was he in some way responsible for his daughter's death? Seemed strange that he'd just cut off his family back home like that? But Nikki was well aware that families did cruel things to one another.

The links between Maria's death and Adam Glass's were compelling, yet nothing seemed to take the investigation further forward. She didn't want to rely on Springer to wake up and give her a crucial clue, but deep down, she was definitely clutching at that straw. Right now, she'd take any damn straw.

'You organized the death notification for Glass, didn't you?'

Saj paused and popped the lid back on the whiteboard pen he was using. 'Yeah, soon as we got the ID. Official identification took place earlier this afternoon.'

Nikki tapped her finger on her lip. 'Glass's sister waffled on to me about laundry – money laundering? We need to find out more about what that little scrote was up to. The fact that he was abducted from his mother's house gives us probable cause to look round. Action that, will you Saj?'

Whilst Saj organized a team of uniforms from the evening shift accompanied by CSIs to go through Adam Glass's house, Nikki wracked her brains. How deep was Adam Glass into the criminal underground? Was he a cog in a bigger wheel or a king pin executed by the competition? She suspected the former. Sleazy little git that he was, he wasn't brainy enough to organize on a big scale – certainly not on the larger scale Ali her taxi driver friend had told her about. Which brought her to think about Joe Drummond. He had better come up with the goods this evening, or she'd make sure he felt the Parekh wrath.

'They're linked, aren't they?'

Sajid's words broke Nikki from her reverie. 'Yes, definitely. I just can't get my head round how Springer fits into it all though.'

'Or this rape accusation by this Jackie Dobson?'

Nikki exhaled. There was still a lot to learn and it frustrated her that the pieces weren't gelling together. 'Maybe that'll be clearer tomorrow. I've arranged to meet her in The Cake'Ole café in City Park tomorrow morning.'

She bent over and slipped her feet back into her DMs and proceeded to lace them up. 'Come on, I'll treat you to something in Broadway before we meet Drummond. I need to get Archie a pair of pyjamas and some toiletries. Don't think BRI deserves to be subjected to his shiny white arse, do you?'

'Too much information, Nik. That's an image I'd rather not have.' Sajid lifted his jacket from the hanger where he'd painstakingly placed it earlier, whilst Nikki scrabbled about on the floor to retrieve hers from where it had fallen.

Chapter 40

Nikki was glad she'd brought Sajid with her to meet Joe Drummond. She wasn't exactly scared of him – wary might be a better word choice – but she was pleased to have someone with her and the fact that Saj was so big wouldn't hurt. They'd just had time to nip up to deliver Archie's toiletries to him and before they even reached his room, they could hear him cheering on some football game or other he'd managed to find on the telly. Nikki had asked the nurses how he was and been told 'irascible and annoying'. She understood that, but according to the ward sister, he was also stable and the consultant was going to consider whether he needed an angiogram or not in the morning. He'd tried to hide his pleasure at seeing them and Nikki was once again reminded of how alone in the world he was. She'd definitely try to visit him every day whilst he was in.

Sitting in Saj's Jag in the shadowy part of the Lidl car park on Ingleby Road, Nikki was on edge. She'd made Saj reverse into the parking space so they could drive straight out. It was ridiculous that she felt this way when she was meeting another police officer. But Drummond had a bit of a reputation and although she'd never been on the receiving end of his temper, it was legendary. Plus, he was a bit of a dick. A bit too cocksure and full of himself.

Maybe he'd been undercover for Vice for too long or maybe now that he was back in the office, he'd just seen too much evil to be normal. Whatever it was, she always kept her wits about her when meeting with him in person.

'Dick's gonna make us wait, isn't he?' In between glancing at his watch, Saj fiddled with the radio. 'Got a lovely bottle of Pinot Noir at home with my name on it.'

'He'll make us wait all right, but he won't make us wait too long. He'll want to head off home too. He's just flexing his muscles.' Nikki glanced around. There'd been a couple of homeless folk huddled in the supermarket doorway and Nikki had run out and given them a fiver. Now she could see them trying to cross the road towards McDonald's. The night was bitterly cold and she couldn't bear the thought of them lying there freezing when she and Saj were in his Jag with its heated seats. 'Do you think they'll buy coffee like I told them?'

'They might, though I'm betting McDonald's won't even let them in never mind serve them.'

Nikki huddled into the seat, glowering at the distant lights of the burger franchise. 'Should've got them drinks myself.'

Saj shrugged and took pity on her. 'Nah, Nik. I'm sure McDonald's will serve them – even if they have to go to the drive-thru bit.'

'Need the loo now.'

'For God's sake. You're worse than one of your kids, you are. Just cross your legs. Glad it's not a Sunday night.'

She could hear the smile in Saj's voice. 'Go on then. Why are you glad it's not a Sunday night?'

'All the Pakistani lads would be all over my wheels.'

Nikki understood. On Sundays, after the store was shut, the car park became a Pakistani 'show off the modifications to your car' venue. The weekly gatherings had got so famous they'd featured on a couple of TV documentaries about the city. 'Wheels indeed. What are you Saj, 18?'

'I'm telling you. They'd be all over it. My car's sweeeeeet.' He emphasized the 'ees' in sweet and made the final 'T' into a tut sound.

Grinning, Nikki rummaged in her pocket when her phone rang. 'Williams. I'll put it on speaker. Hey Williams, you're on speaker and DC Malik's with me. What have you got for me?'

'You're on speaker too, boss, and I've got PC Anwar here. Went to Marcovici's address in Frizinghall and got no reply. It's one of those big terraced houses with attic room extensions. Big enough to house a football team.'

'Thing is, boss . . .' Anwar sounded eager when she interjected. 'I'm sure there were people inside. Thought I saw a curtain twitching. Maybe they saw my uniform and that spooked them.'

'Might have, indeed. Tomorrow wear plain clothes. I've brought you onto the team as trainee detectives.'

'Really? Aw thanks, boss.'

Williams butted in. 'So, we had no luck there, so we went to his place of employ.'

Saj mouthed 'place of employ' with a disbelieving smirk on his face. Nikki nudged him. Okay, so the lad was a tad pedantic, that didn't bother her as long as he got the job done.

'Any luck there?'

'Well, sort of. It's one of those open twenty-four-seven factories with an agency bussing in most of the shop floor employees. The majority of the workers are Eastern European. On the face of it, it seems legit. The night manager was happy to talk to us. Checked Marcovici's employment record and confirmed he was employed via the agency, but had gone home early on Sunday and reported in ill today.'

'So, the day before his daughter turns up dead, Marcovici slouches off work early and hasn't been seen since?'

'Yeah, that's about it. Thing is, we both thought there's something off about the whole set-up. The workers all look . . .' Williams paused and Anwar took up the thread.

'They look knackered and skinny and . . .' She paused too and

227

Nikki could imagine her screwing up her nose trying to articulate her thoughts. 'Scared . . .?'

'But the manager was happy to accommodate your questions? Show you his paperwork and everything?'

'Yes.' Williams sighed. 'On the face of it everything's kosher.'

Nikki heard Anwar giggle in the background and say, 'actually it's halal.'

She rolled her eyes at Saj, grinning at the weak joke. It was good that the two of them were getting on so well. They made a good team. 'Did you get the agency's name?'

'Oh yes . . . very creative. It's called Employ Me.'

'Do a check on them tomorrow first thing, see what they have to say about Marcovici and also say you want to check their employment records. I'll get a warrant for that if necessary. We can't be too careful nowadays.'

'You thinking modern-day slavery boss?'

'Right now, I'm not thinking anything, but I want it checked. It's all too easy to manufacture a hold on people. That's why all those ads about modern-day slavery are hitting the media at the minute. We need to keep our eye on the ball. Good work you two. Go home, we'll see you tomorrow.'

Placing her phone on the dashboard, Nikki exhaled. 'More and more possibilities are opening up in these investigations. We'll keep an open mind, but I'd put nothing past Adam Glass. Whoever offed him and tortured that poor girl to death, assuming for now it was the same perpetrators, is even more of a sadist than him.'

As she spoke, a shiny new BMW glided into the car park and parked next to them. 'Looks like we're up.'

The two of them got out of their car, as Joe Drummond got out of his. Walking round to the front of Saj's Jag, Joe eyed it up. 'Nice wheels, Malik. Pity you're such a pussy.'

Rolling her eyes, Nikki stepped in front of Saj who'd taken an angry step forward. 'Cut the crap. We're not here to trade insults. I want to know what's going off in Bradford. We've got Adam Glass on a mortuary slab as well as a tortured girl. What's going on?'

Drummond took out a cigarette and took his time lighting it. Cupping his hands round the flame he inhaled and then blew smoke from the side of his mouth. Almost as tall as Sajid and leaning a bit more towards fat than muscle, Drummond's bulk was still impressive. Unlike Sajid, who preferred casual chic, Drummond wore suits and ties. It was as if his days undercover had made him detest the sordid well-worn clothes he'd been obliged to wear then. Mid-forties, his weather-worn face bore testament to his days pretending to be homeless, living on the streets. He took another drag of his cigarette before speaking.

'You never heard this from me, okay?'

Nikki and Saj nodded. They both knew how these things worked. So much for departmental co-operation. It was becoming more and more like every department for themselves, trying to get all the credit for every investigation to justify their applications for more funding.

Leaning on the bonnet of the Jag, the smirk that pulled his lips upwards indicated that he was well aware that Saj was pissed off with him. He winked at Nikki and she wished he'd just get on with it. It was bloody freezing.

'There's a big man at the top and nobody can identify him. We're getting whispers of modern-day slavery, gun and drug dealing and prostitution rackets – organized crime at its worst. Your Romanian whore probably got on the wrong side of someone.'

Nikki let the 'whore' comment go, although she could sense Sajid bristling beside her. Drummond was always after a rise and she wasn't there for point-scoring. 'You must have an idea of who's behind it though? I know you Joe. Ear to the ground, finger on the pulse. There's little goes off in Bradford without you knowing about it.' Much as she hated doing it, a bit of arse-licking could often cut through Joe's abrasiveness – make him chattier as he played to impress.

Sticking out his chest, Joe grinned. Nikki smiled back, trying her best to hide the fact that she wanted nothing more than to wipe the cock-a-hoop look off his face. Working with Saj had taught her that sometimes it was easier to get the enemy onside than to fry them with threats. Just a shame they had to consider a fellow officer an enemy.

'It's above your pay grade, Parekh.' He flicked his cigarette butt in Saj's direction. 'And it's certainly above pretty boy's pay grade.' He pushed off from the bonnet of Saj's car and began to stride towards his own vehicle. 'Best I can tell you is, worrying about Glass and that little dead bint is the least of our worries. That's why you're on those cases, Parekh – it's because they can't trust you and that old Scottish git with anything more than low-level stuff.' He opened his door and slid into the driver's seat. 'Word of advice – leave the hard stuff to the big boys. You're way out of your league on this one.'

And with a jaunty wave and an insincere smile, he reversed from his parking space, getting so close to Saj that he had to dive backwards and drove off.

'Dickhead!'

'My thoughts exactly,' said Nikki getting back into the car where the pull of the heated seats had never been stronger. 'You notice his mistake?'

Getting in beside her, Saj snorted. 'Yeah. How did he know Maria Marcovici was Romanian?'

'Precisely. Either they were aware of her and are steering clear of the investigation so as not to scupper a bigger sting or . . .'

'Yeah. It's that that worries me. You don't think Drummond could be a bad cop, do you?'

Nikki had worked with a bad cop before and it had taken her a while to work out that her boss, Kowalski, was rotten. It made her naturally suspicious, but she just didn't know with Drummond. He was a prick, certainly. Was he also playing both sides? She didn't know, but she was determined to find out. *Above her pay grade indeed.*

Chapter 41

Stefan's eyes flickered, but even in his confused state, self-preservation kicked in. He lay perfectly still, trying to work out just how safe he was. The sounds of low mumbling voices nearby told him he wasn't alone and that worried him. Who were these people? Friends or foes? The voices appeared to be coming from behind him, so he risked opening his eyes, just a little, but closed them again immediately when a wave of nausea engulfed him.

He was lying on something soft and even the weight of what felt like a duvet covering his lower body caused him pain. But at least he wasn't freezing any more. For the first time in months, he wasn't shivering and despite the tingling in his extremities it felt good. So good. Instead of the nasty smell that had assaulted his nostrils every time he re-entered the barn, this room smelled of furniture polish, wood fires and food. His stomach rumbled and saliva gathered in his mouth. When was the last time he'd eaten warm food?

He wanted to risk letting them know he was awake, but something held him back. These people could be part of Bullet's network. They might be keeping him here till Bullet arrived with his dogs. And he knew that, this time, Bullet would take his time with him.

Someone hammered on the door. Loud! Stefan's heart thumped against his chest. He tried to sit up, but his legs got tangled in the cover. Dizziness washed over him, but still he forced his limbs to move. There were voices approaching now. He needed to escape. He needed to get up.

Then hands were grabbing his arms, pushing him down, immobilizing him. He strained against them, weakly hitting out, and then a pin prick and he was, once more, dead to the world.

Chapter 42

Nikki wasn't sure what had brought her here. It was just gone ten at night and she'd been on the go for over twelve hours already. After their meeting with Drummond, Saj had dropped her by her car, which she'd left just near Ali's Taxis and she'd been determined to go home. It had been a long day and she wanted nothing more than to have a bubble bath and go straight to bed. However, her thoughts kept going back to Springer's wife, Stevie.

When they'd dropped Archie's stuff off, they'd swung by the Critical Care Unit to check on Springer's condition and Stevie – one hand caressing her swollen abdomen, the other holding Springer's lifeless hand – had looked so lost. Saj, as only he could, had convinced her to allow the FLO to take her home for the night, arguing that Felicity would want her to look after their baby.

Perhaps it was the anguished look on Stevie's face as she'd looked at her unconscious wife. Perhaps it was the silent tears that had rolled down her cheeks when she told Nikki over a lukewarm cup of coffee that she and Fliss – *shit, I'll never get used to that name* – were on their own – no support network, no doting granny or aunties-in-waiting to help out, only a few friends, none of whom had children of their own yet. But something had prompted Nikki to drive over to check on the woman.

Much as she disliked Springer – well, the woman had been an absolute bitch to her, hadn't she – seeing her pallid and diminished, clinging onto life with a fragility that was punctuated by rhythmic beeps and flashing lines from the machines that were keeping her alive, had affected Nikki.

When she'd been pregnant with Charlie and Khalid had disappeared off the face of the earth, Nikki had plummeted so low, she thought she'd never recover. Everything had seemed too much to bear, the hurt too deep to heal and she'd withdrawn from everyone. It had been her mum and her sister, Anika, who had nurtured her, brought her back, had helped her through her pregnancy, cushioned her and been her support, till her natural survival instincts had kicked in. But, with Springer comatose in BRI, Stevie had no one and it played on Nikki's mind.

Still uncertain whether she'd actually knock on the door or not, Nikki got out of the car and walked to the gate. It was late, after ten and maybe Stevie had been able to grab some much-needed sleep. If so, Nikki didn't want to disturb her. The curtains were shut in the living room, but light escaped from the sides, telling Nikki that Stevie was probably still awake. Not surprising really. Nikki had been unable to sleep for weeks after Khalid had gone, the night times dragging more than the days. It was in the silent hours of the dead of night that the darkest most self-destructive thoughts could take hold. She pushed open the gate and walked down the path. She would tap lightly on the door and if Stevie didn't answer, then she'd go home and leave her be.

However, when she approached the porch door, it was open. She stepped into the box-sized space and noticed that the main door was ajar too. A spurt of adrenaline shot from her stomach to her heart. Why would Stevie leave the door open like that? Surely the FLO would have made sure the house was secure before leaving? On high alert, she glanced around her to see if anyone was in lurking in the shadows in the garden or in the street, but the area was deserted. She forced her anxiety down. So what if

Stevie had forgotten to shut the door? She was in shock after all. Her partner was critically ill in hospital and she was heavily pregnant, she was entitled to be a bit erratic. Even as she tried to convince herself that all was right, a nagging doubt persisted. Springer had been abducted . . . kept prisoner in a van, shot and narrowly escaped with her life. No way would Stevie not shut, lock and double lock her front door. Something was definitely off.

Taking out her phone, Nikki dialled. When it was answered, she spoke in a low tone.

'Saj, get here now. Springer's house. Suspected intruder. I'm going in.'

Then she hung up and dialled 999. 'This is DS Parekh, I need a back-up team right now, suspected home invasion.'

Listening to the despatcher's request for details, Nikki pushed open the door and peered into the hallway, whispering answers as she moved. The hallway light was on, a dim uplighter that cast what in happier circumstances might be described as a gentle ambient glow around the space. The coats, hanging on hooks along the wall, cast sinister shadows, but Nikki was focused on the carpet. *Oh shit!*

Ignoring the despatcher's insistent questions, Nikki stepped back, pulled the door shut a little and once more spoke in a whisper. 'Send an ambulance too. There's blood at the scene, and signs of a struggle. I'm going in.'

'No . . . No, protocol demands you wait for back up, DS Parekh. Officers are ten minutes out and I've just requested an ambulance. Please do not enter—'

Nikki interrupted her. 'Look, I'm going to put my phone in my pocket now. I won't disconnect the call, but I *am* entering the building.'

'No—'

'Look, just listen. You will be able to hear everything. I suggest you tell the units to get their lights flashing and get here. I'm going in.' She thrust her phone in her pocket.

Pushing open the door once more, she surveyed the scene. A small table near the bottom of the stairs had been upended, a vase of flowers spilled on the middle of a damp patch where its contents had absorbed into the carpet. A trail of blood stretched from the table further along the corridor towards the living room. Outside the living room door, larger stains had soaked into the carpet. On the wall, about a foot from the skirting board, was a bloody handprint. Nikki swallowed, trying to focus. The hammering of her heart increased – a thurrump thurrump thurrump – that reminded her of a countdown. Her training kicked in, brain focusing her. She needed to act.

Looking around her for a weapon, Nikki grimaced. Nothing. She backed into the porch and saw a large ceramic containing an assortment of brollies. She quickly rummaged through it. *For God's sake, doesn't everybody keep a baseball bat or at least a golf club by the front door?* She picked up a clear plastic brolly with colourful splotches on it and shrugged. In the absence of anything else, this would have to do. Its three-inch metal point was blunt, but it could still be effective with a bit of force behind it and Nikki would be sure to use force if necessary.

With her impromptu weapon grasped in both hands, Nikki entered the house, straining for any sounds of movement. The first thing she heard was a low moaning. She paused and, head on one side, listened again. There it was. This time she discerned it was coming from the front room. Okay. She took a deep breath. She should call out a warning. Indicate her presence and, if back-up was here, that's exactly what she would do, but bearing in mind the level of violence used by the people she suspected were the cause of the blood smears in Stevie and Springer's home, she felt that would give them an unfair advantage.

Sticking to the edge of the carpet, she tiptoed forward, pausing at the bottom of the stairs. The upstairs lights were all off and that helped her decide to clear the downstairs area first. The moaning was louder now, but Nikki swallowed her instinct to go into the living room first. It could be a trap and she couldn't help Stevie if she too was caught. Instead, she crept past the living room and into the kitchen, umbrella held ready to whack anyone she came across. A quick glance told her it was empty.

Tense and alert, she retraced her steps and approached the stairs. Back against the wall, she climbed sideways, so she could, at a quick turn of the head see either the downstairs hallway or the upstairs one. At the top, she got her phone out of her pocket and activated the torch function, using the opportunity to whisper, 'I'm clearing the upstairs now,' for the benefit of the despatcher.

Using her hand to shield its glare, she did a quick survey of the upstairs rooms. Four doors, all slightly ajar. With a final glance downstairs, Nikki moved to the one on her left and pushed it open with her arm. It was a bathroom. Using the brolly, she swooshed the shower curtain to the side, and satisfied the room was empty, she pulled the light string, dropped her phone back into her pocket and leaving the door ajar, proceeded to the next room, glad of the light behind her. She had no sense that there was another presence upstairs, the air felt empty, unshifted. Still, she followed her plan and quickly cleared the other three rooms before heading back downstairs.

'Stevie?' Although convinced the intruders had left, Nikki kept her voice low. 'Stevie, I'm coming.'

Walking along the blood-spattered hallway, Nikki dreaded what she would see. The moans she'd heard earlier had stopped and she cursed herself. She should have gone to Stevie first . . . that's what she should have done. The living room door was half-open with another smear of blood on it near the bottom. Someone had dragged themselves into the room. Every nerve tingling, Nikki took her phone from her pocket and stepped through the doorway dreading what she was going to see. 'The house is empty – no assailant detected. Oh fuck!'

Dropping the phone, Nikki fell to her knees by Stevie's prone body.

'What is it? What has happened . . . are you in danger? DS Parekh . . .?' The tinny voice from her discarded phone echoed in the room.

Stunned, Nikki, her breath coming in wheezy rasps, tried to focus. She was kneeling in a pool of blood that seemed to be getting bigger by the second. 'Get the ambulance here now. I have a pregnant woman who is haemorrhaging. There's so much blood.'

'Is she breathing? Is the mother breathing?'

Nikki crawled frantically towards Stevie's upper body so she could check her pulse and her own heart nearly stopped. Half on her side, one of Stevie's arms was wrapped round something. She was unconscious but her chest was rising and falling slowly. 'Stevie's breathing – just – shit, what should I do? The baby's here. She's had the baby! She's holding it. What shall I do? Where's the sodding ambulance?'

'It's nearly there, DS Parekh, stay with me! It's two minutes out. What you need to do is check the baby's airways, check if it's breathing.'

Nikki crawled closer and gently lifted the baby. It felt limp, although it was still warm. Grabbing tissues from the coffee table, she dabbed at its face, clearing blood and mucus from its nose and mouth. 'I don't think it's breathing. It's not breathing. Tell me what to do. This baby can't die.' Aware that her voice was rising in panic, Nikki swallowed, took a deep breath and focused on the despatcher's calm voice.

'Lay baby on the floor. Raise its chin up and place two fingers on the centre of baby's chest, about an inch down from the nipple line. Got it?'

Nikki laid the inert bundle on the carpet and followed the despatcher's instructions. 'Yes, what now?'

'Just press firmly, but not too hard. I'll count with you. Are you ready?'

'I can't do this. What if I kill it . . . kill her? It's a girl . . . it's a bloody girl and I don't want to kill her.'

238

'You won't, but you need to try to save her. Start the compressions. With me now.

One . . . two . . . three . . . four.

One . . . two . . . three . . . four.

One . . . two . . .'

Nikki, tears streaming down her face, began to press. '. . . three . . . four.

One . . . two . . . three . . . four.

One . . . two . . . three . . . four.

One . . . two . . . three . . . four.'

Then, just as she registered sirens wailing and the flashing blue lights dancing through the curtains, the baby took a gulp of air and let out a cry. 'Did you hear that . . . did you fucking hear that?'

'Well done, DS Parekh! I'll let you go now. The ambulance is here. You are in good hands.

'But wait, what's your . . .?'

But the despatcher who'd talked her through had gone and the living room was filled with paramedics, hooking Stevie up to oxygen and drips and wrapping the baby in blankets and checking her vitals. Nikki got to her feet and wobbled, before an officer guided her to the couch. She was vaguely aware of someone coming in and declaring it a crime scene and demanding a CSI team. Nikki leaned back in the soft cushions and closed her eyes. When she opened them again, there were police officers all around her and CSIs swam in and out of focus, their voices hollow, their faces looming over her as they spoke senseless words. Then someone forced a mug of something warm into her hand and sat next to her. Saj. 'Drink. You're in shock.'

Nikki looked down at her hands holding the mug. They were still covered in blood. Stevie's blood. Stevie's baby's blood. Her breath started to speed up and focusing on the steam rising from the drink, she slowed it down.

One . . . two . . . three . . . four.

One . . . two . . . three . . . four.

One . . . two . . . three . . . four.

It wasn't till Saj took the drink from her and replaced it with a tissue that Nikki realized she was crying. Shit . . . she rarely cried. She lowered her head and scrubbed her face. *Get a grip Nikki, Get a damn grip!* Someone had placed a blanket round her shoulders, an incongruous fleecy one with pink unicorns all over it – and she was shaking – huge spasms wracked her body. It was the aftershocks of the adrenaline rush. She knew that, but that didn't help. She wanted the fuzzy cotton wool in her head to dissipate. She needed to focus. With a shaking hand, she reached over and retrieved the cup from the coffee table where Saj had placed it. Ignoring his low soothing tones, she lifted the drink to her lips and breathed in its sugary sweetness. For a second she thought she was going to heave, but she forced herself to sip. Tea. Ghastly and only lukewarm now. Still, the sugar would do her good, so after her stomach had accepted the first sip without complaint, she forced herself to take more sips and gradually, the shivering abated and her thoughts became clearer.

'Do you know what happened Nik? Why were you here?'

Nikki exhaled. The scene she'd arrived in told two possible stories. The trouble was she didn't know which narrative fitted best. Had the stress of Springer's abduction and critical state sent Stevie into early labour? Had she crawled her way along the corridor after opening the front door in order to get help, but collapsed? Or – and Nikki wished this last thought didn't niggle quite so loudly – had she opened the door to someone who'd beaten her, pushed her over and left her bleeding out, causing her to go into early labour?

She stood up, and leaving the blanket on the couch, she walked to the doorway and poked her head out. How long had she been sitting like a wreck on the sofa? The crime scene investigators were nearly done, so it must have been over an hour . . . more than an hour since she'd pushed life back into Springer and Stevie's baby.

One . . . two . . . three . . . four.

One . . . two . . . three . . . four. Its little chest moving, it's face screwed up, covered in mucus, the cord still attached. One . . . two . . . three . . . four. One . . . two . . . three . . . four.

She walked back along the hallway, past every numbered marker, every surface covered with grey printing powder. She stopped at every blood drop and smear, the upturned table near the door, the bloody handprints and factored in the bruises on Stevie's face, the cut by her lip . . . the blood.

Saj, trailing her, his eyes clouded with worry, repeated his earlier question. 'Do you know what happened here?'

We should have kept her safe . . . I should have kept her safe. She exhaled. 'No . . . No idea . . . we'll have to wait till she comes round . . .'

She left the words '*if* she comes round' unsaid, but the way Saj glanced down at the floor, avoiding her gaze, told her that he too doubted they'd ever get Stevie's story.

Chapter 43

Saj had phoned Langley to drive over to Eccleshill. He was worried stiff about Nikki. He'd never seen her quite as disorientated and he wasn't about to let her drive home on her own. Marcus would kill him if he did. Why the hell did she decide to head over to Stevie's on her own? He'd have gone with her if she'd asked. Mind you, it was just as well she had, otherwise Stevie and Baby Springer would both be dead rather than occupying space in the neo-natal unit and CCU. Was this nightmare ever going to end?

When Langley arrived, Saj was too concerned about Nikki to worry about what anyone else would think and gave him a quick hug. Langley's reassuring presence calmed him. 'She's in a bad way, Lang. You okay to drive her poxy car over to Listerhills? I'll take her in mine and we can pick yours up later.'

Langley cast a glance at Nikki's blood-soaked jeans and bloody hands and quirked an eyebrow. 'You sure you want to take her in your car, Saj?'

'Heated seats. She loves the heated seats. She's shivering.' He handed his partner Nikki's car keys and gently guided Nikki into the passenger seat, wishing she wasn't so compliant. Wishing she'd snap at him and tease him about getting blood on his posh seats.

Halfway there, Nikki exhaled and stretching out her hand,

she squeezed Sajid's arm. 'You're a good mate Saj, but don't you ever tell anyone the state I was in tonight, eh? I've got standards to live up to.'

Relief flooded through him. Parekh was back. 'Depends really, I think my silence is worth a month of cakes at the very least.'

Nikki snorted. 'Two weeks tops, take it or leave it.'

She might still be pale but her spirit was certainly returning. Saj pulled up outside her house and almost before he had the chance to pull the brake on, Marcus was at the passenger door, helping her out.

'Get off. I'm okay. Not a bloody scratch on me.'

Marcus glanced at Saj who gave a discreet nod. 'She's uninjured . . . and she's a hero. Saved a baby tonight. Gave it chest compressions to keep it alive.'

She shrugged. 'All in a day's work, you know?' Then as a yawn escaped, she looked at Marcus. 'You gonna run me a bath, I'm dead on my feet.' She turned to Saj. 'We'll start at half eight tomorrow, yeah? We could both do with a decent night's kip. It's been a long, long day and I need my full eight hours tonight.'

Blowing a kiss to Langley who handed her car keys to Marcus, she walked up the steps to her house, Marcus beside her.

'She's a trooper, isn't she?'

Saj nodded. 'Yeah, she is. Frustrating, annoyingly irritating, but definitely a trooper. Come on. I want my full eight hours' kip too. I think I deserve it.'

Chapter 44

'Eh, Nik?'

Now that Saj and Langley had gone, Nikki leaned into Marcus, allowing him to help her up the steps to the front door. Although she wouldn't admit it, her knees were shaking and she was dog-tired. 'Mmm?'

'Hate to do this to you, but we've got a visitor.'

A groan escaped Nikki's lips. Bloody hell – really? A visitor at this time of night? Then it clicked. 'Anika?'

''Fraid so. She's in a state. In the end I told Haqib to kip in Sunni's room. Told him I'd deal with her. I did try to get rid of her but you know what she's like.'

Nikki did know what her sister was like. A bloody nightmare, that's what she was like. 'I can't cope with her tonight. Any other time, just not tonight.' And in a rare moment of frankness she looked up at Marcus. 'I'm shattered. I just can't do Anika tonight.'

Marcus hugged her close. 'You go straight upstairs, have a shower and get cleaned up. Think those jeans need to be binned. I'll try and get rid of her and I'll make you a nice milky drink to help you sleep. That *elaichi doodh* your mum makes.'

Nicky cupped his cheek with her palm. Warm, sweet cardamom and saffron milk was her mum's go-to comfort drink and it was cute to hear Marcus use the Gujarati words. 'Love you. I don't say it enough, but I do.' With a rueful smile, she sighed. 'I'll shower and then come downstairs. She won't go till she's ranted on to me, anyway. Might as well get it over with whilst I'm drinking my milk.'

Ten minutes later, snuggled in her hooded warm dressing gown, thick socks on her feet, Nikki straightened her spine and walked into the living room. Her sister was huddled into the armchair nearest to the fire, her legs folded under her, a pile of used tissues was scrunched up on her knees. Her eyes were red and her fingers shredded a tissue as she peered listlessly at the stove. Marcus must have lit it earlier and Nikki was glad of the warmth. The lights were dim and one of the candles Charlie had taken to lighting of an evening emitted a light floral fragrance. A few of Sunni's Xbox games were scattered in front of the telly and a scattering of nail varnish bottles on the coffee table alongside one of those nail dryer things told her Charlie had been experimenting on Ruby again.

Everything seemed so normal after the bloodbath that she had witnessed at Stevie and Springer's home earlier that evening and she was thankful. Even Anika bundled up looking sorry for herself was normality for Nikki. Shuffling over, Nikki dropped onto the sofa opposite her sister and pulled a fleece throw over her legs, just as Marcus walked through from the kitchen carrying a tray with three steaming mugs on it. She smiled her thanks at him as he handed her one before placing Anika's on the small table next to her and settling himself onto the couch beside Nikki.

'Want to tell me what's up, Ani?'

Tears began to roll down Anika's cheeks and she grabbed a handful of tissues from the box beside her and scrubbed them away. 'It's Yousaf.'

Nikki resisted making a smart-ass comment, contenting herself with throwing a meaningful glance in Marcus's direction before waiting for Anika to continue.

'I told him all about Haqib and that girl. That Glass girl. Little

245

whore that she is. And all he said was, he was "busy". Too busy to help me with his son. Too busy to talk to Haqib.'

But not too busy to turn up for a booty call! Nikki scowled but refrained from saying anything. She'd learned the hard way that pointing Yousaf's failings out to her sister was a complete waste of time. She'd tried, her mum had tried and even Marcus had tried. Instead, she sipped her *elaichi doodh*, savouring its sweetness.

Anika sniffed and looked over at Nikki. 'Thing is, with that toe-rag of a brother dead, who knows what'll happen? The little bitch will be putting my Haqib in danger and he won't listen to me. Says he's in love. For goodness' sake. In love! With a little slag like her. Can you believe it?'

Now wasn't the time to reveal that she was already aware of Haqib's Shakespearean love story. 'How did you know Glass is dead? Has it hit the news?'

Anika shrugged. 'Haqib brought the slag round to the house, asking if she could stay at ours because your lot were all over her house.' She glowered at Nikki as if this was her fault.

Nikki sighed and took another sip of milk. No way was she going to allow her sister to get a rise out of her. She was too knackered for that. 'Take it you sent her on her way?'

'Course I did. I've got standards. Don't want a racist little scumbag in my house, do I?'

Nikki exchanged another glance with Marcus, whose twitching lips told her he was thinking the same thing she was; Ani might not want racists in her house, but she wasn't averse to slimy, cheating councillors sharing her bed, ones who wouldn't even take responsibility for their own son.

'So, Yousaf?'

'I know he's busy. I know he has responsibilities and I know his wife is an unreasonable bitch but . . . I just wish he'd put us first sometimes.'

Draining her mug, Nikki yawned and placed it on the table. 'Yeah, would be good if he did that, right enough.'

Ani glared at her. 'You hate him, don't you? You always have. You just don't understand the pressure he's under.'

Nikki lifted both hands and rubbed her eyes. 'Not now, Ani. I've had enough for one night, okay? I'll talk to you tomorrow.'

Jumping to her feet, Anika towered over her. 'That's so typical of you, Nikki. Selfish to the core. Always thinking of yourself . . . you're a complete bi—'

Marcus was on his feet, voice raised. 'Stop right there, Ani. Don't you dare say another word. It's time for you to leave. We'll talk about this tomorrow, but you need to start dealing with Yousaf on your own instead of letting him walk all over you.'

Ani opened her mouth to speak, but Marcus, eyes sparking, shook his head. 'Go home. Go home now.'

With a dramatic flounce, Anika slammed out of the house, leaving Nikki and Marcus alone in the living room.

'Well, that went well,' said Nikki scrambling to her feet. 'Let's lock up and get to bed. I've had enough drama for one night.'

'You want to talk about Springer's baby?'

'Tomorrow. All I want to do is sleep.'

TUESDAY 17TH MARCH 2020

Chapter 45

A moment after he regained consciousness, Stefan was gripped by panic. He couldn't move his body . . . his legs . . . his arms. He was completely immobile. When it finally registered that for the first time since his beating, he wasn't in pain, he had the surreal thought that he'd died and was in heaven. Then reality sunk in . . . he wouldn't be in heaven. Not after what he'd done. He'd be in hell and this didn't feel like hell.

He listened to the regular beeps that came from somewhere to his right and smelled the distinct disinfectant smell. Could he be in a hospital? He remembered two figures holding him down. Had they been dressed in green . . . in uniforms? Were they paramedics?

He opened his eyes. The lights had been dimmed and only moonlight filtered through the closed blinds. It was the middle of the night. How long had he been unconscious for? He lifted his head, but it pounded, so he lowered it to the pillow, glad of its softness. He was in a room with another three beds. The two opposite appeared to have people in them and a light snoring to his left told him the third bed was also occupied.

A fuzzy thought that he had to speak to someone – tell someone something – something important – nagged at him. Denis? Was it something to do with Denis? It was fading now – drifting just out of reach and for the first time in months, Stefan Marcovici felt safe as he drifted back into unconsciousness.

Chapter 46

'You're drooling.'

The words were accompanied by a nudge to the ribs. *What the hell is Saj doing in my bedroom?*

'Wake up, Nik. We're nearly there.'

Nikki groaned as it all came back to her. The call at 2 a.m., her forcing herself out of bed, downstairs, out of the house and all but falling into Saj's car. Her body ached with the desire to go to sleep. Saj's damn heated seats had seduced her and now, as she blinked, her eyes gritty and her head pounding, she wanted nothing more than to remain precisely where she was. Whatever awaited them when they reached their destination was not going to be pleasant. Surreptitiously wiping her mouth with the back of her hand, Nikki straightened in her seat and looked around her, trying to place where they were. 'Wasn't sleeping. Just resting my eyes . . . thinking, you know? That thing you never do very much of.'

'You were snoring. Like a bloody Dyson hoover gone rogue!' And he gave a fair rendition of an asthmatic vacuum cleaner.

Choosing to rise above his nonsense, Nikki stifled her grin and instead looked out the window. Sleet hammered in near horizontal lines obscuring her vision, but she recognized the turn-off from the A65 onto Addingham Main Street. In the summer, she and

Marcus had driven this way a few times with the kids to visit Bolton Abbey. She risked a glance at her watch – two-fifteen in the bloody morning. Sleet. Eerie moonlight. And an anonymous call to Trafalgar House, specifically asking for her and leading them on what she had initially hoped would be a wild goose chase. However, the first responders had knocked that hope into touch.

'Got to be linked to Glass and Maria Marcovici and maybe even Springer and Stevie, don't you think?'

Nikki did think that and it chilled her. The anonymous caller mentioned her by name; this had become even more personal and she didn't like it. Someone was playing games with human lives at her expense and that frightened her. It made her wonder just how far they would go to satiate their sick needs. Pinging the elastic band on her wrist, Nikki watched as Saj drove through Addingham and then veered off onto Long Riddings, a road that was bordered on both sides by acres of fields lined by huge trees. The road led only to a disused farmhouse that had already been checked over and was completely empty with no signs of recent use.

As the road veered to the right, Saj slowed down. The narrow lane was lined with police cars, CSI vans and was lit by a couple of spotlights. Much to Nikki's annoyance, Lisa Kane's jaunty little vehicle was positioned just in front of the outer cordon. 'Who the hell told that lot?'

'Apparently the same person who notified us.' Saj bumped onto the narrow grass verge and switched off the engine. 'Covered their tracks well though. Used a burner phone and voice distortion. They wanted to make a big deal of this, didn't they?'

'Hmm. Makes you wonder why though, doesn't it? They didn't exactly draw us a map to Glass or Springer, did they? So, what's changed? I don't like this, Saj. I don't like it one little bit.' She cracked open the door and closed it again as an icy blast hit her face. Taking a deep breath, she thrust it open once more, allowing a gust of cold air into the toasty interior and stepped out onto mushy snow-covered grass. Could this night get any worse?

Saj opened the driver's door and huddling into his thick coat, waited for Nikki to join him on the road. 'Now you've got the DI gig, you'll be able to invest in a proper winter coat.'

Nikki scowled. Any money she got from her temporary promotion would go on a service for her car and the kids with maybe a little left over to add to the leaky windows' fund. Head-down, she barged past Lisa Kane who was ready with her microphone and her thug of a photographer lurking behind snapping away. Nikki ducked under the outer cordon and signed herself and Saj in.

'What else do you *not* see?' Nikki's tone reflected her grumpiness and Saj smiled as he responded.

'CCTV?'

'That's right. There's no bloody CCTV here, but maybe there's some along Addingham Main Street.' She turned to the uniformed officer. 'Get someone on that. I want to see what vehicles could have diverted down this road before say one-thirty this morning.'

Gracie Fells headed up the lane towards them accompanied by two familiar figures.

'Looks like you made a good call with Williams and Anwar. To say they don't officially join the team for—' Saj looked at his watch '—another six hours, they're very keen.'

'Just the way I like them.' Nikki accepted a crime suit, gloves, face masks and bootees from the officer in charge of logging the crime scene activity. 'You extended the scene at the other end too?'

The officer nodded. 'Yeah. It's a dead end down there and we secured the farmhouse but we've got a couple of officers there just in case.'

By the time she'd struggled into her onesie, Gracie had reached them. 'You want to tell us what you got, Gracie?'

But Gracie was looking over their shoulders. 'For God's sake Saj, couldn't you have given your boyfriend a lift over here? You could have all come in the one car.'

Beside her, Nikki saw Sajid tense. His nostrils flared and with his breath turning to steam in the cold air, he looked like a bull ready to charge. Nikki darted a glance behind them and saw Langley walking towards the outer cordon. For fuck's sake. Gracie had just outed Saj. Her gaze swept the periphery. Lisa Kane was smirking, microphone at the ready, and already making her way towards Langley. Anwar and Williams studiously studied their feet pretending not to have heard Gracie's announcement whilst a group of CSIs and uniformed officers displayed no such inhibitions and openly gawped at Saj.

'Who the hell do you think you are, Gracie? The resident "outer"?' Nikki's voice came out in a hiss and Gracie flushed, her mouth falling open in a shocked 'O'.

'Shit, Saj. I thought everybody knew. It's so damn obvious to me. I mean you and Langley are great together. I thought you were just a bit distant at work for professional reasons. Didn't realize it wasn't common knowledge.'

Gracie shuffled from foot to foot, her distress evident in the tension around her mouth and the pleading glances she sent in Saj's direction.

Exhaling, Saj pulled the mask over his face and nodded. 'Forget it. It was bound to come out at some point. Just wish we'd been the ones to decide when.'

Satisfied that Saj wasn't about to knock Gracie flying, Nikki darted back towards Langley and all but dragged him under the cordon, signing him in double quick time and darting a 'back off' glare at Lisa Kane. Under her breath she brought Langley up to speed. 'Gracie just outed you and Saj. It'll be round the office in no time and what's worse is Kane, the bane of our lives, overheard.'

Langley's face paled as he glanced at Saj who offered a weak smile in return.

Taking control, Nikki clapped her hands together. 'Let's get this show on the road. Take us to our victim, Gracie.' She turned to Langley. 'Glad you could make it, Langley. By the sounds of it, seeing the body in situ might be beneficial.'

As the little troupe headed away from the cordon, Nikki jogged back. Stopping in front of Kane she glared at the woman. 'I know you won't hesitate to find some way to make mileage out of that little revelation, but here's the deal. You forget you ever heard it and I'll speak to you later on today, on the record. Fuck me over and I'll make sure you never get so much as a whisper of a scoop, okay?'

Kane took a moment to consider and then extended her leather gloved hand. 'Deal.'

Nikki glanced at the hand, then with a curt nod said 'Deal.' She left Kane's hand hanging and jogged back to catch up with her team.

By the time they'd walked down the lane, Nikki was drenched and frozen. The whole thing with Kane overhearing Gracie's unintentional outing had placed extra pressure on an already charged situation and nobody was speaking. Langley had waited till they were out of sight of the journalist and grabbed Saj's hand for a quick squeeze. Nikki's relief when Saj returned the gesture with a tight grin was almost palpable. About two hundred yards from the initial cordon, Gracie stopped and gestured to a gap in the foliage to her left. Through the gap, drifted the sounds of the CSIs at work and the beams of the powerful lights that had been set up for the CSIs to work the scene properly. 'We've been accessing the area through here, although the actual entry spot was a bit further on. We wanted to preserve it and I've got some of my team working on that area now.'

Following Gracie, they squeezed through the gap in single file and followed the treads laid by Gracie's team towards a crime scene tent that had been erected about three hundred yards over the field.

As she walked towards the tent, Nikki looked at the ground around her. 'Footprints?'

'None worthwhile. The ground is too mucky after all the recent rainfall to hold decent prints and, with the addition of the sleet, we've not been able to obtain any conclusive tread marks.'

'So, who do we have in the tent?' Nikki was getting a little pissed off with Gracie's insistence that they view the body for themselves. Her secrecy was bordering on coyness and with her earlier faux pas with Saj and Langley, Nikki was in no mood to put up with her dramatics.

'You're nearly there. Just see for yourself.' She branched off on a set of treads that led towards a group of her team, leaving the four detectives and Langley on their own.

Nikki moved forward muttering under her breath about 'loose tongues' and 'consequences'.

Saj laughed. The sound reverberating in the artificial eeriness of the field. Nikki turned around and looked at him. 'You bloody losing it, Malik?'

He shook his head. 'No. Just thinking that only I could be outed by a woman in a bunny suit in the middle of nowhere with the most vicious journo in the region within earshot and Mr Camera-always-ready Ashton in sight. Okay, it wasn't how I wanted to do it, but it's done and there's nothing we can do about it. I couldn't go on . . .' He briefly brushed Langley's upper arm. 'We couldn't go on like this forever. I'll just have to man up and face the consequences.'

Pleased to see Saj taking such a positive slant on things, Nikki snorted. 'Right then. Now we've sorted out your personal dilemma, do you think we can focus on the victim?'

When she pulled the door open and stepped inside, moving round the treads that were placed around the periphery of the tent to allow 360-degree access, Nikki understood why Gracie wanted her to see the victim with fresh eyes. After the first blast of bleach that made her stomach churn, Nikki took slow breaths through her mouth and directed her thoughts towards the body. The victim was male, probably no more than early twenties, if that. He was naked, and had been hog-tied and gagged. She could see that his blood had begun to pool where his stomach touched the ground. She expected Langley to confirm that he'd either been left here to die or had been positioned here shortly after death. His body was a mass of bruises and cuts. So many that it was difficult to see where one ended and another began.

'May I?' Langley had waited, allowing them time to view the body, but now he wanted to get closer.

Nikki nodded. The waste of a young life was always upsetting, but to see one so deliberately tortured and punished was just evil. The desire of some humans to cause maximum pain for their own enjoyment was nothing new to Nikki. She'd spent the first years of her life living with someone like that, but she'd never grow used to it. Never stopped being upset by it. Never stopped fighting against it. For if there was one thing she knew, it was that those sorts of people would never stop unless someone stronger made them. Inflicting pain was their raison d'etre.

'Apart from the bleach, there is evidence of multiple canine bites which links to the other bodies I've PM'd. The torture is similar and I'm getting faint whiffs of dog faeces. I suspect that when I swab his feet we'll find traces.'

'If they've used bleach how will you be able to get traces of the doggie poop?'

Williams' question was valid and Langley smiled at him. 'I think it's squished between his toes. I reckon they tortured him in the same place their doggies had their toilet.' He turned to Nikki. 'Whoever's doing this is a sick fucker. If the CSIs are done with him, I'd like to get him back. I'll start the PM as soon as possible. This bastard needs to be stopped and I'll do what I can to help.'

Nikki nodded and then grimaced as both her and Saj's phones started to ring at the same time. *What now?*

'Yeah?' Nikki caught Saj's eye as they both listened to their caller.

Nikki hung up and turned to Williams and Anwar. 'Make sure this scene is airtight, get the body expedited to the morgue for Dr Langley and then when that's done you can meet us at the next crime scene.'

'What?' Williams' surprise was echoed in Anwar's expression.

Expression grim, Saj said. "Yep, looks like we've got a BOGOF tonight.'

Williams' eyebrows drew together. 'BOGOF?'

Hitting him on the arm, Anwar snorted. 'Buy one get one free.'

Nikki was already heading from the tent. Another anonymous tip off. Another body. A team of CSIs are heading there and the first responders are nearly there. I'll text you. Langley, you coming?'

Langley jumped to his feet. 'Yep. Count me in. Sleep's overrated anyway.'

Nikki yawned. She wasn't sure about that, but maybe a catnap snuggled in Saj's car would be enough to refuel her for a bit. It seemed like days ago that she'd been pressing life into Stevie and Springer's baby, but it had only been a few hours and here she was with another two victims on her plate. Would this night ever end?

Chapter 47

Nikki, unable to get the vision of the hog-tied boy out of her mind, couldn't even snatch a few minutes sleep on the way to the new crime scene. Every time her gritty eyes drifted shut, they jerked open again straight away. This scene, like the scene in Denholme the other night, would be one of the ones that stayed with her for a long time. The lad had looked only a few years older than Charlie and Haqib and, perhaps it was her bone-aching tiredness or maybe she was going soft, but she found it hard to dissociate herself from these scenes. It had been the same with Stevie and the baby. Before she'd been wakened, her sleep had been fitful as she tossed and turned, relaying her actions over and over, wishing she'd gone straight to Stevie and not cleared the rest of the house first; after all, rules were there to be broken – sometimes. If she took the time to analyse it, Nikki suspected she'd find that this newfound sensitivity was all to do with finding out the truth about her dead husband, Khalid, last year. That and the close shave her family had survived with a serial killer.

Staring at the mesmerizing swirling sleet, Nikki wondered what the hell was going on in Bradford. She suspected that the positioning of the body of the young man, displayed so emotion-lessly in Addingham, just inside the Bradford district, followed by this new body near the Ponden Reservoir, again just within the district's boundaries, was no accident. Whoever had orchestrated this was playing with them and Nikki wasn't about to let them get away with it. 'This is really fucked up, isn't it, Saj?'

'Funny you should say that; I was just thinking that myself. Two bodies, miles apart, reported anonymously within a couple of hours of each other with your name mentioned. That's not even mentioning the leak to Kane and her sidekick. No coincidence.'

Nikki glanced at her phone, willing it to ring. She'd prefer to have a bit of a heads-up before they reached the scene, but it was unlikely the first responders and the CSIs would have had time yet. 'They're spreading us thinly, aren't they? Forcing us to stretch our already over-extended resources. They must have something else in mind. Something explosive.'

At that point her phone rang, eliciting a groan from Nikki. 'It's the DCS.'

'Well, you better jump to it. You're the DI, after all, and Archie will be sleeping like a baby up at BRI, so you're the one in the hotseat.'

Shit. She'd forgotten she was DI. In Archie's absence she should have been keeping the DCS up to date on this. Now, as well as having a banging headache, she was going to have to endure the acerbic tongue-lashing of DCS Clark. She pressed *answer* and immediately held the phone away from her ear.

The DCS's voice wasn't loud but it was assertive and it was certainly unhappy. 'I had reservations about offering you even a temporary promotion, but DCI Hegley assured me you would be up to the task. However, it seems that even the most basic of routine communications to your line manager is beyond you.'

Ignoring Saj, who had taken his hand off the steering wheel to mimic a hanging, Nikki took a deep breath and modified her tone. 'Excuse me, ma'am. I was just on the point of contacting you . . .' She threw a 'shut up' look at Saj who'd snorted just a little too loudly. 'Perhaps you're unaware but the Addingham crime scene was very rural and as such had no phone signal. We've had to use the police radio for communication purposes. DC Malik and I are en-route to the second crime scene but, I'd like you to be aware, that the signal there is likely to be patchy too. I suspect that's exactly why our perpetrator selected these two areas. Shall I update you before I lose the signal again?'

Seemingly mollified, DCS Clark agreed and Nikki spent the next five minutes updating her, ending with reassurances that she would keep her apprised of developments where possible. Hanging up, she exhaled. Her headache was worse, but she'd survived her first run-in with Clark.

'Dodged a bullet there, Nik.'

'Yeah, but there's only so many bullets I can dodge. Hope Archie gets back to work ASAP.'

Saj stopped at a junction on the A629 and indicated right. 'Scar Top Road. How apt.'

Despite the heat in the vehicle, Nikki shivered. 'Ominous indeed. Look, there's the outer cordon. We're going to be popular, blocking off this road for the foreseeable future.'

Up ahead, a couple of police cars and a CSI van blocked the road. Nikki presumed they'd taken similar action beyond the crime scene in the other direction. 'Again, a lack of CCTV once you leave the main A road and what's the odds that whoever dumped this body used the back roads?'

They got out of the Jaguar amidst whirling sleet and Nikki shuddered. Her boots hadn't dried out from the Addingham scene and every step she took reminded her of how sodden her socks were. As they approached the cordon, monitored by a uniformed officer and signed themselves in, a white-suited CSI approached.

'Hi, I'm the crime scene manager, Carter. Pleased to meet you, DS Parekh. Gracie told me you were heading this way. We're short-staffed. I'm not even supposed to be on call tonight, but what with the other scene in Addingham and the incident at the farmhouse, we're really stretched.'

Not sure if Carter was his first name or surname and too knackered to care, Nikki looked round at the two police cars and the four officers that were drifting around taking notes and speaking to the other two CSIs. 'Tell me about it. We're all stretched. I take it it's too much to hope it was a prank call?'

''Fraid so. Suit up and I'll take you down. We've erected a tent and put some treads down, but to be honest, I'm not sure what evidence we'll be able to pick up. It's a quagmire down there.'

Even the cold wasn't enough to stop Nikki from yawning as she donned the coveralls. She suspected that if she didn't keep moving, she'd fall asleep standing upright. Saj looked nearly as tired as she did, but his face lit up when Langley approached. With two bodies to post-mortem, Langley took the rare opportunity to see both in situ before heading back to the hospital. After Langley was suited up, the three of them followed Carter along the glistening main road. The strong CSI lights from behind the roadside bushes gave their surroundings a ghostly aura.

A couple of hundred yards along, a small track, barely wide enough for a Range Rover, let alone a transit van, veered off over a bridge that spanned the reservoir.

'Nothing much up there. Just an arts centre further up that road, but it's been closed since 5 p.m.'

Nikki looked around, hoping that a business may have installed some security cameras, but there was nothing. If the lights from the crime scene hadn't been on, visibility in the area would be poor. They stuck to the treads, positioned to the side of the bridge. 'Do you reckon they drove over this bridge?'

Carter nodded. 'Almost certainly. They wouldn't want to risk being seen if they parked up on the main road, I don't think, and there's enough space for them to turn their vehicle round here.'

They'd reached the end of the track and Nikki realized that the action was down the side of a shallow embankment, leading to the reservoir. The smell of vegetation vied with the crisp freshness of the cold as they scrambled down the edge, well away from the area already marked out by Carter's team that showed where the body had been carried from.

Carter led them over to a tent and pulled the flap open allowing them entry. 'It's not a pretty sight, DS Parekh. However, if you just stick to the treads, you won't contaminate anything.'

The first thing Nikki noticed, perhaps because she was expecting it and had braced herself for it, was the bleach smell. The second was the boy, again hog-tied and naked, his head pulled back by the rope that bound his neck to his feet, his mouth filled with something. 'Shit, they're either twins or brothers.'

Her fingers fluttered to her neck, stroking her scar. The cold and her nitrile gloves made it impossible to feel its roughness, disorientating her for a second. She inhaled, allowing her hands to fall to her sides. 'There's no point us being here, Saj. This is a distraction. We need to get back to Bradford. Need to find out what's going on there. Williams and Anwar can keep an eye on things here when they arrive.'

Leaving Langley behind to wait for a chance to view the body more closely in situ, Sajid and Nikki retraced their steps, stumbling slightly on the slippery slope. Neither felt the need to joke about it this time. Too many people were being hurt and they hadn't got a proper handle on things. When they reached the bridge, a voice from further along made Nikki jump.

'Well, well, well, if it isn't DS Parekh and her little sidekick. Fancy seeing you twice in the one day. How lucky are you?'

Nikki groaned inwardly. What the hell was Joe Drummond doing here? Maintaining a neutral expression, Nikki ignored his comment and instead said, 'My crime scene Joe. You're gonna have to shift it back up to the outer cordon.'

'I'd have thought you'd have been begging for my help, Parekh. You must be knackered after the evening you've had playing midwife with Springer's lesbo bint and now two fresh crime scenes.' He laughed. 'What am I talking about? You've had more bodies over the past couple of days than I've had sex . . . and you know how often I get my leg over.'

How the hell did Drummond know about Stevie and Springer's

baby? Never mind that, how did he know personal details about the pair of them? It wasn't common knowledge, yet he knew. She exchanged a glance with Saj, who looked like he'd happily throttle Drummond and the two of them walked towards him, forcing him to back up.

'Come on, let's get you back where you belong, out of my crime scene, eh?' Nikki kept her voice pleasant and with a shrug Drummond acquiesced.

By the time they reached Scar Top Road, reinforcements in the form of Williams and Anwar and another CSI team had arrived. With her luck, there had to be a downside too. Nikki growled under her breath when she saw Lisa Kane and Max Ashton. Presumably their anonymous caller had been true to form and notified Kane too. Never mind, Nikki would enjoy annoying the woman with her 'no comment'. Her phone rang and expecting it to be Clark again, desperate for another update, Nikki nearly ignored it, but when she realized it was the phone Ali had given her, she decided to take it. Signalling to Saj to escort Drummond away, she turned her back on them and answered. 'Hi Ali, you're phoning early. It's not even half four yet. You got something juicy for me?'

'Hmm, you could say. There's a lot of activity in Bradford. A lot of clearing things up. A couple of businesses shutting down but loads more opening up . . . and I'm not talking the legal sort. My drivers are telling me that as well as the big new knocking shop on Thornton Road, with thirty girls on stand-by twenty-four-seven, there's another one opened near one of the mills in Manningham and another in West Bowling. One of my drivers picked up a girl who'd been beaten. He dropped her at BRI, but she told him her pimp had left Bradford and that she'd been told she had to pay his debt off. When she was better, she was to contact some thug called Bullet.'

Bullet? The name wasn't familiar to Nikki, maybe he was new to the city. 'Have you heard of this Bullet before, Ali?'

'Nah. I'm assuming he's part of the new sweep. My lads will

keep their ears open on this one, Nik. We don't like this sort of crap happening on our doorsteps.'

'Where the hell are they getting so many women?' And more to the point, how many pervs were out there living normal lives, yet not thinking twice about treating these women like rubbish. If there was one thing Nikki knew about the prostitution trade, it was that it relied on the laws of supply and demand . . . and that sickened her.

'My guess is people-trafficking. Eastern Europeans. That's what Haris was told.' Ali's voice was full of disgust and Nikki could imagine the anger lines marring his features. His expression was probably pretty similar to hers. Haris was Ali's cousin and he had his own network for gaining information. If he didn't have a handle on this Bullet character, then that indicated that the new gang were even deeper underground than she would have expected. That thought made her uneasy as it implied someone with some sort of inside knowledge of how the city's gangs worked. Someone with enough nous to operate under their noses without leaving any tracks . . . someone who wouldn't arouse any suspicion. 'Haris know who's behind it?'

'Nah, he's pissed that his network's holding out on him. They're running scared. There's been too many messages left . . . too many bodies, so nobody will step out of line.'

Nikki understood that. She'd seen two of those messages tonight and then there was also Maria Marcovici, Adam Glass, Springer and Stevie. She had a feeling that if she didn't get ahead of this, things were going to get much worse and quickly too. Ali's mention of other businesses was intriguing. Just how far-reaching was the criminal hold on her city? 'What other businesses, Ali?'

'Underground, unregulated gambling venues. Drug distribution centres. It's like whoever's behind it has built up their workforce and are now ready to freeze out the low-level pimps and dealers. Haris said that your lot had shown too much attention to that halal chicken factory on Thornton Road and now it's shut down.'

Nikki frowned. 'You sure Ali? It was open just last night.'

'Yeah well, according to the guy Haris picked up, it's shut now. Something kicked off the other night and now it's shut. Look, got to go Nikki. My bed's calling for me, it's been a long night. I'll keep my ears open and keep you informed, okay? But be on high alert. Something's gonna kick off. If not tonight, then tomorrow night or the night after. Whoever's behind all of this shit, they're tightening the vice.'

Ali's talk of bed elicited an involuntary yawn from Nikki as she took a moment with her own thoughts. This all added up to something huge. The only trouble was, she wasn't entirely sure how, or who was behind it and right now, her brain wasn't functioning. Logic told her that with sunrise only an hour or so away, nothing else would kick off tonight. So, she should update Saj and they should try to recharge their batteries for a couple of hours before the morning briefing, at half nine. After that, she had to meet this woman, Jackie Dobson, to find out more about the high-profile rapist and find time to check in on Archie, Springer and Stevie. At least the three of them were under the one roof, so that would make things easier for her.

On the drive back to her house, Nikki first updated DCS Clark and then Sajid. They spent the rest of the journey trying to get their head round things. 'You heard of this guy Bullet?'

Saj shook his head, 'No. Maybe you should run it by Drummond, see if anyone on his team knows anything about it.'

'Hmm. Not sure I want to. He's not playing it straight with us. And I'm a bit suspicious about where he's getting his information. He seems a bit too interested in my investigations and knows a lot more than he should.'

Saj parked up outside Nikki's house. 'Yep. I think you're right, Nikki. Tomorrow's another day. Surely we'll get something to move us forward after we've had a couple of hours.'

'Tomorrow is today though Saj, tomorrow is today.' She got out and looked up at the house. Marcus had left the light on for her and as she walked to the door, her entire body protesting at the effort, she smiled. It was good to be home.

Chapter 48

As soon as Xavier had realized it was Parekh leading up the investigation, he'd been pleased. She'd been a thorn in his side for a while now with her eye always on the estate and what was going on there. Publicly he'd had to interact with her and he found her rude and disrespectful. It made him happy to think that she would be the named officer when everything went tits-up for Bradford police.

Xavier had only been waiting for ten minutes for DS Nikki Parekh and her sidekick to turn up. He'd dragged himself from his mistress's bed just for the satisfaction of seeing how much strain his antics were placing on Parekh. It was bitterly cold, yet adrenaline seemed to give him inner warmth. His contact had informed him when she left the last crime scene and he was filled with the urge to see how much he'd broken her. Risky? Sure, but if she did happen to catch sight of him he was well wrapped up and he could blag his way out of almost anything. It was part of his job after all.

She looked like an old granny as she pulled herself out of the car and stood for a moment looking up at the light shining from her home. For a moment, she wobbled and Xavier's heart jumped. Would she fall over in the street? Was she *so* tired? But, as Malik drove off in his flashy Jag, she stepped forward, her gait unsteady, as if she was half asleep already. Xavier swallowed his disappointment. It would have been delightful to see Nikki Parekh on her arse in the snow, but it wouldn't be too long until he brought her down. He could wait. He was a patient man.

Poor Parekh, you've had a night of it, haven't you? No wonder she was dead on her feet. He'd seen to it that she'd had no reprise. That was the only way to wear your enemy down; Keep the pressure up, keep turning the screws, keep them guessing, unsure where they were or where to turn next. She'd be trying to link all the dead bodies and he wasn't about to make it any easier. He had big plans for her . . . huge plans to squeeze her till she popped. *If you feel pressure now, DS Nikita Parekh, then you are soon going to think today was a holiday at the seaside. For, as the weather gets colder, things are just going to keep right on hotting up for you and I'm not sure you're up to the challenge.*

Smiling, he watched as she tried a few times to insert her key in the lock. Stupid bitch didn't even dress for the inclement weather. No gloves, no scarf, no hood, no decent coat. She was a walking disaster area. No wonder she couldn't open the door. If he'd been so inclined, he could have taken her out there and then. She had no idea she was being observed. No idea just how vulnerable she was right now. In a heartbeat, he could snuff her out, or one of her brats or that layabout of a gardener boyfriend of hers, and she wouldn't even see him coming.

Finally, she got the door open and stumbled inside, slipping off her leather jacket before the door even closed behind her. He was going to enjoy taking her down . . . but only after he'd shown her just what a failure she was. Just after he'd flooded the streets with drugs . . . keep the cost low, get them hooked and then crank it up. That was his business model and he was sure it would work. Besides, he was diversifying. Gambling, drugs, whores – all the illicit stuff that people would pay over the odds for, but didn't want their families to know about. He kept his overheads low and raked in the money. Soon Bradford would have only one kingpin and Xavier would be it.

Today was the day they trimmed all the deadwood and planted it afresh. Parekh might have thought last night had been bad, but by the end of today, she'd be finished and he'd decided he was going to be the one to deliver the killing blow.

He pulled his coat collar up and began to walk back to where he'd parked his car. There was one loose end that niggled him and he wondered if it had been dealt with yet. He took out one of his phones and dialled. 'Cyclops? Has Bullet found him?'

'He's still looking, boss. I've expressed your annoyance to him in no uncertain terms and now his other jobs are out of the way, he's focusing on Marcovici.'

Bullet was becoming more of a liability than an asset. Letting Marcovici escape was a rookie mistake, but not discovering his escape for hours was unforgiveable. 'I want to be updated as soon as he has him.'

'He can't have gone far, boss. He was all but dead when he left him in the barn. I reckon he's crawled out and got covered in the sleet somewhere. He can't have survived these temperatures and he's got nothing on him to ID him. Nothing to link him back to us.'

'I hope you're right.'

'Sure I am. When am I ever wrong?'

Xavier laughed. Cyclops was a cocky bugger that was for sure. But Bullet's days were numbered in his operation. There were plenty of other willing lieutenants ready to take his place.

Chapter 49

Nikki was on the stairs when the doorbell rang 'I'll get it. It'll be Saj.'

She'd arranged for him to pick her up and so what if he was a little early. They could have a caffeine hit before heading into the station. Still tired and well aware of the bags that drooped under her eyes, she glanced at her watch. Eight forty-five. He was early, but he could join her for a coffee and some breakfast before they left for Trafalgar House. She could barely remember the last time she ate anything and the inside of her head had that fuzzy 'I need caffeine' buzz going on.

She swung the door open and froze as déjà vu drifted over her. When she didn't say anything, nor move back to allow Sajid access, Marcus yelled from the kitchen, 'Let him in then Nikki, you're freezing up the house.'

Nikki shook her head, hoping the last vestiges of fuzziness would dissipate and turn the person standing on her doorstep into her work partner Sajid. It didn't work, so instead she closed the door, turned and leaned on it, before sliding down, her feet crumpling up the small rug that covered the wooden floor as her bottom hit the surface.

Marcus, a frown tightening his forehead, took one look at her and strode through.

Before he had a chance to say anything, Nikki, shaking and pale, looked at him. 'Marcus?'

'What the hell's up? You're exhausted, that's what it is. You need a bit more sleep. Delay the briefing for a couple of hours.'

'It's not that.' She gestured to the spy hole in the door and Marcus leaned in and peered out at the person still standing on the doorstep.

'Aw . . . for f—' He cut off the sentence and put out a hand to pull Nikki to her feet.

'Why now, Marcus? Why fucking now, when I've got no time . . . or energy to deal with this?'

Marcus exhaled and then pulled her into his arms for a quick cuddle. 'There'd never be a good time for this, Nik. You know you have to let her in, don't you?'

Against his chest, Nikki snuffled. 'S'ppose so.'

'I'll be here though. You're not on your own.'

Nikki leaned away from him and trying out a tentative smile, nodded. 'Okay, let's do this.'

She turned around and once more pulled the door open. The woman standing on the step was tall, slim and elegant. She wore Western clothes that, even to Nikki's unpractised eyes, looked expensive. A scarf covered her hair and her chin was raised arrogantly, Nikki thought. Whilst her dead husband Khalid had shared features with his father, it seemed he also shared some with his mother; his sculpted cheekbones and the shape of his eyes. Nikki realized that the older woman's arrogant tilt of her chin was one that her own daughter Charlie sometimes adopted. However, in Charlie's case it was often a cover-up for uncertainty. It remained to be seen whether Charlie's grandmother possessed any uncertainty.

'You could have told us you were coming.' Nikki was aware her voice sounded petulant and it irked her. She had every right to be annoyed at having been given no notice of her ex-mother-in-law's visit, but she would have liked her tone to portray superior annoyance rather than childlike petulance.

273

'I was worried you might not let me see Aadab . . . Charlie, so I came unannounced. After all, you were less than keen to allow my husband to see his granddaughter, weren't you?'

'Your husband accused me of murdering Khalid. Are you going to do the same?'

Enaya Abadi's lips quirked. 'No, Nikita. I know you did not kill my son. I come in peace. All I have left is your daughter and I want to get to know her.'

Nikki studied her for a moment. 'Well, we'll need some ground rules then. The first is that my daughter's name is not Aadab. It is Charlie and you must call her that. The second is that before you see Charlie, she has to agree.'

Anaya's lips tightened but then with an abrupt nod she turned and began to go down the stairs to the path. 'Okay. Let me know when I can come back.'

Marcus nudged Nikki who waited till she'd reached the bottom step before saying, 'Charlie's gone to school already. You can come in for some tea, if you'd like.'

Slowly, Enaya turned back and a smile that was so similar to Charlie's broke out over her lips. 'Thank you, Nikita. I'd like that.'

Chapter 50

'Bitch. Absolute bitch!' All thoughts of Nikki's earlier encounter with Charlie's other grandmother had been driven from her mind when Sajid showed her the morning headlines from the *Yorkshire Enquirer*. Now, almost at Trafalgar House, she was still venting whilst Saj, knuckles white on the steering wheel, kept a stony silence.

Nikki flicked her phone on again and enlarged the image of Sajid and Langley, suit hoods down at the Addingham crime scene. Sajid and Langley were looking lovingly at each other, their fingers entwined. Nikki narrowed her eyes and tried to view the image impartially. Would other people see two men in a relationship or two colleagues offering mutual support? With a sigh, she scrolled up to the headline again and groaned. Lisa Kane had been clever with it; *Support amid the horror at the fourth Bradford murder crime scene.* She was worried. Saj had sent her the link and told her to open it, but otherwise had said nothing. A pulse at his temple throbbed and his face was tense, his eyes dull and dark with anger. 'Talk to me, Saj. What does Langley say about this? What does it mean for you?'

In a rare display of temper, Saj slammed his palm on the steering wheel. 'What the fuck do you think it means, Nik? I've already had my sister on the phone this morning.'

'Aw Saj, I'm so sorry.' This was one of those moments that Nikki wished Marcus was with her. He always knew exactly the right words to use, whilst all she wanted to do was curse and kick and punch – but that was Saj's prerogative, not hers. She had to support her friend. Cursing herself, Nikki wondered how much her recent run-ins with Kane had influenced the journalist's decision to use this headline rather than the meatier, more sensationalist ones headlining the other broadsheets. 'What did she say?'

'Never answered it. Don't need to hear the family's thoughts. Don't need guilt and shame and shit piled on. Not right now when we're in the middle of this.' He waved his hand in an all encapsulating gesture.

Conscious that he hadn't mentioned Langley in all of this, Nikki considered how to broach that subject again, then decided just to go for it. No point in pussyfooting around – that wasn't her style and Saj knew her well enough to sense that. 'Aw, come on. What about Langley. You've avoided mentioning him, so spit it out. Have you two argued over this malicious crap?'

Saj blushed, he lips tightening as he gave a tense nod. 'I yelled at him. Blamed him for touching me at the crime scene, said it'd be all his fault if the pair of us ended up with our balls chopped off and dumped in the canal where Adam Glass was found.'

Nikki closed her eyes for a moment before replying. 'Oh, so you handled it quite well then. Kept it real. That's good.' She cast a glance at her partner and smiled when his lips twitched. Saj would be okay and so would Langley. They'd work through this.

'I'm an idiot.' He pulled into the car park entrance, waited for the gates to open and drove through.

'Yeah, mostly, but I still like you. Send him a text before we go inside.'

When he pulled into a space, Nikki jumped out of the Jag, turned and poked her head back inside, 'Oh, and speak to your sister, eh? Do it soon before things spiral. Take it from me, delaying the hard conversations is never the best way forward. Look how much damage I did to my relationship with Charlie last year by not making the time to talk to her. See you inside in a bit.'

The first thing Nikki did on entering the incident room was to phone Charlie and leave a voicemail. No way was she going to repeat her mistakes from last year. Charlie needed to know her grandma was in town. She'd be in her second class of the day so wouldn't get her voicemail till break. She'd be shocked, but at least she'd know Nikki wasn't keeping secrets . . . not like last time. They could speak about it later, but she deserved to know right now. She turned her thoughts to the day ahead and wondered about Springer's little family. If there had been any marked change in her, Stevie or the baby or Archie's conditions she would have been notified. Still the urge to speak to someone was overwhelming and she wouldn't be able to concentrate on anything else until she'd been updated. As expected, there was little change in any of their conditions, which, so she was informed, was a good thing. Archie, on the other hand, was apparently being a 'royal pain in the ass'. This last piece of information raised her spirits a little and as Nikki plonked herself on the desk nearest to the investigation boards she smiled.

Williams and Anwar had been updating the boards when she arrived and now they had added photos of the two lads found overnight, with the limited details they had on them. She smiled her appreciation and looked at the congregated team. Most of them looked how she felt – knackered, disillusioned and angry. In addition to Sajid, Williams and Anwar, about fifteen uniformed officers sat around the room looking expectantly at her.

For a moment Nikki's throat became uncharacteristically dry. *What the hell?* She was more than familiar with these briefings, so why did the simple fact that she was now acting DI make her nervous? The one saving grace was that DCS Eva Clark hadn't appeared. Rumour had it, she was upstairs with the top brass, no doubt mouthing off about how they should give the SIO job to someone more competent than Nikki Parekh.

'Right, as you can see . . .' Nikki waved her hand at the boards, some of which had been pinched from other incident rooms and now took up almost the entire back wall. 'Things are escalating, we're stretched, the CSIs are stretched, we're all pulling double shifts and still we don't have much to go on. However, some intel came my way overnight and I need it looking into.' She explained about the illicit brothels, gambling facilities and drug production factories and the supposed takeover by some as-yet-unidentified kingpin. 'My source is reliable, so I'm inclined to follow this up. Clearly, Adam Glass was a known weapons and drugs distributer. Maria Marcovici fits the profile for being forced into prostitution and the two lads found last night were definitely execution-style killings. All the bodies are linked by four distinct forensic discoveries: Dog bites, traces of dog faeces present, the use of bleach as a forensic counter measure and of course the similarities in their prolonged torture prior to death.'

'In't this more summat for vice? I mean, they'll be able to get info from their snitches. Surely nowt much happens in Bradford without them knowing?'

Nikki exchanged a quick glance with Sajid before replying to the officer. 'Ordinarily I'd say yes, but I have reached out to my contacts and they are up to their ears in it. I want us to work our own contacts. Get our own intel on this. We can't rely on them. Like every department they're short-staffed.' She snorted her annoyance. 'Increased budgets isn't high on the top brass's wishlist. We're on our own on this.'

She nodded towards Saj. 'DC Malik will allocate jobs, but here are the main ones. I need a team to check out their contacts in West Bowling, Manningham and Thornton Road for any info on these brothels or on pimps who are being squeezed out by the new boss. Williams and Anwar will be on post-mortem duty. The halal chicken factory needs checking out pronto. I want owner and past employees interviewed. Need info about why it closed down and what kicked off the other night. We need information about any changes in drug distribution in the district – have the suppliers and or dealers changed, have prices and or quality altered . . . you know the sort of stuff. Also, Maria Marcovici's mother is flying in later today. I want a FLO allocated to her and I want to be with her when she IDs her daughter.'

The door barged open, slamming against the wall and reverberating there for a moment. Nikki jumped, sure it was Clark come to stick her oar in. Instead it was a uniformed officer holding his notebook and panting as if he'd taken the steps double-time. 'Sorry ma'am, my boss said to get this info to you straight away.'

A titter of laughter spread round the room and the officer's face flamed pillar-box-red. Nikki glared at the laughers, who shut up straight away, before turning back to the officer with a smile. 'Let's have it then.'

Straightening up, he held up his notebook and licking his index finger flipped over a few pages and cleared his throat. 'Got a callout to BRI last night. Paramedics had been called to a farmhouse in the Dales. The owners opened their door and found a badly beaten unconscious man on their doorstep. They got him inside, covered him in blankets and called the ambulance.'

From the corner of her eye, Nikki spotted Sajid's smirk and studiously avoided looking at him. She wished the officer would hurry up and get to the relevant bit, but he was nervous and the last thing she wanted to do was dent his confidence. To succeed in this job, you needed all the confidence you could muster

'He was taken to BRI unconscious and in a critical condition. He's had an operation to stop internal bleeding and to remove his spleen and he's got some sort of sepsis. Thing is, he came round for a short space of time an hour ago and one of the nurses got his name.'

A spasm of hope contracted Nikki's stomach. Could this be the breakthrough they'd been waiting for? She wanted to shake him to spit it out, but managed to contain herself and instead offered a tight smile. 'Go on.'

'Stefan Marcovici. Soon as my boss heard the name, he connected it to the BOLO issued by your team and sent me up here.'

Thank God for that! They needed a break in the case. Shame it hadn't come to her attention last night, but to be fair, she had been otherwise occupied, first with Stevie and her baby, then the two crime scenes at Ponden Reservoir and Addingham. Despite wanting to jump up and high-five the young officer, Nikki remained perched on the desk, limiting herself to a grin and a, 'Well done. Tell your boss I owe him a coffee. Now, what else can you tell me about the incident?'

'A CSI team was sent up to the farmhouse to see if they could get anything last night to tell us where he'd appeared from, but the conditions were too bad and the paramedics and the old couple had messed up the scene. The old man had gone out with his gun to check for intruders round the property, so the area was compromised.'

Nikki all but cheered. *At last.* If Marcovici survived long enough they might be able to find out what led to his daughter's death. Maybe even get some leads about the others. At this point she wasn't sure if Marcovici was a pawn or a player. However, the fact that he'd been beaten to a pulp seemed to indicate the former. She would take no chances. 'I need that report. What are his chances of survival?'

'Still up in the air. The doctors aren't prepared to commit.'

'Right. Saj, we need an officer up there. No one in or out except medical care and us.'

'At this rate, Bradford police might need to take out shares in BRI. We've already got two officers there looking after Springer and Stevie, five victims including the poor old man who died of hypothermia, in the morgue and Archie lording it in a ward.'

He wasn't wrong, but just at that moment the door slammed open again, hitting the young officer in the back and in walked DCS Clark. Not stopping to issue an apology, her stony face indicating the foulness of her mood, she stormed through the room heading towards Archie's office with an arrogant. 'Parekh. Now.'

Tightness pulled Nikki's shoulders back. *How dare she speak to me like that in front of my team?* Resisting the urge to storm after her and say just that, Nikki turned to the waiting officers, some of whom were gazing in discomfort at their shoes, others looked suitably shocked and a few were grinning. Nikki shrugged. She wasn't the most popular detective and that didn't bother her overly much. However, she hated when superior officers thought they could demean less senior officers publicly. She pasted a smile on her face. 'Trouble in paradise, I assume.'

Deliberately not knocking, Nikki opened the door and marched in. DCS Clark was sitting in Archie's chair and had swept his paperwork to one side of the desk in a muddled heap. Archie wouldn't be impressed by that. There was order amongst the chaos – or so he often told Nikki. Not waiting to be asked to sit down, Nikki pulled a chair close to the desk and plunked herself in it, wondering what exactly she was about to be dragged over the coals for this time.

Clark studied her over the desk, her fingers steepled on her chin, her eyes direct and inscrutable. 'I told DCI Hegley that I didn't think you were up to the interim DI job.'

Ah, so that's what this is all about! Nikki inclined her head. 'Yeah, I told him the same thing. He wouldn't take no for an answer though.' She splayed her hands before her, palms up, 'So, here we are.'

A smile tugged at Clark's lips. 'He also told me you were direct. Seems he was right.' She paused. 'On both counts.'

Nikki frowned. This wasn't how she had expected things to go.

'This is a bugger of an investigation, Parekh, with so many incidents converging and that's without the additional business of Jackie Dobson's allegations.' She stood up and walked round to the front of the desk and rested her bottom against it. 'DS Springer's rape kit test showed evidence of trauma. The perpetrator used a condom, so no DNA from that, I'm afraid. They managed to pick up a few hairs that didn't belong to Springer. We're waiting for the results for that and the scrapings they found under her nails to be processed. With her blood test proving positive for Rohypnol, we feel that it's safe to assume that this Dobson woman's assertion was true. You're meeting with her later today?'

Nikki glanced at her watch. 'In about an hour.'

'You okay with that? I could divert this element of the investigation elsewhere. There's no evidence to assume Springer's abduction and the rape are linked in any way.'

This was a hard one. Nikki was completely swamped, on the other hand, if the rape and the abduction were linked – and the attack on Stevie left that open to debate – then Nikki didn't want to lose time. 'Look. Let me and DC Malik interview this woman. She's expecting to meet with me and she seems a bit jittery anyway. If I feel there's no link to the wider investigation, I'll write it up, pass it to you and you can reassign.'

'Okay, that seems fair. Now catch me up on everything else. I missed your briefing talking to those bloody stuffed shirts upstairs. That's why I was in such a shitty mood earlier.'

Nikki smiled. Maybe she and DCS Clark would be able to work together after all.

Chapter 51

Saj had felt his phone vibrate with a flurry of texts during the briefing and, with each new one, his heart sank a little. He'd spoken to Langley and made it up with him, so none of them were from him. He'd texted his sister, Fozia, saying he'd phone later, so he doubted any of the texts were from her either.

Taking the opportunity when Nikki headed to her slaughter at the hands of DCS Clark, Sajid slipped off to the loos to check his texts. Locking himself in a cubicle, he grimaced as another three texts arrived in quick succession. This did not bode well. He inhaled and opened up his messages. Ten of them! A reply from Fozia – just saying 'speak soon'. Flicking down the list he opted for his older sister's two texts first:

Bushra: WTAF, Sajid. Do you want to kill M & D? You can't be one of them. Contact M & D and tell them you're not.

Bushra: Makes me sick, Saj. Ashamed of you.

Sajid blinked twice. It was bad, but not as bad as he'd expected. What did they expect him to do? Live a lie? Of course, that's exactly what they did expect. Might as well get the others out of the way. News had travelled quickly through Dewsbury. It was all about honour for his family. How his lifestyle would reflect on them. He started with his brother Zeeshan and progressed down the list to his cousins and friends.

Zeeshan: You need to stop this, Saj. Bringing shame on the family. Allah will not tolerate this. You are no longer my brother.

Iqbal: Dirty perv. Shame on you. In the name of Allah, we will punish you.

Well, that was to be expected. He was one of his Birmingham cousins, mouthing off about the No Outsiders curriculum. Standing with megaphones outside a primary school, for God's sake. Full of vitriol and hate.

Fareed: Sinner you deserve to rot in hell . . . makes me sick that we had sleepovers together when we were kids.

That last one hurt – really hurt. Fareed was his oldest friend. On many occasions he'd wanted to tell him. To share his secret. Now, he was glad he hadn't. It seemed that even though he'd helped Fareed escape marrying his first cousin and had defended his decision to marry a Gujarati Muslim girl from Batley, taking on a lot of crap on his friend's behalf, Fareed couldn't return the favour.

Saj had expected this backlash. There was no point in trying to speak to them about it. Things would escalate, the community would stir things up and he'd be a target. He wasn't the only Muslim-born gay in the world, but none of that mattered to his family. In their eyes he had shamed them and the best he could hope for was to keep his head down and let it all blow over. He'd lost his family, yet he wouldn't beg. He'd been a good son and brother to them, but this was one thing he would not deny himself. Even if it meant being estranged from his family forever, he would not forsake his true identity.

One by one, he deleted the texts, deciding there and then to change his number and cut himself off from his family. At least that way he could minimize the hurt he inflicted on his parents. Thoughts of his mum and dad and their bewilderment at the shitstorm that had descended on them brought tears to his eyes.

It was for the best, but he just wished he'd been able to do things a little differently, that he'd had the chance to say a final farewell. Nikki was right about Lisa Kane. She was toxic and if he ever got the chance, Saj vowed he'd get his own back on her.

Slipping his phone back in his pocket, Saj pushed open the cubicle door and went over to the sink. Leaning his hands on the porcelain he studied his reflection. Earlier he'd had heavy bags under his eyes, but he'd known regular cups of coffee would set him up for the day ahead. The bags were still there, but no amount of coffee could penetrate his exhaustion or the darkness in his heart. He wondered how Nikki had got through the case the previous year. At one point he thought she might give up, but she hadn't. Did he have Nikki Parekh's strength? Her willpower? Then it occurred to him. Nikki had Marcus and her kids. That's what had pulled her through the fog, and he had Langley. It was Langley who would pull him through this hellish time. They'd help each other through it.

He leaned over, turned on the cold tap and splashed his face with water. Things were bad, but he had a partner who loved him, good friends, a job he loved and he was alive. Time to man up. They had a job to do and he had stuff to organize before they headed into town for their meeting.

Chapter 52

A few minutes after eleven-thirty in the morning and the prospect of a long day ahead filled Nikki with dread. This case was taking it out of her. They were running around chasing their arses – running on fresh air and caffeine and not a lot else. The whole team was knackered and nothing was coming together for them. Maybe this meeting would give them some sort of angle to work on. That's all they needed, just a single little loose thread that she could pull and untangle the whole bloody mess.

'Okay, we need to work out what we're going to say to her.' Nikki glared at Sajid wishing he'd look a bit more like he was with her. He had a lot on his mind. He'd not said a lot about the texts from his family, but he'd nipped out and got a new SIM for his phone saying he was breaking all ties with them and that his future lay with Langley. She sympathized with him. It was a hard decision to make and she didn't know if she could do that. Then again, after all she, her mum and Anika had been through together, she was sure she'd never have to face such an ultimatum. He was playing absentmindedly with the sugar sachets, yet she really needed him to focus. 'HOY! You here, Saj?'

Sajid sighed and looked up at her. 'Well, if I'm not, I must be a figment of your imagination. Just give me a minute to think, yeah?'

Nikki snorted, took a spoonful of her extra-large chocolate cake with vanilla ice cream and glanced round the café where they'd agreed to meet Jackie Dobson. Despite the steady snowfall, the Cake 'Ole was bustling and they'd been fortunate to get a good table at the window. The view across City Park was delightful. Too cold today for the fountains, still the park had a steady flow of people strolling through in their winter coats and scarves. The dull weather was offset by the new spring daffodils that had just begun poking their heads up from the raised beds.

As they'd driven into town, Nikki thought of their Holi celebrations earlier in the month. With her mum living it up in India it had been up to Nikki to lead the way, so she had invited her sister and Haqib to celebrate with her family. Ever since she could remember, her mum had tried to make the different Hindu festivals special for Nikki and Anika and, even though for a long time they were estranged from her mother's family, she'd made the effort. Nikki had tried to continue the tradition by instigating a colour fight in the street. Ruby and Charlie had pretended to be too old for it all, but soon had mucked in with Sunni and it was one of those special days she savoured, despite missing her mum.

This year, after all they'd been through, she was determined to make it even more special than usual. This was part of her and for so long she'd railed against it – thinking that by acknowledging her Indian heritage, she was weakening herself. No more. Her mother, resilient and loving, deserved better than that from her and although she would never be devout, she would celebrate this part of her heritage and share it with her children.

The café door opened, admitting a short woman in a bobble hat, matching gloves and a long coat. Nikki waited to see if she'd meet her glance and when she did, she stood up and gestured to the third chair at their table.

'DS Parekh?'

Nikki smiled and nodded. 'You must be Jackie Dobson and this is DC Malik. Coffee?'

When Jackie asked for a cappuccino, but declined a cake, Sajid jumped to his feet and went up to the counter to order it. Nikki waited for him to return with the drink, before continuing. When the other woman had finished removing her outer wear, sugared her drink and stirred it, Nikki began. 'DCI Hegley tells us you have evidence that DS Springer was drugged and sexually assaulted on Saturday night.'

Glancing out the window, Jackie lifted her mug and blew on it before replacing it on her saucer without drinking. 'That's right.'

'Okaaaay. So, could you tell us who you think drugged and assaulted her?'

'Well, that's the thing. I'm not prepared to put my neck on the line if she isn't around to confirm it. The only reason I went to you lot was because it had happened before to other women.' She dipped her head down and in barely a whisper added, 'and to me.'

Nikki, eyebrow quirked, glanced at Sajid, before speaking again. 'So, you say you are the victim of this person too and you have evidence of other women being victims of this unnamed man.'

Jackie pushed her coffee away and lifted a napkin from the table. As she spoke, she shredded the napkin with trembling fingers. 'He drugged and raped me over a year ago.' She glanced up and her deep blue eyes bore into Nikki's as if daring her to deny it.

Nikki held her gaze for a long moment and then nodded. 'We'd like to hear what you have to tell us, but because DS Springer is currently unable to communicate, perhaps we could start with that for today and then progress from there. You've already given DCI Hegley a statement about the other incidents, and we will revisit them later as our investigation into this progresses, but for the moment, we need to focus on anything you can tell us that may have some bearing on DS Springer's abduction.' Nikki reached over and gently squeezed the other woman's arm. 'When you're ready.'

Pulling her chair closer to the table, she began. 'I knew the Community Liaison Conference was just the sort of place he'd try it on. You know, a multi-disciplinary conference with people from the mayor's office, the police, social services, education and more . . . the pickings were ripe for him. He'd used that sort of event in the past and I knew he'd be too arrogant not to use it again.'

Nikki risked a glance at Sajid, hoping he would be able to stick to their plan. He was busy jotting things down in his notebook and only the tension along his jawline told Nikki how hard it was for him to keep his emotions in check. They'd both discussed this at length after they'd gone over Jackie Dobson's statement to Archie. Like Archie, they were concerned that this woman reported having documented another eight women including Springer who, she asserted, were victims of drugging and sexual abuse by an unnamed high-profile person. Neither could get their head round the fact that after being one such victim herself, she'd supposedly witnessed these women being drugged and guided off to hotel rooms to be abused over a period of months and yet had not intervened to prevent it . . . eight times!

Nikki was no stranger to the extent victims would go to deny what had happened to them or to keep it hidden. Yet this woman had apparently systematically stalked the man with the sole purpose of compiling evidence against him, yet had allowed eight women to endure unspeakable abuse rather than come forward. Much as she wanted to get into the head of the woman and understand her motivations, a secret part of her wanted to scream at her. *Why didn't you speak up sooner? Why let so many women suffer?*

This woman had escaped the situation and had not acted to prevent other women being subjected to the same thing, but had rather documented their abuses for over a year. This was her way of dealing with it. Her way, presumably, of ending it for good. In some ways, Nikki couldn't blame her. Rape was still one of the least reported crimes and conviction statistics were low, with many cases reported yearly of the victim being subjected to additional trauma during trial. Who was she to judge this woman who was making every effort to make sure her rapist would be punished?

Nikki encouraged her. 'Go on. You can tell us. Who is the rapist?'

But Jackie Dobson shook her head. 'I can't tell you. Not yet. The other women won't stand up, so until DS Springer comes round and supports my case, I won't tell you.'

She reached over the table and gripped Nikki's arm, her eyes wide, like a startled deer. 'Has she been raped? You must have done the rape kit. You must have evidence.'

Nikki kept her voice level, but removed the woman's hand from hers. 'I'm afraid I can't discuss DS Springer with you. You really need to tell us the name of the person you are accusing. That way we can start investigating and—'

But Jackie Dobson jumped to her feet, grabbed her coat and tears streaming down her face, ran out of the café. Saj and Nikki watched her scuttle across the empty Mirror Pool towards City Hall.

'Well, what do you make of that?'

Still watching the woman's progress, Nikki shook her head. 'I've no idea, but we can't do anything without a name. Maybe Springer will be able to give us one when she comes round.'

'Hey, isn't that Yousaf? Looks like he knows Jackie.'

Nikki watched as Anika's boyfriend said something to Jackie before Jackie scurried past, leaving Yousaf to head towards the Starbucks.

'Come on. I want to get up to BRI – check in on all the bodies, both living and dead that we have up there.'

Chapter 53

'Good news or bad news, boss?'

At Cyclops's words, Xavier's earlier good mood evaporated. The last thing he wanted was bad news. Bad news had no place in his plans and the urge to throw the phone to the ground and trample it to a million pieces was strong. He was tired. Instead of wasting time getting his oats last night and then stalking Parekh in the early hours, he should have grabbed some sleep. Truth was, he had too much adrenaline fizzing round his system and it was that – and caffeine – that was keeping him going. After tonight, he'd be able to take it easier. After tonight, the transition would be complete. But now he had to deal with bad news. This was unacceptable. He paid a fair wage so he didn't have to concern himself with 'bad news'. Still, it wasn't Cyclops's fault.

'Okay, tell me.'

'It's Marcovici. He managed to make it to another farmhouse about three miles away from ours. Word is, he's in a critical condition in BRI.'

Pressing two fingers against the bridge of his nose, Xavier took a moment to think. 'What clean-up steps have you taken?'

'I'm heading up to BRI, but they've cleared the farmhouse and moved them to the third location. We'll be putting most of them to work tonight. I've got Bullet and his team sorting them into workers and deadbeats. As agreed, we'll go ahead with killing and dumping the deadbeats around the district at intervals from around four this afternoon and transporting the workers to their various workplaces.'

The deadbeats were the men deemed unproductive – the disposable assets. They'd made him a fair amount of money over the months with their wages taken straight from their accounts, laundered and siphoned off into one of Xavier's safe accounts. They were no loss to him or his business and their final contribution to the project would be to stretch the police resources so thinly that they wouldn't notice the movement of his assets around the city to safer accommodation and working environments. And he certainly did not want the police poking their noses in when he moved the assets that he'd stored near the port in Hull to Bradford. 'Marcovici needs to be disposed of. He's the only loose end. Can you sort that?'

'On it.'

'Lieutenants in place, ready to convince any dissenters?'

Cyclops laughed. 'Oh yeah. They're chomping at the bit. Most of the pimps have flown the city. We've closed down the factories and will direct the pigs to raid them later on – they're always so damn keen to splash their raids over the front pages of the *Yorkshire Enquirer*. By the time we're in play, their paltry snatches will be laughable. Bradford oink oink switchboard is going to be exploding, it's gonna be busy busy, busy later on.'

Xavier's mood lifted again. In the overall scheme of things, Marcovici was a gnat waiting to be swatted. Most things seemed to be in control. 'The Huddersfield gun dealers been subdued?'

'Yep, threw them some dosh and made an example of a couple of their toughest – the rest were easy to convince after that.'

'And the party?'

'It's set. Whilst everything is lighting up the city centre, the auctions are all going ahead in Ilkley. You approved the different lots yesterday. We selected only the crème de la crème and they're already at the venue. Invites have been accepted, some from as far away as Scotland and others from the South of England. We expect a substantial turnover.'

'Keep the other girls at the safe houses till tonight blows over and then set them to work tomorrow. Feed them some smack to keep them sweet for now, but get the men working at the packing plants. I want enough Skunk, Blow, Spice – the lot – ready to hit the streets tomorrow. You got some people lined up ready to deal? Only the ones with enough English.'

'Chillax, boss. We've been over the plan a hundred times. It's all good. By this time tomorrow we'll have made our mark and will be heading up the trade in the North of the country. Talk about a Northern Powerhouse – we're it!'

Xavier grinned. Cyclops was right. They were 'it'.

'One last thing, boss. What about Bullet?'

By rights, he should dispose of the thug. He was to blame for the Marcovici issue, on the other hand he was an asset who took great enjoyment in his work. 'Use his skills for now. We need men like him to police the auction. We'll see how he performs today and I'll decide his fate tomorrow.'

Chapter 54

Nikki, moaning under her breath about the cost of parking at BRI, thrust another coin in the slot, pressed the green button and snatched her ticket. The unspoken agreement was that if they used Sajid's car, she paid for parking. At these rates she reckoned he was quids in, for although she could claim it back on expenses, filling in the forms was a job that she never seemed to get round to.

He took the ticket from her and nodded towards the hospital entrance. 'See who's over there?'

Nikki followed his gaze and sighed. The last thing she needed was a confrontation between Sajid and Max Ashton. The bastard had managed to snap a photo that substantiated the short snappy article written by Lisa Kane. If Ashton was sniffing around BRI, Kane wouldn't be far away. What was it with her that she couldn't just show a bit of common decency? No doubt she was here hoping to worm her way onto one of wards to get an exclusive with one of their key witnesses. She was glad she'd assigned officers to the hospital. It wouldn't be the first time that Kane had got information from loose-lipped hospital staff.

Ashton flicked his cigarette onto the ground and stamped it out with his foot. Saj slammed the car door shut with more force than was strictly necessary. 'Could get the tosser for littering.'

'Yeah and how good would that look? Kane would have a field day about how, with budget restrictions, a member of the Major Incidents Team managed to find time to arrest a respected photographic journalist for littering. What happened to the low profile you told me you wanted to keep, not ten minutes ago?'

Head hunched into his coat collar, Saj grunted and headed for the entrance. 'Archie, Springer, Stevie or Marcovici first?'

'Well, I expect there's no change in the condition of the first three, but I'd like to lay eyes on Marcovici before I see his wife later and as they're all in the ICU, it makes sense to look in on them all. We can always pop back up after we see Archie, if there's any change.'

For sake of ease, Stevie and Springer had been put in a room together and so only needed one officer by the door. The nursing staff had provided a chair, but the officer jumped to her feet as Nikki and Saj approached. Nikki waved her back to the seat and then reconsidered. 'You want to go for a toilet break or a leg stretch? We'll stay for ten minutes.'

Once the officer had disappeared down the corridor, Nikki peered through the window. Two beds stood within arm's reach of one another, each with its own collection of monitors with flashing green and red lights. The frail figures in the beds had been intubated and had face masks on. Nikki twanged her elastic band on her wrist. If neither of these two women survived, the baby in the neo-natal intensive care unit would become an orphan. Nikki found herself willing Springer and Stevie to make it.

'You okay?' The smiling nurse looked from Nikki to Saj and then back again.

Nikki flipped out her warrant card and introduced herself and Saj. 'We sent the constable off for a quick break. Just wanted a bit of an update on these two.'

The nurse opened the door and slipped into the dimly lit room. The sound of the beeping monitors was loud in the otherwise silent room. Nikki followed her, whilst Saj sat down in the chair outside the room. Stopping between the two beds, Nikki was pleased they were together. Maybe they'd be able to sense each other's presence and take strength from that. She pushed the thought out of her mind, glad she hadn't shared it with Saj. She was being fanciful. She studied Springer's face and arms, which were the only visible parts of her. Her colour seemed better and the restraint marks on her arms were fading. But Nikki was aware from personal experience that the physical marks would be easy to heal. It was the mental scars that caused deeper problems. She was torn between hoping Springer never remembered a thing about the rape and wishing she could identify the man Jackie Dobson said was a serial rapist.

As the nurse moved around the room, noting oxygen levels and blood pressure details in charts, Nikki turned her gaze to Stevie. All cleaned up now, Stevie looked much better than she had twelve hours ago. Her face was bruised and swollen, but her worse injuries were hidden under the covers. She reached out with both her arms and squeezed the nearest hand of each of the unconscious women before taking a step back. 'How are they?'

'They're both in an induced coma, but both are doing well considering the extent of their respective injuries. Their stats are improving and now it's just a matter of time, I'm afraid. We'll call you if there's any change.'

Nikki nodded. There was nothing she could do here. Next stop, Stefan Marcovici.

The officer had returned when she left the room, so Nikki and Saj walked further along the corridor to where another officer stood, or rather, sat guard by another room. After sending that officer off for a break too, Saj and Nikki opened the door and walked in. A nurse sat next to the bed, indicating how serious Marcovici's injuries still were. Nikki flashed her warrant card and made the introductions. The nurse nodded and gestured for them to approach the bed.

If she had had to ID the man lying in the bed as Stefan Marcovici, Nikki would have denied it was him. However, she'd been told that blood and a Familial DNA comparison matched his to Maria's. The man in the bed was undernourished. His cheekbones were pronounced, his cheeks sunken. His wrists were so tiny, Nikki suspected she could circle them using only her thumb and index finger, his paper-thin skin barely covered the bones and where it wasn't bruised, it was sallow.

Nikki had no doubt she was looking at yet another victim. She'd seen the list of his injuries and many of them had been sustained over an extended period of time.

'What's his prognosis?'

The nurse bit his lip and lightly brushed Stefan's hair from his forehead. 'Not good, but at least for now, he's holding his own.'

'His wife is flying in from Romania later on in the day. I'll bring her to see him. Poor woman has to identify her dead daughter first.'

'It never ceases to amaze me how much hurt humans can inflict on other humans. Makes you wonder just how much evil is out there in the world.'

Nikki couldn't disagree with him. She saw more than her share of inhumanity, yet she also went home to a loving family every night and had some good friends. The world wasn't all bad, although on days like today she found it hard to convince herself of that. She leaned forward and laid her hand on Stefan's. 'You hang in there Stefan. Your wife is coming to see you this afternoon and she needs you to get better. Can you do that for me?'

She didn't expect a response, still, she was disappointed when she didn't get one.

Nikki could hear Archie before she and Sajid were halfway down the corridor to his room.

'Wonder what's up with the perfect patient?' Sajid's tone was bland.

'He must be a nightmare. They'll be glad when they can discharge him.'

Poking her head round the door, Nikki took in the scene before her. Archie, fully dressed, was making a ham-fisted attempt to fold the pyjamas she'd brought him the previous evening, whilst Nurse Olson, whom Nikki recognized from the other day, stood arms on hips, glaring at him.

Giving the folding up as a bad job, Archie rolled the pyjama bottoms into a ball and tossed them into a bag that lay open on the bed, before repeating the process with the pyjama top. 'You medical people dinnae't always ken what's best for yer patients, you ken? Take me, for example. Getting back tae work's the only tonic I need. Dinnae need yer pills, dinnae need tae rest and I certainly dinnae need to be in here. Dinnae need anyone looking after me.'

'Mr Hegley—'

'That's DCI Hegley to you.'

'We've been through this, *Mr* Hegley. You're not at Trafalgar House now. Besides, you told me your wife was at home to look after you. You can't just discharge yourself unless there's someone at home. The doctors aren't happy with your decision. Are you sure you've got a . . .?'

Glowering at Archie, Nikki stepped into the room. 'No, he doesn't have a wife at home to look after him and more to the point, what do you think you're doing discharging yourself before the doctors are happy to let you go?'

She stepped up to the bed, ignoring the nervous glances Archie kept darting in the nurse's direction. Nikki snatched the rumpled pyjamas from the bed and thrust them at him. 'I never had you down as a liar, Archie Hegley. Now get those bloody things back on right now. No arguments.' And she stepped back and lined herself up with Nurse Olson, mirroring the other woman's hands-on-hips stance.

Archie looked at Saj as if for help, but Saj shook his head and sat down on a visitor's seat. 'Don't look at me. I'm only here for the entertainment factor.'

'Bloody useless lump, that's whit you are, laddie. A damn traitor.'

Saj smiled and nodded. 'Yep, that about sums me up, but I've still got my money on Parekh winning this argument.'

Archie sighed and turned to Nikki. 'I wasn't lying, Parekh!'

'Hmph. You know as well as I do, your wife died a good ten years ago – got remarried without telling anyone? Hmph. Nobody would have you, Archie. Not if you're such a big baby you won't even take the doctor's advice.'

'Ah didnae lie – well, no exactly. My wife *is* at home.'

Nikki's eyes widened. Had he lost his bloody marbles? 'What are you talking about?'

'She's on the mantelpiece, beside Uncle George and my mum.'

Nikki opened her mouth, but no words would come out. Then a huge laugh filled the room, startling everyone. It was the nurse. 'It's their ashes he's got on the mantelpiece. Silly man. How in heaven's name is your wife going to look after you from a cremation urn, tell me that?'

Archie sagged down onto the bed with a sigh. 'I hate hospitals.'

Anger dissipating as quickly as it had arrived, Nikki pulled up a chair beside her boss and squeezed his arm. 'You're a stubborn old fool you know, Archie Hegley. Even if I have to barricade the door, you're staying put till the docs give you the all clear!'

'Might even be tomorrow if you're lucky. They only want to do a stress test and redo some bloods. Now, I'll leave you with your visitors and shred these discharge papers, okay.'

'Woman's a bloody tyrant' said Archie, but he had a twinkle in his eye as his gaze followed the departing nurse.

'Pyjamas.' Nikki's tone was insistent, but Archie straightened up and sat in the comfy chair next to the bed.

'I'll put them on when you've gone. I'm allowed tae sit here if I want.'

Moving his bag to the bedside cabinet, Nikki settled herself on the bed and without Archie having to ask, filled him in on everything from Stevie and the baby to the two murdered boys, to Stefan Marcovici and their meeting with Jackie Dobson.

'Crap. You've got a lot on your plate, Parekh. Why don't you send me all the files and I'll spend some time reading through interviews and statements and the like. See if anything pops.' He leaned over and took his laptop out of his bag and placing it on the table, booted it up. 'I've been doing some work myself this morning. Although you didn't get much more information from Jackie Dobson, I took the liberty of reading through her initial statement to me and DCS Clark. During the statement I identified four of the events where she asserts these rapes occurred. I took it upon myself to get uniform to access the guestlists for each of the conferences and cross match to see which males attended all four of them.'

Nikki slammed the heel of her hand against her forehead. 'Why didn't we think of doing that, Saj?'

'Maybe because we've been running all over Bradford to numerous crime scenes and can barely catch our breath.'

'Hmm.' Nikki wasn't about to let herself off the hook so easily. This was routine police work and she should have caught it. 'What did you find?'

Archie grinned and turned the screen towards her so Nikki could see the list of names. Saj got up and looked over her shoulder. 'Six names . . . all either high-profile or high up in their respective organizations, from local politicians to businessmen, members of the judiciary, clergymen and police officers. How the hell do we narrow it down?'

'Well, I bloody hope you can knock at least one name off the list.'

Chapter 55

Tiredness catching up with her again, Nikki insisted on a drink and a late lunch in the BRI Costa. Nursing a black, heavily sugared coffee and a tuna wrap, Nikki wished her eyelids weren't so heavy. If she slumped in her seat she was sure she'd doze off. She took a sip, burning her mouth in the process, but welcomed the jolt it gave her. *Come on Nikki, focus.* 'We can't discuss this back at the incident room. Jackie Dobson's allegations are still top secret, but what do you make of the list?'

Saj had jotted the names in his notebook, which he now placed on the table between them.

Bishop Graham Banks OBE

DI Joe Drummond

DCS Archie Hegley

Yousaf Mirza local Lib Dem councillor, businessman and Lord Mayoral candidate

Joseph Norton, Labour MP, Bradford Central

Imam Khurram Ul Haq, religious leader and youth charity worker

'You notice Yousaf's on there?'

Nikki nodded. She had mixed feelings about that. She disliked the man intensely, but was he capable of multiple rapes? Were any of them? Of course, they could count Archie off the list, which still left five. She didn't know what to do with the information. Unless Jackie Dobson had a change of heart or Springer woke up and gave them a name, all they had was a list – nothing more. 'Keep it in your notebook. We can follow up on it, if and when we get more information.' She paused. 'Do me a favour though, get someone to check when the next one of those sorts of events is taking place. I think in my new position as interim DI, I should perhaps show my face at one, what do you reckon?'

'Great idea, Nik. Catch the bastard in the act . . . that'll solve it. I'll be your plus one if you like.'

Nikki's phone rang. It was Williams. 'Hope you've got something good for me Williams?'

The officer's voice was excited and his words came out in a rush. 'We got an ID on the two boys from last night. They were brothers. First of all, Dr Campbell linked their DNA to the cigarette stubs we discovered by the canal where Springer and Glass were found, and then got a rush through that national DNA data thing they have.'

'NDNAD, the National DNA Database.'

'Yeah, that's the one. We got a hit on one of them. Danny Boy Bramhope, 21-years-old, and Jason Bramhope, 19-years-old. They're from Newcastle. I got in touch with the local nick, who were well familiar with the lads for low-level drug dealing and suchlike. Said they'd gone AWOL a few months back. I gave them the heads-up on our investigation and they've sent a couple of officers to notify the mother. They said that if anyone knew anything about what they were up to in Bradford it would either be their younger brother Chris or their best mate Jon. They're going to see what they can get from them too and get back to us in a bit.'

'Good work, Williams. Well done. Keep me informed. The PMs go okay?'

The lad's voice lost some of its animation and Nikki understood that. PM's weren't her favourite part of the job either. 'They were beaten pretty badly. The dog shit – I mean faeces – matched the samples from Maria Marcovici and Adam Glass, as did the bite marks. Dr Campbell reckons they were beaten till they were almost dead and then left, hog-tied to strangle themselves before being moved to the dump sites.'

The thought of the terror those boys went through was too hard to think about. Hopefully, they were so far out of it that their death was less traumatic than she imagined. She shuddered, again thinking of her nephew who was only a little younger than those boys. She would enjoy locking up the monster who'd committed these crimes for a very long time.

'Get it written up and take a couple of hours' downtime. You need to conserve your energy; I have the feeling we might be in for another rough night.'

Chapter 56

Nikki reported back to DCS Clark about her meeting with Jackie Dobson and when she'd done, she allowed the other woman to vent for a bit.

'What the hell is it with the woman?' Clark's agitation had brought a flush to her cheeks. 'Springer's in hospital fighting for her life and Dobson has details of at least another *eight* women who've been subjected to this, including herself and still, she won't give us a name.'

It was frustrating, no doubt about it, but the way the woman had scurried out of the café spoke volumes to Nikki. She was scared and felt disempowered. Being victimized could do that to you, especially when the perpetrator was someone in an entitled, powerful position. 'I don't think she's being deliberately obstructive, you know?' Nikki kept her voice calm, willing herself to make her point in a way the DCS could relate to. 'I think she's petrified. Everyone knows the rape statistics. Every woman is all too aware that when they accuse a man of rape, *they* go on trial at the same time. It was only recently some pillock lawyer in Ireland gave the victim's thong as evidence of her willingness to have sex. As for Epstein and Harvey Weinstein and upskirting . . . well, can you blame her for being scared and cautious? It's 2020 and women are still subjected to crap!'

As Clark sighed and her anger subdued for now, Nikki drew out the list she'd copied and printed from Saj's notebook and handed it over. 'Archie's managed to cross-reference four events from Dobson's statements and cross matched it with male attendees. These were the six names that were at each of the four events. I'm sure you've been to events with this motley crew, do any of them jump out as being a bit dodgy?'

Clark took the list, popped her reading glasses on and as she studied it, a small frown formed between her eyes. With methodical care, she folded the sheet in four, placed it in the top draw of her desk and shook her head. 'Can't say any of them strike me as being candidates for rape.'

Nikki frowned. Was it her imagination or was there a worried look in Clark's eyes? Did her hand shake as she folded the paper? Had there been a slight quiver in her voice?

Clark stood up and inclined her head. 'Well, if that's all, DS Parekh . . .?'

It was clear she was being dismissed, and the use of her old title wasn't wasted on Nikki. However, she'd never been one for kowtowing to the subtle rules of communication with superiors. Something was off here and she couldn't let it go. Nikki owed it to Springer, who may lose her own life, her wife and possibly their baby. She owed it to Jackie Dobson and the other women who were too scared to come forward. If Clark knew something, then she should share it. Before she could talk herself out of it, Nikki stood up, chin raised. 'I think you're withholding. I think you know something about one of those men, DCS Clark, and you need to tell me what it is.'

Clark's eyes sparked and her lips tightened. Nikki took a step back. *Okay, so that could have come out less confrontational.* She tried again, hands splayed before her in silent appeal. 'Look, I don't mean to imply that you're *lying*. I just mean – well.' She dropped her hands to her side. Where the hell was Saj when you needed him?

Nikki lowered her head, aware that she was making a real dog's dinner of this. 'Look, I noticed your reaction when you read that list. I thought that indicated that you knew something relevant and I just want to do the right thing. Springer and I aren't friends. I doubt we could ever be friends, but she was raped and Jackie Dobson says it was at the conference and each of those men attended it. It's not conclusive, I know it's not, but if someone on that list is a predator, then we're duty-bound to do something about it. It's our job.'

As Nikki spoke, Clark sank back into her chair, her fingers tapping a gentle rhythm on her desk top. Nikki waited. She didn't know Clark well enough to judge what she was thinking, but she fully expected to be lucky to leave the room with her DS status intact, never mind her interim DI one. She waved a silent goodbye to a service for her car and new DMs. She didn't care. If she hadn't said something it would have gnawed at her gut –like a bloody rat and if the past year had taught Nikki anything, it was that peace of mind was important.

'Do you trust me, DS – I mean DI Parekh?'

So, she wasn't losing the interim post, that was a good sign, although she supposed it depended on her answer to the question she'd just been asked. She screwed up her nose and considered it. Did she trust Clark? She wasn't a hundred per cent sure she did, but then Nikki didn't trust many people. Wishing she was more of a pragmatist, Nikki shrugged. 'You've not done anything so far to make me *distrust* you. That's the best answer I can give.'

Clark smiled and once more rose to her feet. 'I value your honesty, Parekh. Archie told me you were direct.' She paused, frowned and then added, 'Well, in the interests of full disclosure, what he actually said was, "she can be abrasive, infuriating and downright stubborn, but she's honest through and through." Seems like he was right. Anyway, I'm going to ask you to trust me – just for a short time – till this evening should be long enough. I have a decision to make and then we'll look at this list one more time.'

It went against the grain for Nikki not to push for more. Perhaps some of Saj's diplomacy was rubbing off on her. Whatever it was, she sighed, gave a curt nod and left the room, hoping she hadn't made a decision she would regret.

Chapter 57

Signalling to Saj to follow her, Nikki moved to the side of the incident room, near the window that overlooked Nelson Street. The room was only half full. Most of the officers assigned to Nikki's investigation were out on the streets and the few that were in the room were busy at their computers. Taking care no one could hear them, Nikki told Saj about her meeting with DCS Clark.

Running his fingers through his hair, Saj released a long breath of air. 'Do you reckon she fancies one of the men as a rapist?'

Nikki shrugged and leaned her forehead on the window, enjoying its coolness. She was flustered and that had overheated her. 'I just don't know. Whatever it is, she's got till tonight to sort it out and get back to me. Just wish I was sure I've done the right thing.'

'Don't be daft. What else could you have done? She's the big boss.' He leaned forward, pressing his own forehead on the window and frowned. 'You don't think she's seeing one of them, do you? I heard on the office grapevine that she's divor . . .' His voice tailed off and he stood on tiptoe, pressing his face closer onto the glass. 'Shit, that's my best mate, Fareed, down there. Maybe he's reconsidered what he texted me this morning.'

Before Nikki could stop him, he was off, tearing out of the

room, tie flying behind him as he ran. She hesitated. Should she go after him, stop him? She wasn't sure that his friend would have come round to accepting Saj's sexuality so quickly and she thought that his turning up at Saj's place of work wasn't necessarily a good thing. Why hadn't he come in and asked for Saj instead of loitering about outside?

Nikki peered this way and that along the street and noticed a car parked up further along. Inside she could see some men and as she watched, Saj's friend Fareed approached the car, yanked the door open and got into the back seat. This was definitely not a good sign. Nikki turned around, saw two officers and said, 'Get your extendable batons at the ready and get down the stairs after DC Malik. I want you to make sure he's safe.'

She kept her eyes on the car full of men and phoned down to reception in the hope that she could relay a message to Saj before he left the premises. Just as the phone was picked up, she saw Saj, coatless, standing on the pavement peering up and down the street. Further along, the car doors opened and four men got out. It was then she noticed the car number plates were muddied over, but what made her heart accelerate was the weapons they carried in their hands. *Shit, Saj.* 'DC Malik is under attack outside the station on Nelson Street, get out there now.'

Taking to her heels, she too left the incident room, yelling to the remaining officers, 'Officer down in the street, phone an ambulance and then get your arses downstairs. It's Saj and he needs help.'

Nikki didn't wait for the lift, which was slow at the best of times. Instead she took the stairs two at a time propelling her body round each landing by grabbing the handrail. By the time she burst through the outside doors, her chest hurt and she couldn't speak. A crowd of officers and civilians had gathered in a group, blocking her view. She barged her way through, ignoring the protests from people twice her size and manoeuvred herself to the front. Sajid lay, eyes closed, his feet dangling off the pavement, his pristine shirt covered in glistening blood. A bystander pulled his tie off him and tied it round Saj's arm. It was only then Nikki noticed the slash marks on his bicep. His eyes fluttered open and with a weak grin he said, 'Don't think my friends and family are going to come round any time soon.'

Nikki smiled back at him. 'Bloody attention seeker, that's what you are. Phew, you nearly gave me a heart attack! That'll teach you to go running off on your own without back-up.'

An ambulance siren approached and Nikki looked around the scene. One officer was cuffing Fareed whilst another one cuffed someone else who looked enough like Saj to be a relative.

Nikki clenched her fists and stormed over to the two men and pummelled Fareed's chest. 'Fucking homophobic bastards. He's worth a million of you. He'd never betray his friend or his family the way you've done.'

The man who looked like a relative spat in Sajid's direction as he was led inside. 'He's an animal. He has betrayed Islam. We'll be back.'

Nikki watched as the paramedics treated her friend.

'I don't want to press charges Nik. That's my cousin and Fareed.'

'They tried to kill you, Saj.'

'Yeah, but they didn't. The other two drove off and left them and Fareed didn't even lift his weapon. It was just my cousin and he only did it cos he panicked – idiot. He's hot-headed. Keep them in overnight and send them on their way. Warn them that if they set foot in Bradford again, they'll be done.'

Nikki looked round at the group of officers who circled them. 'We all saw what happened, Saj, we can't brush it under the carpet.'

Sajid's face took on a stubborn expression, Nikki was all too familiar with. 'I won't testify. I can't. It's only a damn surface wound anyway and look at it this way, we've taken another few knives off the streets.'

A hand squeezed Nikki's shoulder. It was one of the older uniforms, one whose name she couldn't remember, but who was often on desk duty downstairs. 'Let it go, lass. It's what the lad wants. We'll give them a talking to, keep them in the cells overnight and get rid tomorrow. You've enough on your plate right now.'

Nikki looked at the three other officers, all of whom were part of her team. One of them spoke up. 'It happened like Saj said. Us coming tanking out panicked them and the gobby one lashed out. Otherwise Saj would've talked them down. The other two were already getting into the car as they saw Saj on the pavement. Might make things worse if we do owt else.'

Sighing, Nikki gave in. 'Okay ... but if it ends up on the internet, we'll have to report it.'

Saj grinned. 'Glad you see it my way. Now help me up. We've got work to do.'

Chapter 58

Nikki was heading out with Saj. Ali had phoned and wanted to talk to her face to face. Saj wouldn't let her drive his Jag and *she* wouldn't let him drive full stop, so she'd had to sign out a pool car. Ali had information, but he was being all cloak and dagger. He'd agreed to meet her at The Hare and Hounds on Toller Lane. Ali didn't drink much, but when he did, it was The Hare and Hounds he frequented.

'Before you go, boss, I've got something.' The uniformed officer was checking back in and judging by the grin on his face, he'd found something, 'We managed to track down the halal chicken factory owner.' He glanced at the officer with him. 'We decided to do good cop/bad cop with him. Maggie does a grand bad cop so it wasn't long before he admitted that half of the employees came through the agency Employ Me and that he suspected it ran illegal immigrants. Immoral dickwad. Tried to back pedal and was all –' the lad's voice took on a whining tone as he mimicked the factory owner's excuses. '– "I wasn't certain, so my hands were tied' and "I asked the men if they were okay, but they said nothing, what could I do?"' The officer tutted, his expression saying everything. 'Like he hadn't heard the adverts on the radio about people-trafficking or seen the billboards all over town. Some folk just see what they want to see – especially when dosh is involved. Anyway, he admitted that there had been a disturbance the other night. One of the men had escaped and the minder, a bloke called Bullet, went after him with his dogs.'

Nikki's ears perked up with that little titbit. Bullet was the name Ali had given her last night and the mention of dogs might be a bonus. 'And . . .?'

'Well, this Bullet found the immigrant and the boss reckons it was that Stefan Marcovici because he didn't turn up for work the next day. The owner was pissed with that Bullet bloke though because he kept letting his Rottweilers shit in the car park.'

'Is it too much to hope that you—?'

'Yes ma'am, we did.' Maggie, as eager as her partner, high-fived him and took up the narrative. 'We went to the car park and took various samples of dog turd and dropped them at the lab – and . . . it's a bloody match!'

Their enthusiasm was contagious and Nikki's face broke into a wide smile. 'And did you . . .?'

Maggie nodded again, putting Nikki in mind of the bobbing dogs some car owners had on their dashboard. 'We brought the owner in and he's working with the police artist now. Hopefully, we'll get an E-fit of this Bullet guy soon. We told him he wasn't in the clear because he lied to the officers who questioned him last night. He's bricking it.'

Laughing, Nikki shrugged her jacket on. 'Well done, you two. That's good work. Send me the image when it comes through.'

Trailing out of the incident room after her, Saj tried to convince her he was good to drive.

'Look, you're lucky I'm even letting you stay on the job. If Clark knew what had gone off she'd have sent you home, so stop moaning. You're only saying that because you don't want your nice new Hawaiian shirt smelling of whatever fragrant whiff the pool car is impregnated with.'

Saj's shirt had been ruined after the knife attack and the only shirt available was one borrowed from one of the younger recruits. The rather lovely, bright orange, short-sleeved shirt with palm trees and pineapples all over it was more suitable for a stag night than a major investigation. Saj had tried to convince Nikki to make a detour to Next, but still pissed off with him for digging his heels in about his cousin and his friend, Nikki had dug *hers* in too and insisted they had no time to 'prance about in clothes shops when he had been given a perfectly lovely shirt.'

Buttoning his coat right up to the collar, Saj threw her a dirty look. 'Okay, you take me back to my flat to grab a clean shirt after we meet with Ali and you can drive the Jag.'

Nikki, walking ahead of him grinned. *Result!* She shrugged in a 'oh, I suppose so' sort of way. 'Well, if you insist, Saj, but you know me. I'm happy enough with a pool car.'

'Humph, yeah right. Just quit while you're ahead, eh.'

Nikki took the keys from him and singing Madness's 'Driving In My Car' under her breath emphasizing the word 'Jaguar', she pressed the button for the lift.

'You feeling the cold there, Sajid?' Ali, sitting next to the roaring fire in the quiet part of The Hare and Hounds, studied the sheen of sweat across Sajid's brow. 'Coming down with summat?'

Nikki grinned. 'Come on Saj, take your coat off, Ali won't judge you.'

Saj glared at Nikki, yet, clearly feeling the heat, unbuttoned his coat and slipped it off.

'Bloody hell, lad. Need my sun specs for that. Couldn't have gone for a brighter shirt, could you?' Ali finished the dregs of his pint and stood up, 'What can I get you . . . Pina Colada, DC Malik?'

'Eff off, Ali. I'm on duty, so I'll have a coke and so will she.' Burrowing further into the corner of the table, Saj glared at her. 'Whatever Ali has, better be damn good. My street cred's flown right out the window in this abomination.'

Head on one side, Nikki studied it. 'I think it suits you. Think I've got an idea for your birthday pressie now.'

Flipping his idle finger at Nikki, Saj accepted the glass of coke Ali handed him.

Nikki took a swig of hers and waited till Ali had sat back down before speaking. 'Please tell me you've got something for us, Ali. We're desperate.'

Glancing round, Ali leaned over the table and pushed a folded scrap of paper towards Nikki. 'Found this on the doorstep this morning. Not at the office – at my home.'

Before picking it up, Nikki scrutinized her friend. He kept casting quick looks all round the pub and his shoulders were set and tense. Ali wasn't often rattled, but he was today. She pulled out the nitrile gloves she always kept in her jean pockets and once they were on, she unfolded the paper and angled it so Saj could read too. '*If you know what's good for you, keep your cars off the streets today. Tomorrow is a new day and things will change.*'

Sensing what Ali's reply would be, Nikki had to suggest it anyway. 'We can take it in and get it printed.'

Before she'd even finished her sentence, Ali shook his head. 'Nah, no point Nik, no point at all.' Then surprising Nikki, he added, 'Take it, if you want though. I suppose you never know what you might find.'

Saj handed Nikki an evidence bag and she inserted the note. 'Any idea what it's about or who sent it?'

'I'm not the only one who got a note, Nik. Shipley, Great Horton, Thornbury, Barkerend, Eccleshill Taxis – they all got one. All delivered to their homes, not their businesses. They know where we live and the threat is implied. Plus, they were smart enough to know we all have CCTV at our offices. It's worrying, Nik.'

'What are you going to do, Ali?'

'Nothing I can do – we've all decided to shut for the day. A couple have decided to shut for good. Our men have all got families . . . no way can we risk anything happening to them and there's no way to protect them. No one likes how the wind's blowing in Bradford at the minute.'

Anger surged through her. Whoever was doing this had effectively managed to shut down a substantial amount of business in the city; it didn't bode well and she was helpless to protect everyone. 'I'm sorry, Al. You know if I could, I'd have a team staking out every taxi firm in the city, but that wouldn't do any good. It wouldn't protect your men when they're picking up fares. Besides, this goes wider than this, doesn't it?'

'That's the other thing I had to tell you. Since last night, the dealers, the pimps, even the sex-workers have all gone underground. I sent a couple of my men round to check out some of the known ones in Heaton. They're not there. Houses are empty, like they've been scared off – tellies are still in their living rooms, laptops and all still there, just no sign of life. Half the druggies are in withdrawal and screaming under the arches at Foster Square, the other half are near overdosing. Whenever the storm breaks Nikki, it's going to be bad – really bad.

Nikki had to agree. No way in hell was any of this a big 'clean up Bradford' campaign – it was the move of a very clever and organized takeover bid and time was running out for Nikki to pull the plug on them. She needed to identify this Bullet character and find out who his boss was. He was too visible to be the big boss – too much brawn and not enough brains. No, whoever was behind this was clever and had a widespread network. How else could they have cleared everyone off the streets so effectively?

Chapter 59

'The streets are nearly clear now, boss.'

Xavier had hoped that Cyclops had good news and although he trusted his deputy, he was well aware of everything that could go wrong. It was all in the timing, but phase one had been completed efficiently and that was a good omen. 'Good work! Let's keep focused. Stage Two is trickier. It's imperative that this part of the plan is executed and co-ordinated perfectly. There's a lot of money at stake, but more than that, my wider reputation relies on the success of this stage. We don't want our achievements to be confined to Bradford and a satisfactory completion of Stage Two followed by an equally successful coup tomorrow will allow us to expand.'

'It's all in hand. The first part will start at 5.30 p.m. followed by action every thirty minutes till 9.30 p.m. Nothing will go wrong. I promise.

'And Marcovici? Is he sorted yet?'

'I tried, but I can't get near him. Don't worry, word is he's gonna die anyway. I'll take my chance tonight though. They won't be able to keep a guard there when the city's on fire, will they?'

Xavier laughed. 'Bonfire night all over again. Speak soon.'

Leaning back in his chair, head resting on the head rest, Xavier smiled. He'd dreamed of this for a long time and planned for it for almost as long. Tonight he'd introduce himself to the party-goers. They were the ones with the money and if they liked his services, he would be more than happy to provide auction tours. Many liked to bid online, but there was nothing quite like seeing the goods first-hand – touching them, smelling them, seeing their reactions.

Of course, he would wear his balaclava. The whole reason the business worked so well, was that the secrecy surrounding his identity, his alias, his untouchability carried an implied threat. He scared people and he liked it that way. Too often in the real world he was overlooked, ignored or dismissed even. His family some-times disrespected him, his mistress made unacceptable demands, his business was hard work and so was his high-profile public life. But as Xavier, he was powerful beyond any mutant. He was the man. He would continue to use his public persona to manipulate and feed his private one. This was just the beginning . . . what was it they said? 'The best is yet to come.'

Chapter 60

After their talk with Ali, Nikki asked Saj to assign some uniforms to check in on their known drug addicts, sex-workers and pimps in their patrol areas. The same messages were coming in from uniformed officers all over Bradford; no sex-worker, pimp or drug dealer activity to be found. The ambulance service was almost stretched to breaking, dealing with call-outs to drug addicts going through painful withdrawal or overdose. Reports of eight sex-workers from different parts of the city being found beaten to a pulp as well as a couple of their pimps came in.

'The city's on fucking meltdown, Saj, and we're running around like headless goats.'

'Chickens.'

'Goats, chickens – it's all the same; if they're headless they don't know where they're going, do they?'

She didn't have time to drop Sajid off for a change of shirt because as they left the pub, they got an alert saying a body had been reported in the Thornton Industrial Estate. They got into the car and Nikki headed towards Thornton.

'How many more bodies are we going to have to deal with before this is over?'

Holding onto the edge of his seat as Nikki drove, slightly

faster than was strictly necessary, Saj spoke through gritted teeth. 'Probably at least two more if you don't slow down.'

'Ha bloody ha, Malik. Just because you drive like Fred Flintstone.'

'Fred Flintstone? What are you talking about?'

'As if your feet are stuck out the bottom of the car and you're jogging along.'

Saj rolled his eyes and opened his mouth to retort when his phone rang.

'DC Malik, how can I help?'

Annoyed that he hadn't put it on speakerphone and well aware that he did it just to annoy her, Nikki listened to the one-sided conversation.

'He has. Oh, that's good news. Yes, I'll tell Acting DI Parekh. Someone will be there shortly.

'Well?' The question shot from Nikki's lips like a greyhound chasing a bunny.

'Marcovici's come round. Wants to speak to the police. What do you want to do?'

Nikki thought for a minute. It was just gone five o'clock and they were closer to BRI than Thornton. 'Get Williams to take a uniform and contain the scene. We'll see Marcovici and then head to Thornton. Why do I think it's going to be another busy night?'

Driving to BRI, she enjoyed the power of the Jag, despite Sajid's almost constant girlie yelps every time she grated his clutch or braked too hard. By the time she parked up, ignoring Saj's groan when she tapped the driver's door into the car in the next bay, she'd had enough – she missed her own little car.

'Right, that's it. No more. Keys!' Saj glowered at her from over the Jag's roof.

Nikki moaned a little, but handed over the keys. Although it was enjoyable to drive the Jag for a short time, she actually preferred to be a passenger. That way she could get things done. Besides, Saj's relentless gasps and moans had done her head in.

* * *

The police officer stationed outside Stefan Marcovici's room stood up as soon as she saw Nikki and Sajid walking along the corridor. Her smile told them that Marcovici was still conscious. 'He's awake, but he says he wants to speak only to the police bosses. I thought you'd want to hear his story first-hand anyway.'

Nikki was indeed eager to hear what Maria Marcovici's father could tell them. 'His wife is en route from the airport as we speak. I want to take Stefan's statement first and when his wife arrives, I want to take her to identify Maria before bringing her to her husband. Hopefully that way, they'll be able to support each other.'

Nikki and Sajid entered the room and walked towards the bed. Marcovici was sitting up slightly, his head raised on pillows and though he still had an oxygen mask over his mouth and nose, he was no longer intubated. His eyes followed them into the room and he lifted a skinny hand to remove the mask from his face. The nurse, although still in the room, was not hovering over him any more. 'Try not to be too long with him. He's still weak although his stats are improving rapidly now he's come round.'

Nodding, Nikki pulled a chair close to one side of the bed, whilst Sajid did the same at the other side. 'I'm DS Nikki Parekh. I'm a police officer and myself and DC Malik are looking into what happened to you. I very much want to hear your story, Mr Marcovici. I think you've been through hell and the people who did this to you need to be punished. Will you tell me what you can remember?'

Marcovici swallowed and gestured to a glass of water on the cabinet beside him. Nikki lifted it and held the straw steady so he could take a sip.

'They killed my Maria. Those bastards raped and killed my daughter. Of course, I'll help you catch them.' His voice was hoarse and a single tear trickled from one eye.

Nikki patted his hand. 'I'll record your statement if that's okay.'

When he nodded, she set her phone to record close to his mouth and introduced those present in the room.

'Can you tell us what happened to you, Stefan?' Nikki's tone was gentle. Her heart went out to the man before her. He'd lost his daughter and been beaten badly, yet still he wanted to fight back.

'I am so glad to break my silence. I have much to tell. They tricked us into coming here, took our passports and made us work for them; me in that chicken factory with other men – we are prisoners. Maria, my daughter, took away with the other women.' He stopped and Nikki offered him another sip of water. They'd need to ask more detailed questions later, but for now she wanted the bare bones of Stefan's story. They could fill in the details when he was stronger.

'It my fault she was killed. I tried to escape. I heard on radio about people like us being kept. They gave us bank accounts – but no money. We work hard, but we still owed money. I put the phone number in my head and I run away. Bullet came after me with his dogs. They want to teach everyone a lesson so they take me to a big building. Maria is there, on the floor, dressed like a whore, crying, begging for a fix.' Another tear trickled down his cheek and Stefan stared into space as if he could see this image. 'They make my Maria a whore and a druggie. Right in front of me they inject her with heroin. They took turns with her, Bullet and his thugs. They made the dogs bite her, they beat her and all the time they made me watch. I beg them "Please let her go. Hit me instead." Bullet agree and I was glad.' He paused for a second and his eyes met Nikki's. 'He lied.

'He beat me and beat me and I don't care. They kick me and the dogs bite me, but my Maria is spared so it okay. Then, they tied me to a chair and they kill my baby.' He stopped and closed his eyes, tears seeping from his lids, his breathing laboured.

Nikki held the mask to his face and dried his tears with a tissue. 'You're doing really well Mr Marcovici, really well.'

When he was ready, he opened his eyes and signalled for Nikki to take the mask away. 'They left my Maria in a puddle of blood. They smoke and laugh and talk – oh they talk. I listen. I listen good.' He shook his head. 'One day I want to make them pay.'

He began to cough and the nurse moved closer, looking at the monitors. 'That's enough for now. Come back tomorrow. He's too tired for more.'

Stefan shook his head, his fingers gripped Nikki's arm and he pulled her closer. 'No, I must tell you. The nurse say today is Tuesday? Yes?'

Nikki nodded.

'Then . . .' His breathing became more laboured and Nikki gently replaced the oxygen mask over his face. 'It's okay Stefan, we'll come back tomorrow.'

He gripped her hand again, shaking his head. Nikki looked at the nurse who nodded. 'Let him have a few minutes of oxygen and then I'll let you have five more minutes. He seems determined to tell you something and it might make him calmer if he does.'

Over the sound of the ventilator and monitors Saj's phone rang, whilst Nikki's vibrated on the bed where she'd left it recording. Nikki nodded towards the door and Sajid left the room to take the call. If they were both being called, it must be something important.

With a trembling hand Stefan pulled the oxygen mask away from his mouth. 'Xavier – he is big boss. Big auction. Midnight Tuesday. Farm in Likely Moors, they say. Lots of men come to buy. Women . . . kids . . . men all . . . Xavier, big boss, will be there. Say Bradford burn. Say piggy piggy oink oink too stupid to work it all out. Wednesday Xavier bring drugs and whores to city. You must get there. Denis . . . he's so young . . . thirteen. They will sell him. You must save Denis.'

Stefan's eyes drifted shut and Nikki had a momentary compulsion to shake him. She needed more details. Was Likely – Ilkley? It seemed probable. Could what he heard be true or was it just something being fed to them to waste their time? How did all of this tie in with the information Ali had given her about the pimps and dealers. Stefan was spent. He'd given them as much as he could for now. The trouble was Nikki wasn't sure how the information tied into everything else – Adam Glass, the Bramhope brothers, Springer, Stevie and now she had another name. Xavier – who the hell was he?

She leaned over to smooth Stefan's hair from his forehead when the distant sound of an explosion made her look up. *What the hell was that?*

The door opened and Saj poked his head in, 'Firebomb at the Interchange taxi rank, Nikki. Someone just threw it at the waiting cabs. We need to go.'

With a final squeeze of Stefan's hand and a whispered, 'Your wife will be here soon,' Nikki ran after Saj, stopping only to tell the police officer to stay there and make sure nothing happened to Stefan. Running towards the car, she speed-dialled Anwar. 'I can't accompany Mrs Marcovici to view her daughter. You need to accompany her to ID Maria and then take her straight to her husband. Saj and I are heading to the Interchange. Can you believe it, it's only half four and we've got a reported dead body and an explosion!'

Ambulance, fire engine and police sirens filled the air. They ran to the car, Saj holding his injured arm. It was going to be one of those nights and she still had to tell Saj what Stefan had said.

Chapter 61

Five-thirty came and went with no notable impact. The body in Thornton was just a small distraction . . . a warm-up. That was only to be expected and Xavier wasn't disappointed. He was, however, becoming increasingly anxious as he paced the floor of his office, counting the minutes down till the next planned event. He was tempted to have a small whisky – just to take the edge off – but decided against it. Tonight wasn't the night to be even slightly impaired.

Another glance at the clock, then at his watch. They were synchronized, so it was only habit that made him look at both. Barely a minute to go. Xavier could hardly wait. If this one was a success, then he could be sure things were well underway as planned.

Thirty seconds . . . twenty . . . ten, nine, eight, seven, six, five, four, three, two . . .

When it came, it was even louder than he'd expected. The windows rattled and from the window the rising cloud of deep dense smoke was visible even in the foggy March air. Cars ground to a halt. Outside people were running, excited voices, chattering in higher pitches than normal. He opened his door and followed them as they took to the stairs, mobile phones held to their ears as they phoned their loved ones. Last thing he wanted was to look conspicuous by not following the crowd, so he took his phone out of his pocket and pretended to be deep in conversation as he too spilled out with the rest of the crowd onto the pavement. Sirens descended on the city centre from all directions and the Bradford sky was lit up like never before.

This had worked out even better than he'd expected. He couldn't wait now till six-thirty.

Chapter 62

As all the ambulances flew out of their bays at BRI, Sajid put his siren on and followed them whilst Nikki tried to phone Charlie, Ruby and Haqib to check they'd got home from school okay, but got no reply from any of them. Their bus stopped at the Interchange and she really needed to check they were okay. Sweat was beginning to gather under her armpits as she tried to quash her panic. She twanged her elastic band three times sharply on her wrist, then, running her fingers over her scar, she tried Marcus – engaged. She hung up and her phone rang immediately. *Marcus* flashed on the screen and with a sob she answered.

'They're okay, Nic. All of them are okay,' Marcus said before she had a chance to ask. 'They're back home, pissed off that they missed all the excitement and are Snapchatting their friends to find out what's gone on.'

His calm voice stilled the panic in her chest and she took a deep breath and sent a wobbly smile to Saj. 'Is it on the news, Marcus?'

'Yeah, local news and internet. A taxi driver was hurt, but the buses and trains are running as normal. It was only one lone idiot with a homemade petrol bomb, and from the reports I'm seeing, relatively ineffective bomb. You on your way there?'

Nikki glanced at her watch: 6.25 p.m. 'I reckon I'll check in with

Trafalgar House. We caught a reported dead body in Thornton earlier, might as well be heading there, if the Interchange is covered by the emergency services.'

'Keep in touch, Nik. This sort of thing unsettles the kids, you know. They worry about you. Sunni's here. Wants to speak to you. Love you.'

As Sunni's voice came over the line, Nikki smiled, the tension drained from her shoulders as the little boy rattled on nineteen to the dozen about bringing the bloody hamster rodent home at the weekend. For once, Nikki couldn't care less if he brought home a football team of them. She was just glad her family were safe with Marcus.

When she'd hung up and Saj had done an illegal U-turn on Duckworth Lane in order to head to Thornton, she played Saj the part of Stefan's recording that he'd missed. 'What do you make of it, Saj? Is this explosion at the Interchange just coincidence or is Stefan right?'

'He was pretty spaced out and he'd been beaten badly. Who knows what he remembers or what he's made up in his delirium?'

Nikki wasn't convinced. Even in his frail state, Stefan Marcovici had gripped her hand really tightly. His account of Maria's death tallied with the injuries Langley reported. His attempted escape also tallied. She picked up her phone and rang the incident room. 'It's DS Parekh – I mean DI Parekh.' She couldn't get used to using DI and she suspected that was an indication that she didn't really want to. 'I want you to access the file on Stefan Marcovici and locate the farm where he was found on near Haworth. I then want you to look for farms within a ten-mile radius and get local officers to pay a visit. You're probably looking for unoccupied or derelict properties. Do that as a priority please. We need to find out where Marcovici was held. There may be other men held captive there.'

As soon as she hung up, her phone started to ring again. Trafalgar House. 'Yep, DS Parekh.'

'Just had word of another body being reported in Undercliffe Cemetery, who have you got to send?'

Nikki exhaled. She was rapidly running out of officers and decided that it would have to be her and Sajid. 'DC Malik and I will go, but can you pull in some uniforms to assist?'

'For fuck's sake, Nikki, Undercliffe now?' Sajid slowed down and turned back to Duckworth roundabout.

'This is madness. In the space of just over an hour we've had two dead bodies reported and an explosion in the city centre. Do you really think Marcovici's intel is flawed?'

Saj shook his head 'No, it's looking less likely that he's making stuff up. Add that to the information Ali gave us and what have we got? This city is a melting pot and we are seriously stretched.'

Nikki bit her lip 'I'm going to give him the benefit of the doubt, Saj. Rather be safe than sorry.' She phoned through to Ilkley police station and explained that she wanted them to send her a list of all farmhouses on the moors around Ilkley, that were remote enough to conduct illegal activity in secret and that could accommodate many vehicles and large numbers of people. 'This is urgent, so if you manage to narrow the list down to a manageable number, get back to me right away. Also, if some of your undercover cars could just do some drive-pasts on the moor roads looking for any upmarket vehicles and vans and snag their number plates for me and check them out, I'd be really appreciative.'

'Happy to do it, was he?'

'She actually and yes, she was. Soon as I mentioned slave auctions, she was all in. She'll get back to us, ASAP.'

'Still not sure if its actionable intel, Nik. Stefan was in no fit state to be sure of anything. Poor sod's been through it; it's not surprising he's all flustered.'

Nikki shrugged. She'd wait and see, but for now there were things to do in Bradford.

Chapter 63

Nikki and Saj were nearly at Undercliffe Cemetery. With so much going on, they'd switched on the police radio and were trying to make sense of all the activity around the city as they drove. Interwoven with the air of resolute protocol and focus emanating from despatch control, there was a barely suppressed aura of panic from those on the ground. The police radio channels had been deemed the main means of communication so that despatch had an overall picture of what was happening in the city and were able to relay updates efficiently to those who needed to know.

'DS Parekh?' The voice crackled over the airwaves, calm and reassuring.

'Yes.'

'Two officers found the farmhouse near Haworth where Marcovici was held. It is deserted, but evidence of inhumane sleeping and overcrowded conditions in an outbuilding support Stefan Marcovici's statement. In light of the current situation in Bradford I directed the officers to secure the scene and redirected them back to the city. All available CSI teams are currently employed at the Interchange. Images taken at the farmhouse scene have been emailed to you.'

'Thanks, let's hope—'

But the despatcher had already moved on to another call.

Saj pulled up at the side of the road near Undercliffe Cemetery. The car park had been cordoned off and a single officer stood by it with two CSIs. He was about to turn off the ignition, when a crackle of static followed by a flurry of staccato reported:

'Firebomb reported at Barkerend Taxis . . . any available officers able to attend?'

'Great Horton Taxis firebombed . . . urgent assistance needed, casualties reported . . .'

'Reports of a fire at Ali's Taxis, Toller Lane . . .'

Nikki pounded the dashboard with her fist. 'Those are the taxi firms that Ali told us had received similar warnings to him. What the hell's going on, Saj? What are we missing? What's the purpose of this?'

'All I know is that if this continues, Bradford will implode. It'll be anarchy, even worse than the London Riots of 2011.'

Nikki looked at her watch. 6.37 p.m. She frowned. 'Things are happening every half-hour, Saj. Things to stretch the emergency services and have us pulled all over Bradford, first the body reported in Thornton Business Centre, then the Interchange explosion, the anonymous report about the body here at the cemetery and now a series of fires in the inner city taxi ranks . . . What the hell are they playing at?'

'And what the hell's going to happen next?'

'Don't know, but we don't have time for this!' Nikki waved her hand towards the cemetery. 'It's just a distraction. Tell the lad to process it on his own.'

Saj opened his window and beckoned the officer over. 'You seen the body?'

'Yes sir. Malnourished middle-aged male – looks to have been badly beaten.'

'Okay. You're in charge. When the CSIs are done with him, you need to arrange transportation to the morgue. With all that's going on, we're too strapped. Think you can manage that?'

Puffing his chest up, the officer grinned. 'Sure can, sir.'

Closing the window again, Saj looked at Nikki, 'Where to now, Nik? Got a plan?'

'Not a plan – just thoughts.' Idly twanging the elastic band on her wrist, Nikki concentrated. All of this disorder had a purpose. This was organized, disciplined chaos. She just had to work out what it all meant. Finally, she turned sideways in her seat, leaning her back on the car door and began counting things off on her fingers. 'Number one, we received two anonymous calls reporting dumped bodies, both of which have been described as male, malnourished and beaten, and therefore, to my mind, could be victims of the same people-trafficking ring Stefan Marcovici fell foul of, do you agree?'

Inclining his head, Saj pushed his seat back to give himself more leg room and angled his body towards Nikki. 'Yes, disposable goods, just like Maria Marcovici, her dad, Adam Glass and the two lads from Newcastle.'

'Exactly. Number two, we know the taxi firm bombings were pre-meditated because they each got a note warning them off working today. We can assume the Interchange bomb was also premeditated . . . what does that tell us?'

Saj thought about it. His face lit up. 'They didn't want to cause casualties at the taxi firms or at the Interchange.'

Squirming in her seat, Nikki grinned. 'So, the bastards view their captives as assets . . . slaves . . . not worthy of respect. We've seen how much disregard they have for human life, so why not just set off the bombs? Why give warnings? What was that all about?'

Nikki glanced at her watch again. '6.52 p.m.' She looked at Saj. 'Whatever they've got planned for 7 p.m., I doubt we'll be able to stop it. Let's put that aside for now and focus. What is the result of all this? What have they gained from this? It's a taken a lot of planning for them to implement such well-co-ordinated attacks, but what the hell are they getting from it, Saj? We're missing something. Talk to me. What are they gaining other than making us look like fools and being the catalyst for the breakdown of law and order in the city?'

'Smoke and mirrors.'

'Eh?' Nikki's face screwed up. 'There's plenty of smoke, I'll grant you that, but mirrors? What are you on about?'

'It's all a distraction. Whatever they're up to, they want us off-kilter.'

'Exactly. They're forcing us to deploy all our resources around the inner city, so, whatever they're really up to – and it must be that something really huge is happening elsewhere and –' Nikki was refastening her seat belt. '– my guess is that it's Ilkley – Stefan Marcovici must be right. Come on, Saj we're going to Ilkley.'

Chapter 64

'Operation Taxi Ranks went off without a hitch, boss.'

Xavier had just parked up in the drive outside his house, when Cyclops phoned. He'd passed one of the burning taxi offices on his way home and had been surprised by the tightening in his crotch. *Who'd have thought fire could evoke such raw emotion?* Glancing in his rear-view mirror, he grinned at himself. Things were certainly falling into place. Tonight was going to be a good night. 'You've done well, Cyclops. Where are you now?'

'At the Interchange. It's heaving here, emergency services, journalists. The Lord Mayor even turned up with one of the local politicians in tow – that weedy one with the nasal tones, you know who I mean?'

Xavier did. He hated both the politician in question *and* the Lord Mayor – who the hell thought it was okay to have a *woman* as Lord Mayor? The very title Lord Mayor meant it should be a man in that job. Bloody political correctness gone mad – Snowflake Culture – but now wasn't the time to get started on all of that. 'Yes, I know who you mean. You all set to slip away? You can't be late.'

'Don't worry, there's no way I'd miss out on tonight. No way. Leave it to me to dump my work colleague – shouldn't be too difficult to get rid of her. I'll be there in plenty of time. What about you? Are you all set?'

'Yes, I'll leave around seven, walk down to where you left the car for me and I'll be there in plenty time, whilst behind us, the fireworks will just keep on popping.'

The laugh died on his lips as he caught his wife peering out at him from behind the curtains. *Bitch.* Why couldn't she just mind her own business? If he didn't need to get showered and changed before leaving, he'd teach her a lesson, but there would be plenty of time for that later. For now, he wouldn't allow even her miserable face to affect his mood.

Chapter 65

As Saj drove away from the city into the leafy suburbs, Nikki worked through her thought processes again. Deep down she was sure that she and Sajid were right; still, the thought that she may have missed something made her heart flutter. What if they were wrong and she directed resources away from where they were most needed? Her experience and her gut instincts told her that her logic made sense. She took a deep breath, focused on clearing her head and then exhaled. With a tight grin to Sajid, she dialled a number and put her phone on speaker. 'Anwar? I need you and Williams and anyone else from our team you can grab to head to Ilkley. Meet at the police station there as soon as you can.'

'We've all been directed to different areas, ma'am. Williams is heading to Barkerend, I'm at the Great Horton taxi rank . . .'

'Look, I know what you've been directed to do. I'm overriding that. This is more important. Get in touch with Williams and head to Ilkley.'

There was a moment of silence, except for the background noise of shouting and car horns beeping. Nikki wondered if Anwar was going to defy her. She'd be perfectly within her rights to and Nikki wouldn't hold it against her.

'Okay, ma'am. I'm on my way . . . but before I hang up.

You need to check your emails – the Newcastle police sent the transcript of the interview with the Bramhope boy's friend and brother. Interesting reading.'

Nikki took another look at her watch. 7.30 p.m. With another senseless distraction of a whole load of fire crackers set off in City Park at 7 p.m., Nikki dreaded to think what would be next on their agenda. 'Just give me the details, I've no time to read it.'

'Okay – basically, Danny Boy's mate says Danny was going on about being in the big bucks after Tuesday night – that's tonight. Said he'd be driving Porsches and holidaying in Bermuda. Said his big boss – the X-Man, Xavier – was pulling out all the stops and that he, Danny, was his right-hand man. He told his mate that "Bradford was going to burn whilst they were raking in the big bucks and the pigs, that's us, wouldn't know what had hit them."'

Anwar paused for breath then, 'Shit . . . that's what this is all about. I'm on my way and I'll get Williams too. You can count on us.'

When she hung up, Nikki rolled her shoulders to ease the stiffness that had gathered there. 'Put the police radio back on, Saj. It's after 7.30 p.m.'

After a few moments of uncertainty, Nikki and Saj understood that the attack had targeted Lilycroft Police Station. The police station was purely administrative, but had a lot of staff working in the building and the building was directly opposite the flats where Saj and Langley lived. A young lad had been seen hanging around and at dead-on 7.30 p.m., he'd lit a rocket and hurled it through the automatic front doors of the police station. Before the police had time to react, he followed through with a whole load more, which fortunately were contained in a flash of cordite and colour between the two sets of doors.

'Bloody tossers are really yanking our chains.' Saj's knuckles were white on the steering wheel. Until the news had come in that it was only a firework display, Saj had clearly been concerned about Langley. This concern now changed to anger as he bit out his next words. 'You better get on with those calls, Nik. I want to get those bastards! They're making us look like fools.'

Nikki grimaced and thought for a moment. She had three more calls to make and two would be more difficult than the other. She opted for the easiest one first and dialled. 'DI Shepherd? We spoke earlier, it's Acting DI Parekh.'

'Ah, I was just about to call you. Seems like there's a lot going on over in Bradford. Your bosses have just been on the blower wanting to direct my limited resources to Bradford City Centre.'

Shit, she should have realized that they'd be calling in officers from outlying districts. If she was right, that would be part of the criminal's plan too – to rid Ilkley of all its police for the evening. Nikki's next words were crucial. She had to convince DI Shepherd to keep her officers in Ilkley and she had no concrete evidence to supply the other officer with. She needn't have worried though because Shepherd's next words told her she'd found an ally.

'After your earlier call, I did what you asked. There's really only one obvious location that meets all your specifications. It's a farm-house near Spicey Gill. There's an overgrown access lane, stretches for about three miles from Keighley Road and then another one dipping to the right, takes you to the old Smithson Farmhouse. It's barely accessible now, but with Land Rovers there wouldn't be a problem. I took the liberty of checking the land sale records and the farmhouse itself was sold only three months ago. It's huge, with loads of intersecting barns and well secluded from the main road. I think the cost of making it accessible put many buyers off.'

'That sounds like the sort of place we're looking for. You didn't by any chance take note of the buyer's name, did you?'

'Yes, I did as it happens. It was such a strange one; Xavier – Charles Xavier.'

'X-Man,' mumbled Nikki.

'Sorry, what did you say?'

'That's the one we're looking for. Can I ask you for one last favour . . .?'

'You want me to hold off on sending my officers to Bradford, don't you?'

Nikki hardly dared hold her breath. What she was asking was well out of line and she suspected that if the roles were reversed, even she would think twice about such a risky decision. 'I am. I suspect that as we speak, a whole load of men are using the distraction in Bradford to ensure that the auction, which I am now convinced is happening at your farmhouse, goes off without a hitch. The name Xavier has now come up more than once, in the course of our investigation and, I don't know about you, DI Shepherd, but I don't believe in . . .'

'Coincidences. Neither do I, Parekh. I'll expect you here soon.'

Her legs shook. That had gone better than expected, but she still had two calls to make that would determine how the rest of the evening would pan out. It was now almost 8 p.m. and she wanted to speak to DCS Clark *before* the next attack, but her other call was more important.

She took the burner Ali had given her out of her pocket. 'Wish me luck.'

Saj grinned 'You won't need it. Ali's always got your back.'

When Ali replied within two rings, she suspected he'd been waiting for her call. 'What do you need, Nik? The minute they fire-bombed our business, they took on more than they anticipated.'

Nikki exchanged a glance with Saj, who said, 'Told you so.'

'Hang on a minute, Ali.' She covered the phone with one hand. 'Saj, are you sure you're all right with this? It could all go disastrously wrong and our jobs will be on the line, not to mention the risk to our lives – these fuckers take violence to a whole new level.'

They'd spoken about it earlier and Saj hadn't hesitated. Nikki, however, wanted to give him one last chance to back out. Not only were they breaking rules, but they would be defying direct orders.

'What, you want all the fun for yourself, Nik? That's just selfish. We're partners, okay?'

Nikki went back on the phone and explained her plan to Ali. With Nikki and Sajid going to Ilkley, she wanted to be sure that there were eyes on the ground in Bradford. 'If you see owt suspicious, you're not to intervene, Ali. You got that? You're only there to pass on info to the police.'

Nikki could imagine Ali's eye roll, but she insisted. 'I mean it Ali. No heroics. I shouldn't be asking this of you, but we're seriously stretched. Promise me?'

'Okay, Nikki. We'll just scout round, keep an eye on things and if we see owt we'll phone it in.'

Exhaling, Nikki exchanged a relieved glance with Sajid and hung up.

'Right Saj. Now for the big one. Let's hope I can get this done quick. She took up her phone and dialled. Again. 'DCS Clark, I need to speak to you.'

Speaking quickly, Nikki explained that she and Saj were on their way to Ilkley and what she suspected was going to happen there that evening, leaving out that she'd enrolled Ali and his friends as back up. She laid all her suspicions out, the repeated mention of Xavier, and her suspicions that what was kicking off in Bradford was to distract from the auction.

For long seconds after she'd finished putting her case, the only sound from the phone was Clark's even breathing, Then a loud gush of expelled air, 'Shit, Parekh. Archie wasn't kidding when he said you were stubborn. We're under-prepared for any sort of stakeout. How am I supposed to get any armed officers to you in the next few hours, everything is focused in Bradford and . . .'

Her voice tailed away. Another exaggerated sigh. 'Give me the co-ordinates of this farmhouse. I'll see what I can do, but Parekh?'

'Yes ma'am?'

'You need to swear that you won't go in alone. You'll wait for back-up.'

Nikki gave Clark the co-ordinates and then said, 'Oh, my signal's breaking up.' She rubbed her phone along her trouser leg.

'Sorr . . .' Another rub. 'Breaking . . .' Another rub and then she disconnected.

Saj laughed. 'You, Acting DI Nikita Parekh, will likely now be relegated to Trafalgar House loo cleaner after that performance.'

Grinning, she shrugged, 'Let's hope it'll be worth it.'

Chapter 66

Showered and filled with nervous anticipation, Xavier slammed the door shut and walked past his car. He had a ten-minute walk to reach the car Cyclops had procured for him. It just meant there would be no evidence of him leaving home. Especially if he followed the route they'd planned to avoid CCTV. Once en route to Ilkley, he'd be anonymous anyway. The registration number of the vehicle couldn't be linked back to him.

Two more attacks – the co-ordinated setting-off of the fire alarms at BRI had caused chaos. It was pure genius to pay some lads to set them off exactly at the same time and then run. As he'd been watching Look North, they flashed to the BRI incident. Patients were being wheeled out into the car parks, some on trolleys, some in wheelchairs.

In a series of bizarre attacks at various sites throughout Bradford, the city's emergency services are being stretched to the limit. With Bradford Interchange being targeted, followed by a hoax bomb attack resulting in fireworks at Lilycroft police station and this most recent attack at BRI, the city lives in fear wondering what and where will be targeted next. According to a police spokesperson, no one has claimed responsibility yet. People have been advised to stay at home and await further advice from police as the struggle to get things under control continues. Officers and other emergency workers from other districts have been deployed to help. The prime minister has issued a statement condemning the series of attacks as terrorism and has pledged a 'sizeable, yet unspecified amount of aid to help return safety and stability to Bradford.

His wife was full of sympathy, but he'd found it funny, politicians trying to capitalize on it, hoping to make a good impression, chief of police trying not to look like a rabbit caught in the headlights; it all made for a good night's viewing. He didn't have time to hang around though, so he'd had a shower and changed before leaving just after the seven o'clock event which was parked cars being set alight behind the National Science and Media Museum. *Bradford was on fire tonight.*

He phoned Cyclops. 'Everyone in position at the location?'

'Yes, you on your way now, boss?'

'Yes, and you?'

'Just sneaking away now. I'll meet you there. It's all systems go.'

Chapter 67

Half past nine, the moonlight casting eerie shadows over Ilkley moors and the tension was palpable. It had taken ages to drive from Bradford to Ilkley. The roads were clogged with near stationary traffic and Nikki and Saj had been forced to take a circuitous route.

The rendezvous point at the car park was far enough away from the track leading to the farmhouse, yet close enough to get there quickly when necessary. Apart from Saj's Jag, a couple of Ilkley-owned patrol cars, which Nikki had insisted park up out of sight of the road, a couple of undercover cars and Williams' and Anwar's, the car park was empty – and eerily still. If Marcovici was right, they had two and a half hours till show time, but Nikki reckoned they'd see some activity beforehand. The buyers would have to make their way to the farm in time for the auction and Nikki was determined to catch those perverts as well as the organizers.

Nikki and Saj got out of their car and joined the group of officers gathered under a tree. She'd no sooner opened her mouth to introduce herself when another vehicle turned into the car park. As one, the group tensed and then swung round towards the arrival.

'Fuck's sake.' Nikki stormed over, dragged the driver's door open and glared in. 'What is it you don't understand about staying in Bradford, Ali?'

Swinging his leg out, Ali joined Nikki on the tarmac, towering over her as Haris got out of the passenger side.

'And you brought Haris. What is it with you two? Got a damn death wish or something?'

'Aw, calm down Nik. Did you really think we were going to leave you on your own to take this lot of sickos down?'

'Er . . . in case you missed it . . . I'm here.' Saj strolled over to join Nikki, the rest of the group of officers, relaxed now that their visitors had been identified as allies, just behind him. He gestured to the other officers. 'And so are these.'

Haris snorted and Ali sent a warning glare in his friend's direction. Spreading his arms placatingly he said, 'Look, we won't get in your way. Just consider us back-up.'

Shepherd stepped forward, her face taut, colour high on her cheeks. 'You are civilians. You can't be here. I'm going to have to ask you to leave. As it is, you're holding us up. Now please just get back in your vehicle and head on back to Bradford.'

'But . . .'

Ali wasn't allowed to finish his sentence before Shepherd interrupted. 'Go home . . . I don't want to have to waste time arresting you or sending officers to escort you back, so just go.'

With a quick glance at Nikki, Ali shrugged and then nodded to Haris. 'Let's go. We're not welcome here.'

As Ali started up the engine, the group turned away, leaving Nikki to watch her friend depart. With a sharp toot, he headed for the entrance and winked at Nikki. Smothering her smile, she raised her hand and turned to join the others.

Both Shepherd and DCS Clark had requested armed back-up and were awaiting an ETA. As Nikki had stressed, this extraordinary situation called for extraordinary measures and although seeming a little more anxious than Nikki would have liked her to be, Shepherd was still on board, although with the proviso that she would not authorize her officers to go into an unknown situation without armed back-up. That said, she'd despatched two officers to hike cross-country to a peak that allowed them to view the farmhouse from a safe distance.

Clark had cursed quite a lot, and echoed Shepherd's proviso that Nikki wait for back-up. Clark had informed Archie of what was going on and he'd weighed in with his own instructions that Nikki and Saj were 'not to be heroes' during a heated phone call. He'd also, after Nikki had laid everything out for him, gone quiet for a moment before saying, 'I want to check something out. I'm sure I've come across that Xavier name before. I'll get back to you.'

The longer they waited, the more edgy Nikki got. Her wrist was red raw with the number of times she'd twanged it and Saj had threatened to take the band from her. Even her glower hadn't made him back down. When she thought she wasn't going to be able to take much more, Shepherd's radio kicked in. She and her officers were using an encrypted airwave to communicate. 'What you got?'

Nikki, huddled up beside Shepherd, was counting on them having the right place so much, that she was holding her breath, only realizing it when she was forced to release it in a whoosh.

'Eyes on the farmhouse, ma'am. Vehicles approaching from Keighley Road. Parked up by the barn are three transit vans, can't see their reg numbers. Various men with guns are roaming the area. There's at least three Rottweilers tied on extended chains at intervals round the perimeter. Can't see the rear of the premises, but a sort of ad hoc parking space has been sectioned off and one of the guys with guns is checking with the drivers before sending them to park up. I can see six vehicles parked already and three . . . no . . . four en route.'

'Can you ID any of the occupants?'

'No, they're all bundled up in coats and hats. Most look male, but I can't be a hundred per cent sure. What shall we do?'

'Stay put, keep notes of anything that might be useful and

report back at twenty-minute intervals . . . oh, and don't get yourselves bloody killed. If you feel even remotely under threat, back up.'

'We were right.' Nikki high-fived Saj. Now that her suspicions had been confirmed beyond a reasonable doubt, Nikki was keen to get going. She phoned Clark back and updated her. 'Any word on the back-up?'

'Not yet Nik, but—'

'Yes, you said, boss. I'm not stupid.'

'No but you *are* sometimes reckless, Parekh. Don't let this be one of those times . . . that's an order.'

Clark hung up before Nikki could respond. *Bloody cheek!*

Chapter 68

It was after eleven and Xavier was pleased. The disruption he'd left behind in Bradford, meant that there would be no distractions here. Soon, the buyers would arrive and things could begin. He could hardly wait. Driving up to the farmhouse was a bumpy ride. No doubt there would be complaints about that, but, if you made it too accessible you could end up with every birdwatcher in the area traipsing in. No, better to keep it . . . rustic . . . yes, that was the word the estate agent had used. Good job he'd been able to bounce the balance around the world a few times before the cash landed in their account. Further down the line, if someone should decide to enquire about that transaction, they wouldn't be able to link it to him.

Cyclops had done a good job. A designated parking area for their clients. Bullet welcoming his guests and checking they had the correct code word. Didn't hurt to put the wind up them a little. Keep them under control. Bullet wasn't someone anyone would choose to argue with and it was always worthwhile to have a show of strength at the start of proceedings. That way, when it came to parting with the green stuff, they'd be more inclined.

He'd slipped his balaclava on before turning into the rugged road and had his code word ready. Bullet had been told to expect him and to make sure he was taken immediately for one last show of the merchandise. The car in front of him moved on into the car park and Xavier stopped and ran down his window. As usual when wearing his mask, he deepened his voice and injected a disinterested tone to it. 'Magneto.'

Bullet frowned as if that wasn't the word he'd expected, then something must have clicked in his thick skull and he straightened, twisting his mouth into a smile that was more threatening than his passive look. 'Yes sir, follow me. He will park your car.' He gestured to another armed man who came over and without saying a word, slid into the driving seat vacated by Xavier. The man who didn't look like any parking valet Xavier had ever seen, parked his car next to the vans. Xavier and Bullet waited until he returned, then Bullet barked instructions. 'Take Mr Xavier to Cyclops . . . and be quick about it.'

Walking over the uneven surface, Xavier was oblivious to the cold. The thought of the night's proceedings was enough to warm him and even the mud ruining his shoes wasn't enough to dampen his mood. They reached a door which led to the byre. The cow shed was smaller than the hay barn, but spacious enough to store the cattle. He smiled.

The girls were all dressed up in cheap Primark tat that barely covered their tits and asses. Smiles painted red, eyes wide and drug-fuelled. The boys were dressed in ball hugging boxers with plain white t-shirts. Goose bumps speckled all visible skin and Xavier said – 'get a heater in here. We can't show them if they're shivering like that.'

Each sale lot had been given a top-up of their special fix. Not enough to space them out entirely, just enough to make them compliant. Cyclops had pinned a number on each of them and they sat on rugs that had been placed on bales of hay, waiting for the off.

He stepped through to the side room, where a small heater cast a cosy glow and sat down with a glass of whisky to wait. Outside he could hear the faint sounds of vehicles arriving, the soft burr of talking and footsteps as the buyers settled themselves in the large arena.

Bullet poked his head round the door. 'We're nearly there, Xavier. One more client to arrive and then we can kick off. Are you going to greet them?'

Behind his balaclava, Xavier smiled. 'I wouldn't miss it for the world.'

He emptied his glass in one swallow and walked over to the door that connected to the hay barn. Opening it slightly, he peeped through. There was a buzz in the room. Xavier's visitors sat on rug-covered hay bales that were positioned in a sort of amphi-theatre shape around the barn, sectioned off by low metal trestles. Gas heaters and ambient lighting created intriguing shadows.

Although most were male, Xavier detected a few female shapes. Perhaps they were agents sent to order on their boss's behalf. The thing that everyone had in common with Xavier was that their faces were covered. Xavier recognized Boris Johnson, Donald Trump, Scream and Mickey Mouse masks. Others had balaclavas, like his, and some had chosen superheroes like Batman and Spider-Man. Another thing they had in common with him – their penchant for superheroes. The door on the far side opened and all eyes turned to it. A small man in a Donald Duck mask walked in, looked round and selected his seat. His visitors were all here.

Xavier looked at Cyclops who obediently handed him a microphone. Xavier threw his shoulders back and entered the semi-circle. He waited in the centre till an expectant hush settled round the room. Throwing his arms wide, he spoke into the microphone as if he was a circus ringmaster. 'Welcome, ladies and gentlemen. Tonight, we have something for everyone's tastes, but . . . not everyone will go home *with* something. We have selected an exquisite range of goods, but the competition will be fierce, so to avoid disappointment, I suggest you dig deep.'

He waved to the side-lines and Cyclops walked in carrying a stack of cards on which they'd recorded the item specifics for each lot. Taking the first card, Xavier cleared his throat . . . and Bullet appeared pushing the first girl in front of him with his gun. She stumbled and looked round the hushed room, eyes wide. She attempted to run back to the byre, but one of Bullet's thugs yanked her and pushed her forward. With Bullet following, prodding her if she slowed down, the girl was forced to circle the crowd whilst Xavier spoke. 'Lot one is a dainty little thing. Low-maintenance, but well broken-in and amenable to every, and, ladies and gentlemen, I mean *every* fantasy. Natural blonde hair, as you can see . . .' He strode over, yanked her skirt up and tugged at her pubic hair, making the girl yelp. The audience laughed and, it was at that precise point that Xavier knew he had them eating out of the palm of his hand.

WEDNESDAY 18TH MARCH 2020

Chapter 69

Just after midnight a report came through from the officers with eyes on the farm. 'Looks like they're about to kick off. About twenty minutes ago a bloke drove up and was escorted into the side entrance, ma'am. Soon after that a final car arrived. Most of the guards with the guns have entered the premises through either the main or the side entrances. There's three that I can see still outside, plus those damn dogs.'

'How many who're not guards?' Nikki couldn't stop herself interrupting.

'Probably about thirty or so.'

'And the total number of armed men is . . .?'

'Unless there's some who arrived before we did, I'd estimate fifteen or sixteen with weapons.'

Shepherd turned to Nikki. 'That's not good odds, Parekh.'

She was right, it wasn't good odds and according to Clark, the armed response team were about twenty minutes out.

'What do you reckon, Saj?'

He shrugged, 'Well we could just get in position where the track forks down to the farmhouse. We'll be far enough away not to be seen, but a lot closer than we are now. When the armed

353

unit comes, we'll be ready, and if anyone tries to leave . . . well
. . . we're blocking their exit.'

'Yep, okay, everyone get vests on.' She began to hand out
tactical vests.

Nikki turned to give her little team of four instructions on
safety and parameters. Anwar and Williams were buzzing. Sajid
less so. 'Your arm okay, Saj?'

He nodded. 'I'm not a damn wimp, you know. Bring it on.'

'You're taking up the rear, Saj. Don't want you being injured
again tonight.'

They all climbed into Williams' car which they reckoned was
the most durable and in a convoy of three cars made their way
towards the fork in the track.

Chapter 70

'And now for lot three.' Xavier was in his element. Playing to the crowd, spurred on by the amount of money that had been bid. Untraceable assets always attracted the big bucks. Resources no one was looking for, that society turned a blind eye to, invisible chattels that could be disposed of when they ceased to be profitable or when they'd lost their appeal or just 'expired' at the hands of their owners. It was all part of the deal and judging by the deep pockets here tonight, his brokerage service was a major attraction.

'Ladies and gentlemen, this one is a specialist interest lot. Guaranteed pre-pubescent male, brunette with striking blue eyes and a taut derrière . . . who's going to kick off the bidding for Denis?'

The boy looked petrified, his eyes darting round the room, his hands cupped over his groin as if that would protect him. This only added to his attraction. The people here, willing to go to such lengths to feed their disgusting perversions or those of their clients, in the main, wanted subservience. The lad's panting breaths filled the silence and, before Bullet had even prodded him to take another step forward, three hands were in the air.

'A hundred thousand!' – Spider-Man.

'One fifty!' – Mickey Mouse

And, surprise, surprise, Donald Duck – 'One seventy-five.'

Xavier could barely conceal his excitement. Sweat trickled down the back of his neck and gathered under his armpits – sheer adrenaline. He was raking it in and they'd barely started.

'Look how, cute he is. The way he shivers. Which one of you will be lucky enough to break him in? Come on now, don't be shy.'

Bullet prodded him with his gun and the boy stumbled forward, pissing himself.

For an instant, Xavier was cross, thinking that would end the interest in him. He was wrong – more hands raised, larger and larger amounts were pledged. The boy's fear had piqued their interest even more. *Always thought JustGiving was overrated – seems I'm right!*

Bouncing on his toes around the arena, Xavier's patter became more and more teasing, more and more flirtatious as he played to his audience. The more hands that shot in the air, the more he revelled in the attention. This was business, purely a supply and demand transaction that both parties found mutually beneficial.

Xavier made a final circuit of the arena, when a slight ruckus broke out near the back of the barn. He glanced over, but kept his endless chatter going as he peered into the shadows. Nothing to concern himself about. His men were more than able to deal with anything. A couple of the armed guards made their way towards the sounds, but the audience was engrossed in Xavier's performance.

Bullet left the boy cowering near one of the metal barriers and made his way to join his men at the back of the room. The boy glanced round and before Xavier could anticipate his intentions, the lad took to his feet and ran towards a barrier. He hurdled right over it and kept going, jumping over the hay bales, till he got to the exit. Xavier ran after him, tried to grab his skinny arm, but missed. Unable to jump the barrier, Xavier pushed it aside and took off after the boy, yelling to his men for help. All at once, the barn was filled with activity. Excited yells and squeals filled the air, until everyone was silenced by the single shot that reverberated around the building.

Chapter 71

Gathered in a huddle around Shepherd's car, Nikki and everyone else waited with increasing impatience for their back-up. The not-knowing what was going on, was killing Nikki. Her imagination was in overdrive. She'd read reports of these sorts of events in other parts of the country and the mere thought of what the victims might be being subjected to made her feel raw. She'd begun scratching her arms until Saj had grabbed her hand and with some force twanged her elastic band. She took a deep breath and nodded her thanks. Shit, this was taking its toll.

Nikki was on the point of hijacking Williams' car and driving up the track herself when a number of things happened in quick succession. First, Archie phoned.

'Parekh, I've got a link to that Xavier character. You'll never believe it but, I spotted that one of the bright sparks on your list signed out of one of the conferences using a false name. I just put it down to him being a dick, but when you mentioned Xavier it clicked. I went back and double checked. The room was allocated to—'

Then, before Archie could finish his sentence, a gunshot echoed over the silent moorland. Nikki spoke rapidly before hanging up. 'Gotta go Archie, text me the name.'

This was followed by the crackle of Shepherd's radio and one of her two lookout officers' voices came over the airwaves. 'Shot fired, we're moving closer.'

Nikki glanced at Sajid, but he was already running back to the car with Williams and Anwar on his heels. Glad they were all on the same page, Nikki caught them up and flung herself into the passenger seat as Williams started the engine. 'Looks like we're heading in folks, but keep your bloody heads down. I don't want to lose any of you.'

Williams gunned the engine and was off down the track, making no attempt to avoid the holes and stones as he drove. Behind them, one of the other cars followed and Nikki assumed the third had remained to meet the armed response team.

The farmhouse came into sight, light spilling from a large building and a series of portable low amber lamps dotted around the car park area. Masked figures were streaming towards the parked vehicles and unmasked men with guns were trying to herd them back, by prodding them with their guns. The three dogs were snarling and yanking against their chains, determined to get in on the action and Nikki hoped the chains were attached to something secure.

A few cars were attempting to back out of their spaces, but were being hindered by other vehicles not willing to give way. Two men in balaclavas stood to the side yelling orders at the armed men. By the door to a smaller building stood a guard, focused on keeping two masked figures away from the door.

In the chaos no one had yet noticed the cars approaching, so for now they had an advantage. Nikki phoned Shepherd. 'We're going to park sideways across the track, to try to hold them there till back-up arrives. Can you do the same? Hopefully, none of them will be stupid enough to try to off-road it.'

'Okay, will do.'

As Williams positioned the car and the others slipped out to use the car for protection, Nikki spotted activity from behind the farm. She nudged Saj, 'Look.'

Two burly figures with weapons in their hands, probably base-ball bats, were sneaking up from the rear.

'Is that Ali and Haris?' Saj glared at Nikki. 'You knew they'd hang around, didn't you?'

'Course not. How could I? But where's the damn back-up when you need them? Ali and Haris need a distraction at the front of the farm if they're going to get in at the back.'

Before Sajid could reply, Nikki had yanked Williams' keys from his hand and clamoured into the driver's seat. Revving as loudly as she could, she activated the police light and huddling over the steering wheel to minimize how much of her body could be used for target practice, she headed straight for the biggest group of people. Her hand pressed on the horn for added affect. If she could buy some time for Ali and Haris, then she would. Maybe they'd be able to free some of the kids before it all kicked off big time

Some of the masked men at the front of the building scattered, whilst others with guns took aim, letting off a few shots as Nikki got closer, before also scattering. As Nikki pressed her foot harder on the accelerator, she saw Ali had disposed of the man guarding the smaller barn. Nobody was paying any attention to that building, everyone was focused on escaping from the car park or escaping Nikki's erratic driving. When she caught sight of Haris leading a group of frail looking figures round the back of the barn, she grinned. Back-up would soon be here and everything would be—

A bullet smashed through the windscreen. Nikki's head jerked to the side, her foot came off the gas and her hands slipped from the steering wheel as the car headed straight for one of the transit vans.

Sajid hadn't needed to say a word to Shepherd. She jumped back into her vehicle and didn't object when he climbed in beside her. 'I've heard the gossip about how stubborn Parekh is, but I thought it was exaggerated.'

Saj gave a humourless laugh as they gained on Nikki. 'No – no exaggeration.'

Shepherd tutted, 'And I suppose those figures leading those poor people from the side building are her friend Ali's men.'

'Can't see anyone leading them. They must've just decided to get out themselves.'

Saj grimaced as his shoulder throbbed with every bump they went over and then, when he saw Nikki's car veer straight for the van, he groaned. 'She's been hit. The bastard's hit her.'

He was out of the car and running towards Nikki before Shepherd had stopped. As he dragged Nikki's door open, light flooded the entire area as a helicopter circled above. A tinny voice spoke through a loudhailer. 'Put down your weapons! This is the police, you are surrounded!' And from all directions, officers in full riot gear, carrying guns, approached.

Ignoring the scene around him, Saj heart accelerated at the dribble of blood by Nikki's temple. He tried to find a pulse on Nikki's neck.

'Gerroff, Saj. I'm all right. Fucker couldn't aim straight if he tried. It's just a graze. But, I thought that if I played dead, they'd leave me alone, but hey, ho . . . the cavalry's here.'

'Not before bloody time, Nik. That was a close call.'

The armed response team got the scene secured and weapons confiscated in record time. Although Nikki wanted to unmask each of the predators who'd participated in the auction, she was more interested in unveiling the organizers, particularly Xavier. As she approached the side barn, where the organizers and their thugs had been secured, a figure appeared beside her in tactical gear. He flipped up his visor and Nikki glared at him. 'What the hell are you doing here, Drummond?'

His lips curled in an arrogant sneer. 'You could've fucked that up, Parekh! We had it all under control. The gunshot that you heard was me giving the signal for this lot to descend, your interference could've made it all go tits-up. When will you learn to keep your nose out of other people's business?'

As Nikki glared at him, Saj took a step forward. 'Maybe if you got the idea of co-operation and working as a team, instead of keeping things from us, then this could have been handled more efficiently. If it hadn't been for Ali and Haris, who knows what would have happened to those people who were about to be auctioned off.'

Nikki rested a hand on Saj's arm. 'Leave it Saj. Let's just go and see the coward behind the mask.'

Drummond grabbed her by the arm and yanked her round. 'Oh no, you don't. This isn't your investigation.'

Nikki shrugged his arm off, her face flushed, her fist itching to finds its mark on his face. She moved closer and snarled. 'Don't you ever lay hands on me again or I will have you up for assault.'

A voice from behind interrupted them. 'No need for that, Parekh. Drummond will be perfectly happy to allow you access.' Nikki turned around. DCS Clark stood between two uniformed officers in a light-coloured coat that had become speckled with mud during her short walk from the police car she'd arrived in, to where she now stood. Her face taut and pale told Nikki she'd brought bad news with her.

'Stevie?'

Clark's smile widened. 'She's not come round yet, but she's improving. Springer's spending time with the baby. It'll all work out. In light of your stellar contribution to this investigation, I have spoken to Drummond's superior officer and we've agreed that you deserve to make the arrests. We're going to prosecute this as a joint case – pool our evidence and resources.'

Nikki began walking to the door when she stopped. 'Is Drummond taking care of the Bradford end of things?

'Something like that.'

Nikki nodded, then . . . 'I do have a condition, DCS Clark.'

The other woman quirked an eyebrow.

'I want to be demoted to DS again. I'm not cut out for this DI stuff.'

Grinning, Clark inclined her head. 'Yes, you're a little too impetuous for a DI, but you do make an excellent DS. DCI

Hegley will just have to find his own sidekick when he comes back to work.'

Just before she and Saj reached the door, Nikki took her phone from her pocket. Archie had sent her a text. She frowned. There was only one word on it. What the hell did that mean?

As she opened the door and walked through to face Xavier, the mastermind behind the entire operation, Archie's message made perfect sense.

'Yousaf?'

Anika's boyfriend, the father of her nephew, Lord Mayoral candidate and local do-gooder businessman looked back at her, his face tight. He lunged towards her, but was hauled back by two of the response team. Disgust filled Nikki – disgust and other things too, but guilt lurked right at the top. Guilt that she hadn't spotted this when he spent so much time in her backyard. And fear that even after all he'd done, Anika would still blame her if she arrested him.

Nikki stepped back and, seeming to sense her thoughts, Sajid stepped forward and made the arrest in her place. 'Bitch! You always think you're so fucking smart, don't you Parekh? But I had you and that whore of a sister of yours fooled for years, didn't I? Not so fucking smart after all, are you?'

'Perhaps not Yousaf, but I'm not the one in handcuffs, am I?' Nikki turned her back on the man before she was tempted to rip him apart.

Eyes averted, Nikki walked past Yousaf to a man huddled over on one of the hay bales. He was cuffed and as she came closer, he looked up at her. Nikki had no room for surprise left inside, so she just nodded once as she looked at Lisa Kane's photographer Max Ashton – Cyclops. 'You really are a sick son of a bitch, aren't you? Wonder how Kane's career will pan out now with her sidekick going down for his part in the biggest people-trafficking organization in the UK? If I were you, I'd sing, because I know for a fact how wily that little shit Yousaf can be and he'll try to pin everything on you.'

Chapter 72

Nikki insisted on driving through Bradford before going home.

They'd rescued twenty victims of trafficking from Ilkley and now that Bullet and Ashton and some of the other low-level operatives were squealing, officers had been sent to various addresses in the district to release other victims of modern-day slavery. The number of victims shocked Nikki. Nearly two hundred and rising. Victims of all ages had been subjected to varying degrees of abuse and forced into doing all sorts of things whilst kept in abominable conditions. Social services, BRI and the other emergency services continued to be stretched as they tried to care for everyone.

Processing the various crime scenes, building cases against Xavier and his gang, as well as against the predators they'd captured in Ilkley, would be months in the making. Hundreds of people would be convicted by the end of the process and it stuck in Nikki's craw that most of them were entitled well-off public figures.

Stefan Marcovici had been reunited with his wife, but the scars for both ran deep. They'd only wanted to do the best for their family but it had ended in disaster. The one glimmer of light for Marcovici was that it was down to him that they'd been able to blow up the whole operation, releasing his friend Rogin and the young lad Denis. Nikki had made sure to have both visit Stefan as soon as they were well enough.

Nikki vowed to meet with as many victims as she could, but the sheer numbers made it unlikely. Still she'd try. She'd already spent time with the ones from Ilkley however, most had been groomed onto drugs and the road ahead was going to be a hard one.

Five brothels, hidden upstairs from legitimate businesses, were discovered. Remote buildings throughout the district were identified as drug production and packaging plants. Nikki was sure many more would come to light before the investigation closed.

Now, staring through the darkness, exhaustion making her bones heavy, Nikki regarded her city. Bradford had burned last night, still, she was standing. She totted up the damage. Apart from the Interchange and the taxi ranks, three pubs had been petrol-bombed, and a couple of the all-night supermarkets had had cars driven into their windows as well as the firework attack on Lilycroft Police Station. The physical damage to the city wasn't the worst part of it though. It was the emotional fallout that would follow. Bradford folk were resilient, but the knowledge of the extent of the exploitation masterminded by a man they'd trusted as a councillor and charity worker would have far reaching repercussions.

Closer to home, Nikki dreaded the inevitable confrontation with Anika. When she'd called Marcus, Anika was already at their house. Someone, Nikki thought it may have been Sajid, leaked Yousaf's name. Marcus had put her sister to bed in the spare room and given her one of her sleeping pills. Tomorrow she'd have to face what had happened and Nikki was going to make damn sure that her sister's first priority was Haqib.

'Take me home, Saj. We both need our partners. Tonight's been the worst ever.'

Chapter 73

There was still so much work to do, so despite Marcus's hope that she'd have one day off at least, Nikki went into work. Anika had refused to speak to her and that was fine with Nikki. Perhaps they both needed time . . . time to heal . . . time to process everything. Nikki had found it almost impossible to sleep even though her brain and her body both cried out for it. Every time she closed her eyes she saw one of the victims. This was going to take time and, even before Marcus had suggested it, she'd booked an appointment with her counsellor. Over the last year Nikki had learned she couldn't do everything on her own and that knowing when to accept help and support was a strength.

Sajid was there when she arrived and by the looks of his face he'd fared no better than her in terms of sleep.

'DCS Clark wants to see you, Nik. She's in Archie's office.

Nikki looked over. The blinds were shut and she hoped that Clark wasn't going to try to convince her to stay on as Acting DI. Right now, Nikki wasn't sure she had the strength to argue about it. She moved over, rapped on the door with her knuckles and walked in. DCS Clark sprawled in Archie's chair, her feet up on the table and a blanket over her. As Nikki entered she straightened up, blinking furiously, her face smudged with mascara and a trail of drool on her chin. She wiped it away and exhaled. 'Come in Parekh. I need to talk to you.'

She gestured to a chair opposite and waited till Nikki sat down. 'I asked you to give me till yesterday evening, didn't I?'

'Sorry?' Nikki frowned, wracking her brains to make sense of what the DCS was talking about. Then she got it. 'You mean you've . . .?'

Closing her eyes for a moment, Clark, put her elbows on the desk and nodded. 'Drummond, Nikki. It was Drummond.' Her voice shook, yet she looked straight into Nikki's eyes. 'I've made a statement, Jackie Dobson has too and some of the other women are prepared to make statements too, including DS Springer. Forensics, as you know, confirmed she'd been roofied, but the DNA from the hair found on her body and DNA extracted from under her fingernails match with Drummond's.'

Nikki was numb. She'd disliked Drummond, found him arrogant and sexist, but he was a police officer. Rape was about control and power and Nikki saw that the women Drummond had targeted had been strong women. Women he must have felt threatened by. She was glad they'd found the collective strength to come forward at last.

'How did you get Dobson to talk?' Nikki asked, as the car containing Joe Drummond reversed before heading back to Bradford.

'I didn't. In and among all the chaos that took off in Bradford tonight, two things happened. The first was that I realized I couldn't remain silent any longer about what I suspected had been done to me. What you said to me and the thought of Springer and all his other victims, made me decide to tell my ex-husband and daughter what had happened, so I could testify against him. Then, Springer woke up – groggy and sore and she's got a long fight back to health ahead of her – but she named Drummond and of course we had the Rohypnol evidence and the rape kit to corroborate. I phoned Dobson, said the name and she burst into tears. We will prosecute him.'

Nikki stood up and smiled. 'You did the right thing. Thanks to you one more scumbag will join the ones we arrested last night.' She leaned over and squeezed Clark's arm. 'I'm here if you need to talk.'

And she left the room, her heart heavy with thoughts of the long process ahead.

One Month Later

'I still don't understand why we had to host this pre-Easter drinks thing, Marcus.'

Marcus pulled Nikki to him and kissed her. 'Because it's spring, because our friends have been through a lot, because we've been through a lot and we need to celebrate each other and try to put some of the past behind us.'

Nikki's face clouded. Every night since the one when Bradford almost burned, she'd had nightmares. True to her word, she'd visited as many of the victims as she could. She'd been to every building that had housed them and she'd held it together during every interview she'd conducted with the likes of Bullet or Ashton or the slimy perverts who'd tried to buy human beings like they were lollipops. But she felt dirty – contaminated by the filth, tainted by their inhumanity and almost broken by the ceaseless despair she encountered every time she opened a file, or spoke to a witness or encountered the heartless arrogance of the perpetrators. Maybe Marcus was right. Maybe this would help to cleanse them all a little bit.

Her mum, back from India now, was in the kitchen with her ex-mother-in-law, Khalid's mum. Surprisingly, the two had hit it off and so far, Enaya had been a real pleasure to be around.

She'd had the sense to realize that if she wanted to be part of their family, then she needed to be grandma to not just Charlie, but also to Sunni and Ruby too. Nikki smiled when she caught sight of Sunni sitting on her lap. Anika sat at the table. She'd lost weight and was still prone to weeping at the drop of a hat, but she was trying. She still held back with Nikki. Couldn't look her in the eye, but it was still early days. Haqib had, so far, taken things in his stride. Who could have thought that his father's persistent disinterest would someday be a benefit to the boy? Nikki and Marcus were keeping an eye on him though. He'd insisted on bringing his girlfriend and they were snogging in the front room. Loves young dream might still make it.

The doorbell rang and Ruby ran to answer it. 'It's Uncle Saj and Uncle Langley and some other woman.'

When would Ruby learn to be a bit more tactful? Nikki stepped into the hallway, hugged Langley and Sajid and grinned at the young woman who stood slightly behind them 'Hi, I take it you're Fozia?'

Before Fozia could reply, Charlie, halfway down the stairs, said, 'Oh you're the one that dun't mind Uncle Saj being gay. That's cool.'

Nikki opened her mouth to tell Charlie off, but Fozia laughed. 'Yep, I'm the cool sister. Where do you think he gets it from?'

The front door opened again letting in a rush of cold air and a tetchy Scotsman carrying a baby in a car seat. 'Let us in. Let us in, we've got a bairn wi' us and I'm freezing ma proverbials out here.'

Everyone moved into the living room as Archie and the baby entered with Stevie and Springer. No way could Nikki bring herself to call her Fliss. Both were still painfully thin and Stevie relied on a walking stick, but they were alive and so was their baby.

Before Archie had the chance to put the baby down, Nikki's mum bustled through from the kitchen and pushing Archie out of the way she unstrapped the wide-awake child. 'Aw, my little cherub. My little lovely Amy Nikita, *beti*.'

Nikki caught Springer's eye and they shared a tight smile. Stevie, grateful to Nikki for saving her baby's life, had insisted on calling the child after Nikki. Neither Nikki nor Springer wanted that. Although the situation between them had changed – when you save someone's kid and wife you pretty much become linked – they'd never be close friends. Nikki, on the other hand, rated Stevie, which was why she and Springer had worked out the compromise. Nikita could be her middle name.

The only thing was, Nikki's mum wouldn't let it lie. 'Her name's just Amy, Mum. Not Amy Nikita.'

Her mum glared at Nikki. 'Don't be silly, Nikita. You saved this baby and they've called her Amy Nikita – I'm sure Fliss and Stevie will soon be asking you to be her godmother too.'

As Nikki and Springer both simultaneously choked on the glasses of wine Marcus had handed them, Saj, Langley and Marcus bit back their grins.

Desperate to find out what happens to Nikki and her team? If you want to be the first to know about the next gripping D.S. Nikki Parekh case, sign up to Liz Mistry's email list here:

hyperurl.co/lizmistrysignup

Acknowledgements

There is a real team effort to getting a book ready for publishing and as usual, I have been surrounded by a fabulous team. From my editor, Belinda Toor, who keeps my spirits up with her never-ending positivity, tenacious dedication to pulling the best writing from me that she possibly can and a great sense of humour, to all the HQ Digital team who work tirelessly behind the scenes – I hope you know how much I value your contributions.

Before I even send the manuscript to my editor, my friend and first reader, Toria Forsyth-Moser always gives constructive and invaluable feedback. I couldn't do it without her input.

My family make it so easy for me to find the time to write. Nilesh is always there with food when I need it and Ravi, Kasi and Jimi are a constant source of inspiration when I ask them random questions.

The crime fiction community is a joy to be part of and some of my friends from that community have kept me on the straight and narrow with their eternal optimism. There are too many to mention, but a few have been particularly supportive over this past quite difficult year. Thanks to Rob Ashman, Tony Forder, Malcolm Hollingdrake, Kerry Richardson and Anita Waller.

Dear Reader

Thanks so much for taken the time to read *Broken Silence*. The inspiration for this novel came after attending a talk on Modern-Day Slavery by Baroness Lola Young and Kevin Hyland as part of Bradford Literature Festival. What I learned on that talk made me go away and research more about Modern-Day Slavery – the result was Broken Silence.

This may have been a harrowing read for some of you, but, believe me when I say, I toned my research down quite a lot.

If you suspect that there is Modern-Day Slavery happening in your city, town, road, or area, then please contact this number 08000 121 700

These links are to organizations which work with trafficked people and can provide much more information:

https://www.antislavery.org/slavery-today/spot-the-signs-of-slavery/

https://www.unseenuk.org/helpline-appeal

If you enjoyed reading Broken Silence, I would love it if you could leave a review, recommend it to friends and family, or just sing about it from the rooftops.

If you want to connect with me, you can do so on:

Twitter: @LizMistryAuthor

Facebook: @LizMistrybooks

My website: https://www.lizmistry.com/

Looking forward to Nikki Book 3? – It will be out later in the year.

Happy Reading

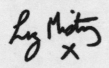

Dear Reader,

We hope you enjoyed reading this book. If you did, we'd be so appreciative if you left a review. It really helps us and the author to bring more books like this to you.

Here at HQ Digital we are dedicated to publishing fiction that will keep you turning the pages into the early hours. Don't want to miss a thing? To find out more about our books, promotions, discover exclusive content and enter competitions you can keep in touch in the following ways:

JOIN OUR COMMUNITY:
Sign up to our new email newsletter: hyperurl.co/hqnewsletter
Read our new blog www.hqstories.co.uk
: https://twitter.com/HQDigitalUK
: www.facebook.com/HQStories

BUDDING WRITER?
We're also looking for authors to join the HQ Digital family!
Find out more here:
https://www.hqstories.co.uk/want-to-write-for-us/
Thanks for reading, from the HQ Digital team

DIGITAL HQ

If you enjoyed *Broken Silence*, then why not try another gripping crime thriller from HQ Digital?

Born in Scotland, made in Bradford sums up **LIZ MISTRY's** life. Over thirty years ago she moved from a small village in West Lothian to Yorkshire to get her teaching degree. Once here, Liz fell in love with three things; curries, the rich cultural diversity of the city . . . and her Indian husband (not necessarily in this order). Now thirty years, three children, two cats (Winky and Scumpy) and a huge extended family later, Liz uses her experiences of living and working in the inner city to flavour her writing. Her gritty crime fiction police procedural novels set in Bradford embrace the city she describes as 'Warm, Rich and Fearless', whilst exploring the darkness that lurks beneath.

Having struggled with severe clinical depression and anxiety for many years, Liz often includes mental health themes in her writing. She credits the MA in Creative Writing she took at Leeds Trinity University with helping her find a way of using her writing to navigate her ongoing mental health struggles. Being a debut novelist in her fifties was something Liz had only dreamed of and she counts herself lucky, whilst pinching herself regularly to make sure it's all real.

You can contact Liz via her website https://www.lizmistry.com/

Also by Liz Mistry

Last Request